I0761900

OF GODS AND GODDESSES

BOOK 3

THE LORDS AND COMMONERS SERIES

LYNNE HILL

Second Edition 2019

Created with Vellum

OTHER BOOKS BY LYNNE

<ins>The Lords and Commoners Series</ins>

Of Lords and Commoners Book 1

Of Princes and Dragons Book 2

Of Gods and Goddesses Book 3

A Gods and Goddesses Novelette

<ins>A Woman's World Series</ins>

A Woman's World Book 1

Lost Powers Book 2

A Collision of Worlds Book 3

This book is dedicated, with much love, to Sheryl.
Thanks for always being there and believing in me!

This chalice contains the new covenant in my blood, which is poured out for thee.

Luke 22:20

The precious blood of our Lord Jesus Christ, preserve my body and soul unto everlasting life.

St. Augustine's Prayer Book (1947)

PROLOGUE

There are many theories about how the world will end. For at least a couple of millennia, if not longer, people have tried to predict how and when the world will end. Some believed that humankind would be destroyed by an asteroid that would black out the sun's life-giving power. Many speculated that humans would be destroyed by a great flood or another ice age. Still others predicted that it would be humans themselves who destroyed one another. They were all wrong. …

CHAPTER 1 COPENHAGEN 1664 AD

How can we leave this place? It has been our home for centuries, Vallachia thought. She went to her chambers for the last time to double check — or was it triple check? — that nothing of importance had been left behind. She found a note on her pillow.

Meet me in the town square. T

Six simple words — yet they caused her mind to race, as they meant much more. Val knew from whom it came and she knew why he wanted to meet. She had a sinking feeling in her stomach. She guessed what he would say — this was a goodbye. Teller would be leaving them. He would be leaving *her*. She crumpled the note and threw it into the fireplace as she ran to the balcony. She checked for signs of humans. None could be seen or heard so she leapt into the air. She flew high, in case any humans happened to be looking up at this late hour. They would think she was a bird or a bat in the distance.

Why did I burn Teller's note? It is not as if we are forbidden lovers. We are simply old friends — who were once engaged. But that was briefly and a long time ago. Surely, we are allowed to meet in the town square — alone — at midnight. Are we not? In our hearts it is as if we are lovers — what does that make us? Nothing, simply friends, she tried to convince herself.

Val tucked her wings in tight and dived head first, speeding toward the city center. She could not see or smell any humans, as she landed gracefully on the head of the massive statue of an angel in the center of a large fountain. The angel had several chips; her nose was mostly missing. Furry green moss had formed in places. The statue had seen better days.

Ironically, the statue had been a wedding gift from Teller. Val had donated it to the City of Copenhagen.

She spotted the burly figure of a man as he emerged from the shadows. She leapt with ease, landing near him.

"What is this about?" Val said.

"Are you alone?" Teller asked.

"Yes."

His emerald eyes held an ancient sadness. He quickly stepped forward and pressed his lips to hers.

Once she recovered from the shock that ran through her entire body, she pushed him away with a shove that would have sent a human ten lengths back but it was only enough to put some distance between them.

"What are you doing?" Val tried not to panic.

"I'm going to the Far East. Come with me." There was desperation in Teller's voice.

Val inhaled sharply. As she had feared, he was leaving. *This is one instance where I do not want to be right,* she thought. "You cannot leave the Court. We need you."

Teller took her hands. "We both know that is not true. I am no longer of use to the Court. We are at peace and it has been that way for some time. There has not been so much as a whisper of a threat and we have heard nothing of Neacsa. She is most likely dead."

Val frowned at the mention of Teller's ex-wife, Neacsa Dracula.

"There is no logical reason for me to follow you to the New World.

However, you could come with us." Teller tightened his grip on Val's hands.

Tears rolled down Val's cheeks. "You know I cannot leave our people. I will not abandon them."

"You mean you won't leave Elijah," Teller said.

"I will not leave him either."

"That is what I feared but I had to try one last time. I had hoped to persuade you with one last kiss. I can't do this anymore — watching you with Elijah. You will go to the west and I will go to the east. I must get as far away from you as possible if I ever hope to get over you."

He was finally giving up on Vallachia — on them. She had won. She was more stubborn than Teller. This was not a competition she wanted to win. *First place is awarded to Vallachia, for being the most tenacious of all.* Her mouth curved in a weary smile at this thought. She forced the tears to stop and gathered her thoughts. *I must not be selfish. It is torture for Teller to have to watch me with my husband.*

Val gave a resolute nod. "I wish you happiness. I hope you find someone who will love you forever." Unfortunately, her voice faltered. *I waited for Teller for two hundred years. Now he has been waiting for me for equally as long. We are even, in a sick and twisted way. That is the world we live in — sick and twisted.*

Teller turned his gaze to the statue he had given Val so many years ago. "I'm glad you understand." His normally vibrant green eyes were darkened with pain. "I love you."

"And I love you." Val wrapped her arms around his neck and kissed him. She had to feel the unusual shock of his lips one last time. She did not want to pull away but forced herself to. "When will you leave?"

"Now." Teller gazed toward the east. "Abdullah, the twins and a dozen or so of my men are waiting for me outside of town.

"How did the others take the news of you leaving?"

"I have not told them."

"You are going to leave without saying goodbye!"

"I almost left without telling you. I did not know if I could withstand your rejection for the millionth time."

"Mari will be furious with you for leaving without telling her."

"It does not matter, as I hope to never return. If we see each other again it will be because peace has ended. No one wants that, so let us hope this is a final goodbye. Unless, of course, you change your mind … someday." Teller kissed her forehead. "Mari has been a dear friend. Will you tell her and the others for me?" He wiped a tear from Val's cheek.

Val leaned into Teller's touch and put her hand over his in order to hold it tight to her cheek. She cherished his special touch, as she might never feel it again. For a brief moment she had the urge to fly away with him — forever.

"Besides, not all of your friends will miss me." Teller tried to lighten the mood. "Riddick will be glad to learn that I am gone and even Elijah — with all his graciousness — will be relieved that I am out of your life. You are in good company; otherwise I could never leave you."

Riddick and Teller had never been able to get on well and Vallachia's husband, Elijah, had grown to tolerate Teller with a cautious dignity.

"I am glad you have loyal companions, as well. Still, I will worry about you," Val said.

"I'll be fine. Surely we can manage on our own."

Val knew this was true. *Teller survived for two hundred years without me — I mean the Court.* "Even if I cannot see you, will you write from time to time?"

"I suppose I will need to stay informed on Court affairs."

She was relieved that Teller would not cut her out entirely, even though he made it sound as if it was all business. "Take care of yourself and I pray you find happiness." She kissed his cheek.

"I have to leave now or I may never be able to."

Val had to force her hands to release him. She closed her eyes tight as a swish of air engulfed her. A gentle puff of sweet breeze flowed through her long golden hair. It cooled her face. Normally, she would have welcomed it but this time it was a sign that Teller was gone. On the outside was a soft whisper but inside was a violent windstorm that would bring the driving rains. She sat on the edge of the water fountain and let the tears fall.

He has to go. It is time for him to move on. This is for the best, she told herself over and over as she tried to rub the pain out of her chest. It was as if her heart had been torn away when he took flight. She cursed him for the emptiness that remained.

CHAPTER 2 COPENHAGEN 1664 AD

Vallachia sat on the edge of the water fountain for too long. She could not pull herself together. It felt as if half of her was missing — Teller was truly gone. As if this wasn't enough, she had to face leaving her beloved home. This very well could destroy the other half of her — leaving nothing. The violent wind inside would keep bringing the rain until she was washed away in the flood.

All her dearest friends would be gathering to leave before the people of Copenhagen began their day. Val had to return to the castle, as she had already put them behind schedule. She knew she must go, so she stared blankly ahead and slowly stood. She made herself go numb, forcing herself not to feel anything. *Life goes on.* She took a deep breath and let the bitter numbness consume her. She headed home with determination. By the time she joined her companions on the balcony, she was emotionless — it was the best mask she could muster.

Over time, Copenhagen had grown up around Elijah and Vallachia's castle. Initially they had built a large wall around their grand home to keep humans from wandering too close. The tall stone wall had helped to ensure that their kind, vampires, remained a secret. Once they had become completely surrounded by the city, they could no longer take flight from the castle during daylight hours without the risk of being spotted. In order not to reveal their true nature to humans it was best that they move. As difficult as this would be, Elijah and Vallachia decided that they would prefer to live freely in a remote location rather than stay in the city and pretend to be human.

Under the pretense of being a wealthy merchant, Elijah sold the Castle to Frederick III, King of Denmark. Frederick was all too happy to take over the grand estate, which was many times larger than his castle.

Elijah and Vallachia were curious about the mysterious new land that had been discovered across the great sea. They were in search of wide-open space so they could spread their wings whenever they liked — literally. They longed to be themselves. Europe had closed in on them, suffocating them.

The Court already had their important possessions packaged and shipped to America. Now it was time for Vallachia and her friends to take flight for the last time from their home. Val had been excited to see this new land, which had all of Europe in an uproar. She had not thought about how hard it would be to walk — or fly — away from her home of four hundred years. There were many wonderful memories. Val and her dearest and oldest friend Mari had each been wed in this castle. Celebrations and grand times with friends and family, learning a new instrument or language, this had all been done right here, in their home. It was where they worked, played and loved.

Elijah had to remind her of the not so joyous times, such as the Court's vampire beheadings. He appeared to be ready to leave it all behind.

Yet, the place Val would miss the most was Elijah's clandestine cave. It was their sanctuary — where they could go to get way from the world. Elijah promised that he would find his wife another such place to call their own. However, Val was skeptical that they would be able to find such a truly secluded place. Riddick, their commander in chief, could find them anywhere, except when they were in that cave. The long narrow water tunnel leading to it made it difficult for even vampires to track.

Elijah looked relieved when he spotted Vallachia. "There you are. We have been looking for you. Where are Teller and the others?"

"They are not with you?" Mari asked. She looked around as if she had somehow overlooked their presence.

Val shook her head no. "I don't know where they are." Her voice was flat.

From the look on Mari's face she clearly did not believe Vallachia.

"I don't know where they are but they won't be coming with us," Val continued.

"Surely that is not true." Mari twisted her face in confusion.

"Teller said it was time for him to move on."

Mari placed her hands firmly on her hips with a stubborn huff. "He is not coming with us to America?"

Val could tell that Mari did not want to accept that Teller was gone. Val understood precisely how she felt. "No. He said he hoped never to return to us."

"What!" Mari's cheeks turned crimson, as Val had anticipated. "He cannot leave without so much as a farewell."

"He told me to tell you all goodbye for him. So you are hearing it from me," Val snapped.

"What an arse!" Mari said. "We have only known each other since we were babes. We grew up together for heaven's sake and he doesn't have the decency to let me know that he is leaving — for good? What a selfish —

"Because we would not have let him go," Val interrupted.

"Yet you let him go?" Elijah smiled and wrapped his arms around his wife.

Val laid her head on Elijah's chest, which was usually a place of great comfort but this time there was little comfort as her mask of numbness threatened to give way.

Mari's anger faded with Val's last comment, as she realized that Val was right — she would have tried to convince Teller to stay. Mari wrapped her arms around both Elijah and Val. "I'm sorry he's gone," she whispered.

This did not help Val to keep her mask intact. She could feel it crack and flood waters threatened to spill out of her eyes.

"All right, that is enough." Riddick was all business. "We should already be in the sky. Daylight will soon be upon us and this place will be crawling with humans. It is time we move out."

Teller was right — Riddick is not bothered in the least by Teller's disappearance, Val thought.

Riddick was also correct — it was past time for them to leave. There was no way Vallachia could delay their departure any longer. Her feet felt as if they were boulders. She did not know if she could take flight. Elijah had to pull her into the air. Val could not stop herself from looking back.

Elijah squeezed her hand. "Don't. Only look forward — to America."

Val wondered how Elijah could leave so easily. He had lived there longer than she had, upwards of six hundred years. Elijah's father, Lord Chastellain, was buried in the catacombs beneath the castle. So many memories, so much history and they were leaving it all behind because the world had grown in around them. It would be easier to keep their dark secret if they left their beloved home.

CHAPTER 3 LONDON 1664 AD

As Elijah and Vallachia had predicted, they had been able to enjoy a long period of peace after the dreaded vampire war of 1551. Elijah was the king of the High Court of Elders. He inherited the throne from his father, Lord Chastellain. With Vallachia by Elijah's side they ruled the vampire world. It was a small world compared to that of humans. The Court's main objective was to ensure that vampires kept themselves hidden from humans.

Vampire populations had been greatly reduced in the war of 1551. With fewer vampires, humans began to flourish. They emerged out of the stagnant and dark times of the middle ages. This gave rise to a new era and the Renaissance was born. With this came new technologies, arts, music and philosophies. Thus transforming the hackneyed culture of Europe.

Time — like vampires — had previously floated along unchanging. As this new era fell upon these ageless creatures they had to learn to adapt. This was not an easy task for timeless immortals. Medieval Europe had been a time of strict social norms, monarchies and religious rule. The world stood still, which was comfortable for Queen Vallachia and her Court.

Many vampires found this new world more difficult to maneuver.

They had to adjust their ancient thinking in order to comprehend concepts such as the earth not being the center of the universe. Vallachia and her companions had tried for a couple of years to convince Samuel, Elijah's closest friend, that the world was indeed a giant ball. In the end it was not Vallachia who persuaded him but rather the works of Galileo. Samuel pored over Galileo's charts and maps of the stars. He spent endless nights studying the sky. He would often mumble to himself, "It simply cannot be. The world is not as we once thought."

Samuel and Aaron visited Galileo while he was under house arrest for heresy against the Church. Galileo's outlandish ideas were the reason for his arrest. It appeared that it was difficult for humans to accept change as well. After all, the church was a large vessel that did not easily alter its course. It was as ancient and stubborn as vampires.

ELIJAH'S ENTOURAGE stopped in London to meet with the members of the British Court and to pick up their dear friends, Mary and Elizabeth. Vallachia had been overjoyed when Mary and Elizabeth agreed to join them on their journey to America.

"There is a British colony, recently won from the Dutch. It is called New York, named after our very own Duke of York. It is a small, yet prosperous city," Lord Alexandru said. Lord Alexandru was the head of the British branch of the Court.

"Are you suggesting we settle in this ... New York?" Elijah asked.

"I have heard that it is lovely." Alexandru unrolled a large map and others moved closer to examine it.

"Our belongings have been shipped to Jamestown." Elijah pointed to the map. "Where is New York?"

"Farther north. It is easy to find because of the long island that protrudes outward." Alexandru ran his finger along the jagged coastline and stopped at New York's location. There was much discussion as they studied the map.

"We do prefer the darker winters in the north," John said. John had once been Elijah's father's most trusted companion. Since Lord Chastellain's death, John had become Elijah's advisor and more. John had helped to raise Elijah, which made him a father figure.

"I have heard that America is lush and green, like our very own Motherland," Elizabeth said.

Val hoped this was true.

In the end, it was decided that they would travel to New York to see what it had to offer.

Lord Alexandru promised that he would visit and that he would tend to Court affairs in Europe. His castle was also surrounded by the ever-expanding city. He said he would not leave London; even if that meant he would have to live under the pretense of being human.

Val was glad Alexandru had chosen to stay behind and look after the vampires of Europe. Elijah bequeathed him with the full power of the High Court of Elders to act on Elijah and Vallachia's behalf.

There were still occasional outbreaks of small vampire "plagues" across Europe. This was usually caused by a handful of unruly vampires. Such cases were not a threat to the Court. It was a simple matter of newly-turned vampires who could not control their thirst. Lord Alexandru was perfectly capable of dealing with them — which often meant removing their heads.

It was difficult for Vallachia to leave London as well. It had been her second home over the years. She hovered high over the city to take it in one last time. The glistening River Thames snaked its way through the sea of rooftops.

"This is far from a final farewell. We will visit." Once again, Elijah had to take Val's hand and lead her westward.

They were leaving all they knew. It felt as if the mask of numbness had become her true self. She wondered if this emotionless state might consume her.

In contrast, Elijah's eyes shone bright with the light of adventure. They were more blue than grey and Val knew this meant that he was excited to explore new places.

They flew through the night seeing nothing except endless ocean.

Val spotted the massive body of a fish; but it was not simply any fish. It was larger than anything she had seen before.

"Look!" Val pointed to the large creature. The fish broke the surface and water shot into the air, as it was forced out of a small opening.

Val tucked her wings in and dived into the water. In doing so, she was transformed from a winged beast to a young woman with gills on her neck and webbed fingers and toes. She could see the fish was much bigger than she had originally thought. It was wider than a common house and many times longer. Swimming alongside it, she ran her webbed hand along its body. Its skin was smooth except where crustaceans had gathered. It was incredibly graceful for its size. With her vampire ears, she could hear the lonely and eerie sounds it made. She imagined that it was calling to a lost love — or was that her own heart making that sound?

The others had followed Val.

"What was that?" Mari asked, as they tread water.

"I have heard seamen speak of such large fish but I always thought they were exaggerating. Now I see they were being modest when describing these magnificent creatures," Samuel said.

"Whatever it was, it was beautiful," Val mused. Seeing the water giant allowed a hint of excitement to creep in. *Think of all the wonderful things we will find in America.* Her mask of numbness began to crack.

Mari studied her companions — floating or swimming about gracefully in the water, far from any land. "I don't know what that thing was but I would wager that the myth of mermaids originated from vampires."

"What are you talking about?" Samuel said. "We are nothing like the mythical sea creatures with fish tails from children's stories."

"Think about it, dear. What would sailors think if they came upon us now?"

"I suppose they would think we were a group of…fish-people."

"Precisely — mermaids."

Samuel furrowed his brow. He was either convinced that Mari was right or he had long since learned that it was not fruitful to argue with his wife. Having been married for a good four hundred years, he had learned a thing or two.

CHAPTER 4 AMERICA 1664 AD

Elijah's entourage had been at sea for two nights and a day. The sun was on the rise when land appeared in the west. They were weary, as there had been no way to take their customary brief rests while at sea.

"That must be America," Elijah said.

As they flew closer, Val could see that the land was indeed green. It reminded her of home. Two equally powerful emotions hit her. First, there was a longing for home that settled deep in her stomach and made it turn. Yet there was relief that Elizabeth was right. *Maybe this place could become our home after all.* She took Elijah's hand.

Elijah scanned the horizon until he found what he was looking for. "There." He pointed to the northwest. "That must be the long island Lord Alexandru showed us on the map."

They landed outside a populated area and walked the streets.

"This is New York?" Val asked.

Elijah nodded his confirmation.

"It is so … small." Elizabeth frowned as she surveyed the town. She was clearly unimpressed.

"There must be no more than a couple thousand people," Aaron said.

"That cannot be. London supports upwards of four hundred-thousand," Mary said.

"The fact that it is not overly populated should be a good thing. I thought we came here to get away from humans," Riddick said.

"I'm beginning to reconsider," Mary said. "I thought there would be at least a good number of people."

"Yes. I feel homesick already," Elizabeth added.

"Give it time. We can be free here. Perhaps it will grow on you," Val said.

Only the main road was cobblestone. All other streets were dirt. The buildings were of a modern architecture as they were all new. They were much more modest than many European homes. There were none of the old elaborate structures found in Europe. No large stone buildings rose high into the sky. Even the churches were simple wooden structures.

It reminded Val of the village where she was born. "It's perfect," she whispered. She was already falling in love with New York. She found the infancy of this place fascinating. She was witnessing the beginning of a new town. The surrounding lands were wild, vast and open, largely unaltered by man. This was exactly what they were looking for.

The Court built a home far to the north of town. It was a one hundred and fifty room mansion surrounded by a thousand acres. The iron gate leading to the home consisted of an elaborate Chastellain family crest with a gold letter "C" in the middle. Its many rooms were for the vampires who came and went from the premises. There were anywhere from fifty to a hundred vampires living there at any one time.

Once settled in, the Court lived as they had before. Elijah and Val continued to seek out new allies and maintain existing alliances. They made it their business to know who their fellow vampires were. In order to stay apprised of the happenings in their world, they frequently traveled across this new land. They were continually on the lookout for any threats to the Court.

Thankfully their reputation had followed them from the old

world. They rarely had to intervene with vampires who revealed their true nature to humans. Once every decade or so, they would have to execute a small coven of vampires for revealing themselves.

Teller stayed true to his word and did not return to the Court. He wrote to Val at least once a year, informing her of his latest adventures. He always made a point to let her know where he was. This made it possible for her to write him in return — or find him, if she were to change her mind. As the years slipped away, his letters came less frequently. She hoped this meant that he was letting her go — or did she truly want that?

Teller spent several years in India with Shantanu's family. He eventually made his way to China.

October 7, 1672

Dear Vallachia,

I have slowly wound my way across Russia. We have found a coven in Beijing. They are friendly and eager to learn how to feed without killing. They are relatively young, with the oldest being no more than one hundred. The leader of this coven wants to train her men to fight. They have agreed to help enforce the Court's laws throughout this land. They want to help protect humans from our kind.

It appears that vampires are few in number in the Far East. I am a giant in this land — over a head taller than the natives. Plus I am easily twice the girth of the locals. I wish you could see how they react to Abdullah. They quickly step aside and sometimes scatter when they see him. [Val could almost hear Teller laughing.] *As you can imagine, this makes blending in difficult so we largely keep to our own kind.*

I have to warn you. I spotted Neacsa, [Val's heart jumped into her throat.] *or at least it was a woman who greatly resembled her. She was in a crowd of people. I ran after her but she vanished. There is a good chance that it was Neacsa, as it appeared that her faithful companion was at her side. What are the chances of seeing two women who looked exactly like Neacsa and her maid of old? The fact that they were able to disappear also makes me wonder. Perhaps I only imagined them, as I caught no scent of vampires.*

The Chinese language is odd but we are slowly getting more proficient. Recently we visited some of the Southern lands. You would love the Karst Mountains. They are like nothing I have ever seen. They are more beautiful than the Carpathian Mountains of home and I never thought I would say that. I wish you would come to me, then I could show you all of China.

Tel

October 15, 1672

Dear Teller,

I am glad you are getting to see the world. It is wonderful to hear from you and to learn that you are safe! It is grand news that the coven in China will join the Court. I'm glad they will help to keep the delicate balance between humans and vampires. That is very concerning news about Neacsa! I hope it was only someone who resembled her.

We are continuing the Court's work here as well, with regular diplomatic efforts. The world is much bigger than we thought. It is working out perfectly, with Lord Alexandru watching over Europe and now you watching over the Far East.

We all miss you. I miss you. I wish there was a way we could be together. I suppose you being gone is for the best. It is easier on both of us.

Much Love,

Val

This was all the news the Court received about Ramdasha's wife — or lover — Elda. Or perhaps she still went by Princess Neacsa Dracula. Whoever she was or whatever name she went by, no one appeared to know what happened to her after Elijah ended the greatest of vampire wars by killing Ramdasha.

Ramdasha had been the Court's longtime adversary. He did not like the Court's laws restricting vampires. Ramdasha and his followers didn't want to hide their true nature from humans. They wanted to rule the world. As the dominant race they wished to make humans their slaves.

As soon as Vallachia dared to hope that Elda was dead, another vague sighting of her would reach the ears of the Court. She remained a ghost and Val prayed that they had not been true sightings.

Overall, the vampire world was quiet; there was not so much as a whisper of anyone moving against the Court. As far as they knew, no one was rebuilding an army or planning to attack. If Elda was out there and continuing Ramdasha's legacy, she was successful in keeping it a secret. The Court had many allies throughout the world and the vampire world was many times smaller than the human world. News traveled fast — as vampires traveled fast — and there was no talk of a rebellion against the Court.

CHAPTER 5 AMERICA 1860 AD

Slavery had been around since the beginning of time — so it seemed. Yet there was a fundamental shift occurring; the world was waking up to concepts long forgotten or suppressed during the middle ages. A sense of fairness and justice swept across Europe and America.

Val had always abhorred the idea of humans owning humans but Elijah was adamant that the Court should not intervene in human affairs. So they did not interfere unless they happened upon someone they could help without revealing their vampire nature.

Val was reminded of one such occasion. While enjoying a walk through the now-bustling city of New York, she and Elijah had come upon a woman being harassed by two men. Elijah took it easy on the attackers as he fought them off and Val helped the woman to safety. They had tried to appear as human as possible while saving the young woman. This sort of intervention was accepted by the Court's ancient laws. However, a larger confrontation or an outright war with humans was forbidden, as it could not be accomplished without unveiling the existence of vampires.

On a mission to visit a small coven in Georgia, Vallachia saw for herself how badly slaves were treated. When they arrived in Georgia,

Elijah and Val were greeted with Southern hospitality. Servants entered with a tray of steaming hot tea. Val was surprised to smell that they were human.

As a man placed a cup in front of Val, his hands trembled. She noticed that he had two raw puncture wounds on his wrist. She looked to his neck to find the same marks. His lips were ashen, which was an odd contrast to his dark skin. Large dark circles could be seen under his eyes. *These vampires are slowly draining him of life.* She quickly stood and took his wrist, trying to remember to be gentle. He shrank away from her.

"I won't hurt you." Her words were as gentle as a mouse's footsteps.

The servant struggled to release his wrist from her steel grip. He did not succeed.

"What is this?" Val demanded as she held up the man's wrist to the leader of the coven.

"He is my slave. We do what we wish with our property," he replied.

Val let go of the human. He stumbled away.

"This is disgusting. That poor man is living in terror. One person cannot *own* another. They are people, not property to possess."

"I have papers that say otherwise, My Lady." The leader smiled with confidence.

"I'm sure you do." Elijah gave Val a pointed glare that told her to back down.

Val could not. "You're revealing who we are to humans. That is against our laws." She reached for the ever-present dirk at her side.

Elijah swiftly moved to stand between his wife and the leader of the Georgian coven.

"I assure you, my slaves will not tell anyone about us. They know that that would result in certain death." The man spoke only to Elijah.

"He looks as if he is not far from death as it is," Val said.

"That is true. Our slaves do not live to old age. Soon he will die and he will take our secret to his grave. No one will find out about us. You have my word."

This satisfied Elijah.

~

UPON THEIR RETURN to New York, Val paced in the Great Hall. Her bright blue eyes danced with an angry flame. "How could you defend that ... that *man?* Though I hate to insult men by calling him one."

Elijah was amused by Val's anger; it was in contrast to her usual calm, rational self. She was like the keel on a sailboat, the one who kept their kingdom upright at all times. He thought it was about time that she allowed the ship to heel. "That coven has always remained discreet. They are not breaking our laws. If they do, we will intervene, as always."

"Meanwhile their slaves are forced to live a nightmare," Val said.

"It is the way things are in the South. Slavery is as old as time. There is nothing you can do about that. You know why we cannot intrude upon human affairs."

"Because it is difficult not to reveal who we are," Val chanted Elijah's mantra — one she had heard a thousand times.

"Yes. Remember Joan of Arc. She should not have been fighting with humans. It got her killed. Not to mention, she risked revealing the existence of vampires."

"Maybe we were given this power for a reason. It is our duty to help." Val was not going to give up this time.

"We *do* help humans by keeping our kind out of sight. That is enough and it should be enough for you as well." The light blue in Elijah's eyes was replaced by stormy grey clouds.

"How can you turn your back on human suffering? It is not simply this coven but all of the South. Slaves are treated horribly. Their living conditions are miserable and they are beaten in order to keep them from rising up against the plantation owners."

"Wonderful!" Elijah rolled his eyes. "Now you are going to take on all of the South? That will surely end in your death. As soon as they discover you are a vampire, they would burn you alive."

"Well I had hoped I wouldn't be alone."

"We have had this conversation before. We must leave humans to their own affairs. We have our hands full keeping our kind from revealing who we truly are. We can't fight human wars as well. We also can't restrict our kind any more than we already do."

"Why not? We could enforce a law prohibiting vampires from killing humans. All of our kind can learn to feed as we do."

"It is a vampire's nature to kill; such a law restricting them would turn too many of our allies against us. That is precisely what our enemies would want."

Val crossed her arms. "Then why do we exist? Surely, we were not put on this earth simply to feed upon humans."

Elijah paused thoughtfully for a moment then shook his head. "You know very well that we have no idea where we came from or why we're here. Vampires have no origin story and we can only speculate as to our purpose. For you and I, as rulers, our purpose has always been simple — to uphold our ancient law."

"Maybe simple is no longer good enough for me."

The muscles in Elijah's jaw bulged as they glared at one another.

"Very well, *Elijah*! I will go south alone."

"You are so ... stubborn, *Val*! It is not our responsibility to play God. Will you not listen to reason?"

It is time for her to lower the keel and steady the ship. Elijah was no longer amused. *She is taking this too far. What has gotten into her? Surely she is not insane enough to head south alone ... is she?*

Their raised voices attracted the attention of John and Riddick.

John studied the King and Queen. "In all the years I have known you, which is quite a few, I have never heard you two fight — not like this. What is this about?"

"She is so ... Maybe you can talk some sense into her." Elijah stormed off.

"Aye. She is obstinate but you were well aware of that long before you married her," John called after Elijah.

With narrowed eyes, Val watched Elijah leave. She turned her furious glare to John and Riddick.

CHAPTER 6 NEW YORK 1860 AD

"We can't have the two of you fighting. You are our leaders. We need unity and stability from you at all times." John spoke to Val with the tone of a concerned father.

John often reminded Val of the late Lord Chastellain, which unnerved her. *Forever* the *Chastellain's minion.* She clenched her teeth. "I want to help. We have the power to do so, which makes it our obligation."

"That is admirable, My Lady." John said, "but you know why we cannot. Imagine what it would be like if humans found out about us. This is what our enemies would want. This is the only thing that keeps vampires from taking over the world. The Court and its just laws are what maintain the balance. Yet, you already know this, my dear."

Val issued a frustrated moan. "You always take Elijah's side; yet that is your job, is it not?" She turned to leave. There was no point in wasting time on John. He would never go against the king.

Riddick placed his hand on John's shoulder to keep him from following after Val. "Let me talk to her."

"Be my guest." John swept his arm outward as if clearing a path for Riddick.

"My Lady." Riddick caught up with Val. He grasped her arm to stay her.

The concern in his dark eyes lowered Val's defenses.

"There are other ways to help — less dangerous ways. Find some other means, one where you don't risk exposing us," Riddick said.

This was a good point, which aggravated Val all the more.

"I know what it is like. We are warriors living in a time of peace. It is nice at first but then —

"What are you saying?" Val snapped.

"There is no reason to go looking for a fight."

"I'm not *looking* for a fight, Riddick. I expected John to agree with Elijah, but not you." Val yanked herself free of his grip and strode away. She needed a woman's perspective on this matter, so she went to find Mari. *Surely she will understand.*

MARI WAS READING a newspaper in her chambers. "What is the matter?" she asked when she saw the look on Val's face.

"Elijah and I ... had a fight."

"That must be a first?" Mari smiled with amusement.

"I suppose so. We tend to agree on many things or we are willing to compromise but not this time. You should have seen what that Southern coven is doing to their slaves. It is atrocious. They feed from them until they become too weak and then they kill them."

"Those poor dears! They must live in absolute fear." Mari lifted her chin high. "Slavery is so primitive. At least we have always been civilized enough to pay our servants."

Val sighed with relief. *I have found an ally.*

"Perhaps this is the problem with living for an eternity; we tend to grow restless."

Val narrowed her eyes. "I am not *restless*. Slavery is immoral. We must do something!"

"Yet, there has always been human suffering. Why are you

concerned with this issue at this particular time, if it is not that you are bored? You must find something to occupy your time."

"You may not care enough to help but I do," Val scoffed.

"Very well. What ... exactly do you propose we do — go to war with the South?" Mari said.

"Perhaps."

"You know that we could not accomplish that without making it obvious that we are not human. That would require breaking our principal law. There are other ways —

"Now you sound like Riddick." Val crossed her arms and tapped her foot on the floor. "What 'other ways' do you propose?"

"Perhaps lobby the government or send money to organizations that are fighting slavery. Now is a good time. This country is on the brink of tearing itself apart over the issue of slavery."

"We have always donated to worthy causes but I want to do more than simply throw money at this problem."

"Here, take a look at this." Mari held up the newspaper and read the headline, "Volunteers and Donations Needed." She went on to explain, "This article is about an orphanage in downtown New York. They need money and volunteers in order to be able to keep the place open. This article is about how colored children are frequently kidnapped from their beds at night. It is suspected that slave-traders smuggle them to the South to sell them. Orphaned children are particularly easy targets for slave traders."

Val snatched the paper and skimmed it. "This is awful." *Of course! I am needed right here — in my own city.* Without another word, Val left to dress.

Modern-day dresses were even more uncomfortable than the large silk brocades of medieval Eastern Europe. *In fact, corsets may be the worst invention in the world.* Val dreaded giving up her comfy breeches for a dress that was puffy everywhere but the waist, which was suffocating. But she had to blend in — appear as if she were a normal woman, though be it a wealthy one.

~

VALLACHIA KNOCKED on the door to the orphanage but there was no answer. She let herself in. It had most likely been a warehouse, which was now used to house children. Small beds lined one wall. Tables and a play area filled the other side of the room. The play area consisted of a frayed rug and a handful of well-used wooden toys.

Val could hear children playing outside. At the far end of the large room sat a simple desk where a woman rummaged through a stack of papers. She wore the long black and white robes of a nun. With her mouth downturned and three vertical creases visible on her forehead, the woman focused on her work. She did not notice Vallachia as she approached and Val deliberately walked loudly, as humans did.

"Excuse me," Val interrupted.

The woman started.

"My name is Vallachia and I would like to help." Val set a leather satchel on the desk.

The woman picked it up slowly, as if there might be a snake inside.

"I was also hoping to volunteer here," Val continued.

The woman opened the bag and her mouth fell open. It was full of gold. She simply blinked at the shiny coins until she decided that they were not an illusion. After a long moment she shook her head, closed her gaping mouth and stood. "Pardon me, where are my manners? I am Sister Gwendolyn Godfree but please call me Gwen." She held her hand out to Val.

Val gently shook her hand being extra careful not to hurt Gwen.

"Bless you, my dear and praise the Good Lord above. Now we can pay our bills." Gwen gestured to the papers on the desk. Her brown eyes had a light in them that had not been there moments ago. "We will be able to stay open and make some much needed repairs. I did not know how we would buy food next week, let alone pay the rent. Come, let me show you around."

The restrooms and kitchen were small and inadequate for all the people they served. The grounds were also insufficient, as they were overgrown and had nothing for the children to play on or with. Despite this, the children romped merrily. It pleased Val to hear their innocent laughter.

"We have seen the number of orphans increase many fold over the years. It is very difficult for us to keep up. So many need our help and we have so little."

Val felt a heavy stone form in her chest at the thought of so many children without parents. *Where would I have been without my father?* Her heart ached for these children. They needed her — or did she need them?

Val spent the rest of the day with the children. She read to them and tried to help some of the older ones with their reading and writing.

A small colored boy tugged lightly at Val's dress. "You are funny looking," he kept his head down.

Val laughed and put her finger gently to his nose. "Not funny — simply different."

"Papa used to tell me stories about you."

Val shook her head. "Surely you are thinking of someone else. What is your name?"

"Kitch."

"It is a pleasure to meet you Kitch. My name is —

"I know who you are." The boy put his tiny hand in Val's. "I will show you." Kitch led her across the room to the beds. From under his pillow he pulled out a book. He flipped through the pages. "Papa used to read this to me." He stopped at a picture of a woman in a long flowing white gown. She had large white bird-like wings and a golden-jeweled crown on her head. The crown resembled Val's — one that had not come out of the vault in their dungeon for many years. The angel in the book was surrounded by a flurry of snow. It appeared she was standing on top of a mountain but what was most shocking was that the woman in the picture had a clear likeness to Vallachia.

CHAPTER 7 NEW YORK 1860 AD

"She's the Great Snow Queen of the North," Kitch explained. "I used to stare at this funny looking lady a lot. I thought she was sick with her pale skin and yellow hair but Papa used to say that she was an angel and that she would save us."

"Save you, how?" Vallachia asked.

The small boy shrugged. "By ending slavery, I guess."

Val had no idea where this book had come from. It most likely had roots in the old European tales about the snow queen who ruled with love and compassion — the ageless Queen of the North. It appeared that these old stories about her had continued to morph and spread over the years. The boy's story made her heart even heavier. She sat down on the bed. "Please listen to me. You should not believe such fairy stories. It will be a long and difficult fight against slavery and one person alone will not be able to stop it."

Kitch lowered his head in disappointment.

Val was not sure what had changed her mind but she knew that what she said was true. *People of color will have to fight for their freedom. I will help all I can. However, I will not be able to save them on my own,* Val thought.

"But this is you in the picture. I always knew I would find you someday. Surely you have come to save us," Kitch said.

"I wish that were true. But no one person can do that. People must stand together — if they do they will be strong enough to end slavery."

There was pain in the boy's eyes. Val had crushed his dreams.

"Let's get you ready for bed, Kitch." Val smiled in hopes of reassuring the boy that things would be fine.

Val helped to get the children to sleep and finally headed home. *I was terrible to Elijah earlier. He is right — as always. I will help but in a different and safer way*. She could not stand it that he was upset with her.

Elijah did not look up from his book when Val landed in front of him. "I was afraid you headed south," he said. "I was debating as to whether or not I should gather Riddick and the others and head out as well."

"Elijah, I'm truly sorry. You are right, we can't restrict our kind anymore and we can't go to war with humans. So ... I have found another way to help."

Elijah turned his gaze to Val. His expression softened. "And what might that be?"

Val smiled with relief. She took the book from his hand and curled up on his lap. She needed to *feel* that he was no longer upset with her. He put his arms around her and she told him about the orphanage and little Kitch.

"My Snow Queen," Elijah whispered in her ear after hearing the boy's story.

Thankfully the storm was gone from Elijah's eyes; they held love and longing. Val pressed her lips to his.

"We are deprived of the entire human experience," Val said. "This endless life without children is ... lonely at times. I think that's what was truly upsetting me. Humans have always treated one another poorly and of course, vampires are known to be cruel. Yet as long as I'm helping I will be content. I have found children who need me."

"The *entire* human experience is not all you make it out to be. We get to experience the best parts; eternal youth, health, strength and speed, not to mention we can fly. And don't forget about being able to breathe under water. We get to experience the best parts of being a human and much more and we get all this forever. We don't grow old or sick. It doesn't get any better than this."

"When you put it that way..." Val laughed.

"I am grateful that you did not head south. I dreaded the thought of having to follow you." He kissed her lips and her neck as he unbuttoned her dress. "Let me help you get out of this uncomfortable thing." He untied her corset.

After all these years Elijah knew exactly how to please Vallachia. They knew every inch of each other. They took it slow and enjoyed each other to the fullest.

EVERY MOMENT VAL could spare was spent at the orphanage. The first time Elijah came to visit he was dressed in his best. He looked beyond handsome in his tailored black suit and top hat.

"May I help you, sir?" Gwen asked.

"I am looking for my wife." Elijah said. "Apparently I have to come here if I want to see her."

"You must be Vallachia's husband. I imagined her husband would be handsome ..."

Val chuckled, as Sister Gwen appeared lost for words. Val had been preparing the midday meal for the children but could easily hear what went on in the orphanage. Val headed for the main entrance. They had moved Gwen's desk so that it was by the front door. Val had suggested this change in hopes of deterring slave traders from slipping in and taking the colored children.

"Darling, I'm so glad you decided to visit. This is Sister Gwen." Val gestured to the nun behind the desk.

Elijah took Gwen's hand and kissed it. Gwen's cheeks turned the color of roses.

"It is an honor to meet you. Vallachia has told me about you."

Elijah swiftly moved around the desk and took Gwen's arm in his. "Perhaps you could give me a tour."

Gwen looked as if she was going to faint. *Elijah could make a nun want to reconsider her chastity vows."*

As he was being shown around, Elijah made it clear that this place would simply not do.

"Tell me Sister, who owns this building and how do I find him?" Elijah asked.

Val knew that Elijah was planning to buy the place. *When he set his mind on something there was no stopping him.*

The next day Elijah came in with the deed to the building in his hand. Renovations began at once. They added a separate large kitchen and larger bathrooms. Riddick and Samuel built wooden forts and climbing structures on the playground. Mary and Val made bookshelves. They were not fancy but they did the job. Soon they were filled with books of all kinds.

The children were completely terrified of Riddick. They stayed well away from him. Riddick worked to gain their trust, usually by bringing them sweets. Such delicacies the kids would only have seen in candy store windows, yet never could have afforded. This worked well to win the children over.

Once the children became used to Riddick they loved to climb all over him. They constantly asked him to twirl them around and toss them up in the air. He would then take turns spinning or throwing each child high into the sky and gently catching them.

The first time Gwen observed this she screeched and ran to stop Riddick.

"Don't worry he will not drop them," Val said.

"How do you know that?" Gwen asked.

"He has ... very sure hands."

A little boy chimed, "My turn! My turn!"

Riddick started to pick the boy up but pretended the boy was too heavy. "You are so big. I don't think I can lift you."

Gwen shot Val a concerned look — terrified might be a better word. Val tried to ease Gwen's mind with a smile. Eventually Gwen had to smile as well, as the little boy squealed with joy while flying through the air and landing safely in Riddick's arms.

"It is surprising that you don't have children of your own," Gwen said one evening while they cleaned up after putting the children to sleep.

"There will be no children for us." Of course Val still wanted children more than anything but she had let that dream slip away long ago. There was no pain in her chest and no tears formed in her eyes.

"I'm terribly sorry to hear that." Gwen's eyes were filled with sorrow. She was a kind soul and cared deeply for others.

"Don't be sorry. There are plenty of children who need us. In fact, I have sixty children now." Val smiled.

"You know, you act as if you are much older than you are."

Val nodded — Gwen had no idea.

Elijah and Val carried on managing the orphanage for many years. They watched the children grow until it became apparent that they were not aging. After a couple of comments about their continued youthfulness, they became less active in the direct happenings of the facility. In order to keep their ancient secret, the Court only funded the orphanage from afar.

Without the children to occupy her time Val moved onto her next obsession. She sought out any references, person or text, that might provide a clue as to where vampires came from. Who were the first vampires? Why do they exist?

She consulted historians at the most prestigious universities under the ruse of being a student interested in "mythical creatures". She devoured every historical text she could find, which was not much. Elijah's father and John were the oldest vampires she knew; therefore, their origin predated at least 500AD. There were not that many books or even scrolls still in existence from this time and beyond. Even stone carvings such as hieroglyphics did not offer any clues as to where they came from. All she found was a history of humans and truly mythical creatures, of which she already knew.

Mari, Mary and Elijah watched with concern as Vallachia poured over some ancient parchments.

"Maybe she is having some sort of existential crisis," Mari said.

"Or she's going bloody mad … again." Mary chewed on her fingernail.

Elijah let out a heavy sigh. "Ever since the great vampire war she has been concerned with figuring out where we came from but this is severe, even for her."

Val paid no attention to her concerned friends as her eyes skimmed the fragile scroll.

CHAPTER 8 NEW YORK 2000 AD

Vallachia and her friends thought the world had changed quickly throughout the Renaissance and beyond, yet they could never have predicted the changes that were to come and how fast they would be upon them — like an avalanche. And there was nothing that could have prepared them. Slavery ended, cars were invented, humans learned to fly!

Many of these new technologies were incredibly useful. The two greatest inventions, as far as vampires were concerned, were blood banks and sunglasses.

The Chastellains owned the world's largest company supplying blood to hospitals and of course, to the Court. They no longer had to hurt humans in order to feed. This made life as an immortal all but perfect. There was nothing for Vallachia to feel guilty about. In fact, life could not have been better for the leaders of the High Court.

Thanks to UV sunglasses, the sun was no longer a nuisance. Even though life was easier in many ways, they struggled to keep up with this changing society. Once again, the city grew up around the Court's manor, as it had back in Copenhagen. They turned their home into a resort for humans and the Court left New York City. Since they did not feed directly from humans anymore it was better for them to remain largely isolated. This helped to ensure their secret was kept. They built a new two hundred room mansion in upstate New York to accommodate the growing vampire population. Like humans, vampires were growing in number. Of course, humans were being turned to vampires at only a fraction of the rate that humans were born. Everything appeared to be in balance.

Vallachia's exhaustive search to find where vampires came from slowly subsided as the resources ran out. Her ears were always pealed for information, such as when the Dead Sea Scrolls were discovered. She and Elijah snuck into the museum where they were on display so Val could study them. Still, nothing had been discovered about the origin of vampires.

Vallachia entered her new bedchambers to find Elijah resting on the bed. He had obviously been waiting for her. She appeared on top of him in a flash and lowered her lips to his but he pushed her away enough to look her in the eyes.

"There is something I need to show you," he said.

Val tilted her head in confusion.

Elijah pulled his shirt off and there was a large white bandage above his right chest muscle.

Val jerked back. "You're hurt! What happened?"

"It should be healed by now." He ripped the bandage off to reveal a large red and black tattoo of the Chastellain coat of arms.

"You ... you got a tattoo ... and you did not tell me?"

Elijah frowned. "Do you like it?"

Val ran her hand over the tattoo, tracing the large "C" with her finger. "It's beautiful."

He exhaled with relief. He gave her that look that still made her weak in the knees.

She brushed her lips over the tattoo and then her tongue. She pushed him down with her hands on his shoulders. She continued to kiss down his chest and slowly worked her way down his stomach. As she went lower he moaned with pleasure ...

~

Elijah slept soundly. Val studied the elegantly detailed tattoo. When she laid her head on his chest, she noticed something sticking out of the pocket of his jeans, which lay on the floor beside the bed. She gently unwound herself from him, trying not to disturb him. She pulled the paper out to find that it was a drawing of the Chastellain Crest. A receipt that read Matrix Tattoos accompanied the picture. This gave her an idea. As carefully and quietly as possible she dressed and left.

Val knocked on Mari and Samuel's chamber door.

Mari answered the door in a robe and her hair was a mess.

Val smiled at the sight; it was odd to see Mari when she was not perfectly groomed.

"What do you want?" Mari whispered with a hint of irritation.

Val laughed. "Sorry to bother you. I was hoping you would come to the city with me?"

"Right now?"

"Yes, now. While Elijah is asleep."

"What are you up to?"

"You will see." Val gave her a mischievous crooked smile.

"Very well. Let me dress." As she shut the door Val could hear Mari tell Samuel that she had to go and he moaned in frustration.

Val also convinced Mary, Elizabeth and Sonia to accompany her. They made their way through the crowds on 52nd Street as if they were normal humans.

Men openly gawked at this assorted group of lovely "young" women.

"I may never get used to how rude men are nowadays. Men used to have to be discreet when they ogled women. Now they outright stare and make obscene comments or whistle. It is disgusting," Mary complained.

"At least our breeches and your short hair are no longer novelties that attract attention," Vallachia said.

"That's true," Mary said. "At least now we can wear our hair and clothes however we see fit."

"In fact, I don't know how we survived without blue jeans," Elizabeth said.

"They sure as hell beat corsets," Sonia added.

"I can't believe you pompous ladies ever wore such evil contraptions," Mary said. "I never would have been caught dead in such a thing."

"We have tried for centuries to help you gain a sense of fashion but you are simply hopeless," Mari said.

"What exactly is it we're doing here?" Sonia asked.

"Hopefully Val is taking us to a new clothing shop," Mari said.

"Here we are." Val pointed to a sign that read *Matrix Tattoos*.

Mari's mouth fell open.

CHAPTER 9 NEW YORK 2000 AD

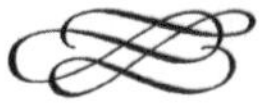

Vallachia laughed at Mari's expression. "Don't worry. You don't have to get a tattoo. I'm getting one and you all may do as you wish. I didn't want to ... do this alone."

"I have not been drinking nearly enough for this," Mary said. "Hopefully they sell booze?"

A young man, completely covered in tattoos, greeted them. Pieces of metal adorned his face. He gave the attractive ladies a broad smile. "How can I help you?"

"It looks as if he fell face first into a tackle box," Mary whispered.

Val chuckled.

"Apparently, she wants a tattoo." Mari gestured to Val.

"Great. Is this your first?" he asked.

"Yes," Val replied.

"Awesome, virgin flesh," he said.

Val rolled her eyes and Mary let out a disgusted sigh.

The tattoo artist was not deterred. "Pick the one you want." He pointed to several thick binders full of artwork.

"I know what I want and where I want it," Val said.

"I like a woman that knows what she wants."

"You mean, a woman *who* knows what she wants." Val corrected his poor English.

The boy's stare was blank.

"Never mind." Val pulled out the picture of the Chastellain Coat of Arms she'd stolen from Elijah's jeans and handed it to the tattoo artist. "With a red C and black surroundings. I want it right here," Val placed her hand above her right breast. She wanted hers to match Elijah's.

"I did this same tattoo on someone else."

"Yes, that was my husband and you did an excellent job. That's why we are here."

The man frowned. "Husband? You're too young to be married."

"Sometimes I feel as if I am seven hundred years old," Val said.

Her companions laughed.

The man didn't know what to make of this odd comment. "Well, your husband is lucky. This way." He led Val to a well-worn chair. It looked like it belonged in a dental office.

The man went right to work. The needle was a bit irritating but not painful to a vampire. Val was careful to hold perfectly still. Since she would have this on her body for an eternity, she wanted it to be perfect.

"I can't believe Elijah got a tattoo. Is that what started all this nonsense?" Mari said.

"I'm only surprised because the two of you are such prudes," Mary said.

"We're *not* prudes!" Val retorted.

"Please," Mary snorted. "You two act as if you're from the thirteenth century or something."

"We were quite progressive for the thirteenth century," Val said.

"My point exactly," Mary said.

"What in the hell are you talkin' about?" the tattoo artist asked.

"Nothing." Val glared at Mary, warning her to drop it. "Besides Elijah is far older than the thirteenth century, and he was the first of us to get one." Val spoke quietly so only vampires would hear.

When the artist was done, he handed Val a mirror and wiped the drops of blood away. *It is superb,* she thought — exactly like Elijah's, only slightly smaller.

"It is quite lovely," Mary said.

"I want the same," Elizabeth declared.

"No way. You're not going to get a tattoo before I do," Mary said. "I'm next." Mary had always been overly competitive. She had to be the best or first at everything.

"You're all going to get tattoos because your king and queen have them?" Mari crossed her arms. "You're nothing but a bunch of sheep."

Val glared at Mari, trying to shut her up.

"You girls are weird," the tattoo artist said.

They were clearly making the poor young man uncomfortable. He was the one who was used to freaking people out, with his piercings and his tattooed body. "You didn't even flinch," he said to Val. "Most first timers, girls anyway, find it very painful."

"I suppose I have a high tolerance for pain."

"Who's next?" he asked.

Mary and Elizabeth fought each other for the chair. They wrestled each other to the floor. It looked like a serious fight until Mary pressed her lips to Elizabeth's.

The artist's mouth hung open.

"That is quite enough ladies. Remember your manners." Val easily pulled Mary off Elizabeth with one hand.

"Unless I can join you." The artist looked hopeful.

"No chance in hell." Mary quickly took the chair before someone else could.

"Very well. Mary will go first," Val commanded.

Elizabeth issued a disappointed sigh. "I wanted to be first for once."

"Your Queen has spoken," Mary said.

"Would you shut up?" Val smacked Mary's arm.

Mary turned to the tattoo artist. "Do you have any scotch?"

"Uh, we don't sell alcohol here." He turned to Sonia. "And I'm gonna need to see your ID."

The ladies broke into a fit of laughter.

Sonia presented her fake ID.

Mary had the Chastellain C inked on her upper arm.

Mari ran her finger over Val's healed tattoo. "I do like it. Yet, I'm afraid Samuel will be furious."

"Surely not," Val said. "He will simply have to get one as well."

"Why would you all get the same tattoo? What does it stand for?" the tattoo artist asked.

"We're all kin and it's our family coat of arms," Val answered.

"'Coat of arms?' Where are you from?"

The women all answered in unison…

"London," Mary said.

"Ludus," Val said.

"Copenhagen," Mari said.

"Constantinople," Sonia chimed.

"Const-what?" The tattoo artist said.

"Never mind all that," Val said.

"And you're all family?" He looked confused and skeptical.

"Yes, we're family," Val confirmed.

He shook his head and went back to work on Elizabeth's ankle. This group of odd ladies was more than he could make sense of.

Mari gave in. She decided to get the C on her right shoulder blade. She thought it would be easier to hide.

"You know, Samuel will see it," Val said.

"I know. I hope he approves." Mari twirled a strand of hair around her finger and paced as she waited her turn.

"He'll love it." Val tried to reassure her. "In fact, he'll head straight down here to get one for himself, followed by Riddick and Aaron," Val said.

"I hope you're right," Mari said.

"What about John? Do you think he will get a tattoo?" Sonia asked.

"Never," Val laughed.

Five hours later they were done. Val tipped the man a couple extra hundred dollars.

"Come back for your next tattoos."

But Val had the feeling he was not sincere. He looked relieved that they were leaving.

CHAPTER 10 NEW YORK 2000 AD

Val found Elijah reading on their bed.

"There you are." He barely looked up from his book.

Now that it was done, Val was worried. *What if he doesn't like the tattoo?* She stood in silence at the foot of the bed.

When she didn't say anything he stopped reading to give her his full attention. "What's going on?"

Here it goes. With one hand and in one quick motion she pulled her shirt off, revealing the new tattoo.

Elijah's lips parted. In a flash he stood in front of her.

"You didn't," he stared at the blood red C above her bare breast.

Oh no. He doesn't like it. Her heart beat faster. "What do you think?"

He ran his finger across it. "It's real?"

"Of course."

"You truly are mine?" he whispered.

This took Val back. She had to push his head up with her fingers on his chin to get him to look her in the eye. "What's that suppose to mean?"

Elijah pressed his body to hers. "Sorry, my love. I didn't mean to say that out loud. I know you love me and that has always been enough. Yet you also love him."

"Why on earth would you bring Teller up at a time like this?" They hadn't seen Teller in well over three hundred years. He hadn't even written in a long time.

"I shouldn't have. The tattoo is amazing and I'm grateful you're mine. Sometimes I still can't believe you chose me, that's all," Elijah said.

"Of course I chose you. I could not ask for a better friend, husband and lover."

It was as if Elijah had been forcing himself to look at her face and he could no longer resist. He had to see if his mark was still on her — a mark that would never disappear. He kissed the tattoo and ran his hands gently over her exposed breasts. He grabbed her waist and picked her up. She wrapped her legs around him and he carried her to the bed. That was when they heard the arguing.

"What's that about?" Elijah asked.

"Well ... we all got tattoos." Val gave him a sheepish smile.

"Who?"

"Us girls."

"It sounds as if Samuel is not happy about it." Elijah jumped up and pulled his shirt off. He put it over Val's head just as their door flew open. Val pulled Elijah's shirt down to cover her.

Samuel stopped short at the sight of Elijah's tattoo. "So it's true; you did get one."

"It is just as I said." Mari appeared behind Samuel. She too stopped short at the sight of Elijah. "Oh my, it's bigger than I'd expected."

Elijah shifted uncomfortably under their stares. He went to the dresser and quickly put on a black t-shirt.

Mari pulled the collar of Elijah's shirt down revealing Val's tattoo. "You see."

Samuel's frown deepened. "Simply because they did something foolish, you had to as well? I don't approve of that *thing* on your body. We live forever and now you all will be stuck with that ... that ... so called art, for an eternity. People don't even know what true art is anymore." He spun on his heal and was gone.

"Give it some time. Perhaps it'll grow on you." Elijah said to Samuel's back.

Val whispered, "Sorry," to Mari.

"I don't care," she said. "I like it. It's *my* body after all."

Val smiled. *There's Mari's stubborn side.* "Elijah's right, Samuel will come around. I know it's hard to accept new things. Some of us don't want to let go of our old ways."

Riddick and Aaron appeared in the doorway.

"What's all this talk about tattoos?" Riddick asked.

Mari pulled Val's shirt collar down again to reveal the "C".

"That's …" Aaron started.

"Cool." Riddick finished his sentence. He stared at it for a bit too long.

Elijah pulled the shirt up to cover his wife.

Aaron boldly lifted Elijah's shirt to inspect his tattoo.

"Since when do we undress one another?" Elijah said.

"We can't very well be the only ones without tattoos." Riddick said to Aaron. They headed out at once.

"Wait." Val pulled Elijah's drawing of the "C" out of her pocket. "You'll need this."

Riddick took it with the slightest bow. "Thank you, My Lady."

"Will you stop calling me that? It sounds ridiculous in this day and age." Val had not cared for the title 'My Lady' even back when it was common and proper.

"Old habits are difficult to break, *My Lady.*" Riddick winked.

Val sighed.

Riddick and Aaron disappeared.

"I fear I may have created a monster," Elijah said. "I'm going to join them … to make sure they stay out of trouble."

"Good luck with that," Mari spat.

If the vampire ladies freaked the poor tattoo artist out, Val could only imagine what the human would think of these strange men.

The men were out until late that night. When they returned the old friends drank and played games as usual but this time the coven's new tattoos were the main topic of interest.

Val raised her glass of well-aged wine from their cellar. "To being a member of the Chastellain family."

"To the High Court of Elders," Elijah added.

"So we have to get a tattoo to prove our loyalty to the Court?" Samuel sneered.

"Of course not, my dear friend," Elijah said.

With reluctance, Samuel raised his glass and tapped it against the others.

CHAPTER 11 NEW YORK 2000 AD

Samuel did eventually get the Chastellain tattoo. This was only the beginning of tattoos for Riddick. Eventually he had sleeves covering both arms. More ran across his chest and back.

Vallachia decided that it was long overdue that she had professional photos taken. Pictures were a neat technology but when one never changed, they were not of great importance.

When Elijah entered their room, he caught the scent of a human. He raised his eye-brows in question.

"I hired a photographer. After all, we never had wedding photos taken." Val gave Elijah a knowing look. Of course they had no wedding photos, because no one could have dreamt of a camera back in 1462.

"Well at least we did take a honeymoon. One of the first ever, I'd imagine." Elijah said.

Val smiled at the memory. "That we did, thanks to Riddick's crazy idea about newlyweds getting away to be alone. The concept of honeymoons did take off after all."

Elijah chuckled.

The photographer struggled to make out what they were saying.

So Val continued in a louder voice, "So you're fine with having our pictures taken?"

"For you, my dear, anything," Elijah replied.

"Anything?" Val issued a playful grin. "You may want to amend that after you find out what I have in mind."

The photographer had them pose in different positions first inside and then on the balcony.

"I want pictures of our tattoos," Val said.

"Isn't that a bit personal, honey?" Elijah said this quietly so the human would not hear.

Val unbuttoned his Ralph Lauren dress shirt. "Please, darling. You promised — anything."

They had come from a time when the body was to be kept completely covered. They were both uncomfortable at first. But once they became accustomed to being mostly naked, they got some wonderful shots. The photographer positioned them strategically so that Elijah's arm would be covering Val's breasts or they were intertwined sensually with each other.

The photographer appeared to be greatly enjoying himself. "Are you like — models or actors or something?"

"No." Val laughed.

"Well you should be," he said.

"We have too many scars to be models," Elijah said.

Elijah had several thin lines across his face from the explosion in Ramdasha's cavern and many others that were barely visible. Val had more scars than Elijah; her back, hip and arm contained the worst of them. If one survived several centuries of medieval vampire wars, one was bound to have some nasty scars.

Val had the best photos framed and used them to decorate their bedchamber walls.

TIME CONTINUED TO FLOAT ALONG. They had to do something to pass the endless years. They all had their favorite hobbies. Val had always

loved to dance. She and Elijah learned the latest moves. Circles would form around them as the crowd stopped to watch the handsome couple.

Val's friends were expert musicians. They spent countless hours playing together — singing and dancing. Sonia was the best singer amongst them. Mari grew to be a spectacular artist. Her paintings hung all over the manor. Aaron had always been a writer. He started by documenting children's fairy stories from around the world. His immense collection grew to contain many histories and anthologies. These were the grandest of times — but nothing lasts forever.

CHAPTER 12 NEW YORK 2020 AD

The High Court of Elders had, in some ways, let their guard down. Everything changed one sunny morning when Val woke after an uneasy rest. Elijah sat next to her, his head rested in his hands and his back heaved with each breath.

"What's wrong?" Val rubbed his shoulders to calm him.

When he lay down, he wrapped himself around Val. "It was only a dream," he whispered.

"About what?"

"Surely it's nothing."

"You're not usually this upset over a dream." In fact, Val could never remember a dream disturbing him before.

"It was … incredibly vivid. There was a large red dragon. It was after you. I tried to fight it off but in the end it swooped you up in its talons and flew away, taking you from me."

Val was reminded of her dreams about a dragon, in which Teller had become a ferocious winged serpent. They too had seemed real. This was madness though, as they had not seen Teller in ages — three hundred and fifty-six years, but who was counting? Still the dream worried Val. She never told Elijah about her premonition dream of Teller and the dragon, which she'd had the day before they learned that Teller had become Vlad the Impaler. Elijah looked worried enough and she didn't want to burden him more, so she decided it was best not to tell him.

"It was simply a dream. Everything is fine." Val was not only trying to comfort Elijah, she was also trying to convince herself of this. *Yet Teller is the only one who stood any chance of taking me from Elijah. If he returned it would be positively wonderful to see him ... and feel his electrifying touch. Would I still be strong enough to resist him?* Then she chastised herself for being arrogant enough to think that Teller would still want her after all these years. *It's been so long since he was with us; surely he has moved on. Of course, he must be happily married by now, so there is nothing to worry about — right?*

Unfortunately, Elijah was thinking along the same lines. "Dracul means dragon, correct?"

"Aye," Val said with a heavy sigh.

"That's what I was afraid of." Elijah stood and dressed. His brow was furrowed with determination.

"Where are you going?" Val asked.

"For a walk."

"Do you want me to come with you?"

"No." The unusual sharpness in his voice caused Val to recoil. Elijah softened his expression. "I'm sorry. I need some time to gather my thoughts." He kissed her forehead before he took flight from the balcony.

Vallachia watched him go with a sinking feeling in her stomach. She could not fully place it. It wasn't only Elijah's dream; there was something else bothering her. She could not shake her uneasiness; it hung over her the entire day.

At dusk Val could no longer stand it, she called him — no answer. She went to the Great Hall and found no one. She headed to Mari and Samuel's room.

Mari frowned when she saw Val's face. "What's wrong?"

"Have you seen Elijah? He left this morning. He was ... troubled. I haven't seen him since."

"We haven't seen him today. Why was he upset?" Mari asked.

Val's heart quickened. *Don't panic. He is fine.* "I must find him." She headed out.

"Wait. I'll go with you." Mari sped after her.

On the way to the horse stables Val told Mari about the dragon dream and Elijah leaving to "gather his thoughts". All the horses were accounted for. He was not out riding. Val asked anyone she came across if they had seen Elijah. No one had. She called him again — no luck. This was the problem with a two hundred room home — he could be anywhere. They had never found another secret place like the cave they'd had in Copenhagen so Val had no idea where else to look.

Val fought against the helplessness that threatened to consume her. Something deep down in her gut told her that he was in trouble. "Where could he be?" she yelled in frustration.

"Try not to worry. He may simply need more time. Surely he'll return soon," Mari said.

Val hoped she was right but knew that something was wrong — terribly wrong. When the sun was on the rise, Val went to Riddick. "Take as many of our best men as you think you will need and look for Elijah. Split up so you have more of a chance of finding him. I'll wait here in case he returns."

Riddick nodded and was gone. He was always happy to take action. Val paced in their room, glancing at the large balcony doors in hopes of seeing him there. Mari sat on the sofa to keep her company.

"It's not like Elijah to get upset over a dream," Mari said.

"I know — that's why I'm worried. This isn't only about a stupid dream."

Val stepped out onto the large balcony and scanned the horizon for any sign of him. "The winds have changed. This morning they blew in from the north; now they're coming from the south."

Mari stared into the distance as well. "Does that mean change is coming?"

"It feels like it," Val said.

Mari nodded.

Riddick barged in. Val's heart sank even farther at the expression on his face.

"We followed his scent and found this," he held up a cell phone, "then we lost the scent entirely, as if he vanished. Our men are searching the area as we speak."

Val took the phone and slid her finger across the bottom of the screen to open it. She typed V-A-L-L — Elijah's code. The phone opened to reveal the background picture of the two of them, mostly naked revealing their matching tattoos. Val showed the phone to Mari. There was no mistaking that it was Elijah's. "What does this mean? Why would he leave his phone behind?"

"I suppose he could have dropped it," Mari said.

"Vampires don't *drop* anything, not by accident anyway," Riddick said.

"Maybe he doesn't want us to contact him?" Mari failed to hide the concern in her voice.

"Most likely he dropped it on purpose so we would find it," Riddick offered.

"That's what frightens me. Is he telling us that he's in trouble?" Val asked. She rubbed at the pain in her stomach.

They heard a commotion downstairs. The three vampires took off in a flash.

CHAPTER 13 NEW YORK 2020 AD

"Let go of me! I have to see her," a man's voice rang out. This was followed by the loud cracking sounds of vampires fighting. Mari and Val exchanged a concerned look as they recognized the voice. When they reached the main foyer, they could see ten guards trying to restrain Teller, Abdullah and the twins. The guards were not faring very well.

"Stop," Val yelled, "Let them go!"

This the guards did at once. Teller was on his knees so Val joined him and wrapped her arms tightly around his neck. He placed his arms around her waist as the shock ran through them. It was a moment of total pleasure. Val could forget her troubles, even if it was only for a brief moment.

"Apparently he does know the Queen," one of the guards said.

"I've come to warn you," Teller whispered. "You and Elijah are in danger."

Val pulled away enough to look into his eyes. His eyes were dark, he was truly shaken. Val's heart raced. *Elijah is in trouble.* "You may be too late," she whispered. She pulled Teller to his feet as she stood. Val didn't let go of his hand. It was as if she had to feel his electric touch;

it stabilized her, which she greatly needed. Val bowed slightly to Teller's comrades. "It is good to see you all again, Abdullah, Cosmin, Costel."

They bowed deeply in return.

John had appeared at the sound of the commotion. He never missed anything that happened within these walls.

"Gather the leaders of the Court for a meeting in the Great Hall," Val ordered.

With a nod John was gone. Riddick followed after him.

Mari gave Teller a hug. "It is good that you are here. Yet, I'm still furious with you."

Teller gave her a weary smile. "I am truly sorry for not saying goodbye. Surely you understand why I had to leave?" he emphasized his point with a glance to Vallachia.

"Yes, well, I'm relieved that you are alive and well," Mari said. She took Teller's free arm in hers, as they headed toward the Great Hall.

"It's wonderful to see you both. I only wish it were under better circumstances."

Val shot a worried look to Mari.

"I had better talk to you in private before meeting with the entire Court. That way you can decide what to tell them," Teller said.

"Why would we not tell them everything?" Val asked.

"To avoid panic. You may want to choose a … certain level of discretion."

"You're beginning to frighten me," Val said.

"Good. You should be. Listen to my story; then you can do whatever you think is best. Where's Elijah? He needs to hear what I have to say."

"He has been missing for more than a day now. I have men out searching for him."

"Then we can't waste another moment." Teller spoke quickly. "A couple of weeks ago I was walking the streets of Shanghai. I was alone and it was late, when a coven of vampires surrounded me. None of them were familiar, which was odd, as I know everyone in those parts.

The vampires attacked. I fought them off but some of them were chanting in … some strange language. My mind grew blurry, it was as if I couldn't think. One of them injected me with something. I assume it was an incredibly high dose of anesthetic. It must have been enough to knock out a vampire because I slowly slipped into darkness. When I woke, I found myself in heavy chains on a hospital bed. The only faces I recognized were those of Neacsa and her faithful servant — whose name I don't remember."

Val inhaled sharply. "Your wife … or Ramdasha's widow — whomever she is? She is alive." Her heart pounded against her chest as she envisioned this exact same thing happening to Elijah. *He must have been captured by her as well!*

"Doesn't Neacsa go by Elda?" Mari asked.

"I first knew her as Neacsa. She will always be Neacsa to me," Teller answered.

"What happened next?" Val asked.

"They kept me drugged and I only caught bits and pieces when the drug would wear off enough for me to regain consciousness. Then they would knock me out again. What I was able to gather was that they thought they needed my blood. I'm not entirely sure why. In the end it became apparent that it was not my blood they needed after all. Neacsa grew frustrated because whatever they were trying to do was not working. They said something to the effect of, 'He must not be the one. We need the blood of the Queen's true love.' Some of Neacsa's people were certain that I was the one they needed, so Neacsa was convinced to try one more time. They took more blood and she said that if it did not work this time then they would kill me. What was it they said about why I had to die? … 'To ensure that the chosen ones could not come to be'."

The room fell silent. Val was hoping he would go on — to explain — as none of this made any sense. It only raised endless questions. Val looked at Mari and Mari shook her head and shrugged.

"What does this mean? What are our enemies up to?" Val asked.

"I don't know but surely it's a move against the Court," Teller said.

"It sounds like tales of witchcraft." Yet Val had never encountered real witches. She always believed that the witch burnings throughout history were simply excuses to kill strong minded women who did not accept that their place was below men.

"There's no way to know for sure but I don't think they call themselves witches. They referred to themselves as 'the Servants of Aggadad.'"

"How did you manage to get away?" Val asked.

"The morning they intended to kill me, I woke to the delicious smell of human blood."

"I wager that that is an effective way to wake a hungry vampire," Mari said.

"At first I thought the woman holding the blood bag was you." Teller turned his gaze to Val.

Val shifted uncomfortably under his affectionate stare.

"As I downed the blood, my strength came back and my head cleared. That's when I noticed the differences between the woman who saved me and you. She looked to be older than you but definitely resembled you. She wore a long white dress and appeared to … glow. Yet, she smelled like a vampire and something else unidentifiable. This strange woman unchained me and told me to come straight to you. So … here I am."

Val's mind raced. "Who was she? What was she?"

Teller shook his head, not knowing the answers. "That's all I could gather and it makes no more sense to me than it does to you. It does follow that if they were not able to get what they needed from me, then Elijah would be their next target. It appears that Neacsa needs the blood of your true love, to carry out her plan. Sergiu referred to her as a witch. It was not something that I wanted to accept but she does appear to have certain abilities. The chanting that weakened me and her uncanny ability to see the future are clues that lead me to believe that Sergiu may have been right all those years ago."

"It sounds as if Elda is planning to fight us on a different level — one we know nothing about," Val said. "It's unlikely that they will attack with an army, as that tactic failed miserably before. I suppose they intend to challenge the Court in an entirely unexpected manner."

"That is concerning, to say the least," Mari said. "We're always prepared for a war but how do we fight against something we don't understand?"

"That makes it the perfect plan to defeat us," Val said.

CHAPTER 14 NEW YORK 2020 AD

Riddick and John entered the Great Hall.

"The other members of the Court are on their way, My Lady," John said.

"Thank you," Val whispered. Her mind swam with a million questions.

Teller returned Riddick's glare with a condescending smile.

These two will never change. They're like children. Val stepped between them, "That's quite enough, boys. We all have to get along. I'm not sure what to make of all this. But one thing is certain, we need one another. We are on the same side." She looked between Teller and Riddick for understanding.

Teller shrugged. "You're the boss." His tone was sarcastic.

Riddick stepped forward. "You're still an arrogant asshole."

The palm of Val's hand slammed into Riddick's chest as he advanced on Teller. Val gave Riddick a knowing stare and nod that said, "I can handle this."

Riddick took a step back. Val turned her attention to Teller. "In Elijah's absences I *am* the boss and you will do well to remember that."

Teller put his hands up in surrender. "Of course, Your Majesty." He issued a dashing smile.

Val understood how Riddick felt; Teller was infuriating. The look on his face made Val want to slap him and kiss him at the same time. She shook her head to clear it. "Our first priority is to find Elijah. The other members of the Court need to know Teller's story. Some of them may know something about the Servants of Aggadad. Hopefully someone will be able to shed some light on what we're up against."

Samuel had been out looking for Elijah but returned for the meeting of Elders. He greeted Teller as the old friend that he was. Then he went straight to Mari and they shared a concerned glance.

Soon Val was surrounded by her coven; the leaders of the Court from abroad joined the meeting remotely on large flat-screens. This included Lord Alexandru in London, Lord Shantanu in India and Lady Jinlan in Beijing. She was Teller's friend and the leader of the Chinese branch of the Court.

Teller retold his story. Unfortunately no one had heard of the Servants of Aggadad or the mysterious lady in white who resembled Vallachia and who had saved Teller. It was decided, that the number-one priority was to find Elijah. Reinforcements from their allies overseas were to join the Court in America. They were to help in the search for Elijah and to try to discover anything they could about Elda and Aggadad.

Teller had been taken to Zhengzhou, China and held captive in an underground lab. It was decided that if Elda and these "servants" did indeed have Elijah, it was unlikely they would bother transporting him all the way back to Zhengzhou. It was more probable that Elijah was being held closer to where he was captured, as Teller had been. Nevertheless, a small group of Jinlan's men were going to search for the lab in Zhengzhou to see if they could find any clues, before heading this way.

It was decided that Val would set up a base outside New York City in order to more easily coordinate their search for the King. The Court also came to the conclusion that if Elda did have Elijah, then she most likely needed him alive — for now at least. This gave Val hope, she knew he was not dead and that they would find him. They simply had to.

Val headed straight for her room to pack after the meeting. Her girlfriends joined her.

"Don't worry. We'll find him in time." Sonia wrapped her tiny arms around Val's waist.

Val only nodded as she was too choked up to speak. Her other friends joined in the embrace. This got the tears flowing. Val feared the worst. *Was Elda torturing him?* After all, it was Elijah who beheaded her love, Ramdasha. Val was also worried that they may be able to gain the power they needed from Elijah — her true love. They may soon be able to carry out their plan — whatever that might be. Whatever the Servants of Aggadad were up to, Val knew it was not good.

THE COURT SET up a camp consisting of many large tents deep in the forest yet only a short flight from New York City. These were not just any tents. They were tall enough for people to easily stand in. Val's tent held a bed, desk, dresser, table and chairs. Her tent was partitioned off into several different "rooms" by silk tapestries and elegantly carved wooden partitions. Plush rugs lined the floor. This was how queens "camped".

"Riddick is to lead the search," Val announced.

Riddick stepped forward. "Please My Lady, send Samuel to lead the search. You're solely in charge now. I can't leave you unprotected."

"She will not be unprotected," Teller snapped. "I will look after her."

Riddick glared at Teller. "I bet you will. However, it's my duty to protect the Queen ... from all manner of vermin."

Teller narrowed his eyes. He stood from the table he had been leaning on and stepped toward Riddick. "What exactly is that suppose to mean?"

Val shook her head in frustration. She did not understand their hatred for each other. "Please, you two, we don't have time for this." The concern in her voice seemed to bring them back to the task at hand.

"You must heed my advice," Riddick said. "This could be part of Elda's plan. If we put all our resources into trying to find the king it will make it easier for them to get to you. Without you and Elijah everything would be lost. That may be exactly what the enemy wants."

Val nodded. "You're right. ... Thank you." Thinking with only her heart, she wanted to put everything the Court had into finding Elijah but she could not allow their ancient reign to fall apart in Elijah's absence. This was much bigger than Elijah or Val. It was her duty to keep the Court together until the king returned. "Riddick will remain here to guard the camp. Samuel will lead the searches."

Samuel quickly stood — ready to find his oldest and closest friend.

Val placed her hand on Riddick's shoulder. "You do what you must to keep this camp secure."

"Of course, My Lady."

Val wished she could help in the search but her friends convinced her to stay put for two reasons; for her protection and in case Elijah returned. They figured he would seek Val out first and she would be easier to find if she remained in one place.

CHAPTER 15 NEW YORK 2020 AD

The problem was that hanging out at camp was not good for Val's mental health. She felt useless and there was nothing to do. She could not focus on reading or much of anything, for that matter. She conducted searches on her phone for information about the Servants of Aggadad but didn't find anything of use. It was as though they didn't exist.

Val walked with Riddick on patrol around the camp simply for something to do. He had opened his mouth several times to speak, only to shut it again.

"Out with it already." Val said.

"At the risk of offending you, I want to ask you to do something for me — for all of us."

Val tilted her head. "Very well."

"Stay away from Teller," Riddick blurted.

"Oh," Val said. "That *is* offensive. You know I'm worried sick about Elijah and I wouldn't do that to him."

"I know. You say that now but if you deny the power Teller has over you then you will falter. We all know how you two feel about each other and the way he looks at you ..." Riddick shook his head. "It worries me. I mean, can we even trust him? He shows up after all these years with some odd story. It's suspicious."

Val narrowed her eyes. "Of course we can trust him." She took a deep breath. "Thank you for voicing your concern. Once again, you're right and I have every intention of staying away from Teller. You know, I would be lost without you."

"Thank you for the kind words, My Lady, but it's you we would be lost without. You're the solitary leader of the vampire world ... until we find Elijah."

Val gave him a peck on the cheek and headed for her tent. She was going to be tested right away, as she caught Teller's scent before she entered. She pulled the tent flap back just enough to see him. Teller was waiting for her. She watched him for a moment. It was wonderful to see him — to know where he was — to know that he was safe. She shook her head to clear it. She turned on her heel and headed for Mari's tent. Val lay beside Mari on her bed.

"Avoiding Teller?" Mari said.

Val's friends knew her too well. She supposed that was bound to happen after being together for the better part of seven hundred and seventy years.

"Maybe I simply needed to see my oldest and dearest friend," Val said.

"Don't bother denying it. You know I'm right." Mari put her index finger against her lips as she thought. "You know, Elijah would forgive you."

Val's mouth fell open. "For what?"

"Giving in to your desires for Teller."

"I can't believe you said that and at a time like this!"

"I'm simply saying — how long can this go on? Teller has not let go of you in the least and you're equally guilty. The two of you are locked in temptation."

"Where did you get that — from those terrible romance novels you read?"

"Oh, come now, you like the same books I do."

"If only you knew what it felt like to touch him then you would understand."

"I do understand. I told you many years ago, you made the wrong choice."

"Technically you never said that I chose the wrong man," Val snapped.

"Maybe if you two got together then you could finally get over each other and both of you could move on. We all would be happy to see that happen including Elijah. Your feelings for Teller aren't fair to Elijah."

Val stood to leave; this was the last thing she needed to hear. "You're mad you know! This nonsense you're talking is treason."

"Come now, we don't live in the middle-ages anymore. It's the twenty-first century for crying out loud," Mari yelled to Val's back as she left the tent.

Val could not find anyone else to distract her. Mary, Elizabeth, Aaron and Sonia were all out searching. So she wandered around camp alone and tried not to think.

CHAPTER 16 NEW YORK 2020 AD

Elijah mindlessly walked the crowded streets of New York City. *Change is upon us. Things have been perfect for a long time. I have everything, including a perfect queen to rule by my side. She is beloved by the Court's followers and she is my world. Vampires follow her as much as they do me. Together we make this work. We keep the delicate balance between humans and vampires. Yet, I cannot shake the feeling that she will be leaving me and the Court. No, she would never do that. I have no doubt that everything would fall apart if she were to leave — including me.*

A sense of urgency came over Elijah. *I should be with her now. I must try to convince her to stay.*

Elijah turned around to head home when he noticed a number of people closing in around him. He had been lost in his own miserable thoughts and did not see the threat. They had formed a circle around him and it was too late. Some of the strangers chanted, while others attacked. Elijah's fist hit the first attacker in the jaw, followed by Elijah's elbow slamming into his face, sending him flying back.

Elijah spun around pulling out the gun that had been tucked safely in his jeans at his lower back. The members of the Court still did not leave home without being armed. Handguns were easier to conceal than swords, though he wished he had his trusty weapons of old. He shot the next attacker in the chest; the .45 caliber bullets sent his opponent stumbling back. People on the street scattered and screams rang out, mixing with the sound of gunfire.

Elijah's head began to spin and he knew they would capture him. He could also tell that they did not want him dead as the attackers backed away when Elijah fell to his knees. They had attacked only to distract him — to keep him from escaping the spell that rendered him useless. He swiftly dropped his phone. It slid under a drop box outside the nearby post office, thus concealing his phone. His friends would find it and hopefully discern that he was in peril. He felt the sting of a needle enter deep into his lower back. He was unable to move, let alone fight them off. Elijah's world slowly grew dark.

WHEN ELIJAH CAME TO, it was difficult to focus on anything. He could not move an inch as he had been chained to a gurney with heavy shackles. The space around him looked like a hospital room or a laboratory. Something told him that he was deep underground. He was hooked up to an IV bag but instead of injecting fluids into his body, it was taking his blood. He only recognized one face, "Elda," he whispered.

A man in a white lab coat approached with a syringe that was four times the size of those used on humans. It must take that much more anesthetic — or whatever they were using — to render a vampire unconscious. The long needle sank deep into Elijah's arm and once again the light began to fade.

The worst part was that when he was unconscious, the nightmares would return. He endlessly fought the dragon to no avail. Vallachia would call to him as the dragon tore her away — forever.

After several times of being drugged whenever Elijah woke, he decided to keep his eyes closed and pretend to still be unconscious. He overheard Elda, "It's working. We found the right one this time. He must be the Queen's true love. Soon we will be able to take over. We only need a little more of his blood, then we can kill him."

"He should wake any minute," a man's voice said.

"Then give him another dose," Elda ordered.

The next time Elijah came to, there was a tall woman in a long white dress standing over him. At first, all he could make out was long blond hair.

"Drink this. Quickly now," the blond woman whispered.

"Val?" Elijah whispered.

The lady shook her head no.

When he could finally focus on her face, he could see that it was not Vallachia but the woman resembled her. A slight glow encompassed her entire body. The smell of blood was overwhelming. He drank eagerly. The blood helped to clear his head. The woman quickly unlocked his chains and threw them off. Elijah broke the last one in two before she was able to unlock it.

"Good, your strength is back. Elda will be along any moment to knock you out or to kill you. Your people are in a camp north of the city. Go now!" She indicated a door at the other end of the room. "There's an elevator at the end of the hall."

Elijah's mind was slowly coming back to reality. "Valentina?"

She nodded. "It's good to see you again Elijah but we don't have time. You must go now!" She gave him a firm shove toward the door.

Elijah ran out of the room and toward the elevator. He pressed the call button. "We thought you were dead." But when he turned around, he found that he was alone. Valentina had not followed.

"Valentina! Are you coming?" he asked the empty hallway. No answer. The doors to the elevator opened and he had to go. He hoped she would be able to get out. His head swam with thoughts about what this would mean for Vallachia. *Valentina is alive. How can that be?*

The elevator buttons indicated that it was ten stories up to the ground level. A surveillance camera hung in the top corner of the elevator. *Elda's probably already spotted me.* Elijah jumped, grabbed the camera, ripped it from its holder and crushed it on the floor. He looked around for a way out of the elevator. *I'm vulnerable in this damn metal box.*

Elijah broke a roof panel and leapt onto the top of the elevator. An alarm sounded and the elevator came to a screeching halt. He almost lost his balance but quickly recovered. He moved to the thin ledge of the nearest door frame. Up he went leaping one floor at a time until he reached the door marked 'ground level'. The shaft continued upward for many more stories.

They will be looking for me on the ground level. Elijah made one more jump to the second story opening. He began to slowly pull the elevator doors apart, which required breaking them. The doors moaned in protest. The sounds of metal grinding against metal mixed with voices below. Someone was prying the ground level doors apart.

A glance down revealed the barrel of a gun. A man in the elevator door below scanned the shaft. Elijah pulled with all his strength. Bullets whizzed past. The doors came apart enough for him to squeeze through. He took off at a full run across the second story, looking for a window. All he knew was that he had to get out of the building. It appeared to be normal business offices on this level.

Elijah caught a glimpse of sunlight from a window ahead. He did not slow his pace as he ran straight for it. Using his arm to protect his face, he jumped through the glass. He landed on his feet on the street below. The sound of glass shattering on pavement was followed by startled screams from onlookers.

A woman coming out of the main entrance pointed her gun at Elijah. "Stop!" she ordered.

Elijah was gone in a flash. He swerved as the sound of gunfire rang out. He looked around for any sign of where he was. The building he had been held beneath had a large sign that read Pittman's Laboratory Industries.

The woman was a good shoot. Elijah was a fast-moving target, but not fast enough for vampire eyes. She narrowed her eyes down the sight of her gun. She steadied her hands and pulled the trigger. With one well-placed shot she saw blood spray as the bullet found its mark.

CHAPTER 17 NEW YORK 2020 AD

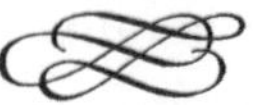

For the first two weeks of endlessly searching the city and surrounding areas, Vallachia had been able to remain hopeful, as Teller had survived that long in Elda's clutches. Val was at least able to keep the panic from consuming her. But now a month had passed since she'd last seen Elijah. The search parties took shifts and covered every inch of the city. They sneaked into buildings and combed the streets looking for any sign of their king.

What good is all this if Elda can see them coming, Val thought. But she couldn't give up. Elijah was missing and they had to do something. She prayed he was not dead. *I can't do this — any of this — without him.* It was easily the worst month of her life.

At first, she was staunch about avoiding Teller but without Elijah to run to, this grew more difficult, as the long days and nights droned on. Eventually Teller caught Vallachia alone in her tent one night.

She stood to leave.

"Please, I only want to talk," Teller said. 'I promise I will behave. I want to be here for you."

This was too good an offer to resist and that was how he got in.

"I do hate it that we can't be friends anymore," Val admitted.

From that point on, when he was not out searching, they were together. He was a shoulder to lean on — to cry on. He made the waiting and the not knowing somewhat bearable. Val didn't know if she could have gotten through this without him. He kept her hopes up that they would find Elijah. Still, as time passed things were looking bleak.

They took strolls around the camp. Teller told Val about his adventures in the Far East. This was fascinating as she had never been. He talked about the friends he'd made over the years, many of whom were now in New York, helping with the search. At this point their camp was bursting with vampires from all over the world.

Val told him about their travels, mostly around the Americas. She told him about trying to help slaves and fighting for civil rights. She told him of the children that she looked after whenever she could, as they still ran the largest orphanage in the city.

"Sometimes I think that things never change," Teller said.

"How so? The world is a vastly different place than the one we grew up in," Val said.

"Is it? During my time as the Prince of Wallachia, I faced all the same issues that politicians face today. I battled a militant Islam. The wealthiest of merchants did not want to pay their fair share of taxes. I dealt with a corrupt yet powerful group of people meddling in politics for their own personal gain. Back in Wallachia we called them the Boyars but today such people would be called the mafia. How best to fight crime and poverty, these are all issues of today and they were all the same issues I faced as a leader in medieval Europe. We haven't solved any of these problems. You see, the world never truly changes."

"Well you did not have to run in an election."

"That's true. That would have been easier."

Val laughed. Teller had won the hearts of the people of Wallachia. She was sure he would have been elected by them. Yet, as it was back then, he'd had to marry a princess and then kill her father. So an election very well may have been easier. That princess now went by the name Elda. *So Teller killed her father and Elijah killed her love. No wonder Elda is after the two most important men in my life.* This thought sent a chill through Val. "We're in big trouble, aren't we?" Val whispered. "I mean ... Elda, she truly has reason to hate us and she's out for revenge."

"Aye." Teller said.

"I'M sorry if I ever seemed disrespectful to you," Teller said.

Val sat curled up in a chair in her tent. She raised her eyebrows at Teller.

"You have never been a queen to me. You're my childhood love and my dearest friend. The one who used to play with me in the fields outside our village. I'm sorry for not treating you like the royalty that you are."

These memories created a sense of longing. The better part of a millennium had passed since they had been children in Ludus. "I know," Val said. Not exactly accepting his apology but acknowledging that things were complicated between them. "I'm grateful for your company," she admitted.

Teller moved to sit in a chair next to her. His muscular arm rested close by. He wore a short sleeve t-shirt and Val could see part of a tattoo on his bicep. She tilted her head to examine it. He always wore a black leather jacket so this was the first time she noticed his tattoo. "What's this?" She lifted his shirtsleeve to get a better look. It was the head of a dragon. *Not a surprise,* she thought.

"Do you want to see the rest?" he asked.

"No! That's not necessary."

Teller gave her a mischievous smile. "Come now. I know you're curious."

He stood and pulled his shirt over his head, turning his back to Val. Her lips parted. The head of the dragon started at his upper arm and covered his large shoulder. The serpent's body twisted and wound its way across his entire broad back. The tail of the beast curved around his waist and ended on his stomach.

Val was mesmerized. "It's beautiful," she breathed. She simply had to touch it. She did not remember standing. Her fingers ran gently across his olive skin. She started at the nose of the dragon on his bicep and slowly ran her hand across the dragon. He flinched at her shocking touch and his muscles tightened as her hand brushed across his skin. She lifted his arm with one hand while she finished tracing the tattoo with the other hand. She ended up standing in front of him with her hand on his stomach.

Teller took her hand in his. She let him pull her close. His lips were on hers.

The pleasure of his touch rushed through her body. *This will be like before, the few times he stole a kiss. It is only a ... kiss.* Val told herself.

Instead of stopping him — or trying to — Val shut her mind off. She let herself go. She became completely lost in his caress, nothing else mattered — a complete escape.

Teller pulled her shirt over her head, he stepped back at the sight of her tattoo. His green eyes darkened with anger and his jaw muscles tightened. "The perfect reminder that you are not mine."

This helped to bring Val back to reality. She shook her head. *Right — not his. Thank God for my tattoo to break the spell,* she thought. She took her shirt from his hand and started to put it back on.

Teller grabbed her arm to stop her. "I don't care. I know you love him but we were meant to be together. I can make you forget about him." He pressed his lips and body to hers.

At his overpowering touch she felt herself slip away once again. There was a voice that screamed for her to stop but soon that part could no longer be heard. She completely let go.

It was different being with Teller. His touch was determined, strong — even rough. Elijah was always smooth and gentle. Maybe it was the overwhelming sensation between them. It was more than she could stand. When Val closed her eyes, she saw thousands of fish making their way to a giant fiery planet in the darkness. An intense feeling of enlightenment consumed her. For the briefest moment she thought she knew the purpose of life. This visceral experience was overwhelming. So she chose to keep her eyes open and focus on Teller's bright green eyes.

One last shudder went through her body. When his heartbeat

began to slow — or perhaps it was her own, she was not sure which — she managed to shove Teller off. She rolled away from him. Once he was no longer touching her, she could think again. Thinking brought the tears; soon she was sobbing. *What have I done? I can never take this back.*

After a moment Teller put his hand on her shoulder to comfort her and the electric touch was so strong it hurt. Val jolted and would have moved away but the painful sensation disappeared. This was enough to distract her from her sorrow. She gazed at Teller with wide eyes. "What was that?"

"I don't know. I have never understood our connection," he whispered.

Val put her hand in his, locking their fingers together. The shocking sensation was gone! It was a normal touch. She felt two opposing emotions at the same time. Half of her was relieved and the other half was devastated. *Our connection is gone. We are no longer linked — we can finally be free of each other. Perhaps we can move on! Yet, that amazing feeling is gone. We may never feel it again.*

"I love you," he whispered.

"I have always loved you. That was never the problem."

Teller laid his head on Val's chest and she ran her fingers through his thick dark hair. That's how Riddick found them.

CHAPTER 18 NEW YORK 2020 AD

In a blur, Elijah headed north out of the city. He clenched at his side where the bullet had grazed him. He took flight as soon as he could. Elda's men were nowhere in sight. *Perhaps I lost them or perhaps they chose not to pursue me,* he thought.

Elijah easily found the camp that Valentina told him about. This was where Vallachia would be waiting for him. By the time Elijah found the camp he was beginning to think that Valentina had only been a figment of his imagination.

Riddick was the first to greet Elijah. He looked relieved at first, then concern flashed across his face when he noticed Elijah's blood-soaked shirt.

"I'm fine or I will be soon," Elijah said.

Riddick gave him a one-armed embrace and a slap on the back. "It's good to see that you are alive. Vallachia will be relieved. I will let her know you're back."

Samuel appeared at Elijah's side. The two old friends grabbed one another's forearms and gave each other a one-armed embrace.

"Let me have a look at your wound." Samuel said.

RIDDICK LIFTED the flap to Val's tent. "Excellent news … shit." He looked between the lovers for a moment. His eyes narrowed on Val. "The King has returned."

Elijah is back! That was all that mattered. Val had to see that he was alive and well. Riddick dropped the tent flap and Val quickly dressed and was gone. She caught up to Riddick and soon spotted Elijah and Samuel. Elijah was in the same clothes she last saw him in, only now they were dirty and torn. His shirt was soaked in blood.

"He will be fine," Samuel said.

Val threw her arms around Elijah's shoulders.

Elijah breathed in her scent but all he smelled was … *him*. Elijah knew in that instant that his nightmares had come true. *I'm too late.* When Elijah looked into Val's bright blue eyes, he saw something new — something he had never seen before. It was guilt. Over her shoulder Elijah spotted *him* — the culprit — the dragon from his nightmares.

Elijah had always thought that "seeing red" was only a figure of speech — a stupid cliché even. But it was as if the sun had suddenly set. The sky turned a deep red. In fact, everything he saw was shrouded in a blood-red hue.

Elijah didn't know if he pushed Val away or if she simply ran off but in an instant Elijah was on top of Teller. His hands were around Teller's neck. Teller gasped for air when Samuel pulled Elijah off.

This is only a dream, Elijah thought.

DAYS PASSED and Elijah's head cleared from the loss of blood and being endlessly drugged. Vallachia, however, was nowhere to be found. Elijah sat at the desk in her tent. He spun her broken cell phone in his hand. Riddick had found it not far from camp. The cover looked like a spiderweb. Someone, most likely Val, had shattered it.

She obviously wants to be alone. She'll let the guilt eat her alive. It will destroy her. I have to find her! She never denied her love for Teller. Even in the very beginning she had always made it perfectly clear that she wanted to be with him. When that did not work out and we finally married, I knew that their love was a part of the deal. It is worth it — to be with her. She is worth it. The fact that she loved him doesn't matter because she also loves me and she chose me. If she were to choose me again then it still wouldn't matter. I have to tell her that I forgive her, Elijah thought.

"My Lord," Riddick said as he entered the tent. "Do you want us to continue the search?"

"Yes. Find her," Elijah demanded.

"Would it not be wise to give her some time, My Lord? She clearly does not want us to follow her." Riddick gestured to the broken phone.

"No. That would not be wise. You know she will beat herself up over this — over nothing. I have to get her back." Elijah put his head in his hands and resisted the urge to scream. *If only I could speak with her, I could set everything right.*

"Of course, My Lord. We'll find her." Riddick turned to leave.

"Wait. Is Teller well?"

"Yes. He's been confined as you requested."

"Bring him to me."

With a nod Riddick was gone. When he returned, he brought with him two guards with Teller secured between them. Teller wore heavy iron shackles.

For a moment Elijah wanted to tighten his fingers around Teller's neck again. *She wouldn't want that. She wouldn't want any of this.* "Let him go."

"My Lord?"

Elijah glared at Riddick and he quickly unchained Teller.

Teller stepped forward rubbing his wrists. "Where's Vallachia?"

"That is *the* question. I was hoping you might be able to shed some light on her whereabouts?"

Teller's eyes widened. "She's not here?"

"She's been missing since the day I returned. Do you know where she would go?"

Teller shook his head. "I have no idea. We have to find her! She may be in trouble."

Elijah thought that Teller appeared to be telling the truth. He didn't know where she was. Elijah nodded in agreement and then waved his hand for Teller to leave. *He knows nothing or would tell me nothing of use.*

Elijah couldn't stand to look at Teller any longer because all he saw was Teller and Vallachia intertwined. This image was enough to bring out the monster inside. If Teller didn't get out of his sight, Elijah was afraid he might kill him. *Then Vallachia would never forgive me.* As Teller left, Elijah gestured for Riddick to approach. "Follow him," Elijah said in a low voice. Then he was alone.

CHAPTER 19 NEW YORK 2020 AD

Vallachia ran. She didn't care where she was running — it didn't matter. What did matter was that she got away from the mess she had made. *Now I've lost Elijah. I've also lost the connection with Teller. I've lost everything. I didn't fully realize that I had so much; now it's all gone. This is a fitting punishment. I don't deserve either of them.*

Lost in her miserable thoughts, Val barely stopped in time when the glowing figure of a woman appeared in front of her. The stranger wore a long white dress and there was a faint light that outlined her lean form. Val almost ran into her. She stood directly in front of Val. For a moment Val thought she was looking in a mirror. But the woman was not exactly a mirror image; she looked to be a bit older than Val.

This must be the woman who saved Teller from Elda. Val stepped away from the woman.

The woman's smile was warm. "Come, my darling. It's time you went away with me."

"What?" was all Val managed to get out.

"My beautiful daughter, it's time for you to come with me."

Val's head had already been spinning from the events of the day.

Now she thought she might black out entirely. "Daughter? That … that can't be."

"We have a lot of catching up to do but for now you must trust me. We have to leave. They'll be looking for you."

"Why … leave?" Val stuttered.

"It's no longer safe for you. Please trust me, my dear. When we get home, I'll explain everything."

The woman took Val's hands. In that instant Val wanted to trust this stranger and she didn't understand why. Val had never been the naturally trusting type.

"It was you who saved Teller?"

The woman nodded. "And Elijah."

I knew it. I can trust her. "Thank you," Val whispered.

"Now," she said with more urgency, "allow me to save you."

Val looked back. "I suppose it would be best for me to go back and try to fix the huge mess I've made."

"You were doing a good job of running away on your own, so please come with me. I have an isolated home where we can be safe."

"Safe from what?"

"Dark times are coming. I'll explain when we have the time."

Val gave a reluctant nod.

"Good. Give me your phone."

Val questioned whether or not it was wise to give her phone to this woman but she handed it over anyway.

The woman dropped the phone and crushed it with her foot.

"No!" Val regretted her choice at once. She should at least let her friends know that she was alive.

The woman took Val's hand again and spread her enormous bat-like wings. Val followed her into the air. Val decided that she would hear what this woman had to say and then return to try to make things right with Elijah — with all her friends. *Surely, they will forgive me.* The thought of losing Elijah and her family, caused a pain in her chest, which she tried unsuccessfully to rub away.

The woman paused in the air long enough to sprinkle dust she had in a pouch tied to her waist. Sparkling particles floated in the air below them.

"What's that?" Val asked.

"So they can't follow us. Our scent will be lost here."

The Servants of Aggadad must have used some such substance to throw us off Elijah's scent, Val thought.

The two vampires flew for hours toward the north. They landed in a large basin that had once been the mouth of a volcano. They were completely surrounded by tall mountains, which formed a perfect circle around them. The center of the basin consisted of a large lake. It was breathtakingly beautiful and very isolated. Humans could not easily get here. They were surrounded by Canadian tundra. Snow and glaciers topped the mountains. Several waterfalls fed the lake in the basin of the volcano. Everything below the snow line was a lively dark green.

"This place is amazing," Val said, as they landed by the lake.

"I'm delighted that you like it." The woman led Val to a small cabin. Smoke rose out of the chimney.

"You don't live alone?"

The woman shook her head no. "Come meet the ladies."

As they entered the tiny home, Val was struck by the scent of humans but not just any humans. They had a distinct scent. Perhaps they were not fully human. There was something different about these people.

The woman claiming to be Val's mother said, "This is Sasha." She gestured to a middle-aged woman who was short with long brown hair.

Sasha took Val's hands. "It's a pleasure to finally meet you!" Her brown eyes sparkled with excitement.

Val only nodded in reply. *Who are these strange people? What are they?*

"And this is Angela." The woman in white pointed to an older woman who looked to be in her sixties. Angela was taller than Sasha and her hair was long and gray. "It is with great pleasure that I finally have the opportunity to introduce you to my daughter, Vallachia."

Val studied the woman. *How could she possibly be my mother?*

Angela put her hands on Val's cheeks. Val resisted the urge to pull away.

"She's lovely, just as you said," Angela said. "Though I did not believe you when you claimed that your daughter was more beautiful than you, Valentina, but I must admit, she is indeed."

"That is her father that you're seeing in her," Valentina said with pride.

Valentina! That was my mother's name!

CHAPTER 20 NORTHERN CANADA 2020 AD

Val gently took Angela's hands and removed them from her face. Val looked at Valentina with wide eyes. "Are you truly my mother?"

Valentina smiled and nodded as if this were a completely normal situation.

Because this happens all the time, right? You find out your mother is somehow alive after ... almost eight hundred years.

"Come, Angela. Let's tend to the garden and allow these two to catch up on the past couple hundred years or so. I'm sure there is much to discuss," Sasha said.

Valentina watched her companions leave before turning to Val. "You must have so many questions. Let me start from the beginning. I was turned into a vampire not long after your brother was born. As you will remember those first years of being a vampire were ... well, difficult at best. I didn't want to hurt my family. Then as the years passed I decided that it was best not to disrupt your life by suddenly turning up. I had faked my death and I needed to remain 'dead', for everyone's safety. Your father did a marvelous job of raising you. It soon became apparent that you did not need me anyway. So I contented myself with watching over you from afar. As a matter of fact, I have watched over you your entire life."

"That's … creepy. If you're my mother then what was my father's name?"

"Adam."

"And my brother?"

"Josiah. You were born in the spring of 1242. Your father used to call you his spring flower. Your brother took over ministering in Ludus after your father's death. They were the most wonderful men. I loved you all very much and it hurt me to stay away but I had to." Valentina had begun to talk in the old Romanian dialect that Val had grown up speaking.

Only Val's closest friends would have known all this about her brief human life. Valentina took Val's hands. When Val looked into the stranger's bright blue eyes she knew that this woman must be related to her and most likely was indeed her mother.

"Mom?" Val ventured.

Valentina threw her arms around her daughter. Tears ran down Valentina's cheeks. "I have dreamed of this day so many times."

"Why did you not come to me after I was turned into a vampire?"

"I knew, without a doubt, that our paths would cross — when the time was right. You didn't need me until now."

"What's that suppose to mean?" Val felt the heat of anger rising in her chest. *My mother was alive all this time and she only now bothered to find me.* "Of course I needed you after I was turned. You could have helped me through … that terrible time … and what makes you think I need you now?" This last part came out harsher than Val had intended.

Valentina smiled and put her hands out as if to say slow down. "When I learned you had been turned I searched for you for a year. I barely missed you on several occasions but you scarcely stayed in one place. When I finally found you, you were in good hands and did not need me. I knew the Chastellains would look after you and take care of you. I didn't want to disrupt your life."

"That's madness. When I was a human I can understand you not wanting to interfere with our life or put us in danger but as vampires you and I could have had a life together."

Valentina frowned and sorrow flashed through her eyes. "It was complicated. I had to stay away. At that point I too had my own life and path to follow, just as you had your own path. Our lives did not cross until now."

"You're talking nonsense."

"We each had to take our own journey in order to find our way back to each other, when it matters most."

What kind of an answer is that? "I don't understand."

"Soon everything will become clear. You see Sasha, Angela and I are Servants of the Great Goddess. As you may have sensed they are not simple humans."

"What are you then?"

"We're something more. We have trained to become Servants of the Goddess."

"Are you witches?"

"No. We don't use or like that term. It's too vague; we serve the Goddess."

"Yes, I got it." Val snapped. "But what in the hell does that mean? Are you like the Servants of Aggadad?"

Valentina flinched at the name. "Absolutely not. They use their power for selfish reasons. We only do as the Almighty Mother wishes. However, the self-serving nature of Aggadad gives them a ... certain strength and this is what you're up against. This is why you need us now."

"So they're stronger than you?"

"It's not that they are stronger, per say, it's that they are willing to do things that we are not. Elda will not fight you in another war. She knows she doesn't stand a chance against your armies. She will attack the Court using other means. She's the strongest of the Servants of Aggadad and with her supporters she has grown very powerful."

"Are you telling me that she will use magic to take on the Court of Elders?"

"I suppose that's one way to put it. Yes, that is her plan. We do not consider it magic. To us it's a knowledge of the energies which lie hidden to most, yet they are there if one knows how to find them and use them. It's more of a spirituality, if you will."

Val shook her head. She did not fully fathom what the woman was saying. "How did you find Teller and then Elijah?"

"Yes, well Elijah was tricky, as Elda's servants blocked our sight after I rescued Teller. You see we keep watch over the world from here, to the best of our ability, anyway."

Valentina gestured to a pedestal that held a large asymmetrical shape draped in a purple silk cloth. She removed the cloth, unveiling a two-foot tall crystal. "This is the seeing stone."

With a closer look Val noticed a metallic silver liquid inside the crystal. It swirled around like a thick shimmering cloud. Right before Val's eyes, the color changed to a sparkling purple and an image appeared. Elijah sat at a desk turning her broken phone in his hand. Val's heart leapt.

"Elijah!" She placed her hands on the large stone. She had the urge to try to go to him, as if she could step into the crystal and be by his side. The image faded and Teller appeared in shackles. "No! I have to go to them." Val started toward the door.

Valentina quickly covered the stone and firmly grabbed Val's arm before she reached the door. "Please, not yet. There's more you must know. Your friends will be fine for now and we'll look after them from here. Let me finish; then you can decide what's best."

"Elijah won't kill Teller, will he?"

"No. He wouldn't do that — he's not like his father."

"You knew Lord Chastellain?"

A dark cloud filled her eyes. "His reputation was … far reaching."

Val nodded. "You're right, Elijah is not his father. He will not hurt Teller." Nevertheless, Val felt she should be there for them. *Yet, how can I be there for both Elijah and Teller? Maybe they are better off without me? This way I won't be between them — messing everything up.*

Valentina surprised Val by putting her hand on Val's lower abdomen. She began chanting and Val was about to step away when Valentina opened her eyes wide and smiled.

"Finally, they're on the way! We have been waiting for this day for a long time."

CHAPTER 21 NORTHERN CANADA 2020 AD

This woman may be my mother but she may very well be insane. Val backed away. "What are you talking about?"

Valentina's crystal blue eyes danced. She headed for the front door and called for Sasha and Angela.

They came running.

"It is time. The prophecy has come true," Valentina announced.

Sasha squealed and threw her arms around Val.

Val held her arms out in surprise. "What in the hell's going on?" She backed away from Sasha.

Valentina had tears of joy in her eyes. "Darling, you are going to be a mother!"

"That's it. I've had enough. You're all mad. There are asylums for people like you. You should all head there now." Val turned to leave.

Valentina gently took her daughter's hand. "I know this is a lot to take in. Please stay and rest a bit. You look tired." Valentina placed an arm around Val.

Val had never had a mother to coddle her. Her father had always been there for her but this was different — a mother's reassuring touch. Val had not known what it was like so she had not missed it. She had been deprived. It was a surprise to find that she liked the attention … the affection — maybe even needed it. Her mother's touch was enough to keep her from walking out the door.

Val's heart sank as it occurred to her, *After father's death, I had always been comforted by the thought that he had been reunited with his loving wife. Yet this was not the case. Valentina is not dead. Father has been denied his long lost love all this time.* Val lowered her head and shook it.

Val was lost in her thoughts as Valentina led her away from the door and across the room to an old couch. Val did feel tired … too tired. This was all too much. *I should leave these crazy people and try to get Elijah back and release Teller from his shackles. I have to warn them about Elda and her demon followers or whatever they are.* She was trying hard to focus on all that needed to be done but she was tired. She had been with Teller the night before and she didn't remember when she had slept last. She had not slept well since before Elijah disappeared. She also had the odd feeling that Valentina had something to do with her drowsiness.

"Let the poor dear rest," Angela said.

Perhaps it was only the power of their suggestion but Val lay down and closed her eyes. …

Two figures slowly emerged from solid white surroundings. They glowed as if they were almost a pure light. They were difficult to focus on in their bright surroundings. Val made out a man's face and a woman's face. The man vaguely resembled Teller only much more handsome — which Val didn't think was possible — and the woman looked somewhat like her but she was perfect and many times prettier. The Bible passage, "Made in God's image," echoed through her head. *They are Gods, perhaps The Gods. The Mother and Father of … us all.*

"So it's true? Are we to see the chosen ones walk the earth?" the man said.

"Yes, my darling," the woman wore a proud smile.

"It's about time. I did not think it would take this long." He smiled with affection. It was perfectly clear to Val that these two had a deep love for each other. A love that went beyond all else. They had transcended time and space together.

"It is a good thing that I did not bet on this one," the God said. "For

I would have lost. I didn't think she could resist him that long. We took great measures to see to it that they would be together."

"Ah yes but this is the right time, my love. The chosen ones were not needed until now. I must say she got her stubbornness from you," the Goddess said.

He gave the woman a knowing smile. "I don't think she got her stubbornness from me, my dear."

The woman laughed, which ended with a sigh. "I will miss them … terribly."

The man placed his arm around the woman. "Don't despair. They'll return to us … one day."

VAL WOKE with a start and Valentina appeared at her side. Val shook her head to try to clear it. *This is all a crazy dream. I will wake — for real — any minute and be back in Elijah's arms, safe at home.* She was still trying to wrap her head around the bizarre dream when her mother put her hand on Val's stomach again.

"Twins, actually, both girls. That is, if you want me to spoil all the surprises for you."

Val sat up. "Stop speaking such nonsense. It's impossible; you know we can't have children."

"Vampires don't but you were given an exceptional gift and it will only happen once. As you may have guessed, these two will be very special. They're the chosen ones."

"Chosen to do what, exactly?" Val's voice was flat, unbelieving, even melancholy.

Valentina frowned. "That's beyond my sight. Only time will tell. You see my dear you were never meant to be able to resist Teller. The fact that you were able to for so long really says something."

"So Teller is the father?"

"Of course." Valentina's frown deepened. "I'm terribly sorry but life played a trick on you two. You were meant to be together all along but your children were not needed until now. It took someone as wonderful as Elijah to keep you two apart for so long."

Val lay back down and put her arm over her forehead as the tears rolled down her cheeks. It was crazy but her first thought was, *If I am truly to have Teller's children, then how will I ever get Elijah back?* It was the only thing that made sense. Gods, Goddesses, chosen ones, none of that was intelligible. Gods who messed with people, toyed with them like tiny ants — played with their hearts. Val felt blood rush to her cheeks as she thought of the couple in her dream. *They caused me to hurt Elijah; they kept me from Teller all those years. This is their fault,* she wanted to scream.

Val rose in one fluid motion. *It was merely a stupid dream and I'm not going to have a baby, let alone two.* "I have to get back to my friends."

Valentina's brow creased and desperation flashed in her eyes. "Please, no, you can't. Your job is to protect your babies. And the best way to do that is to keep them a secret. No one must know about them."

"If any of this is true then why can't anyone know about them?"

"They, well, *you* for now, while you carry them, will be fiercely pursued. You and all your friends would be in grave danger if you go to them. You can protect the Court and your daughters if you stay hidden. The chosen ones are the only chance we have of beating Elda. She was able to get what she needed from Elijah. His blood worked for her dark purposes and soon she will take over. We cannot stop her but they can." Valentina placed her hand lovingly on Val's lower abdomen. "They are all that matter."

"Will Elda allow vampires to take over the world?"

Valentina nodded.

"So you are telling me that the world as we know it is going to come to an end. That my friends are in danger and vampires will soon rule the world. And the worst part is that you expect me to sit here and do nothing. I get to stay here, in your sanctuary and raise a wonderful family ... while my friends fight for their lives — I don't think so." Val moved toward the door.

Valentina appeared in front of her. "I know you're brave. You have never fled from a fight. Please don't think of it like that — you are not abandoning them. It's the only way to save the human race and the vampires you love. Please don't go."

The sheer panic in Valentina's eyes caused Val to stop. "I can't leave them. They're the only family I have."

"You have us now and we'll write to them and let them know you are well. We'll watch over them from here." Valentina pointed to the crystal. "Please trust me. This is the only way to fight Elda. It's the only possible way to beat the servants of Aggadad. We have to ensure that your girls reach maturity. It's the best way to help your friends and save humankind."

"What happens when they come of age?"

"The Great Goddess has told me that this is my duty. I'm here to help you protect them until their thirteenth birthday. I have tried to look into the future beyond that point but we can only see what the Mother wants us to see."

"Your God speaks to you? You do realize you sound mentally ill — hearing voices?"

"It's a type of communication through meditation and having an open mind and heart. With practice most anyone can do it."

Something inside told Val that there was truth in what she said. All of this coincided with what Teller had told them of his encounter with Elda; she'd told Teller he had to die to ensure that the chosen ones could not come to be. The pieces fell into place. Elda also appeared to have magic of sorts and Valentina clearly knew more about this than Val. She could help Val understand what they were up against.

Val went to the seeing crystal and removed the silk cloth. First she saw Teller; he was sitting in a tree outside their camp. She was relieved to see him alive and free. Then she saw Elijah; he threw her broken phone against the center tent pole, turning the device into a million pieces. He sat down hard in his chair and rubbed his forehead with his thumb and index finger. She ran her hand down the crystal. Val wanted to go to him more than anything. "I have to write to him," she whispered.

"Of course." Valentina shoulders relaxed.

She was truly terrified that I would leave, Val thought.

Valentina placed the silk fabric over the crystal. “It is important that we keep the seeing stone covered when it is not in use.”

“Why?”

“Because others can see us through the stone as well. Sometimes the images are of events currently happening and sometimes they are of things that have not yet come to be. But as you have seen, Teller is fine.”

Val could only muster a slight nod.

CHAPTER 22 NEW YORK 2020 AD

Vlad – that name suits him better than Teller. He appears not to know where Vallachia is, Elijah thought. *Teller had not strayed too far from camp. He is waiting for her to return as well.* Elijah wished that he would go back to wherever the hell he had come from. Things had been perfect while Teller was away. It appeared that he was back for good. *Vlad took her from me and now he remains as a constant reminder of why she is gone.* Every time Elijah looked at Teller it ripped the wound open again.

Riddick reported that they could not find any trace of Elda's people in Pittman's Laboratory, the site where Elijah had been held. Not surprisingly, she had vacated the building after Elijah's escape. After all, she had been able to elude the Court for all these years; Elda had to be highly intelligent.

This was where Samuel and Aaron's expertise came in handy. They were the Court's technology experts; both had been fascinated with computers from the time they first heard of them. They even wrote some of the early computer programs that were still in use. Samuel, especially, spent most of his time with computers. He was relentlessly investigating the case at this point. He tracked down the owners of the Pittman building and hacked into their computers to search for any information on the tenants. Yet he came up short, finding nothing of Elda. According to the owners, the floor where Elijah had been held had been vacant for years.

"She's good," Aaron mused with a hint of admiration.

Not long after Elijah's return and Vallachia's subsequent disappearance, Elijah entered his tent to find a large black crow standing on the desk. He looked around and found no one else. The crow cawed as if speaking to him. Elijah noticed what looked like a cigarette fastened to its leg. *It must be a note.* He slowly approached the bird. It anxiously jumped about, yet let him get close enough to untie the string holding the paper. It took flight and headed for the open tent flap as soon as he had the paper in his hand.

Elijah stared at the note with apprehension. He desperately wanted news of Vallachia. Yet, he also had a sinking feeling, as he could predict what the letter would say — that she was not coming back. She would leave him with no way to try to change her mind.

The letter was written in her elegant long strokes. He had no doubt it was from her.

My Dearest Elijah,

I'm truly sorry for everything! I want to be with you more than anything. I hope that someday you can forgive me and we can be together once again. For now, know that I cannot come to you to try to make things right. Though this is very much what I want, I must stay away for a time. This is bigger than you or me and I must do what is best for everyone. Please don't worry about me or look for me. You will not find me. I'm fine. I love you more than anything. I will come to you as soon as I can — to find out if you will have me.

Love always,
Val

Elijah crumpled the letter in one hand and yelled in frustration. *She can't do this!* He had no way of talking to her. No way to get her back.

She left him completely helpless. He was not used to this feeling and he didn't like it. *She must know that I forgive her. All I need is one chance to convince her to come back.*

The worst part was that he couldn't influence her. He had always been able to do this before by looking her in the eyes. *Or did she control me with her bright blue eyes? I suppose it works both ways — we influenced each other. Was that true love?* Whatever it was, it was unbearably painful now that she was gone.

Riddick heard the yell and came to see if Elijah was well. He was not.

"Call off the search, pack up camp. We're going home," Elijah commanded as he left the tent.

Teller appeared at Elijah's side. "You can't do this. We have to find her. What if she's in trouble?"

Elijah shoved Val's letter, which was now a ball in his fist, into Teller's chest. Elijah's shove was a bit too hard as the force pushed Teller back a step. Teller caught the letter as it fell from Elijah's palm. "Yes, I *can* call off the search and she is fine." Elijah took flight for home.

Once back in their bedchamber, Elijah gazed at the pictures of his wife wrapped in his arms. Their matching tattoos mocked him. He ripped the pictures off the wall and smashed them on the floor. Soon the floor was covered in glass. In the beginning she had left Elijah a couple of times but that did not hurt nearly as bad as this because she had not been his. At this point, he had had her for so long. "She's mine!" he yelled. It felt as if he was drowning. Half of him was gone. He couldn't breathe. *I can't live without her.* He fell to his knees. The glass cut deep but he didn't care. *How could she do this to me?*

He was only vaguely aware of Mari and Samuel outside the door.

"Go on. Go talk to him. He needs you," Mari was saying to her husband.

"What on earth do I say? This is beyond my expertise?" Samuel sounded utterly distraught.

Mari moaned in frustration. "Very well. I will talk to him." A soft knock came from the door. When Elijah did not answer she slowly opened it and inhaled sharply at the sight of the room and Elijah on his bloody knees. She walked gingerly across the glass as if it could somehow hurt her through her shoes. She pulled him up by his upper arm.

Elijah pulled his arm loose from her grip. "Leave me alone."

"Elijah, please. Let us be here for you."

Elijah turned his head away, so she grabbed his chin and forced him to look at her. "Listen to me. Vallachia said she would be back as soon as she could. We must trust her. She knows what she's doing. She will come back to us — to you."

Part of Elijah believed Mari or at least wanted to. This was what Val's letter had said. He was suddenly tired. He couldn't remember the last time he had slept. Elijah swayed but Mari caught him.

"Samuel, help me get him to the guest chambers. He must rest and this room will simply not do."

Together they carried Elijah out of that horrible room. Mari gave orders for the room to be cleaned and for the pictures — what was left of them — to be placed in storage.

They laid Elijah in a guest bed and the last thing he heard was Riddick. ...

"They can't see their King like this."

Then there was only blackness as Elijah slept — without nightmares. The nightmares were no longer needed, as he was living them. He was a King who had lost his Queen. He was nothing.

Elijah woke to find Samuel seated in a chair not far from his bed. The glass had been removed from Elijah's knees and they were bandaged. He ripped the bandages off, as he knew they were healed.

Samuel opened his mouth to speak but Elijah spoke first, "I'm fine. I'll be fine." He knew he had to pull himself together. He would move on without her ... for now. He had to — for the Court, for humans and for vampires.

The annoying caw of a large black crow came from the window.

"Fuck," Elijah said as he lay back down putting his arm over his eyes — perhaps this would make the bird disappear — somehow. But it only cawed louder. He could not handle any more heartbreak from her.

"What is it?" Samuel asked with concern.

"It's another note from her. Untie the paper from the crow's leg."

Samuel slowly approached the bird but it flew away and landed on the bed next to Elijah. It cawed right in Elijah's ear and he resisted the urge to knock it away. *Apparently, it only delivers messages to the intended reader.* Reluctantly, Elijah took the paper from the bird's leg and it flew out the window.

"That was … odd," Samuel said.

"She can't use a phone or we could track her. She obviously does not want that." He held the paper in his clenched fist — not wanting to read it.

"Maybe I should follow the bird. It might lead us to her?" Samuel said, as he peered out the window.

"No. She wants to be alone and we will respect that."

Samuel continued to look after the bird. "You're a better man than I."

Elijah slowly opened the letter.

My Precious Elijah,

I must warn you. You are all in danger. It appears that your blood worked for Elda and her followers. She will move against the Court soon. She is fighting us on a different front. Our armies will not help us this time. I wish I knew more and I wish I knew how to stop her but it may be too late now that she has obtained your blood. Please warn the Court. You must be on high alert for whatever she is planning. I wish I could be there to help and I wish we could be together!

Take care of yourself and stay safe,

Your loving wife

. . .

ELIJAH REREAD the note to try to make sense of it. *What is she talking about?*

Samuel looked even more worried. "What did she say?"

"I have no idea. Apparently we're in trouble." Elijah stood and quickly dressed. This was good — there was work to do. "Call a meeting of the Elders."

Samuel smiled and nodded as he left the room. He was glad to see that Elijah was doing better.

It was for show but Elijah knew he had to keep up the façade … until she returned.

CHAPTER 23 NORTHERN CANADA 2020 AD

Vallachia slowly adjusted to her new life. It was nice to live with humans — or semi-humans — whatever they were, as they spent a lot of time cooking. It had been ages since she had cooked anything. Val had forgotten how much humans eat and how much has to be done to sustain them. Valentina and her companions were not completely self-sufficient but close, if resources were rationed. Valentina would make trips to the nearest town from time to time for supplies for Angela and Sasha.

A cooler full of blood bags was kept in the basement of the cabin. The cabin ran on a combination of solar and wind power and when those failed they used a gas-powered generator as a backup.

There was endless gardening and food processing. Large amounts of firewood had to be gathered and stacked, just to name a few of the many chores that had to be done in order to survive this far north. Val was grateful for all the work to keep her busy. This way she did not have to think too much. There was a pain in her chest when she would think about Elijah. As always, no amount of rubbing would sooth it. It took all her willpower not to fly to him when the house fell silent and Angela and Sasha slept.

Although, Val wasn't sure how the two ladies slept at all. It was summer and the sun never set — it simply circled in the sky. Their hidden refuge was above the Arctic Circle. Like Northern Norway, this too was 'the land of the midnight sun'. With twenty-four hours of daylight, Val often did not know what day or what time it was. There was only one endless day. Valentina warned Val of how the winter would be quite the opposite. They would have a period of time in which the sun would not rise. This was ideal for Vampires, though Sasha and Angela were not looking forward to the seemingly eternal darkness of winter.

Val longed for her old friends. They had been by her side for many hundreds of years. It was odd not having them close by. She missed her life in the mansion full of spacious modern rooms. The only place for her in the small cabin was on the old worn out couch. She knew she had been happy but now that her old life was gone, she fully realized how perfect things had been for so many centuries.

Val did not allow herself to believe, even for a second, that she could possibly be pregnant. It would be a dream come true. However, if these ladies turned out to be nothing but a bunch of crackpots — which was a distinct possibility — then it would have crushed Val if she had believed that she could actually have children.

Val had been with them for three months. She sat by the lake with her mom— though she still had trouble calling Valentina by that title. Valentina was only about twenty when she had been turned so she looked as if she were only a slightly older sister to Val, not her mother.

Val was about to give up on these odd ladies and head home. Part of Val wanted to go back and part of her did not want to face all the trouble that she had caused. *The right thing to do would be return and try to fix things*. She had been lost in her thoughts when Val heard something that would change everything. In the peaceful quiet she became aware of a different sound. She could hear something new and faint.

"Shhh," she said to Valentina who was about to say something. Val listened hard. "Do you hear that?" It was the faintest sound like a distant drum — no, drums — two heartbeats. Val put her hand over her lower abdomen. She could feel the slightest vibration of the beating hearts. Val jumped to her feet in shock and excitement.

Valentina got to her knees and put her ear to Val's stomach. She closed her eyes and a tear ran down her cheek. "Finally, heartbeats," she whispered. In a flash Valentina ran toward the cabin yelling, "Heartbeats! We have heartbeats."

Val couldn't move. *It is true! I will have Teller's children, like I always knew I was meant to.* Her feet failed her. She felt as if she were floating helplessly on a cloud. In fact, she had never felt such joy. Everything seemed brighter. In that instant her entire world changed, as nothing else mattered but these new lives inside her. Everything else became a distant second. She was suddenly grateful that she had chosen to stay. *These tiny miracles must be protected above all else. That means keeping them a secret.* "No one must find out about you," Val whispered as she gently rubbed her belly.

"Darling, come here," her mom called.

It was as if Val had been in a trance. She managed to turn and head in their direction.

Angela had been working in the garden — of course. "Oh, thank the Great Goddess! I was starting to worry because in humans we usually hear a heartbeat at six to seven weeks." She then looked thoughtful for a moment and ran inside.

"Angela is our resident mid-wife," Valentina said.

"That's ... convenient." Val said.

Angela returned with a planner. "Okay, you came to us on April second and that was the day of conception." She flipped the pages, "and today we have heartbeats." She marked this on the calendar. "It looks like your little angels may be taking twice that of the average human pregnancy. I will keep track to be sure. Now we will start to see that belly grow." She looked as happy as Val felt.

"I can't wait. It will be fun to grow fat for once."

"Oh, it will be a pleasure to have children around," Sasha exclaimed.

CHAPTER 24 NORTHERN CANADA 2020 AD

After Sasha and Angela went to bed that night Val asked her mom, "How did you know that I was pregnant?"

"We have unconventional ways of knowing things. Ever since I became a Servant of the Great Goddess, I have had a recurring vision. It was that the last of my grandchildren would be twin girls. I saw myself in their lives, helping to raise them. Not like my other grandchildren — your brother's children — whom I only watched grow from a distance."

"I'm glad you found me when you did. After all, I will need help with twins."

Valentina placed her arm around her daughter as they sat side-by-side on the couch.

Val laid her head on her mother's shoulder. Her touch was reassuring — all would be well. "Don't think that I have forgotten about your vague reasons for abandoning me for all those years. You did a good job of changing the subject." Val sat up and looked her mother in the eyes, demanding a real answer.

Valentina sighed. "Oh darling, please don't think for a moment that it was because I didn't want to be with you or because I don't love you. I do love you very much. I have always watched over you. I revealed myself as soon as you and your coven needed me. As you know our …" she searched for the right word "… alternative lifestyle has always been extremely persecuted throughout history. We have learned to keep to ourselves. We live an isolated life. A solitary life can grow to be a habit. Like an addiction, it can be difficult to break. Life's easy here — simple. I'll admit it was difficult to think about leaving to save your men. But I knew I had to. Honestly, I feared you would reject who I had become."

"I would not have rejected you." Then Val thought of how uncertain she had been when she first came here. She had thought there was a good chance that they were mentally ill. She *had* almost rejected them.

"The world has rejected us. So we keep our abilities a secret. I learned a long time ago to keep to my own kind," Valentina said.

Val nodded. "And now?"

"The world is about to change and we are needed. So we may no longer have the luxury of keeping to ourselves. We may be forced out into the open."

"Can you really perform magic?"

"We don't have magic. We simply have a better understanding of nature and its elements. This allows us to do things that may appear magical to people who don't fully understand the world and all its wonders. You've seen us perform the spell to maintain the protective shield around the volcano opening."

Val had thought they were simply praying for protection. "And you can see bits and pieces of the future; what else can you do?"

"You want something tangible — evidence. Well, our gifts come in handy when we need to start a fire." Valentina held out her hand and flames appeared. They hovered just above her palm. She threw the flames at a log in the fireplace and it caught fire at once.

Val's mouth hung open.

"Our powers can also help us to put fires out." Valentina held her hand palm-upward again, only this time water appeared above it. She moved her fingers in a circular motion and the water swirled around. She threw it at the log and extinguished the fire.

"That looks like magic to me."

"Call it what you like. You see, fire and water are natural elements that can be controlled by the mind."

"And you can teach me to do that?"

"Yes. But it takes time and much practice. Angela and Sasha are much older than they appear. Angela is a hundred and forty, while Sasha is approaching her hundredth birthday. They use their powers to slow their aging and they will return to the Great Mother someday as they are not immortal. It took us many years to learn how to use Mother Nature's gifts to their full potential."

"What else can you do?"

"What I just showed you are some of the most basic elements, the easiest to control. There are many possibilities. The brain is a very powerful tool. We can control our internal organs. For example, we can slow our heart rate. We can help to heal others. Then there are all manner of spells and curses, from simple to complex. These require the right ingredients and incantations. Blood is often a powerful medium. Celestial events can aid in the completion of spells as well."

Val could not imagine what all this entailed.

VALLACHIA SPENT most nights reading to her babies as her belly grew. She wanted them to know their mother's voice. They did appear to be growing slowly because at nine months Val's stomach was only about the size of a football. Angela estimated that Val was about halfway through the pregnancy at that point. That was fine with Val. This was her only chance to have children and she was going to enjoy every moment of it. On the other hand, she was anxious to see them come into the world.

Val's only regret was that her friends could not be a part of this. It saddened her to think that her girls would not know their father's voice when they were born. She wished that Teller could be here. One night Val broached the subject. "It's not right that I am keeping them from Teller. He has a right to know."

"Normally I would agree with you," Valentina said. "But you are a vampire and you were not meant to have children. This makes them special. It's not safe for anyone to know."

"Not even their father? He would never hurt them. Surely if we talked to him he would understand that he could not tell anyone."

"It's entirely too risky. It would be easy for others to find out if you were to leave the safety of this volcano. You can't go to Teller because news spreads fast in the vampire world. And there's no news like a pregnant vampire, let alone the *Queen* of Vampires having babies. You have never fully understood how much your people love you and follow your every move. Vampires are always eager to hear any news of their King and Queen. Your enemies are already on the lookout for the chosen ones. It's simply a risk we cannot take."

"Are they to grow up not knowing their father?"

"It's for the best. If Teller were to tell just one person, the secret would be out. For you to remain hidden is the safest way."

Val frowned, as she rubbed her rounded belly. She wished there was a way for Teller to know and still keep her unborn children safe.

CHAPTER 25 NORTHERN CANADA 2020 AD

The heartbeats grew stronger each day. Vallachia's cravings for human food grew as well. She began drinking less blood and eating more. This put a strain on the food supplies and Valentina had to make more frequent trips to town. This was a dangerous time for them. Valentina risked being seen by one of Elda's supporters anytime she was in public; her whereabouts were at risk of becoming known anytime she left the protective barrier, which kept them concealed from Elda's sight.

Once a day Valentina, Sasha and Angela would perform a ritual — the one Val thought was only a prayer. The women would hold hands and chant. They claimed that this put a seal around the mouth of the volcano.

"Why can't I see it?" Val asked one day. She could not tell any difference. It looked like the normal sky above them.

"We can see it and feel it," Sasha said.

"What does it do?"

"It keeps our enemies from finding us. Anyone who means us harm will not be able to see or smell you from the other side of the barrier," Angela said.

"Perhaps you will be able to see it, one day," Valentina said.

"Is this how Elda was able to elude us for all those years — she somehow concealed herself from us?" Val asked.

"Most likely and her sight is strong. She knew the Court was coming well in advance," Valentina said. "She would have had plenty of time to flee."

Late that night while the ladies were fast asleep, Val woke with a start. A familiar rhythm had changed. She listened hard. First she heard her own heartbeat increase, as panic took over. There was her heartbeat — boom, boom — the loudest, and only one other could be heard. It was a four-beat rhythm, not six. One of the babies' hearts had stopped beating!

"Mom!" Val yelled. This was followed by a sharp pain in her lower abdomen, which caused her to scream. Val knew, without a doubt, one of her babies was struggling for its life. Her tiny heart had stopped beating regularly and she was thrashing about, trying desperately to survive.

Valentina appeared from her room in a flash. "What's the matter?"

"It's one of the babies!" A faint irregular heart beat could be heard. This was followed by another wave of pain. Another scream escaped from Val. "She's dying!"

Valentina put her ear to Val's stomach in order to better hear the heartbeats of the babies over the sound of Val's racing heart. "Oh, no."

Angela emerged from her room. She appeared to be half asleep. "Val, wake up. There's something wrong. I can feel it." But Angela's premonition was late.

"There *is* something terribly wrong. Get Sasha at once!" Valentina yelled.

It took Angela a moment to fully realize that they were already awake and well aware that there was a crisis at hand.

"Mom, please save her. I can't lose her!"

"I know, Baby." Valentina placed her hands on Val's stomach and began to chant.

Soon all three ladies had their hands on Val's large round belly and were in deep meditative states.

Val strained to hear the tiny hearts. One was constant — steady … strong. The other would come and go. When the beating would stop the baby would kick and Val would scream, more out of panic than pain.

"It's not working. This is a powerful healing spell. Why isn't it working?" Angela's voice cracked.

Valentina furrowed her brow in concentration. Her eyes opened wide. "It's you, dear. You must relax. Your heart is racing and you are tense. This is not helping your baby. You must calm yourself."

"Take a deep breath," Angela said in a soothing voice.

"Calm down!" Val yelled. "How in the hell do you expect me to do that?"

"We have to put her out," Valentina snapped.

Sasha placed one hand over Val's heart and one hand on her stomach. Valentina remained focused on the baby and Angela moved to place her hands on Val's forehead.

Despite feeling the worst panic she had ever experienced in her long life, Val began to relax. It was as if the ladies had complete control over her body.

"Take a deep breath."

Val did.

"Again."

Soon Val was breathing deeply and evenly on her own. Her eyelids grew heavy and moments later she was in a deep sleep.

~

VAL JERKED awake from a nightmare in which blood was gushing from between her legs. She quickly looked for any signs of blood — signs of a miscarriage. But there was none.

"All is well, my dear. The babies are both fine," Valentina whispered as she ran her fingers through Val's hair.

Val rubbed her belly and listened carefully for a long time — two sets of light heartbeats, steady as a steam engine moving down a track. Six rhythmic beats for her and her two daughters, in perfect sync. A tear fell from Val's eye as she laid her head on her mother's chest. "You saved her."

"Don't worry, both babies will be healthy. I can see it."

CHAPTER 26 NORTHERN CANADA 2020 AD

Angela and Sasha were exhausted after being up most of the night and putting all their energy into saving the unborn children and knocking Val out. They slept for the better part of the next day. Even Valentina slept for a couple of hours.

Yet Val felt energized. *They must have given me and the babies all of their strength,* Val thought. Val made enough breakfast for everyone, which she proceeded to eat the majority of.

"With my appetite for human food, do you think the babies are human?" Val inquired at dinner that night.

"Since both parents are vampires wouldn't that make them…oh, I don't know… vampires?" Sasha's tone was sarcastic.

"I don't think they will be fully human or vampire," Valentina said.

"What will they be then, werewolves?" Sasha said.

"You know there are no such things as werewolves," Valentina said.

"Well there is not supposed to be a such thing as a vampire giving birth either," Angela said.

"Whatever these babies will be, they will be divine. And I'm not just saying that because I'm their grandmother. They will be kind-of-heart."

"You have seen this?" Val asked.

"Yes," Valentina said with certainty.

Val smiled with relief. *My babies will survive. No, they will thrive.* "You said most people can become a ... servant of the Goddess — it takes a pure heart, practice and dedication. How do you reconcile being so religious with being a vampire?"

Valentina gave her a questioning look.

"I mean you clearly don't think vampires are the spawn of Satan?"

Valentina laughed. "I don't know where we came from or if we are inherently evil. Some of us appear to be. What I do believe is that intention is everything."

It was Val's turn to give the questioning look.

"It's simple. If one intends to do harm then that is evil. If one's intentions are to do good and their actions come from a place of love and caring then that is worthy of the Goddess."

"That's seems too simple but I suppose it makes sense."

"Do you want to learn our ways?" Valentina asked.

Val's eyes widened. She was not sure she wanted to go down this religious path. It's as if that part of her died when she became a vampire. Yet, her mother could do some amazing things. She clearly had a lot to learn and that was Val's favorite pastime — learning. Maybe it was time to pick up her religious roots again, or at least see what it had to offer. "I guess I can give it a try."

"Way to commit." Sasha chuckled.

"Good." Valentina rubbed Val's large belly with a gentle caress. "As soon as my grandbabies are born, you will need to learn our ways in order to better protect them. For now, your job is to focus on growing those little ones."

"Do you think I will be able to learn? I've never been very ... spiritual. I don't think I could ever see the future like you," Val said.

"Ah but you already have. You have had dreams that came true, am I right?"

"I suppose so, few and far between." Val told them of how she dreamt of wolves killing her father numerous times and long before he actually died and her dream of finally finding Teller who transformed into a Dragon.

"That's remarkable. You had premonition dreams even when you were a human? I had to practice the ways of the Great Goddess for twenty years before I had my first premonition dream," Angela said.

"Val may become a powerful seer with practice." Sasha appeared genuinely impressed.

"Your human mind could not fathom such a wretched beast as a vampire killing your father, so it made you into wolves in your dream. Wolves were something that made sense to you as a human girl. As for the dragon dream, of course there was no real dragon, yet Teller had become a member of the Dracul or Dragon Family," Valentina translated for Sasha and Angela. "He truly had become a fierce ruler."

Val thought of her dream about the Gods, the perfect man and woman who were waiting for Val's babies, the chosen ones, to be born. Val suddenly understood that it was true or at least partially true. It was what her brain was capable of understanding. There may have been much more to the story or parts that Val could not possibly fully comprehend but it was at least some of the story. "How do I learn to tell the difference between regular dreams or nightmares and the ones that will come true?"

"You most likely already have some feelings about which ones are more vivid, frequent and important but you will be able to understand much more clearly with practice and training."

"Are you as powerful as Elda?" Val asked.

"I'm afraid not. Elda is one of the most powerful soothsayers. It's rumored that she had a strong sight even as a human and her visions come to her during the day, not as dreams. This is very rare. In fact, day visions occur for only the most tenured of servants. But Elda had them when she was still a young human. Who knows how powerful she has been able to become over the years?" Valentina explained.

Val frowned.

"Most intelligent and insightful people can become servants of the Great Goddess if they train daily. They do not have to be born with these gifts, as Elda may have been. But it takes a lot of work to learn how to see outside oneself. One must attain the ability to let go of the self. This is incredibly difficult, as most people spend their lives desperately clinging to the self. Once the self is gone, one must learn to embrace and control the powers we possess."

CHAPTER 27 NORTH AMERICA 2021 AD

On October 7, 2021 Val went into labor. The births of the twins went smoothly. Vampires have a high tolerance for pain and what pain Val did feel was eased by Angela's chanting and Sasha's caressing. Valentina gently guided each baby into the world when she was ready. After seven hours of labor, Val held two glorious baby girls, one in each arm. They were pink and healthy.

Val had not given much thought to names. She knew she needed to see them first. She was right to wait because as soon as she gazed at them for the first time she knew within seconds — the slightly bigger one was Vera and the smaller one was Veva. They had thick tufts of curly golden hair on top of their heads and they blinked at their mother with emerald eyes. Other than Veva being smaller, they were mirror images of each other.

Valentina stumbled, knocking over a tray full of medical supplies.

Val looked up from her babies. "Mom! What's wrong?"

By the look in Valentina's eyes, she was not in the room with them. She was far away, seeing something the others could not. "The chosen ones have taken their first breath. You must warn Elijah. The end is upon us." Her voice was deeper, as if it was not entirely her own.

Val looked to Angela for an explanation. “I’m afraid that is what a day vision looks like, my dear.”

~

IT HAD NOT QUITE BEEN two years since Elijah had last seen his wife. The Court had been on high alert. Like old times, they began training regularly. They increased security. Samuel oversaw a corps of elite vampires, who did nothing but look for Elda. They had no success.

The Court updated their emergency strategies. Their secret meeting places were upgraded and well stocked with weapons and blood. Vampires could survive with little else.

Elijah woke with a start to the sound of a crow. This time he quickly untied the note from its leg. He had not heard from Vallachia in many months and was desperate to know if she was well.

GET OUT NOW

THREE SIMPLE WORDS but it was enough. Elijah did not pause to question it. He tucked his semiautomatic forty-five in the back of his pants, threw on his bulletproof vest, belted on his two favorite swords and his trusty razor-covered whips. This only took a handful of heartbeats. He sped down the corridor rousing everyone and commanding them to get out at once.

As the Court exited the manor they found themselves surrounded by unfamiliar vampires. Again Elijah did not hesitate. He moved forward, taking off the heads of the nearest vampires with his lethal whips. Samuel and Riddick were at his side, as well as Teller, Abdullah and the twins. They rained bullets into the crowd of vampires and then drew their swords in order to finish them off or fight them off at close range.

Explosions came from behind them. Elijah turned briefly to see the manor going up in smoke. He knew the next round of bombs would target them. "Run!" he yelled.

The Court fled in different directions. Explosions sounded off all around. They headed for cover in the nearby forest.

"Head for water!" Elijah yelled. For now they needed to disappear. They sped north to the St. Lawrence River. "Split up and slowly make your way back to our rendezvous point in the city."

Half of Elijah's men headed upstream and half headed downstream. They swam swiftly remaining underwater for miles before they began to break off on either side of the river. Finally only Elijah and Riddick remained.

"Let's head to Lake Champlain and swim most of the way back to the city. That will be safest," Riddick said.

"Smart thinking." Elijah dived back into the river and swam south.

As Elijah and Riddick walked the crowded streets of New York, it became clear that something was terribly wrong. People were muttering things about an attack on Europe and the world coming to an end. Elijah gave Riddick a concerned look and sped off in a flash. He grabbed a phone from a man who had been talking on it. The poor guy did not know what happened other than his cell phone disappeared as a rush of air blew over him.

Elijah quickly dialed Lord Alexandru in London. No answer. Elijah frowned at Riddick and quickly dialed the second in command.

"Who's this?" Hector demanded.

"Hector, it's Elijah. What's happening?"

"Elijah! Thank the heavens. We have been attacked."

"Where is Lord Alexandru?"

A choking sob came from the other end. "He is dead, My Lord."

"No," Elijah whispered. "Hector, what's going on?"

"It's the skeletons."

"What?" Elijah could not help himself. He looked to Riddick for clarification but Riddick only returned Elijah's open-mouthed gape. "Talk sense, man."

"Honestly, My Lord, the people of Europe are fleeing in terror from these … these … skeletons. They have vampire fangs and they cannot get their fill of human blood. They kill one person after another. We were also attacked by … *normal* vampires and one of them killed Lord Alexandru." Hector's voice broke again.

"Hector, where are you?"

"Safe-Haven Seven."

"Stay put. We'll get there as soon as we can." Elijah dropped the phone and crushed it under his foot before taking off in blur.

"Has Hector gone mad? What does all that mean?" Riddick sped alongside Elijah.

"Something terrible has happened. This may be what Vallachia was warning us about all along."

CHAPTER 28 EUROPE 2021 AD

As the first vampire to give birth was holding her newborn daughters, Elda stood high in the Alps, on the ancient battlefield of 1551, surrounded by her servants — the servants of Aggadad.

"We have been waiting centuries for the galaxies to align. It will be more powerful than any singular eclipse or even a planetary alignment," Elda announced.

"During the last planetary alignment we were able to raise a handful of the dead, yet they were weak and did not survive for long," Silvia added. She was once Elda's handmaiden when they had been humans but now she was much more. Silvia was her oldest and most faithful companion.

"But tonight our galaxy will be in the center of the nearest six galaxies as they form a perfect line. Only at that brief moment will we have the power to raise our fallen soldiers. We are more than prepared to take full advantage of this celestial event of the millennium. It's our only chance and we can't make any mistakes or we will be forced to wait another thousand years." Elda's voice rose as she rallied her people. She opened her arms wide to the sky. "Tonight will end the reign of the High Court and vampires will no longer be forced to hide from humans. We will take over the world. Our superior species will finally be free."

Cheers rang out.

"Is this about bringing *him* back?" Silvia whispered to Elda.

"When I first found this spell, I had hoped that it could bring Ramdasha back to me but now I know that raising the dead comes with a price. Whatever we conjure up tonight will not be the same soldiers we lost in the frightful battle of 1551. No. I have no illusions of getting him or Adela back. I am no longer a foolish little girl with childish dreams — they're lost to us forever. These fallen comrades will only give us the numbers we need to take over the world," Elda said.

Silvia lowered her head in sorrow at the mention of Adela. Adela had been Elda's handmaiden a long time ago as well. Yet like Ramdasha, she had not survived the war — only Elda and Silvia remained. They lost everyone they cared about that day. They had been determined to find a way to defeat the Court ever since.

"Our soldiers are ready and waiting in strategic cities all over the world," Elda went on. "As soon as the dead begin to terrorize Europe, our armies will attack the supporters of the Court. We have fighters ready to attack Jinlan's coven in Beijing, Shantanu's coven in India, Lord Alexandru's in London and of course the majority of our forces will attack the Court's headquarters in New York. Not to mention a half dozen other smaller covens."

Elda's commander assured her with a nod that all was in place.

"Good. Surprise is what will make us successful," Silvia said.

"A few hundred angry soldiers who have been brought back to this world from the eternal beyond will definitely be a surprise," Silvia added.

"Do you have the King's blood?" Elda said.

"Of course, My Lady. Thawed and warmed to the perfect temperature." Silvia handed a golden chalice to Elda.

"It is time," Elda's honey colored eyes shone bright with excitement. "We will only have a few seconds when the galaxies will be in the optimal position."

Elda's followers formed a circle around her and each held a milky white crystal high above their head. They began to chant the ancient curse, one they knew by heart as they had practiced this relentlessly for hundreds of years in anticipation of this exact moment when there would finally be enough celestial power to make the spell work.

Elda's scepter held the largest of the crystals in a claw setting. In her other hand she held the chalice filled with Elijah's blood. It was her offering to the universe. She held both to the sky as she began to chant with the others. Their voices started out soft and low. They grew louder and the rhythm grew faster as the brief window approached. When the galaxies were perfectly in line, Elda and her people were yelling over the wild wind that whipped around them.

A thick column of red light came from the sky. It engulfed Elda and spread to the other crystals around her. Her followers were blown back as the light continued to spread, engulfing the battlefield. There was no loud explosion, only a brief vibrating hum. Once the entire field was covered in the bright red light, the light transformed into a thick smoke. The red smoke slowly dissipated into the ground.

Elda lay flat on her back and began to blink as she focused on the night sky.

Silvia was at her side in a flash. "Are you okay?"

Elda relieved Silvia's panic with a mischievous smile. "We did it."

"Of course we did. You knew this day was coming. You predicted it a long time ago."

Silvia helped Elda to her feet.

"Look, the chalice is gone."

"The mighty Aggadad accepted our blood offering."

They watched as a cloud of bright red smoke came from the sky. When it hit the ground it billowed outward. Charred skeletons emerged from the smoke. From the ground, brown and yellow skeletons unearthed themselves.

"It appears that our spell may have worked better than we thought. Not only did it bring back our soldiers who had been burned but it brought back the Court's soldiers who were buried here, as well."

Elda bit her lip. She was not sure if having the Court's soldiers return was a good thing. Her sight had never gone past this day. She was suddenly terrified. She had always known the future. She had always been able to see her enemies coming long before they reached her. Now, for the first time, she did not know what tomorrow would bring.

"My fallen comrades!" Elda yelled. "Please join me in the fight for our freedom."

But the skeletons did not pause to listen to her. They moved quickly in different directions. One of them pushed Elda out of its way as it marched by with determination.

"Where are they going?" Elda asked.

"Perhaps they can't be controlled," Silvia said.

"We have to try."

They chased after the fleeing mob of dead soldiers but their words were not heeded.

CHAPTER 29 NEW YORK 2021 AD

After the attack on the Court's manor in upstate New York, Elijah and his men regrouped in their underground barracks, Safe-Haven One.

"Get what supplies you need. We leave for London as soon as John finds his way here," Elijah ordered.

"I didn't see John leave the manor and he was not with us when we fled," Teller said.

Elijah's brow furrowed with concern. *John was always within earshot. Surely he made it out of the manor in time.*

"I'm afraid we can't afford to wait for him much longer," Samuel said.

"My Lord, what if it's a trap?" Riddick asked.

"That's a distinct possibility. Yet it does not matter, as our allies need our help and Europe is in trouble. It's our duty to protect humans from our kind and it sounds as if Europe is in the greatest peril," Elijah said.

~

John never came to the Court's emergency meeting place — Safe Haven One. Elijah didn't want to leave him behind or believe that he was dead. Elijah's strong sense of duty to humans finally won over his desire to wait for John. The Court had to move on without him.

As Elijah's entourage approached Ireland they knew things had gone awry. Black smoke rose from populated areas as they flew over. Roads were jammed with people trying to flee. They remained high in the sky as it was broad daylight. Any humans who happened to look up in their panicked state would think Elijah and the others were a flock of large birds. They headed straight for Safe-Haven Seven.

Mary and Elizabeth ran to Hector at once. "Is it true? Lord Alexandru..."

Hector's voice left him and he could only nod a confirmation.

"Oh no," Mary said. She and Elizabeth both embraced Hector.

Elijah wondered if Hector might break down entirely. "We're sorry for your loss, Hector. Alexandru was a dear friend and comrade. We all share in your grief. Yet, we need to know what's happening. Please pull yourself together. You're in charge now. The Court needs you."

"Of course, My Lord," Hector's voice cracked as he tried to focus on their dire situation. "The men — what's left of them — are trying to get some rest as the night will bring about endless fighting."

"Who, exactly, are you fighting?" Elijah inquired.

"Not who, My Lord but what? At dusk they will undoubtedly be out to feed yet again. They have an insatiable need for blood. They can kill thousands of people in one night."

"What are we up against, Hector?"

"They are blackened skeletons. It's as if they had been burned. They have long eyeteeth, like us when we feed. They are faster and stronger than humans but they can be easily killed. We spent last night slaying a number of them."

"They only come out at night?" Riddick asked.

"That appears to be the case. We have not seen any sign of them during daylight hours for the past two days."

"At dusk we head out. In the meantime, get some rest from the long journey across the sea," Elijah announced.

"This is awesome. I can't wait."

Elijah turned to see who had spoken and glared at the culprit — Cosmin. "You think this is funny?" Elijah noticed that Costel's fangs were protruding from his lips. "And what's wrong with your brother?"

"Nothing, My Lord. He's excited," Cosmin said.

"Put those things back in your mouth." Elijah turned to Cosmin. "And you, you think this is *'Awesome'?"*

"Yes, My Lord. I have always wanted to kill vampire zombies. It's like a video game or something."

"Except this is *not* a game, you idiots." Elijah gritted his teeth.

"Of all the possible things to have on a bucket list, you want to fight vampire zombies?" Riddick asked in disbelief.

"Well, I don't usually think about dying so it's not a bucket list really, more of a to-do list," Cosmin replied.

Elijah had had enough of their foolishness. As he passed by Teller he said, "Your boys are imbeciles and don't even try to apologize for them."

"I wasn't about to," Teller said.

Abdullah gave a chuckle, as he sharpened his scimitar.

AT DUSK the Court walked the streets of London. All they had to do was follow the screams. Elijah watched in disbelief as dark bony figures emerged out of the shadows. They appeared to have only one desire — human blood. They completely ignored Elijah and the others, as they moved quickly about.

"What is it that you want?" Elijah called to them but they did not acknowledge that anyone had spoken.

Two of the dark figures knocked down the door to a home. It must have been the home of someone who would not or could not flee. Elijah sent his whips through each of them and they evaporated into a pile of ash.

"Just when you think you've seen it all," Sonia said.

"At least they're easy to stop. Spread out and kill as many of them as you can," Elijah ordered.

After a couple of hours of hunting down and killing these creatures, Elijah's men regrouped. They figured they had killed at least ten skeletons and had not found any more in some time.

"Let's split up and move on to the next populated areas," Elijah ordered. "We'll meet at Safe-Haven Four, in Venice, as we clean up yet another plague in Europe."

"My Lord..."

Elijah turned to where Riddick was pointing. The two piles of ash from the first two skeletons Elijah killed were reforming into menacing dark figures. The skeletons moved into the apartment complex. Resuming their business of finding humans as if they had never been turned to ash.

"What the..." Teller said.

"Correction, apparently they cannot be killed, only stopped ... temporarily." Aaron said. He moved to stand protectively between the apparitions and Sonia. This was an old gesture and deeply ingrained in Aaron. Sonia, while a small package, could easily take care of herself, perhaps better than Aaron. Yet the gesture made Sonia feel loved.

"All right!" Costel said.

"We get to kill them again." Cosmin said. The twins raced forward slashing the two figures until only a pile of ash remained.

"Very well, plan B. Head back to every one of these ... things we killed or didn't kill, tonight and do it again; do this as many times as necessary. Stop them from hurting anyone and meet back at Safe-Haven Seven at dawn," Elijah ordered.

"Whoever gets the most wins," Costel yelled as he sped away.

CHAPTER 30 EUROPE 2021 AD

At sunup they turned on the news for information on what was happening around the world. It became apparent that most major cities across Europe were being terrorized by these apparitions.

The news station suddenly shut off and the flat screen turned solid green. Samuel tried to fix it with no luck. "It's as if TV transmission has been stopped all together. Cell service may be next. Check your phones."

"I can't call out," Elijah said.

"I have no service either," Riddick said.

"What's going on?" Elijah asked.

"It must be a cyber-apocalypse," Samuel said.

"You mean we're cut off from the rest of the world?" Mary asked.

"That's the idea behind a cyber-apocalypse," Samuel said.

"It must be Elda. This is all part of her plan to take over," Elijah said.

"What are we going to do? There are not enough of us to protect all of Europe at once — fighting these…whatever they are," Riddick said.

"I like the term vampire zombies," Costel said.

"I vote for vampire zombie, as well," Cosmin added.

Elijah's jaw clenched as he tried his best to ignore the twins. "We need to find a way to kill them … for good."

Samuel set a large metal box on the table, showing them that it was sealed with a thick steel lock.

"What's that?" Mari asked with dread.

"I've locked the ashes of one of those things in this fail-proof container. No vampire could escape it."

"And you brought it in here!" Mari shivered in disgust and put her hand to her mouth as she gagged.

"It's a test to see if we can stop them for good. Surely it will not be able to re-form in this steel box. If my theory is correct, then we can trap them after we kill them."

~

AT DUSK the Court watched the metal box with anticipation. Black smoke flowed out of the box and a black skeleton formed in front of them. Elijah's whip turned it back into a pile of ash.

"So much for my theory." Samuel sighed.

"Apparently they can't be contained either. Two of you set out to stop the other apparitions in the city. We will split up into pairs and focus on the areas that are affected the most," Elijah said.

Cosmin and Costel ran for the door. Cosmin shoved his brother to the side to try and get a head start. Costel stuck his leg out to trip his brother, which caused them both to tumble. They slid through the pile of black ash and landed by the door in a rather serious wrestling match.

"They have it all over them! I think I'm going to throw up." Mari ran from the room.

"Those two must be separated," Elijah said. "I can't, in good conscience, set them loose on Europe. We already have enough problems as it is."

Cosmin jumped to his feet and brushed some of the ash off. "Please, My Lord, we'll try to behave."

"We've never been separated," Costel added.

"Well then, it's long overdue."

The twins gave each other a concerned looked.

"Can you guarantee me that you will not get into trouble?" Elijah narrowed his eyes at them.

"Maybe he's right. We should go our separate ways," Cosmin said.

"Yeah, who can promise that they will stay out of trouble?" Costel said.

The plan was quickly laid out. Pairs of the Court's vampires set out at once for the major troubled areas across the continent. Abdulla and Teller each took one of the twins. Many of the others set out with their significant others; Samuel and Mari, Sonia and Aaron, Mary and Elizabeth and so on.

"We can at least slow them down, even if we can't get rid of them for good," Elijah said. "We can cover most large cities with what is left of the Court. Any word from our allies in Beijing or Shantanu's coven in India?"

"No and now that communication is down, we're not likely to hear from them anytime soon," Samuel said.

"This is a disaster." Elijah rubbed his forehead.

"I'll keep experimenting. I'll find you to let you know if I discover a way to get rid of them for good. Next, I'll try my flame thrower." Samuel, like the twins, had a glint of excitement in his eyes.

"Goodbye for now, old friend." Elijah gave him their signature one-armed embrace.

Elijah and Riddick set out together. They hunted and killed the shadowy skeletons, as they made their way to Copenhagen. This was their ancient home and they wanted to protect it.

Several nights were spent killing and then re-killing the apparitions.

"Is this hell?" Riddick asked.

Elijah gave him a sideways glance.

"Think about it; spending every night fighting something that will never fully die. Endlessly repeating the same thing over and over. That sounds like hell to me."

"We'll find a way to send them back to ... wherever they came from."

"That's the problem, we don't know how they got here or how to get rid of them. Nothing has worked so far," Riddick said.

"We need to find their origins. That may give us the answer to defeating them."

"How do we find that?"

Elijah sighed. "I have no idea." He had never felt so helpless.

LIFE WENT on in this manner for a month. No matter what they did to the skeletons, they would reappear at dusk to drink an endless amount of human blood. Or try to, if the Court did not get to them first.

"You ever see the movie Groundhog Day?" Riddick asked.

"Shut up," Elijah said, as they headed out once again at twilight.

The Court was overextended and tempers were high as they grew beyond tired of this battle that they could only temporarily win, yet never end.

"At least the skeletons appear to be taking longer to come back." Riddick had to try hard to find a bright side.

That night a full moon shone brightly on Copenhagen. Few people remained in the city; many had perished but most had fled. The apparitions had to travel farther each night to find humans to feed on. This made it harder for the two vampires to cover all the ground.

Elijah knew where some of the skeletons would reform. They would remain where he last turned them into ash the night before. He stood with his whips ready, waiting alone outside the city for the black smoke to bring them back to life. This time when the apparitions stepped into the moonlight they turned to smoke that rose high into the sky. They disappeared entirely. No pile of ash.

Elijah took flight, searching for others. Black smoke could be seen floating in the air in a couple of places. He watched as the smoke dissipated. He searched throughout the night for any signs of the skeletons but found none.

"Did you find anything?" Elijah asked Riddick when they met up at dawn.

"No, nothing. They … disappeared. You?"

"It appears they evaporated."

"Do you think they're gone for good?" Riddick asked.

"Let's pray that this nightmare is over."

CHAPTER 31 EUROPE 2021 AD

Elda fell to her knees with a scream. "Did you feel that?" she whimpered.

Silvia hurried to Elda's side. "No, My Lady. What happened?"

"They're gone — the dead — they've vanished. It's not something I can see. It's a feeling. Perhaps since the power that gave them life came to this world through me, I felt the power leave this planet as well."

"We knew their strength was waning but now you are saying that they're gone entirely?" Silvia said. "The full moon must've driven them away for good. This is perfect. We can't have them killing all the humans, otherwise how would we survive?"

"Yes, this is simply marvelous, as they provided a necessary distraction," Elda said. "This made it easier to take out the cell towers and satellites. Plus it weakened the Court by spreading them out across Europe. With my people attacking every major city, humans now know that we exist and soon they will know that I am their ruler. As we speak my forces are rounding up and imprisoning the remaining humans. The world as we know it has changed forever."

Elda and Silvia embraced in celebratory congratulations.

"It's finally here. Our day has arrived!" Silvia said.

"All that waiting and planning has paid off. With the queen missing and the Court scattered, the king will not be able to maintain control."

"Not to mention the losses they endured from our attacks."

"The world knows vampires exist. This can't be undone so the Court's oppressive laws no longer matter," Elda said.

"We have won!"

IT TOOK several days for the members of the Court to make their way to Venice. There was still no cell service and no electricity. The lights in the safe house were dim as they ran off generators. Thankfully Samuel had insisted on having these doomsday hideouts. They had been well supplied and maintained over the years. They were coming in handy now.

"Any word of John?" Elijah asked his comrades.

"No. Perhaps he perished when we were attacked in New York," Teller offered.

"Maybe he has not found his way here yet. He could be at another hide-out waiting for us." Elijah didn't want to entertain the possibility that John was dead.

"If he were alive, he would have checked here by now, as he searched each safe haven for us," Riddick said.

Not knowing John's fate was torture for Elijah. John had been by his side since he was a small boy. Elijah could not remember a time without him. John was always by Elijah's father's side. When his father was killed, John showed the same dedication to Elijah — the most faithful of servants. When Elijah took over as king, John had remained an ever-present obelisk in his life. Elijah could count on him. John filled a hole where Elijah's father had once been. In fact, he had always been a surrogate father. Elijah could hardly bear the thought of life without him. Of course, Elijah had not fully realized all this until John came up missing.

The only logical explanation is that John is ... dead. Elijah conceded with the weight of a stone in his chest.

The flat screen TV clicked on in the other room. A woman's voice rang out. "Attention. May I have everyone's attention?"

Elijah and his comrades filed into the room with the now working TV. They were hungry for any bit of news from the outside world.

It is with great pleasure that I welcome you to the new world. For those of you who don't know me, I am your new ruler, Queen Elda. All will bow to me, as I am the leader of the vampire world. This new world will be one where all vampires are free. We are the superior species and our time has finally come. Under my rule you will no longer have to remain hidden. My fellow vampires, rejoice as you can now taste the sweetness of freedom!"

The camera panned to a crowd of cheering vampires. Then the TV went blank.

"Well that confirms what we already knew; Elda is behind all this," Riddick said.

"How was she able to turn on the TV and get her signal through?" Samuel asked. He immediately moved to investigate the back of the TV. "She must have complete control over the airwaves and now she can send her messages all over the world."

"That will simply not do. We have to find out how she is doing it and hack into her system," Aaron said. He and Samuel went straight to work.

"What are we going to do?" Mari asked.

"The only thing we can do — we must try to help the human race. There will be many ruthless vampires coming out of hiding. They'll hunt and terrorize humans. We'll have to try to protect them," Elijah announced.

"Can we be ourselves at all times, since humans know vampires exist?" Riddick asked.

"I suppose we don't have to pretend to be human anymore," Elijah said.

"That'll be odd. I'm used to keeping my identity a secret in public. In fact, that's all we've ever known," Teller said.

~

ELIJAH WAS APPALLED at the state of affairs when they ventured out of their underground shelter. Vampires were relentlessly hunting humans. They were rounded up and taken to camps that Elda's supporters worked hard to secure. Many people died in the process. If they resisted or if they found themselves too close to a hungry vampire they did not survive.

Then, to make matters worse, there were numerous unorganized bands of vampires who took full advantage of their new freedom by indiscriminately killing humans. This was not always for feeding; at times it was simply for sport.

Elijah and his Court came upon a football field in Venice. Blood-stained bodies lay piled in mounds. The scene reminded Elijah of the slaughtered buffalo across the American plains. On one of his many adventures he and Val had come across the carnage that settlers had left behind. They had destroyed many buffalo herds and taken no meat or skins. They simply left them for dead — for what — a good time or to simply prove that they could? That had been hard enough to make sense of, but this, this was many times more unfathomable.

"How could I have let this happen?" Elijah's stomach felt like it had turned upside down. He placed his hand over it and wondered if he was going to throw up.

"In all our years, we have seen humans commit such atrocities against one another and I'd wager that has been the case since the beginning of time," Riddick said. "Vampires are killers by design — so this new world of Elda's is likely to be even more brutal than the human world."

"This was to be expected if our kind ever took over the world," Teller added.

"I don't give a shit what humans did to one another," Elijah spat. "It's my job to protect humans from our kind. It was our kind who did this, ergo it's my fault. That's the price of being the king. There's no one else to blame when you're the leader. I have failed."

"You did *not* do this." Mari placed her hand on Elijah's shoulder.

Elijah pulled away from her attempt at comfort. "We have to stop this."

CHAPTER 32 EUROPE 2021 AD

Hundreds of humans had been slaughtered and thousands taken prisoner and this was only in Venice. It was assumed that this was happening throughout the world. What was left of the Court could no longer contain all the chaos. After a couple of nights attempting to fight the rogue vampires and Elda's soldiers, it became apparent that the Court needed a new strategy.

Riddick was recovering from a large gash on his arm. Several others were gravely injured as well. Elijah was grateful that they had not lost anyone — yet. He knew losses would be inevitable if they kept this up.

"We need to be smarter about this." Elijah paced to help him think. "We are not winning this battle."

"It does not appear that we're even slowing down the number of humans who are being killed or being thrown into her prisons," Riddick said.

"I suppose it's time for us to go underground. If we cannot beat them in outright battles, then we're going to have to use surprise attacks. We need to go into hiding so we can plan a new strategy."

"You mean guerrilla warfare?" Abdullah asked.

"Call it what you like. We must try to save humans at all cost."

A crow cawed loudly from behind Elijah. He flinched. He had never thought much about crows before but now they were becoming the stuff of nightmares. He gritted his teeth.

"How did a bird get in here?" Riddick asked.

My darling husband,

I must warn you. We have been betrayed by someone very close to us. All we know is that someone we trusted has joined forces with Elda. She knows of every safe house the Court ever created. Her men are systematically destroying each hideout, in an attempt to find you. They will soon attack the safe house in Venice. I'm able to warn you earlier this time. So you have a couple of days at best. Get out and take all our blood supplies to a new and secure location. It will not be long before human blood is the most precious and scarce commodity.

Your loving wife,

V

"What the fuck," Riddick all but yelled. "She knows what Elda's plotting? And where in the hell is she!"

"Who is with her? She wrote, *'we'*. So apparently she's working with informants — perhaps she knows someone who is close to Elda," Mary reasoned.

Elijah had hoped that Val would return to fight. He shook his head. "I don't know but it appears she has no intention of returning at this time."

"When we need her the most! Our world — her world, the one we fought so hard to maintain for all those centuries is gone — apparently she doesn't give a shit anymore." Riddick's face was crimson.

Elijah thought Riddick's head might explode. "I don't understand. It's not like her. She has always begged me to fight for humans — this is her chance and she's nowhere to be found. The world was constant for many years, so many that it seemed continuous … never ending. Suddenly, in the blink of an eye that world is gone. We're going to have to do this without her and we're going to have to … adapt. We are … no longer in control. We're the ones in hiding now." Elijah placed his hand over his stomach as it turned over again. This was the hardest thing he ever had to admit. He had been on top for so long — to let that go required giving up a part of himself. He would have to humble himself. He hoped he was up for the challenge. Raised in aristocracy he had never gone without. This was entirely new territory.

"Do you think she has something to do with this?" Riddick interrupted Elijah's troubled thoughts.

Elijah rounded on him. "How dare you make such accusations against the Queen?"

Riddick put his head down. "Sorry, My Lord."

"You know her as well as I do. She would never have a part in hurting humans. She's trying to warn us. How could you speak such treason?"

"Please forgive me, My Lord."

Seamlessly the two old comrades reverted to their medieval roots and ingrained formalities. For a moment they were no longer old friends but a king and his commander in chief.

"Yet, the queen disappears and then the world as we know it comes crashing down. You can't tell me that that is merely a coincidence," Samuel ventured.

Elijah became thoughtful for a moment. "It's not. She has disappeared for a reason. Whatever it is she's doing, it's for the best. She's helping in any way that she can. I don't doubt that for a second and you shouldn't either. After all, she warned us of the attacks."

"How's she able to do that?" Aaron said.

Mary lit up. "Maybe she's infiltrated Elda's inner circle."

"That is not possible. Elda knows what Vallachia looks like," Riddick said.

"I don't know but I am done worrying about this. We can't do anything about Vallachia. We need to focus on how to save mankind and ourselves," Elijah said.

Riddick turned his glare to the wall.

Elijah knew Riddick was not convinced of Val's innocence but the discussion was over. There were more important issues than Elijah's estranged wife. In a way, this was a guilty relief for him. Humans were suffering and this kept him preoccupied. He had to put all his energy into surviving, so that the Court could continue to help humans. Humans had to make it through this. As the leader, the burden was on him. Having to admit that he no longer ruled the vampire world caused a knot to form in his stomach. Yet this was not as terrible as wondering about Vallachia. He could not fathom why she would not return to him and to her people. He decided to focus on the easier of the two — the end of the world.

"The first order of business is to secure our blood supplies. We leave for London tonight to warn Hector, if it is not too late," Elijah said.

"Then what?" Teller asked.

"We go home."

The Court's main blood banks were in London and New York. They had to get to them before Elda did.

CHAPTER 33 EUROPE 2021 AD

When they reached London, Elijah was relieved to find Hector alive. "You need to get your men out of Safe Haven Seven. Elda knows where these hideouts are and she will be here soon. Take what you need and find a new hideout, one that no one in the Court previously knew about, as someone has betrayed us. Our blood supplies must also be moved and secured. At the rate Elda and the rogue vampires are going, it's likely that human blood will become scarce. You should take what blood you can with you to your new hideout."

Hector nodded in agreement. "I know just the place. We'll ship the blood to Perth. I used to have a secret place there. It was where I would go when I needed to get away."

"No one knows about it?"

"No, not even Lord Alexandru knew."

"Perfect. The Court has a better chance of surviving if we go our separate ways. We'll head back to New York and salvage what we can. We'll send a messenger when we get settled in a new place."

"Just like old times, eh? Before the convenience of modern technology," Samuel said.

"You can't stay in New York, it won't be safe," Hector said.

"You're right, we won't stay there long. We'll retrieve the blood from our banks and stock up on supplies, weapons mostly."

"And then what?" Hector said.

"I don't ... know." Elijah hated to admit it but he didn't know if he could fully trust Hector. *He may be the spy who is informing Elda of the Court's plans.* Elijah felt guilty for thinking this. Hector was an old friend. Yet, someone who was once close to them had to be providing Elda with information. Secondly — and equally discomforting — Elijah honestly did not know where they would go after New York.

"Good luck, my friend," Hector said.

"I wish you the best as well."

They did not waste any time. They parted ways quickly as there was much work to be done.

THE NEW YORK CITY streets were hardly recognizable. No one walked along the usually crowded sidewalks. Many of the subway entrances were filled with water, as the humans who maintained the water pumps were imprisoned or on the run or dead. Sonia sobbed at the sight of the once prosperous city.

They continued to fly north. The safest time to be out was in broad daylight. The daylight would keep new vampires indoors as well as the vampires who had had too much blood the night before. Vampires who drank to excess became intoxicated, not much different than humans who over-drank alcohol. Upon awakening, an overindulgent vampire would have unclear thoughts and the sun would be incredibly painful to the eyes. It was an advantage to the Court that this described a good number of Elda's supporters as well as the rogue vampires.

It was November and winter had fully set in. Elijah was relieved to see this as the cool weather helped to keep their blood supply cold. When they drew close to their main blood-bank distribution warehouse, Elijah kept an eye out for refrigerated semi-trucks to transport the blood. With the region being abandoned this turned out to be an easy task. Samuel and Aaron quickly hijacked a number of semis. If the trucks were full of goods, the contents were dumped in the street. Soon they were fully loaded with boxes of blood bags. One semi was reserved for weapons, ammunition, generators and anything else that might come in handy. They set out in a long cavalcade for the nearest military base.

"It's a good thing it's not the middle of summer or all our blood would have been spoiled," Samuel noted.

"Yes, so far we have luck on our side. Let's hope it holds out. I'll meet you at Fort Drum," Elijah said. He took a handful of men and flew home. It was all but destroyed. The multi-story mansion was collapsed in on itself. In some places it had been largely burned to ash. Elijah went to where the entrance to the basement had once been and they dug out the stairs. He went to a large safe hidden behind a fake wall. Out of the safe he took only one small wooden box. He left the crowns, jewels and gold behind. They would only be a burden in this new world.

Elijah locked the safe and they reburied the entrance. "I suppose the treasure will be as safe here as anywhere." Elijah took flight, leaving his home behind.

The carnage at the Fort Drum army base indicated that a battle had ensued. Any humans who remained were dead. They rounded up more supplies, including military guns, ammunition and camouflage for their base camps. Anything that looked like it might be useful was quickly loaded into a semi. Machine-gun-mounted Humvees became the lead and rear escorts for the long convoy of semis.

Riddick drove, while Elijah sat in the passenger seat rubbing his forehead with his thumb and index finger.

"You don't know where we're going, do you?" Riddick said.

"No. I only hope to avoid Elda and her supporters until we can get the blood to safety."

"Yet you have no idea where to find safety."

"If only Val would tell us Elda's whereabouts — that would be rather useful. Then we could avoid her until the blood is secure."

"Then we could find her and rip her heart out," Riddick said.

"For now, we need to hide at night. We'll travel during the day. This will lower the chances of running into Elda's forces."

"How, exactly does one hide an entire convoy of trucks?"

"We'll have to find warehouses or very remote locations and camouflage the trucks."

This was what they did. During the day they only stopped long enough to fuel the trucks. This had to be done by siphoning the diesel directly from gas station supply tanks.

"You still don't know where we are going, do you?" Riddick asked.

"As a matter of fact, o ye of little faith, I do." Elijah had been searching his memories of his travels for a good hideout. He and Val had toured the Amazon a very long time ago. Some local villagers spoke of secret tunnels that ran through the jungle. Elijah was going to see if he could find them. Yet he was not about to tell Riddick that he was relying on an old legend being true. Elijah had never seen these hidden passageways. Either way, the Amazon was remote, provided lots of cover and hopefully was far away from Elda. This was only a hunch but he did not know what else to do. He was not about to divulge this to his comrades.

CHAPTER 34 SOUTH AMERICA 2021 AD

Elijah knew that crossing the Panama Canal would be dangerous. It was a bottleneck, the perfect place for a trap. If not an outright trap, then it was a strategic place for Elda to have guards stationed. Up until that point they had avoided major cities but soon their path would be limited to one of two crossings.

"We'll use the inland crossing to get over the canal. It is best to avoid Panama City," Elijah decided.

"I have a bad feeling about this. Must we cross?" Riddick said.

"It's the fastest way to get this much blood across while keeping it refrigerated. What else could we do, sneak it over in ice chests?"

Riddick nodded as he pondered the idea.

"I was being facetious! That would take entirely too long. We would be spotted for sure." Elijah could hardly contain his irritation. They had been cooped up together in the semi cab for far too long.

They hid the trucks under green camouflage and Riddick led a recon team to scope out the canal crossing.

Upon their return, Riddick announced, "It's not good. The canal is closed to all transport, water and land. There are a handful of vampires guarding the area. They wear dark green armbands with a tarantula insignia."

"Elda's men," Elijah whispered.

"We could blow up the guard tower." Cosmin's eyes glowed with the light of adventure.

Elijah clenched his fists and took a deep breath, trying to calm himself. It didn't work. He spoke softly and slowly … at first, as if he were speaking to a small child. "We cannot blow up the tower as that would also destroy the bridge." Now he yelled, "The one we have to get across!" He turned to Teller. "Shut your boys up, will you?"

Teller was leaning against a truck with his arms crossed. He turned a hard stare to Cosmin who quickly closed his mouth and diverted his eyes to the ground.

"Thank you," Elijah said. "We'll go in full force at dawn and attack the guards. We greatly outnumber them so an ambush should work."

"That's a much better plan than yours," Costel whispered to his brother. "But, I've always wanted to blow up a bridge." A bit louder he ventured to say. "Perhaps, My Lord, we could blow up the bridge after we've crossed."

"Shut the hell up ..." Elijah rubbed his forehead; this always helped him think. "That may not be such a bad idea." Elijah looked to Riddick and then Teller for confirmation. Riddick and Teller were old and wise. They had vast experience in the ways of combat. Elijah trusted their counsel.

"I don't see why not," Teller said.

"It could lessen traffic from the north to us in the south, or at least make it easier to control the route if the need arose," Riddick added.

"Very well. You two," Elijah pointed to the twins. "You blow up the bridge *after* we are over." Elijah turned to Teller. "I will hold you personally responsible if they screw this up."

Teller grinned. "I'll look after them."

With a jump, Cosmin gave his brother a high-five. "We're checking off that to-do list like crazy now."

Elijah could not help but give the slightest of smiles. Could it be that after all these years the twins were beginning to grow on him? He shook his head. *No, certainly not.*

~

AT DAWN they made their way to the Centennial Bridge. It looked like giant sailboats back to back, as the suspension cables made two large triangles across the long bridge. The bridge rose high over the water, so large ships could pass under it with ease.

Elda's guards had made a makeshift post out of corrugated tin in the center of the bridge.

Elijah and his men were as quiet as lions stalking their prey. Elijah and Riddick were in the lead with Samuel directly behind them. This was an old habit. They came from a time when rulers were at the forefront of battles. If a king expected his men to follow him into war, then he had to be willing to lead the way. If the fight was not worth risking the king's life then others should not make the sacrifice either. *It was a more noble time, in some ways,* Elijah thought. He despised leaders today, who hid in bunkers while their infantry was slaughtered.

Hiding in the shadows, Elijah and Samuel watched two guards patrol the bridge. Samuel aimed his .45 at one of the sentries.

Elijah pushed Samuel's arm down. "You and your modern technology. That's entirely too noisy. You'll alert the others. Not to mention it will not kill them. This is how it is done."

Elijah moved forward without a sound and with the speed of light. After only a couple of heartbeats the guard's headless body wavered. Elijah caught him and lowered him silently to the ground. The other guard opened his mouth but Elijah's whip went through his neck. Again he caught the body before it hit the ground.

"Silent and effective, unlike your gun." Elijah whispered. "Stay downwind so the others don't catch your scent."

On Elijah's signal, they flew under the bridge and ambushed the lookout station and the guards on the other side of the bridge. When all the guards lay motionless and headless, Elijah gestured for Aaron who had remained back.

Aaron moved quickly to the convoy. They were free to move the trucks across the bridge. The twins went to work rigging the bridge with explosives. In no time the bridge was full of the Court's food supply.

"You see? There was nothing to worry about," Elijah said.

"Look!" Riddick pointed.

Pairs of vampires flew toward the semis at full speed. They hit the trailers broadside and pushed the trucks into the low railing. The scraping of metal was all that could be heard. The trucks were being tipped over the edge of the bridge. In no time they would be tumbling into the water below.

Machine-gun fire rained from the Humvees.

"Save the trucks!" Elijah yelled and with the sweep of his right arm, the men on his right side took flight. They began to stabilize the semis by pushing from the side opposite Elda's men. Elijah took flight as he beckoned for the remaining men to follow.

While speeding past one of Elda's men, Elijah snapped his neck. Two others had hoods covering their heads — for protection from the sun — no doubt. Elijah ripped their hoods off on his way by. This caused them to fall to the bridge screaming in pain. He readied his whip in order to finish them off. When the first whip cut through the air it did not find the soft skin it was intended for. It wrapped around something hard instead.

Elijah was face to face with an armored vampire. Elijah's whip was wrapped tightly around his metal-guarded arm. With one jerk of the enemy's arm the whip was yanked out of Elijah's hand. Elijah swung the second whip around the vampire's leg. Elijah tried to pull the winged creature down but, with one kick, Elijah's second whip was torn out of his hand. The vampire dived for Elijah who braced for the impact. But the sound of rocks crashing down on metal could be heard as Riddick tackled the armored man.

CHAPTER 35 SOUTH AMERICA 2021 AD

Riddick and his adversary landed hard on the pavement of the bridge. With one blow to the head from the metal covered arm, Riddick was sent flying off the bridge.

"No!" Elijah yelled. He knew his gun would be of no use against this enemy. *I don't know why I even carry the stupid thing*. He landed and drew his double-edged straight swords. "Who are you?" He yelled over the chaos around them.

"That's why I have the advantage. You don't know who I am but I know everything about you. That's how I knew how to protect myself against you. Honestly, ya oughta get some new tricks."

"I don't need tricks. I have a millennium of experience. How did you know we were here?"

"We're on the lookout for you all over the world, in every major port or border crossing. One of our lookouts was able to hit the alarm and warn us that they were under attack. And now I have you. Our queen will reward me greatly for finding you."

"Your queen is the Lady Vallachia and she is not behind this," Elijah spat.

"She *was* our queen but she has unfortunately disappeared." The sarcasm in his voice could not be missed. "We have a *new* queen and she's not the weak patsy that used to keep us suppressed because of her *love* of humans. We have a powerful queen now and we're finally free of your oppressive rule."

Elijah had heard more than enough. He moved to attack. The vampire shot several rounds into Elijah's chest but it hardly slowed Elijah's advance. Elijah attacked hard and swift with both swords, searching for the weakness in his armor. "I don't go into battle without armor either," Elijah said. They always wore bulletproof vests when there was a threat of any kind.

Elda's vampires managed to push one of the semis off the bridge. This caused Elijah to momentarily back off his attack.

"What is in the trucks that is so important? All your precious gold?" the enemy said as he advanced on Elijah. He raised his arm to strike another blow.

That is it! Elijah thought. In order for the vampire to have any mobility in his arms the armpit of his metal suit was made of cloth — no metal. Elijah found his mark. He drove one sword horizontally into the enemy's armpit. He forced the weapon all the way through his opponent's torso.

The man fell to his knees.

"No," Elijah said. "Those trucks carry something that will soon be far more precious than gold." He swung the butt of his second sword so hard it knocked off the head of his attacker.

Elijah quickly surveyed the scene. Teller, Abdullah and the twins were salvaging what they could from the truck that had been pushed over the bridge. The rest of his men were finishing off any of Elda's vampires who remained. Things appeared to be under control. In a flash, Elijah dived off the bridge.

When he hit the water his gills and webbed feet took over. He searched for Riddick and soon spotted his body drifting face down in the current. Elijah sped toward him. Riddick's gills were slowly moving in and out as they sucked what oxygen they could from the water. *He's alive!* Elijah pulled Riddick out of the water. Once Riddick lay on his back on the shore, Elijah saw his face. It was smashed to pieces by the metal blow he had taken.

"No!" Elijah yelled.

Samuel heard Elijah's cry. He could recognize Elijah's voice from a mile away. Samuel spotted them on the shore and called for their medic.

The medic injected Riddick with a heavy dose of anesthetic. "He needs to remain asleep while I reconstruct what I can of his face before his accelerated healing kicks in any more than it already has."

Elijah locked his fingers behind his head and paced.

"It will be okay. Riddick will be fine," Teller said.

Elijah locked eyes with Teller's then went back to pacing. He would not be content until Riddick was awake and well. He had lost Vallachia, he'd lost his kingdom and he'd lost John — the only constant in his entire life. All he had left were Samuel and Riddick. He could not lose anyone else and keep up this fight. Elijah gave a knowing nod to Teller.

Teller knew exactly what it meant. It meant that Elijah needed Teller to take over. Elijah needed to be by Riddick's side. Riddick was all he could focus on.

Teller took flight for the bridge. "Get the trucks off the bridge at once! Make sure none of Elda's supporters survive! Hunt them down if need be! Elda mustn't get word from her men that we were here! Don't leave any evidence behind."

THREE HOURS LATER, the trucks were across — all but the one at the bottom of the canal. They were dented but still drivable. Elda's guards were accounted for and dead. The bridge was blown, along with the bodies of the fallen.

Riddick began to stir as the drug wore off. Elijah was relieved as he watched Riddick's face heal. Riddick almost looked like himself. There was still some swelling, which would be gone soon. A thick red line remained across his cheek, which would become a scar. One side of his jaw was also slightly deformed. Yet otherwise, he was fine.

Riddick slowly sat up. Elijah pulled him to his feet by the forearm and gave him a one armed hug. Riddick moaned and scratched his mostly-healed cheek. He stopped short as he noticed the bridge was no longer there. "You blew the bridge without me!"

Elijah laughed. It was a good sign if that was what he was most worried about. "Maybe sneaking the blood across in ice chests was not a bad idea after all."

"You should listen to me more often." Riddick went back to rubbing his mostly-healed face.

"You may be right. I'll try to remember that next time," Elijah said.

"You'll look even more dreadful with that big scar down your face," Teller said.

"You do realize that you resemble Riddick?" Samuel said.

"Well, I've always been the handsome one and now that goes without saying," Teller said.

Elijah rolled his eyes. "That's enough. Let's get the hell out of here."

On his way by, Riddick gave Teller a shove that almost knocked him over."

"I suppose I deserved that," Teller said.

CHAPTER 36 SOUTH AMERICA 2021 AD

It was not long before the roads became nothing but jeep trails and that was if it was not pouring rain, in which case the Humvees could barely move forward let alone the trucks. The semis were parked and camouflaged. Samuel used a combination of solar panels and generators to keep the trucks' coolers running. Half the Court remained behind to guard the trucks and the others took flight with Elijah.

"What exactly are we looking for?" Samuel asked.

"It's a small village in the middle of the Amazon forest. Val and I visited there once but that was a long time ago. I don't know if it's still there. If we can find it, perhaps the natives can lead us to secret underground tunnels," Elijah said.

"You mean to tell us that you don't know where these tunnels are?" Riddick said.

"No. But I'll know the village when I see it."

"So you don't even know where the village is and you've never actually seen the tunnels?" Riddick shook his head.

"I told you. I'll find it."

They flew along the Amazon River for hours, not seeing much except dense trees and rivers.

"It may be faster if we dig our own tunnels," Teller said.

Elijah spotted a bend in the mighty river, followed by another. This resulted in a perfect 'S' shape. It was a familiar landmark. "There." He pointed. "That's the village." Nestled safely in one of the curves, surrounded by river on three sides, came the slightest glow of fire.

They landed outside the village and Elijah handed Riddick all his weapons — two whips, two broad swords, the belt of knives from around his waist. He knew he would not need any of these. He would need much more.

Elijah's .45 was always tucked in his pants at the small of his back. He held it out for Riddick to take as well.

"You can at least keep the gun hidden under your shirt. No one will know you have it," Riddick protested.

"I mean these holy people no harm. Besides they will be largely naked and they're human. They're no threat to us," Elijah said.

"What do you mean — naked?" Teller asked with concern but Elijah was already gone.

With no weapons, Elijah felt as if he were naked as well. He took a deep breath. *Having the courage to put down my weapons is harder than I thought.* He emerged from the forest to find a group of humans drumming and singing. Well, it was more of a wailing really. Their golden brown skin was largely exposed. Some wore belts that consisted of thin strings decorated with beads or colorful fabrics. Only a few wore modern clothes and these were threadbare and soiled.

They slowly stopped singing and drumming as they noticed the stranger approach. Only one singer continued his sorrowful cry. He had been lost in the music. It took him several moments longer to become aware that everyone around had fallen silent.

"Please, I need your help." Elijah held his arms out in surrender.

They chattered amongst one another. Elijah tried to make it out. He spoke many — perhaps most — languages but this was largely foreign to him.

When he and Val were here centuries ago, she had won them over with rare gifts. She had sweets for the children and some beautiful fabrics for the women. He did not have to do — well, anything. Val was the one who could win people over with her loving smile. Now he had to do it on his own — somehow, with no sweets or silks and no wife.

A woman approached with a cup of water and a man offered him some dried meat. Elijah realized they thought he was a lost human, starving and thirsty.

"No, no. I'm fine." He tried to reassure them. *These people only want to help me and they don't even know me. Hopefully their generosity remains after they find out what I am,* he thought. He wished he could understand them. If there had been any Latin or Greek base to their language Elijah could have made out what they were saying. But there was not.

Finally the boy who had remained in the trance-like state after the others had stopped singing, stepped forward. "What is it that you need?" He spoke with a heavy accent in British English. He was one of the few who wore clothes. He had on an old Star Wars t-shirt and blue jeans. Both of which had numerous holes and stains.

Elijah sighed with relief. "How is it that you speak English?"

"I lived with my mother in Natal for a number of years. I was taught English there."

Elijah could not help himself. He was curious about this boy. He could not be beyond his eighteenth year. Elijah had to remind himself that he too looked eighteen. "And yet you are here?"

"These are my people. I was born here and this is where I belong."

"You are wise beyond your years." Elijah smiled.

The boy frowned in concentration. "Do you mean that I am smarter than I should be ... since I'm so young?"

"Yes. That is exactly what I mean and ... I need your help. Your ancestors once spoke of tunnels which ran beneath this land."

The boy narrowed his eyes. "My ancestors? You're one of them, aren't you — a creature of the night?"

This boy is sharp, Elijah thought.

The boy turned to his people and spoke. They began to shrink away from Elijah.

"You're aware of what's going on around the world?" Elijah asked.

"My great grandmother spoke about the day the world would end. We've known of your kind for a long time." The boy had taken several steps back as well.

"Please. I will not harm you." Elijah went down on one knee. One thing he had learned from his brief time with these people was that this was a sign of respect.

The boy studied Elijah. "You must face my grandmother. I warn you — she sees all."

Elijah kept his head respectfully lowered. *This is a test. One I have to pass.* Crippled hands reached out to cup Elijah's cheeks. He raised his eyes. The old woman was completely naked. He peered into her cataract-laden eyes. *Her arthritic hands must cause her such pain.*

She stared at him intently for a time and with a toothless smile she declared a verdict to her people.

"Grandmother Tomamacowee has decided that you mean well," the boy translated.

The old woman turned to her grandson with further instruction. The boy nodded and kissed her forehead.

"Grandmother says that I am to take you to our sacred tunnels."

Elijah bowed his head again. He exhaled a breath that he had not realized he had been holding.

From the shadows Mari said, "Why is Elijah bowing to these commoners. They should be bowing to him."

Samuel frowned. "These people are not commoners. They are immortals as well. We are in their world now and that old lady is their leader, their queen, if you will."

"She's no queen and they're not immortal," Mari countered.

"I've read about these people. They live forever through their ancestors. They have an unbroken chain of knowledge and communication with their forbearers. If one's essence remains on this earth, is that not immortality?"

Mari rolled her eyes. "Whatever you say, darling." It was beyond her to argue with him when he began philosophizing. Although she figured there was some sort of difference between these people's "immortality" and a vampire's immortality.

"What's your name?" Elijah asked.

"Marcel," the boy answered. "Grandmother is Tomamacowee but you may call her Tomoc. Your friends may join us now."

"Not much gets by you, now, does it?" Elijah said.

Marcel smiled with confidence. "Well, it's grandmother really. She told me that it's not likely that you are a lone creature of the night. You are their leader and your faithful followers are never far away. She's seen you coming for quite some time."

Elijah was impressed with these people's insight and wisdom. The Court spent the next several hours with the villagers answering questions about vampires, such as if crosses had any effect on them. "No. Garlic doesn't bother us either." Elijah had no idea where that myth had come from. Most of the questions came from Marcel who was aware of the world outside this village. He was incredibly eager to learn.

CHAPTER 37 SOUTH AMERICA 2021 AD

At dawn they set out from the village with Marcel in the lead.

"It will only be a matter of time before Elda finds your people. She's focused on containing heavily populated areas but soon she will send scouts to look for any remaining humans," Elijah said.

"We've already made plans for when that day comes. We have some supplies in the tunnels and we're prepared to evacuate quickly. Don't worry there is plenty of room in the vast tunnels," Marcel chattered away.

In a flash, Elijah sped forward. He grabbed Marcel by the shoulders and lifted him off the ground. He gave Marcel a moment to realize that his feet were suspended in the air. Elijah gently set him back down. "That's how fast they'll be upon you. You won't get away — none of you."

The boy stared at Elijah with wide brown eyes. "Your point is made. I'll speak with my people. Perhaps it's time for us to go into hiding after all?"

"So we're going to be one big happy family? Humans and vampires living together underground," Samuel said. Living with humans was something he had never done. In fact, such an outrageous thought had never crossed his mind.

"Times have changed my old friend," Elijah said.

"It's not so bad," Teller added. He was used to living with humans. He had lived around humans for almost two hundred years.

They hacked their way through the jungle for hours.

"This is tediously slow. Can't we carry Marcel and fly there? Mari whined.

"We're almost there," Marcel said. The idea of being carried through the air was not something that sounded appealing. The few seconds suspended in Elijah's grip had been more than enough. He liked to have his feet firmly on the ground.

"Can we at least carry him on someone's back, so we can move faster?" Mari said. She was not used to being out of her palace. Hiking in the jungle was something she would rather read about from the comforts of home.

"Marcel has to lead the way. Honestly love, try to enjoy the adventure. It's good for you to slow down and see new places," Samuel said.

Yet it took them another hour before they reached the tunnels.

"We're here," Marcel said.

"Thank God!" Mari breathed.

They came to a low rock face. Moss and vines covered the stone surface. Marcel pulled back the vegetation to reveal a small passageway. Elijah was relieved to see that the entrance and surrounding area looked much like the expansive jungle around them. It was well hidden; nothing stood out about this place or gave any indication that it led to tunnels. "Perfect," Elijah said.

They entered the opening in single file.

Mari started and grabbed onto Samuel's arm. "What's that?"

"It's a spider," Elijah said as he pushed past them.

"That's not a spider! It's a monster," Mari replied.

"Well, get used to him. He's your new roommate," Riddick said.

Mari shivered. "I can't possibly live here."

"Did you expect the Ritz?" Teller said.

"All those years spent in castles and grand manors. Now you expect me to live like a caveman? I will not be reduced to this!" Mari said.

"You mean cavewoman," Mary corrected.

"Go ahead, Mari. Try your luck out there in the open. What do you think Elda will do to you when she finds you?" Elijah said.

Mari whimpered.

~

THE COURT BUSIED themselves setting up their new home — or perhaps compound was a more appropriate term. Samuel and Aaron placed large freezers deep within the tunnels. They were powered by solar with a back-up generator. The solar panels were hidden at night to lessen the chances of one of Elda's supporters spotting them. They were largely safe during the day. Yet, Elijah worried that the solar panels would point their enemy to the tunnels eventually. Not to mention fuel for the generators would become more difficult to scavenge as time passed. He would worry about the sustainability of all this later. For now they had plenty of blood and they had a way to keep it fresh.

The tunnels were divided into living quarters. They mined out some areas to make bigger rooms. Teller, Abdullah and the twins installed metal doors, starting with the main entrance. Supplies were brought in for humans. It did not take long for most of the villagers to see the wisdom in moving to the tunnels as well. Gardens were planted within walking distance of the tunnels. They modeled the gardens after the British, planting them with no patterns or rows. From the air the gardens looked as if they were natural vegetation. Chickens and pigs were let out during the day and brought inside to their own quarters within the tunnels by night. Mari was not thrilled about living in an underground barn. Wells and outhouses were dug. The jungle provided much. This would allow them to survive and remain hidden.

The tunnels were like a maze. They were made up of three main shafts with many shorter laterals branching off. Overall there were several miles of underground caverns. The ceilings were low and taller people had to duck their heads in some places. They mined out a main meeting room that doubled as a mess hall. Samuel and Aaron ran wires and lighting throughout the tunnels.

Elijah set official rations on their blood supply. Each vampire was given three and a half pints every two weeks. Vampires preferred four pints, as they felt more satisfied. However, they could get by, without side effects, on three and a half pints. Samuel and Aaron had long since figured out the minimum amount of blood it took to keep vampires healthy. This way they had plenty of strength and they did not become so hungry that they put the humans around them at risk.

"We can donate blood," Marcel offered.

"You would do that … for us?" Elijah asked.

"We're up against creatures that are many times faster and stronger than us. You're our best chance of defeating them or even just surviving against them. We'll do whatever we can to help. If it is as you say and you fought for us for a thousand years then the least we can do is donate some blood."

"That's very generous of you. If we work together it'll increase the chances of both species surviving," Elijah said.

Samuel quickly did the math. "There are not enough humans to sustain us."

"But they can help to keep our blood supply up. It'll give us more time. We'll set everyone who's able and willing to donate on an eight week rotation for giving a pint of blood."

This required them to head to a city for more supplies. Most of the population of Brazil had been on the east coast. This was where they headed. They found themselves in Natal. This time, abandoned hospitals were their targets. They grabbed all they could carry. They secured what was needed to be able to draw blood plus any other medicines that they thought might be useful.

Elijah quietly jerked his head toward a closed door. "Shhh. Did you hear that?"

"I sure did," Riddick said.

Elijah twisted the handle of the locked door until the mechanism inside broke. He swung the door open with his hand on his whip. The scent of a human was strong in the tiny storage room. A woman could be seen behind some shelving. She was curled up in the fetal position.

"We're not going to hurt you."

She flinched at the sudden nearness of Elijah's voice.

She looked up with large brown eyes full of fear. "Are you human?"

"I'm afraid not but —

She made a run for it. Elijah nodded to Riddick who quickly wrapped his arms around the young woman, easily subduing her. This caused her to drop a backpack she had in her hand.

"No! Let me go!" She kicked Riddick's shin with all her might and Riddick did not so much as flinch.

"We'll let you go. I promise, we won't harm you. There's one thing you need to know first. You need to know who we are."

"Please let me go." Tears ran down her cheeks.

Elijah felt terrible for her but he had to try to get through to her. "We can help you. We have a safe place for humans and vampires alike. Not all of us are bad. We have always fought for humans and we'll always protect them."

She continued to struggle in Riddick's grip so Elijah went on, "You don't stand a chance out there on your own. … Wait! I know…" Elijah knew the poor girl was too scared to be reasoned with, so he ran to the reception desk and drew a makeshift map on a prescription pad. In no time he was back. "This is a map that will lead you to our hideout — in case you change your mind."

He tucked the paper into the front pocket of her jeans and nodded to Riddick. Riddick quickly released the girl. She stumbled to get her footing and grabbed the backpack as she ran out the door. Elijah knew that whatever it was in the pack, it must have been important.

"Do you think she'll find us?" Riddick asked.

"If she's smart she will."

CHAPTER 38 NORTH AMERICA 2021 AD

Elda had plenty of time to do this right. After all, if one plans to take over the world, one had better have a flawless plan, with all the details covered. Elda had just that. The next phase was to leave the humans leaderless. Her supporters had long since infiltrated governments all around the world. Only powerful countries were of interest — largely ones with nuclear capabilities. The U.S., as well as Great Britain, Russia, China, North Korea, Japan — these were a few of the most important countries, the ones at the top of Elda's list. She had people in numerous high-ranking positions with top security clearance, ready to do her dirty work. This was how she easily entered the U.S. president's emergency bunker. Her spy had all the security codes, clearance key-cards, I.D.s, retina scans — all she needed to get to the president.

He was hidden deep beneath Pikes Peak, outside of Colorado Springs. Elda and her men managed to make it far into the mountain before they had to kill any guards. Before entering the room she paused to listen to the president and his top advisors.

"We can't bomb these prisons where people are being held. We would only kill a couple of their infantry and numerous innocent civilians would die. Please Mr. President, it's not worth the large amount of lives lost."

"Find out where these *creatures'* leader is located and I will send a nuclear missile right up his ass," the president replied.

"Well done," Elda said to her spy from outside the presidents meeting room. "They don't even know of the security breach." With a mischievous smile she added, "Let's have some fun."

Elda barged into the room with her entourage. "You're in luck Mr. President, as the one you seek stands before you. I do hope you have one of those missiles on you now, as that is the only thing that could possibly save you."

"Who in the hell are you and how did you get in here?" The president stood and leaned on the table in front of him, supporting himself with his fists.

"I already told you who I am. I'm the leader of the *creatures* you were just discussing."

"A woman! Impossible. A woman could never cause this much damage. Get her out of here!" the president yelled.

"You're such a moron. How did you ever get elected?" Elda appeared in front of the president and sank her fangs into his neck. Her followers did the same to the others in the room.

Once the humans were dead, Elda critically eyed her surroundings. "This place is quite nice. It will make a suitable headquarters. Secure it."

A handful of her supporters filed out of the main room.

"Now let's check in with my faithful followers to see how they are faring at eliminating the other human leaders of the world."

CHAPTER 39 SOUTH AMERICA 2021 AD

Bray wound her way through the streets of Natal. She was making sure no one had followed her. Little did she know that this would not stop a vampire from tracking a human. Once back in their most recent hiding place, she set the backpack down in front of a little girl.

"I got it. This is enough insulin to last you awhile," Bray announced.

"You did it! Thank you Bray!" the small girl chimed.

Bray ruffled the thick brown hair on her head. "You're welcome."

"You look like crap. What happened to you?" Bray's cousin Jack asked.

"I was caught."

Jack sat up from the sofa where he had been lounging. "Whoa! By one of *them?* How did you get away?"

"They … let me go."

"I told you not to go alone but you just had to go and sneak off," Jack said.

"Like there was anything you could have done. You would have been caught too."

"So what happened?"

"You're not going to believe this ...

That evening Bray stared at the scribbled map on the piece of prescription paper.

"Forget it Bray. We can't trust them," Ramon said.

"But they let me go."

"It's a trap."

"A trap? How?"

"So you would lead the vampires right to us," Ramon said.

Bray shook her head. "You're wrong. No one followed me and you didn't see him — his eyes."

"I know — he was *really hot*. We're not going to trust your judgment, Bray. I've been told that your taste in men is terrible."

"It's not that. He really didn't want to hurt me. He wants to help."

"Why would one of those monsters help us?" Ramon asked.

"I don't know." Bray shook her head in dismay.

"You see, that's why we're *not* going and that is final."

Bray disliked Ramon but when you're one of only a dozen or so people left in an entire city you don't get to choose whom you hang out with. She was stuck with him.

That night Bray lay in bed staring at the ceiling. She could not get those haunting grey eyes out of her head. *Or were they blue? They were kind and intelligent and ... Ramon is right, he is the most gorgeous man I have ever seen.* She shook her head. *That's not it — okay, that's not ALL of it. He really wants to help and he can help us.* He had been sincere, she saw it in his eyes. By morning her mind was made up.

"I'm following the map. I'm going to find him."

"Well you're going alone," Ramon snapped.

"I know. I also know that he's our only hope. There's a chance that I'm wrong and that's why I'm going alone. I won't put any of you in danger. If they're willing to help then I will come back for you."

"That's if you can get through the jungle on your own and find that vaguely marked place on that tiny piece of paper. Don't you know that the Amazon is humongous?" Ramon scoffed.

Bray grit her teeth. She would not be deterred by Ramon's constant negativity. "I only have to get close. He'll find me."

"I'll go with you," Jack said.

Bray smiled. Her cousin would not let her down. She was relieved that she didn't have to trek for miles on end through the jungle alone.

They packed at once. Jack headed for the Camaro.

"What're you doing? The Land Rover will get us farther."

"But the Camaro will get us there faster." Jack smiled.

This was one advantage of being in an abandoned city, they had their choice of vehicles.

"I know you love the Camaro but we have to be practical. We can pack a lot more supplies into the Land Rover and get much closer to our destination."

Jack frowned. He laid his head and arm across the top of the bright red sports car, "Sorry Baby but I have to leave you for another. I hope you understand. You're my number one girl, though. I'll come back for you."

"Just help me pack the damn Land Rover." Bray was losing her patience. Once they tied down sleeping bags and as much fuel, water, food, bug repellent, flashlights, batteries; anything they could find or thought might come in handy, Bray hit the gas and the Land Rover sped west out of Natal.

Jack yelled out the passenger window, "Wait for me!" The Camaro did not reply.

"Will you knock it off! This is serious."

"One thing my father always said was, 'If you lose your sense of humor then you've lost everything.'"

Bray smiled at her cousin. "He's a smart man."

Jack peered out the window with a longing gaze. "It was an awesome car though."

Bray laughed. "Give it up, already."

That night when they lay on their sleeping bags looking up at the stars through the trees, Bray asked, "Do you think our family is alive?"

"You know what, I do. I think they were locked up."

"Then we have to save them."

"Save them? I don't even know how we'll find them."

"We have to try."

Jack sighed. "I know."

CHAPTER 40 SOUTH AMERICA 2021 AD

Almost a week had passed. Bray and Jack traveled for two days in the Land Rover. Then the roads ran out and they hiked for three more days. On the sixth morning Jack was ready to head back.

"Our food is running low. We may be able to make it back to the city in time if we turn around now."

"I don't know if the blisters on my feet will let me walk all the way back." Bray sat with her back against a tree and her head down.

"Bray!" Jack's voice was full of panic.

She slowly raised her head. Black boots stood directly in front of her. She looked up to find a man in green army fatigues and a tight green t-shirt.

He smiled down at Bray. "You changed your mind." He held out his hand to help her up.

Bray reluctantly took it and he effortlessly pulled her to her feet.

"My name is Elijah."

She could only stare at his unforgettable eyes. *Grey, no blue, no grey.* She tried to define them. They had never left her dreams since she first saw him. She was beginning to think she had only imagined seeing him in the hospital.

"Wow. I've never known anyone to leave my cousin speechless. I'm Jack and this is Bray."

Elijah bowed his head respectfully. "It's a pleasure to meet you." Elijah shook Jack's hand.

"Whoa! You're freezing."

"Yes, well, all is right then, as that is natural for us."

"You mean vampires?" Jack asked.

Elijah nodded. "We're a good day's hike from the tunnels on foot. So we had better get moving, unless of course, you want to fly."

"No way! You can fly?" Jack said.

Riddick stepped out of the trees. Jack panicked and stumbled backwards falling to the ground. "He's huge and…"

"All around terrifying, yes, we know." Teller suddenly appeared, lifting Jack back to his feet.

Bray hid behind Elijah.

Jack looked between Teller and Riddick. "Are you two brothers … or something?"

"Absolutely not!" Riddick said.

"No relation whatsoever," Teller added.

"There will be time for all your questions while we head to the tunnels."

"Are we truly going to spend the entire day walking the jungle at a snail's pace when we could simply carry them?" Teller asked.

"I didn't want to scare them. Not until they fully understand that they can trust us." Elijah said.

"I'm not afraid. I want to fly!" Jack's large brown eyes danced with excitement.

"Flying is not the scariest part." Elijah nodded to Riddick who leapt with ease into the air and transformed. Riddick's iridescent batwings spread out so far on either side that there was hardly room for them in the overgrown forest. His skin was grey and cracked — like stone and the head of the monster had glowing yellow eyes and long sharp teeth.

"Holy shit!" Jack tried to run but slipped again on the wet forest floor.

Bray made a run for it as well. Elijah grabbed her and swung her onto his back. He took flight before Bray even knew what was happening.

By the time she gathered her wits she was high above the treetops. She started to push herself away from the monster underneath her, until she realized she would fall to her death. She clung tightly to Elijah and closed her eyes. *This can't be happening. This can't be happening!* Her concern for her cousin caused her to force her eyes open. She had to know if he was okay.

He too was on the back of a large bat-like, stone creature-thingy. These were the only words that came to her mind to describe them. Jack's mouth hung open in awe.

When he noticed Bray staring at him he yelled, "Bray, you've got to look around. This is the coolest thing ever!"

How can he be so sure that this is all okay? Bray thought. She took a deep breath. Well there was nothing she could do about her situation anyway. Even if they did not die by falling out of the sky; even if they were being taken to a giant cauldron to be cooked and eaten, there was nothing she could do about that now. She slowly ventured to look around. It was beautiful. Rolling green hills as far as she could see, hilltops, rivers ... and then there was the mother of all rivers, which was so wide in places that it looked more like a lake. "Wow," Bray breathed.

She glanced at Jack. He was sitting up straight on the back of the creature with his arms toward the sky. "Try it, Bray. It's like I'm flying all on my own."

"Go for it," came from the creature she was on. "I'll catch you if you fall."

She slowly sat up and even more slowly raised her arms. Eventually she laughed at the thrill.

"Woo Hoo!" Jack yelled.

Riddick spiraled through the air, causing Jack to fall off. Jack screamed as he sped toward the ground.

"No!" Bray yelled, wrapping her arms around Elijah again.

"He'll be fine," the creature beneath her said.

Jack was about fifteen feet from the ground when Riddick swooped him up in his arms and they landed safely on the forest floor.

Jack's knees buckled when Riddick set him down.

"I've always wanted to do that," Riddick said. "You were having entirely too much fun. I couldn't resist giving you a scare."

Bray slid off Elijah's back as they landed. She ran to Jack. "Are you okay?"

Jack finally caught his breath. "That was ... awesome! Can we do it again?"

Bray smacked Jack's shoulder. "You're such an adrenaline junkie. You scared me!"

"You were scared? I was terrified! Seriously, that was better than racing the Camaro through the empty streets."

"This way." Elijah led them out of the trees into a clearing. "Welcome to the tunnels."

Naked women cooked fish over open flames. A naked man was returning from a hunt with his furry kill fastened over his shoulder.

"Don't they have clothes in the jungle?" Jack said.

Bray's mouth fell open. "Is that a ... monkey?"

"What do they do with those?" Jack asked.

"Eat them," Elijah replied.

"That's disgusting." Jack wrinkled his nose.

"Ah, poor cute little monkeys," Bray said.

"You never know. You might like it. You two are obviously American — North American, so what are you doing in Brazil?"

"Our parents are from Brazil and we visit often. Our grandfather, Jack's father's father and my mother's father, passed away. We had to return for the service," Bray answered.

"How did you escape when the vampires attacked Natal?" Riddick asked.

"Well, the morning of the attacks, Jack and I decided to get away from our crazy family and go for a hike. We got lost and that was probably what saved us. We were far away on a mountainside. By the time we found our way back the next morning, the city was empty."

"You see? Once you get her talking she doesn't shut up," Jack said.

Ignoring her cousin, Bray looked at Elijah with large pleading brown eyes. "Do you think you can help us find our parents?"

Elijah had been thinking that that was the next step. Now that they had a secure base, they could think about trying to free humans from Elda's prisons. "There's a possibility that we could find your family. Of course, there is no guarantee that they are alive."

"Did you hear that, Jack? He'll help us. I knew we needed to find him." When Jack did not answer she turned to find him wide-eyed and pale-faced. "What ..." she followed his stunned gaze and screamed.

Elijah drew his sword and turned to see what had startled Bray.

"There's a ... a baby in the fire." Jack somehow managed to spit the words out.

Elijah put his sword away. "That's a monkey, or it was, and a full grown one at that. Now let me fetch Mari and Sonia. They're our official welcoming committee."

"Or unwelcoming committee, is more like it," Riddick added as they left Bray and Jack.

Bray made a gaging sound, as she turned away from the fire. She tried to get the tiny charred figure out of her head. Much to her dismay, Elijah was gone and she was face to face with an attractive dark-haired woman. She stood tall and regal, even though she was in the middle of the jungle and her clothes were stained.

"I heard the terrified scream of a damsel and knew at once that we had newcomers. My name is Mari and this is Sonia." Mari gestured to the young girl at her side.

Bray loved children. "Is this your mom?" she asked Sonia as if she were speaking to a baby.

Sonia frowned.

"Sonia is not a child, my dear and I am not her mother. Indeed she is older than I. Now, allow me to show you around this God-forsaken place. We have a strict curfew. Everyone must be inside the tunnels at dusk and all signs of inhabitance must be hidden or taken into the tunnels each night. We are largely free to move about in the daylight hours. This is the safest time for us, as our enemies will be hindered by the sun — we hope."

Mari and Sonia headed for the tunnels.

"What's going on? Why do they talk so funny and how can the girl be older?" Bray whispered.

Jack shrugged.

Mari looked over her shoulder at the humans. "I must warn you, we have excellent hearing, so whispering will not do you any good."

That night Bray and Jack passed on the barbecued monkey. They ate some canned beans and one of the natives offered them fresh corn and cabbage from the garden — this they devoured. The newcomers watched as the camp prepared for darkness. Samuel and Aaron took down antennas and covered them with giant green palm leaves. Solar panels and farm animals were taken into the tunnels. Fire pits were cleaned out and covered with palm leaves. Bray was nervous about being locked up underground. As the sun set, camouflage was pulled over the metal doors to the tunnels and they were sealed inside until first light.

CHAPTER 41 SOUTH AMERICA 2021 AD

The Court's next move was intelligence gathering. Pairs of vampires were sent out on day missions to find out where humans were being held and to discover how well they were guarded.

"We free them, then what?" Riddick asked.

"It's not our job to sustain the entire population. Humans will have to learn to survive in this new world until we can find and kill Elda," Elijah answered.

"Humans still greatly outnumber vampires. So her supporters are spread thin across the world. Every one of her vampires we take out significantly weakens her forces. That's how we'll win this war. Little by little," Samuel said.

"We have to go back for the others," Bray interrupted from the back of the meeting room.

"What others?" Elijah asked.

"The others who escaped the attack on Natal. I promised them that if I found you, I would come back for them."

"We don't need more mouths to feed. There are probably many humans all over the world who have managed to elude Elda's forces so far. Why should we save this group of humans?" Riddick asked.

"It will be more people who could donate blood," Mary pointed out.

Bray glared at Riddick. She was pretty sure she didn't like him. "There's a sick girl. She needs insulin. She won't survive without our help."

"We're barely surviving. We're not going to be able to care for a diabetic child," Riddick said.

"We must try," Elijah said.

ELIJAH SET OUT WITH BRAY, Jack, Riddick, Mary and Samuel with the goal of finding the humans Bray and Jack had left behind. Riddick tracked the humans from where Bray had last seen them. They had a new hideout, not far from the old one. Once Riddick had their scent it was easy for him to locate them.

Elijah twisted the locked door handle. The mechanisms inside ground and clanked in protest. The door swung open to a plush apartment. The vampires could hear humans scurrying about trying to hide or perhaps escape out the back.

"Ramon! It's me, Bray. It's safe to come out."

They slowly moved down the long hallway.

Ramon rounded the corner at the end of the hall with a gun pointed at them.

"Ramon. Don't shoot. They won't hurt you. They're here to help," Bray said.

As she spoke, Riddick sped forward in a blur. He ripped the gun from Ramon's hand and twisted his arm behind his back.

"You brought them right to us. You traitor!" Ramon yelled.

Riddick patted Ramon down and removed another gun and a knife from his belt. He released Ramon's arm.

"Ramon, please listen to me," Bray said. "Not all vampires are bad. They have a compound deep in the jungle. We can be safe and free there. Please come with us."

"You're such a stupid girl! They can't be trusted," Ramon said.

"I know that vampires took everything from you but you don't have a choice," Jack said. "If you want to remain free for much longer you must come with us. These vampires are our best chance of surviving."

Riddick and Mary sniffed out the humans who were hiding. Riddick found a small girl under the kitchen sink.

She issued a high-pitched scream when she saw Riddick's large form and scarred face.

Bray ran for her. "It's okay." She picked the child up and hugged her tight. "I'm here. I came back for you, like I promised. They won't hurt you."

"Bray, it's really you?" the girl whimpered.

"Yes. You're safe."

"I seriously doubt that. You led them straight to us," Ramon spat.

"You are free to leave," Elijah said. "No one here will stop you. However, we're offering you safety, all of you. It's only a matter of time before Elda's vampires catch your scent and track you down."

The other humans who had attempted to hide, gathered around Ramon.

"I will never trust you monsters," Ramon said.

"Then I wish you the best of luck on your own." Elijah stepped aside and gestured to the front door.

Ramon moved cautiously toward the door. Others followed.

"Wait!" Bray said. "You don't stand a chance out there on your own. They're even more powerful than we thought. You don't have to trust them but please trust me. Come with us." Bray still held the child in her arms.

In the end some chose to follow Bray and Jack and some decided to leave with Ramon.

"You're all a bunch of idiots!" Ramon glowered at the ones who chose to stay.

"Good!" Jack yelled after Ramon as he left. "No one likes you anyway, asshole."

The humans who stayed gathered some belongings and they headed for the safety of the tunnels. The little girl refused to let go of

Bray, so Elijah carried them both in his arms. The vampires were loaded down with humans and their baggage. Riddick alone carried four humans. Yet they managed to fly them to their new home.

~

ELIJAH and his men as well as Bray and some of the other humans stood over a large map of Brazil.

"Our scouts have found a prison outside of Fortaleza, northwest of Natal." Riddick pointed to the map. "This is where most of the surviving humans from surrounding areas are being held."

"Jack! Our parents could be there," Bray said.

"There's a good chance that your family may be there. We'll start with this prison. The goal is to free as many humans as possible," Elijah said.

"I have to go so that I can look for my parents," Bray said.

"You can't go. You'll slow us down. Do you have a picture of your family?"

"No," Bray lied. "I want to be able to search for them myself."

"I'll go instead," Jack offered. "I can find them."

"Why, because I'm a girl?" Bray glared at her cousin.

"Yeah, a weak little girl," Jack teased.

Bray punched him.

"Ouch." Jack rubbed his shoulder. "Okay, not so weak."

"You're both too weak and too slow. Not to mention, if we do somehow find your family it will be difficult enough to get them all back here. If one of you comes this will mean that there will be one less person we can carry on the return trip," Elijah reasoned.

"You're unnecessary baggage. It's too risky. No humans can go on these missions," Riddick agreed.

"Unnecessary!" Bray was starting to despise Riddick. "Fine." She pulled her phone out of her back jean pocket and quickly scrolled through her photos. She stopped at a group picture. "Here are my parents and Jack's are there." She pointed to the tiny faces on the phone.

Elijah studied the picture. "Put a voice memo on your phone. Tell your family that they can trust us. If I find them I will play it for them."

Bray nodded and spoke into her phone, "Mom, Dad, if you are hearing this it's because my friends have found you. Please, trust them. They will bring you to safety … and to me. … I love you." She quickly brushed a tear away before handing the phone to Elijah. "Please, find them."

"I'll do my best." Elijah took the phone and studied the picture again. He handed the phone to Riddick who also studied it. Then the vampires all but vanished before Bray's eyes.

Jack put his arm around Bray. "They'll be back before you know it — with our family."

"There are hundreds if not thousands of people in that prison. I could spot our family from a mile away. I should be going." Bray began to pace.

CHAPTER 42 SOUTH AMERICA 2021 AD

The plan was simple, a good old distraction tactic. Samuel and his men blew up the main prison gates with grenades. Hot chain-link fences with barbed wire around the top lined the perimeter. Destroying the gates broke the electrical current that ran through the fence. Samuel's crew kept the guards busy with more explosions and gunfire.

Elijah and his task force hurried over the fence, away from the main entrances and the guard towers. Once inside Elijah shot any vampire guards they came across, while Riddick finished them off with his straight sword. Once they made it to the main control station, Aaron went to work hacking into the security system. In no time the sound of cell doors sliding open rang through the air. Elijah sped to the entrance of the main cellblock.

"This way!" he yelled as humans emerged from their cells. Some ran for the exits; others were more hesitant.

"Follow him." Elijah pointed to Riddick. "He will help you escape."

"Quietly. Calmly now," he repeated to the humans passing by. He studied each one carefully — looking for a familiar face. He glanced at Bray's phone occasionally when he saw someone who looked like Bray's parents. Yet, upon a second look he would find that it was not them. *There must be thousands of people in here,* he thought. *I may never find them.*

He spotted a familiar face but he was not part of Bray's family. "Hey!" Elijah yelled. "Ramon."

Ramon looked at Elijah and tried to avoid him by moving to the other side of the hallway through the crowd.

Elijah pushed his way through the people. He stopped Ramon by grabbing his arm. "It looks like you did not make it long on your own after all."

"Go to hell!" Ramon snapped.

"I'm looking for Bray and Jack's family; do you know where they are?"

"I don't give a shit about that bitch and her family. She sold me out."

"She didn't sell anyone out."

"I never would have gotten caught if she did not lead you freaks right to me." Ramon struggled in Elijah's grip.

"I don't have time to argue. Will you help me or not?" Elijah said.

"I already told you — you can suck it!"

Elijah let his fangs grow. "That is a stupid thing to say to a vampire."

The defiance in Ramon's eyes turned to pure fear.

Elijah shoved him away. "Jack was right, you are an asshole."

Ramon scrambled to his feet and stumbled away.

Elijah desperately scanned the masses. He began to play Bray's voice message to her parents.

Elijah was losing hope when he heard a woman yell, "Brayanna? Brayanna!"

"Wait," a man called after her.

"It's Brayanna! I hear her," the woman yelled. She made her way toward the voice of her daughter and Elijah. The man struggled to keep up.

Elijah recognized the woman from the picture. He played the message again.

Tears streamed down her face. "Our daughter's alive. She's safe." The woman hugged Bray's father.

"Stay with me. I'll take you to Bray." *If we can fight our way out of here,* Elijah thought. He waited until all the humans were out of the cellblock and Bray's parents found the rest of their imprisoned family, which included Jack's mother.

"And Jack's father?" Elijah asked.

"He was killed when they captured us," Bray's father answered.

"I'm sorry to hear that. We have to get out of here," Elijah tried to console them and move them along at the same time.

On the way out it became apparent that most of the prison guards had been killed. Many humans headed for the city.

"We're going to want to get away from here," Samuel warned, once everyone was out safely and Elijah and his men were reunited. Samuel held a small silver cylinder with a bright red button on top.

Elijah guessed that it was a detonator for a powerful bomb or perhaps many bombs.

Samuel smiled like a kid on Christmas morning. "I'm going to make sure no one can ever be imprisoned here again."

"You work fast," Elijah turned to the crowd and yelled, "Move out now!" He scooped Bray's father onto his back and took her mother in his arms. "Hold on," he took flight. His men did the same, they swooped Bray and Jack's other family members up into the air.

Bray's mom screamed.

Elijah wished he could cover his ears. "Please."

"Sorry," Bray's mom whimpered. She buried her head in his hard chest.

A loud explosion caused the woman to scream again. Elijah looked back to see different sections of the prison collapsing in a cloud of smoke and debris.

CHAPTER 43 SOUTH AMERICA 2021 AD

"Mom!" Bray ran to the woman sliding out of Elijah's arms. Her mother's legs were too shaky to hold her so the two women collapsed in each other's arms as they fell to their knees.

"You're alive," Bray whispered.

Elijah smiled. "Great work today, men."

"And women!" Mary snapped.

"And women." Elijah put his arms over Mary and Elizabeth's shoulders. "This was a successful mission and the first of many. Today was a great setback for Elda. Next we will free humans from other regions so she will not suspect that we are stationed in Brazil. We'll head out as soon as we have gathered enough intelligence and have a good plan. Well done!"

"Hear, hear!" Riddick cheered.

"Hear, hear! Teller echoed. All the men — and women — cheered. Save Jack and Bray who were mourning the loss of Jack's father.

THAT NIGHT FOLKS gathered in the meeting room. They were still excited about the day's mission. Or perhaps they just needed the company.

"Since vampires are real, does that mean Count Dracula was real?" Jack asked.

Teller glared at Elijah.

"I didn't say a word — yet," Elijah taunted.

"Don't go there." Teller put his head down and shook it.

"Oh yes. We'll always go there as long as I'm alive. I hope to always be here to remind you of that time in your life," Elijah said.

"Well then perhaps I should put you out of my misery," Teller said.

"What is it between you two?" Marcel asked.

"A woman, of course; it's always a woman," Riddick said.

"We tolerate each other," Elijah said. "We keep finding ourselves in situations where we need each other. Teller proved to be useful back in the war of 1551 and he has proven to be rather useful once again."

"Wait. So you're Count Dracula?" Jack said.

"It's ancient history, kid. I made many mistakes when I was young and foolish," Teller said.

"Young? You were two hundred years old!" Elijah argued.

"Yes, as I said, young. Don't tell me, *Mr. Perfect*, that you didn't make mistakes when you were in your two hundreds," Teller snapped.

"You call the atrocities you committed *mistakes?*" Riddick said.

"Don't believe everything you read or hear and remember that those were dark times." Teller tried to defend himself.

"They were indeed. It was because of cruel rulers like you that things such as the Geneva Convention, war crimes and human rights were created," Elijah said.

"Yes, what *is* the world coming to?" Abdullah said with a sarcastic smile.

"Indeed." Elijah gritted his teeth.

"Wow. You're the real Count Dracula." Jack's mouth had been hanging open the entire time as he tried to make sense of their conversation.

"No. Not anymore and I was never a count. That most likely came from Bram Stoker's version of my story. There have been many stories before and after Stoker. None of which are true. I went by Prince Vlad. I may have been a vassal but never a count."

"What's a vassal? Is that like a ship or something? Jack asked.

"No. Don't people study history anymore? A vassal is a political puppet or a pawn; in this case for the sultan and I was not willing to be such, so I fought the Ottoman's and I won."

"Who are the Oatmans?" Marcel asked with his heavy accent.

"Ott-o-mans," Teller over-pronounced. He slapped the palm of his hand on his forehead. "Kids these days. They don't know anything, especially about history."

"So then tell us. What was it like to be a ruler back then?" Marcel was eager for the opportunity to learn about history firsthand.

"Well, it was a lot of work. I did have twenty concubines, though."

Jack's jaw dropped even farther.

Elijah chuckled. He hoped this was a good distraction for Jack. He needed it after learning of his father's death.

"That's nothing, the sultan had seven hundred concubines. Trust me, it's not all that great. They are expensive and ... difficult," Teller said.

"Please, tell us more?" Marcel asked.

"As I said, those were dark times. In order to maintain control, most rulers were cruel. I was no exception. I learned much from the Ottomans."

"Yes, what was your mantra? 'Let them hate me as long as they fear me.'" Elijah said.

"And let's not forget your moniker, The Impaler," Riddick said.

The humans all looked to Teller for a response.

"You're all enjoying this aren't you," Teller said.

"Greatly," Elijah said.

"Thankfully those days are over. Politics have not changed over the years. Human rights you say? I don't think so," Teller said.

"How so?" Marcel asked.

"The main problems of my kingdom were militant Muslims and collecting taxes from the wealthy, while not over-taxing the commoner. Sound familiar? It was a delicate balance between maintaining a strong enough army and not taxing the people to death. We fought over resources and religion the same as today. I even had to fight a bloodthirsty mafia. Though we didn't call it that back then. They were called the Boyars. Now look at what vampires have done to the world. It's a battle zone out there. Nothing ever truly changes."

Marcel's shoulders slumped under this grim outlook. And no one seemed willing or able to argue that things were better.

CHAPTER 44 SOUTH AMERICA 2021 AD

From the other side of the room Mari sighed.

"What are they talking about?" Bray asked.

"They're talking politics ... again." Mari paused when she saw the look on Bray's face. "Oh dear. I know that look all too well."

"What?" Bray pulled her starry-eyed gaze away from Elijah and focused on Mari.

"You fancy Elijah."

"No one says that anymore and no I don't. Well I mean ... he saved my family. I'm grateful, that's all," Bray said.

"And I'm a monkey's uncle."

Bray shook her head in confusion.

Mari sighed again. "Never mind. Let me save you the heartache. He's spoken for," Mari said.

"It's not like he could be married or anything. He can't be more than twenty."

"I assure you, he is very old and his heart belongs to another."

"Who is she? I've never seen him with anyone."

Sadness flashed in Mari's eyes. "She is not here but she will return, soon ... I hope. I pray that she will come and rescue us from this place. She is our Queen — our rightful Queen."

"So if she is the Queen, that makes Elijah the King?"

Mari nodded. "The King of the Vampires or he once was. That should not surprise you. He's clearly the leader here."

"I thought your King would be old or something, I don't know."

"Elijah is the oldest amongst us, now that John is gone or missing — wherever he may be."

But Bray was barely listening. The fact that Elijah was a king was not nearly as hard for her to accept as the fact that he had a wife. *But he can't be married.* Bray thought. She was grasping for something — anything to keep her heart from falling to pieces. A tear formed in her eye. She quickly wiped it away, hoping Mari wouldn't notice.

Mari did not notice because a tear rolled down her own cheek.

"What's the matter?" Bray asked.

"Elijah's wife is my dearest friend. I miss her so much."

Bray's frown deepened. She put her arm around Mari's shoulder and Bray was surprised that Mari let her.

"Where is she?"

"No one knows."

Bray waited for an opportunity to speak with Elijah. As soon as Riddick moved from Elijah's side Bray took his place. "So you're married?" Bray tried to sound casual — just making conversation.

"Aye."

"Is it your wife who came between you and Count Dracula," Jack asked.

Elijah chuckled. "It actually sounds funny when you put it that way."

"What happened?" Bray said.

Elijah frowned as the memories returned. What Teller almost did to Vallachia when they found him after almost two hundred years of searching. The pleasure Elijah felt when his hands crushed Teller's windpipe. *The truth is Vallachia has always been between Teller and me — since 1260.* "I'm not going to talk about it, so you can give up now."

Bray noticed that Elijah's hands had tightened into fists.

"Wait, let me guess, you have been married for like … what … a hundred years or something crazy like that?" Bray tried to lighten his mood.

"We were married in 1462," Elijah replied.

Her face fell. "No way. You two must be ancient. And you put up with each other for all those years?"

"We are ancient. We were together for two hundred years before that as dear friends. And there was no 'putting up with her', as you so elegantly stated."

"Well, excuse me for not being able to talk like I'm from the 1800's."

"I was born in the early sixth century — A.D. that is. Of course, we spoke different languages entirely back then."

"You're lying."

"Precise dates have long since been forgotten. They are of little concern. It is easy to lose track after that many centuries."

Bray shook her head in disbelief and fell silent as she tried to wrap her head around this. "I'm not stupid. You actually expect me to believe that you are ... however old that is?"

"It doesn't matter what you believe."

"You must really love her," Bray said. "What's it like to be with one person for that long?"

"It's as if we are one," Elijah said. "We know each other's thoughts. We often do not have to speak, we simply know. We move as one. You see, vampires mate for life and it is not a prison sentence. We truly cherish each other. There is no growing tired of one another. There is only ... caring." He paused and shook his head, as he tried to push away the pain that was overtaking him. "I suppose that is the way it is with all my oldest comrades. Take Riddick for example, he is an extension of me as well. He knows what should be done as soon as I do. We work in perfect unison. Words are not always needed. Often a nod or a look is all that is required."

"Wow." But Bray was not interested in Riddick. "So why did she leave, if you two were so close and ... you know, you're meant to be together and all?"

"Whatever her reasons, she has good cause." Elijah spoke through a clenched jaw. He stood to leave.

Bray's heart sank even farther as she watched him go.

~

THE COURT LED many more missions to release humans from Elda's prisons. Elijah was not sure if the people they set free around the world survived. Perhaps they would eventually be recaptured but at least the Court was doing something to help. The more problems they caused for their enemy the better.

There were other changes that needed to be made in this new world. Elijah declared that it was against the Court's laws to turn humans into vampires. Human blood was scarce and far too precious. Anyone who remained loyal to the Court was to abide by this new law — no new vampires.

Samuel and Aaron were able to hijack a satellite.

"Will this give us the ability to communicate remotely?" Elijah asked.

Aaron nodded. "We can coordinate missions with Hector and his branch of the Court in Australia, as well as Shantanu and Jinlan."

"It's like the U.S. Government — they had their very own secure communications network. They had internet, email, phone access and the like all on their own system." Samuel smiled with pride.

"So no one will be able to access this but us?" Teller asked.

"Correct. Only people with the security codes will be able to use this network," Samuel said.

"What if Elda finds out about the system? Will she be able to break into it?" Elijah asked.

"Not easily. For now the network is so new that she could not possibly know we have it," Aaron offered.

"That makes sense. You can't hack into something you don't know exists," Teller said.

"I'll keep the system operable and maintain its security," Aaron said.

"At least Samuel and Aaron's nerdiness is paying off," Teller teased.

"You should be grateful we're nerds," Samuel and Aaron said in unison.

"Well, I am now," Teller said.

"And you two nerds have clearly spent way too much time together," Elijah added.

"We have all spent far too much time together and now we're cooped up in this tunnel every night. This can't be good," Riddick said.

"It will be a miracle if we don't kill one another." Abdullah chuckled.

Elijah wondered how they had become utterly dependent on modern technology. Most of his life he hadn't known what electricity was. But since the apocalypse, it was all he thought about. Without the cooling units for their blood supply the blood would spoil and all would be lost — the Court, the resistance, everything. Elijah shook his head. "You do realize that we spent the vast majority of our lives without any technology? We could get by without modern communication once again, if we had to."

"Luckily we don't have to," Samuel said.

CHAPTER 45 NORTHERN CANADA 2021 AD

Vallachia watched from afar as the world and her kingdom fell apart. It pained her to know that all was lost but she was not about to leave her babies or expose them to this chaotic world. Protecting them was what mattered most. When her baby girls slept, she worked hard to learn her mother's ways — the ways of the Great Goddess. Valentina was convinced that this was the best way to help her people and to keep her daughters safe.

Vera and Veva were growing slowly, which was still too fast for Val; yet they were healthy and as steady as the sun. Val had wanted to be a mother her entire life so she cherished every moment of her time in the volcano.

Thankfully there were two girls to fuss over, as the babies had four women fighting over them. Valentina, Angela and Sasha would argue about who got to hold them or feed them. However, the diaper changing was often left to Val.

The girls appeared to be more human than vampire. As they grew they ate human food — a lot of it. They slept through the night. They did not appear to have fangs or wings — in fact, they had no teeth when they were born. Val thought of Vera and Veva as normal human babies.

Being a mother was natural and easy. However, Val was lost when it came to her mother's teachings. It was incredibly difficult to learn to calm her overactive mind. She was used to analyzing the world with an intelligent and critical eye. She needed to plan ahead at all times, especially in this isolated volcano where supplies were constantly on the verge of running out. *I need to launder the diapers and it is my day to pick the garden ...* She was used to thinking like this. Now she was told she had to learn to think in an entirely new way. Calming her busy mind seemed impossible — there was simply too much work to be done to sit around and meditate.

Valentina was a patient teacher. "In order to make a mind out of the overactive monkey in that head of yours, you must learn to focus on only the present. The only thing that matters right now is your breath. Let go of the past and do not concern yourself with the future."

Inhale... exhale... It does feel nice to simply breathe. The soft song of a bird rang out in the distance. *Birds!* "Did the chickens get fed this morning?"

"That's not what's important at this time. The chickens are fine. You must focus. Tame that mischievous monkey inside. Focus only on your breath ... in and out."

Val moaned. *It was Sasha's turn to feed the chickens this morning. Did she remember that it was her turn?*

"Gently push all other thoughts away. Inhale ... exhale ..."

"How can you sit here and do nothing when there is so much work to be done?"

"Prayer is far from 'doing nothing'. The work will get done. There is time for both. We work hard and we pray hard — that's our philosophy. It's the key to a balanced life."

"This is not my idea of prayer. This is a waste of time." Val was anxious to check on the chickens.

"When you calm your mind, it opens. You will witness the power of prayer once you are able to control that little monkey jumping around in there." Valentina poked at Val's forehead.

"Then I will be able to help set the protection spell over this place?"

"Indeed and much more. We'll need your help to cast a protective layer over the tunnels as well."

"To protect Elijah and the others — we can do that from here?"

"Yes. The more spiritual energy we have the more powerful we'll be. That's why we need you. With your help we should be able to protect your friends as well."

Now this was motivation! Val was excited about the prospect of being able to help the ones she loved. *Clear my mind. Breathe. ...*

As THE YEARS PASSED, Val improved. To her surprise she found a whole new world once she was able to, "make a mind out of a monkey," as her mother would say. She began to feel and know things in a different way. For example, she could "see" the thin transparent layer of protection that domed the inactive volcano around them, as well as the one they placed over Elijah and the others. She could not see it with her eyes but she could *feel* that it was there. She also knew that it worked to keep Elda from finding them. Val did not know this because her brain told her it was logical. She understood this to be true in her heart. She could feel that it worked.

Val often had dreams that came true. She had a dream that Angela fell and cut her leg. Val had all but forgotten the dream until Angela slipped the next day and sliced her lower leg on an axe.

"I saw that same deep gash in the same exact spot on Angela's leg in a dream last night," Val said.

"Why didn't you tell us? Sometimes we can prevent such accidents," Valentina said.

"I didn't remember the dream until now. I didn't think it was real or ... would become real."

"You're opening your mind more all the time. Your sight will become more powerful as you grow. It's time for you to start writing down your dreams and studying them. With practice you can learn which ones feel real and may come true and which ones are only dreams," Valentina lectured.

Val tried not to breathe in the sweet scent of fresh blood as she cleaned and bandaged Angela's cut. "I'm sorry — if I could have prevented this and I didn't..."

"Don't be sorry, dear. It's my fault. I'm the klutz," Angela said.

"We can help to heal it faster," Val offered.

"No, no. It's a simple cut. It will heal fine on its own. There's no need to fuss over me."

CHAPTER 46 SOUTH AMERICA 2034 AD

Teller was having trouble sleeping. Whenever he dozed off he was awakened by a familiar voice calling his name. Upon awakening, he would be alone. After the third night of fighting this he gave up on sleep and walked the tunnels. He saw candlelight coming from one of the humans' quarters. It was Tomamacowee's room.

Her curtain was pulled back so Teller appeared in her doorway. "Can't sleep either?" He did not have to worry about whether or not she was decent. She was always naked. She rarely even wore the decorative belt that some of the natives preferred.

With all the endless time here Marcel had been teaching any who wanted to learn how to speak the local Tupian dialect. Teller had become quite fluent after all these years.

"I know when someone is troubled," the village grandmother replied.

Teller was still not used to naked old ladies. He wished she would cover herself. "May I join you...Tomamac...?" he asked.

"Please call me Tomoc. Of course you may join me, that's why I'm awake. I'm here to help you."

"What makes you think you can help? I don't even know if anything is wrong."

"Tell me, what's troubling you."

"Surely it's nothing. I have had a couple of restless nights — that's all."

"Is it that you can't fall asleep or does something wake you?"

Teller narrowed his eyes. "Actually, I hear someone call my name. But when I wake no one is there."

"Ah, someone is trying to contact you from the other side."

"The other side?"

"Yes. When one of our ancestors has an important message they call our names in the night to wake us. You see, we are most susceptible to the other side when we are in our dream states. It's the best chance they have to reach this world. They usually do this when they need to warn us of danger or when we are in need of being reminded of our sacred path."

This sounded like gibberish to Teller. "I'm sure it's nothing. After all, I don't have any ancestors who would bother to warn me or remind me of religious beliefs." *This is utter nonsense.* He stood to leave but the crone placed her thumbs on Teller's temples and cupped her crooked fingers under his chin thus securing his face in her hands. He closed his eyes — largely to avoid the sight of wrinkled sagging breasts.

Teller found himself surrounded by hazy figures. His eyes could not fully focus on any of them. They stood in a sea of white. The floor blended in with the walls and the walls blended with the roof — if there was a roof. The figures appeared to speed by him. Teller wasn't sure if he was moving past them or if it was the other way around. From the brief glimpses he managed to sneak, the people appeared to have dark brown skin — naked in their youthful prime. Out of the crowd came a familiar face. It was the only one who came into focus. "Sergiu!"

Sergiu opened his arms wide with a welcoming smile. Sergiu tried to speak but Teller went speeding away from him — back through the crowd. Teller found himself face first on the dirt floor of Tomoc's chambers. "Sergiu!" He jumped to his feet. "Where did he go? He was trying to tell me something. It looked important."

"It most usually is. The other side does not often go through the trouble of trying to contact us unless it's dire." She issued a toothless grin in an I-told-you-so manner. "So an ancestor was indeed trying to contact you?"

"He's not an ancestor. He …" Teller choked. Seeing Sergiu's face was wonderful. Yet, it opened up old wounds that had never fully healed. Now the scars had been ripped off and past wounds were bleeding all over again — not dripping blood but gushing blood. Teller managed to say, "He was a dear friend."

"Ancestors do not have to be in your direct blood line. They only have to be one of your people. This *Sergiu,* he was one of your people?"

"I … I don't know. I don't have any *people*. I don't belong to any tribe."

Tomoc laid herself down. "You poor thing. You don't know who your people are?" There was true sorrow in the crones cloudy eyes.

"No! You can't sleep. You must send me back. I have to see him. He needs to tell me something."

"I can only show you the path. In order to speak with someone who's on the other side, you will have to go there yourself."

"Please! Show me how."

Tomoc chuckled. "That can't happen tonight. That's impossible. It takes many moon cycles to learn how to go to the other side and return safely. I have spent much energy. For now I must rest."

Teller sighed. "Tomorrow then." Teller covered the old woman with a blanket. This was not only out of kindness but also to cover her indecency. *If only she would put some clothes on.*

Before this encounter with the village grandmother, Teller had only been tired. Now he was utterly troubled. His eyes filled with moisture as pain and longing overwhelmed him. "I will find you Sergiu. I promise." He paced the tunnels until dawn. The thought of getting to see Sergiu, of getting to speak with him, soon eased the pain and filled Teller with anticipation.

When Teller heard Tomoc stir from her slumber, he sped to her door. He tried to help her up.

She shooed him away and got up on her own. "Not now, eager one. I have ... human needs that I must take care of." She scratched her bare butt as she shuffled toward the latrines outside — which consisted of a large stick-built outhouse with a green thatch roof. This was barely enough to sustain the growing number of humans. They were regularly having to build new ones and fill in the old holes.

As the Court continued to rescue humans from prisons, more free humans heard about the encampment in the jungle and found their way to Elijah's refuge. The tunnels were now cramped, which made life uncomfortable at times but this was good for their blood supply.

Teller could not help but chuckle at the old lady. However, his amusement was soon replaced by impatience as he went back to pacing.

It seemed as if hours had passed but in reality it was no more than twenty minutes.

"Fetch me some of that lovely brew you make," Tomoc said.

In a flash Teller was off to make tea — his specialty.

TELLER TAPPED his foot as the crone sipped her tea. She appeared to be enjoying Teller's anxious frustration. Finally, Teller could not contain himself any longer. "You have to send me back to ... wherever it was. I have to find out what he wants. I have to see him again."

"Yes, it is a wonderful gift but it must be earned."

"Do whatever you did last night and I will be able to speak with him."

"I already told you. It doesn't work that way. It took all my energy to bring you back from the other side last night. Going is easier, leaving is difficult. If I had not spent much energy you would not be here now. We have lost many to the allure of the other side."

Teller shook his head. "Then let me stay with him."

"Your work here is not done. Besides, then you could not bring back his important message."

Sergiu was gone, Val was out of his life — again. He felt as if he had nothing. He wanted to be with Sergiu.

Tomoc looked at him pointedly, as if she could read his thoughts. *What about Abdullah and the twins?* Teller still had many men who cared about him — who followed him. *What about them?* Teller was not entirely sure if he had thought this or if the crone had whispered it.

"Others rely on you," she said.

Teller nodded. "Please teach me what I need to do to find him *and* return."

"You are smart and wise, so perhaps it can be done. Be warned — it takes most a generation or more to learn what I have learned."

"I can do it. I will make it back to Sergiu."

She smiled. "That's the spirit you'll need. Now you should call me, 'Teacher.'"

Teller nodded. He knew that the word teacher, in her language, meant much more than it did in English. It was a title of great respect. It implied a spiritual master.

CHAPTER 47 SOUTH AMERICA 2034 AD

After a month Teller was beyond frustrated. He knew nothing of meditation. He could not concentrate hard enough. "Focus on how Sergiu makes you feel," Tomoc would say.

Teller could think of many words, *regret, longing, lonely* ...

"Not the words — the feelings themselves," she said as if she were speaking to a child.

"That doesn't make sense. Words and feelings are the same thing."

"No. Words are words and feelings are feelings."

Teller gave a hopeless moan. "Is there a CliffsNotes version or something? Maybe I'm not cut out for this? None of this makes sense. You don't make sense."

She frowned at him. "You're capable of great things. I can see it." She took a deep breath. "Think of how it felt to see him the last time."

This was not a memory that Teller wanted to relive in detail but if his teacher said it was necessary, he had to try.

She slapped Teller upside the head. "Not the bloody, headless time. When you saw him on the other side."

"Oh." Teller said and closed his eyes again. Tomoc could enter his mind. She could read his thoughts and speak to him. It didn't feel intrusive. She was in Teller's head only to guide him. She did not judge him for his past.

Teller's heart beat faster as the fuzzy figures started speeding by him. *I'm doing it!*

"That's better," Tomoc whispered.

Teller scarcely made out Sergiu's face when he was suddenly ripped back to this world. "What are you doing? I found him!"

"That's the first step. Now the hard part," Tomoc said.

"We haven't even gotten to the hard part yet?" Teller put his face in his hands and moaned.

"You found the object you desire. Now you have to find a way to leave your desire."

"How in the hell do I do that?"

"You will need to be able to focus on your reasons to come back. This sounds easy but with the temptation of the other side it will not be so."

"That's simple enough. I only have a few reasons to come back. There's Abdullah and the twins."

"Again, the first step."

"And Vallachia."

"And…"

"My other men."

"Those are the obvious ones."

Teller took a deep breath. "And Elijah."

"Closer."

Only one image was in Teller's mind — Riddick. "No. You mean to tell me that in order to pull myself away from my oldest and dearest friend I have to think of my nemesis ... This is the only way I will be able to return?"

Tomoc crossed her arms in front of her bare chest and smiled.

Teller was no longer bothered by her nudeness. "Shit."

This caused her smile to widen.

"That's why I could not let you rush into this. You still have much work to do."

Teller got to his feet and stormed out. *I hate Riddick and he hates me. That's simply the way it is. There's nothing I can do about that.*

Teller spent another sleepless night. The next morning he glared at Riddick across the morning campfire, where a feast of eggs and potatoes were being cooked for the humans.

Riddick is standing in my way. It was Riddick's fault Teller could not see Sergiu. He knew what his teacher would say, "Is it his fault or yours?"

Teller was restless throughout the day, like a boy who had a huge school project due yet had no idea where to begin. He had to confront Riddick, to make amends, he supposed. *What do I do? I can't simply walk up to him and say, "Hey, will you be my friend?"*

By the time the evening chores of closing up camp were done, Teller had still not found his courage. Now it was too late as they were trapped underground until sun-up. It would be difficult to get Riddick alone in the crowded tunnels. Once again, Teller could not sleep.

As people headed out for the day, Teller followed after Riddick. Teller was determined to get this over with. He had postponed the inevitable long enough. Every day wasted was another day he didn't get to see Sergiu. Even if he didn't succeed he had to give it his best. "May I have a word with you?"

"What is it?" Riddick asked.

"I mean, alone." Teller looked around at all the people and vampires moving about.

Riddick narrowed his eyes. "I have to head out on patrol."

"I know. It won't take long."

Teller led Riddick away from the camp.

Riddick crossed his arms. "What's this about?"

Teller frequently made that same gesture. He slowly crossed his arms in front of his chest and it was almost as if he were looking in a mirror but it was Riddick he stared at, not himself. Teller suddenly laughed as he was beginning to see something he had never noticed — or accepted — before.

"What's the matter with you?" Riddick asked.

"Don't you see it? Everyone is forever telling us how much we resemble each other and I don't think they mean only our appearance but our personalities as well."

"That's ridiculous. I am nothing like you," Riddick spat.

"I always told myself that as well. But in actuality it's not that we're too different from each other to get along. It's that we're too alike to get along."

"You're speaking nonsense. You're spending entirely too much time with that nutty old lady. She has clearly gotten into your head. I recommend staying away from her before she permanently screws up your mind. Now, if you will excuse me, I have to get to work."

"I too prefer to work rather than face uncomfortable thoughts."

Riddick narrowed his eyes and turned to leave.

"Riddick, wait. One last thing."

Riddick paused, although Teller could see that he was tense, as if fighting the urge to run or punch Teller in the nose.

"Where did we go wrong?" Teller asked.

Riddick looked confused.

"I mean, for centuries, since the first time we meet, we have loathed each other. Do you remember why?"

Riddick looked at the ground. He slowly scratched his head. He was searching through centuries of memories for an answer. "I have no idea. Why does this matter to you all of a sudden? We have never gotten along and we never will. That's the way it is. It's not important."

"It must be important. It's a riddle I must solve."

"Well, good luck with that." Before Riddick was out of earshot he yelled. "Tell your new girlfriend I said, 'Hi'."

"Screw you!" Teller yelled back. Teller plopped down on the damp forest floor. Very little sunlight found its way through the thick trees. Teller closed his eyes. The songs of numerous birds were overwhelmingly loud, especially for a vampire. There were too many different types of songs to count.

Teller was on the verge of an insight; he could feel it. He knew now that his mission was not to win Riddick over — per se. *Riddick is right — we will never get along and that's okay. What is it then?*

The image of Riddick standing in front of him with his arms crossed appeared in Teller's mind only this time there was an elegant golden mirror frame in between Teller and Riddick. Teller had always thought Riddick was arrogant, selfish and power hungry.

"And..." he could almost hear his teacher pushing him farther.

"And I can be all of those things as well." How many times had Riddick called him arrogant, which was usually followed by the word ass. Sure, Teller and Riddick had both matured over the years. They were not the same vampires they had been in their youth.

The reason I hate him is because he reminds me of the parts of myself that I don't like. The parts I want to keep hidden. The parts I wish I didn't have. That is it! When Teller looked at Riddick, he was seeing all the things he hated about himself. Riddick was an irritating reminder of who Teller once was and who he could still be at times.

"There — I did it. I admit that I don't like myself." Yet he knew his work was not done. "So I can be an arrogant controlling jerk, now what?" Letting this in made Teller feel empty. *I despise Riddick because I despise myself. It's dreadful to realize that you don't like yourself — the one person you can't get away from.* Utter dismay was consuming Teller.

"Look again," he heard Tomoc's voice, even though she was not there.

"I don't want to look at myself. I'm a wretched person," Teller said out loud, even though he was alone.

"Are you sure?" Tomoc pointed to the "Riddick" in the "mirror". "Tell me what you see now."

Teller slowly raised his head and peered into the mirror in his mind. This time Riddick looked different — somehow. "There's good in him as well. Riddick is strong and brave. He's loyal to his friends and his cause. He has learned to care deeply for others."

"And..."

"I'm all of those things too." Teller could feel the overwhelming dismay start to recede.

"What next?" Tomoc tested him.

"I don't know."

"Think — feel?"

"I have to accept all parts of myself. I have to learn to love them all; the good as well as the terrible."

Teller could almost see Tomoc smile with pride.

"Come to me when you have done this." Her voice rang in his head.

CHAPTER 48 SOUTH AMERICA 2034 AD

When Teller opened his eyes it was almost dark. He slowly made his way back to the tunnels. He watched Riddick in the common area talking with Jack. For the first time, Teller did not feel irritation or hatred. Teller fully understood Riddick and himself. Teller was content with *all* the parts of himself. Riddick no longer reminded Teller of the horrible parts buried inside, the parts he wished to ignore. Teller not only acknowledged the darkness within, he had fully accepted it. The darkness would never completely disappear and that too was fine.

Riddick glanced at Teller. Teller smiled warmly. Riddick rolled his eyes and shook his head. He clearly thought Teller had gone mad and maybe Teller had.

~

TELLER APPEARED at his teacher's door. "I'm ready."

She had fully expected him and simply nodded.

He sat in front of her and crossed his legs.

"You have done much work in a short time. You are a good student. I'm proud of you."

It did not feel like a short time to Teller. It felt as if eons had passed since he first saw Sergiu on the other side. "Do I get a gold star?"

"Even better, you get to speak with your old friend. Now remember, when you feel like getting lost in the other side, it's not Riddick you must return for. You must return for yourself. You are worth it."

A knot formed in Teller's throat so he only nodded. *That may be the nicest thing anyone has ever said to me.*

"I will do what I can to help but I can only guide you. Much of this will be up to you."

Teller closed his eyes and thought of Sergiu. Through the haze of figures quickly passing by, Teller made out Sergiu's faint figure in the distance. Soon Sergiu's arms were around Teller. Teller could feel his touch! "You're really here?"

"Yes it is I. We don't have long. It's not safe for you to linger here. The more time you spend the more difficult it will be for you to leave. First of all, I want to ask that you stop torturing yourself over my death. My dying saved you and that was more than worth it. All I wanted was your happiness. That's how much I love you."

"How could you possibly be so selfless? You gladly sacrificed yourself for me?"

"Yes, because after my death you left the terrible Vlad behind forever. My death saved you from yourself. It was my purpose to stop you, though I didn't fully understand that at the time. If I had not succeeded then you would have continued down that dark path. You would not have been content until you conquered the world. But losing me changed you for the better." He gave a sheepish grin. "Although I must confess, things are wonderful for me here."

For the first time Teller noticed the tall lean hazy figure waiting patiently beside them. A woman slowly came into focus. She was stunning. Long brown hair fell down her back. She wore a flowing white gown.

Teller quickly put the pieces together. "The lovely Empress Theodora." He bowed his head. "The historians were correct. The mosaics and paintings of you do not do justice to your true beauty."

She put her arm in Sergiu's. "We had only met briefly when I was

Empress. I was already married then. But thankfully we've been reunited here."

Teller had never seen Sergiu this … blissful. A huge burden lifted from Teller's shoulders. *I didn't condemn Sergiu to hell. He is … happy.*

"Now before you must return. Lady Theodora has something that will help you. You must go to Petra."

"Petra?" Teller had flown over Petra on a number of occasions.

"You must go there at once," Theodora instructed. "Buried deep within one of the old Bedouin caves in the Rose City you will find an ancient scroll."

"Why do I need this scroll? What does it say?" Teller asked.

"We don't have time," Sergiu said. "The scroll contains the genesis of the vampire race. It will provide many answers and it will show you the path the chosen ones must take."

"What are you talking about? Why does everyone have to talk in riddles around here?"

"You must go — now. The scroll has the answers you seek," Sergiu said.

"No! I can't leave. There's still so much —

"We'll be together again someday but not today. I have one last piece of information that will make it easier for you to leave me. The Lady Vallachia will return soon and with her she brings the two most precious of gifts. Now go!"

The only thing that filled Teller's mind was Vallachia as he began to speed away from Sergiu and Theodora. He found himself lying on the dirt floor of the tunnel. *Val's alive and Sergiu is fine — better than fine! He's in paradise with his true love.*

"You made it back. That's good." His teacher said in little more than a whisper.

Teller helped Tomoc lay down.

Teller heard her heartbeat as it became irregular. "What's wrong?"

Tomoc gave him a weak smile.

"You spent too much energy getting me back. Now you're dying?"

She nodded and her heartbeat slowed.

"Why did you do that?"

"You received important information, no? I'm ready to be with my ancestors. It's my time. You have seen the other side so you know not to be sad for my passing."

Tomoc was right. Teller knew she would be young and beautiful once again. She would be surrounded by her family. Her arthritic hands would no longer cause her pain. "Thank you for everything. I owe you so much. I may never be able to repay you."

"Nonsense. There's no need for payment. You must go to Petra ... whatever that is." She closed her eyes.

"I will." Teller held her hand and knelt by her bed long after her heart beat for the last time. He was surprised to find that while he would miss his teacher, he was relieved for her. He knew for certain that she was free. Free of human pain and suffering. A smile came across his face as he could almost see her being embraced by loved ones who had been previously lost to her — all naked, of course. He chuckled.

CHAPTER 49 SOUTH AMERICA
2034 AD

Teller stayed for the ceremonies for his teacher. Then he made plans to head out at once. "I have to leave. I won't be long and I will need to take some of my men."

"How many?" Elijah looked worried.

"I'll only take Abdullah and the boys."

Elijah would not miss Cosmin and Costel. Sometimes they could be of use but more often than not, they were simply in the way. "How long will you be?"

"It's difficult to say. We'll return as soon as we can."

Elijah nodded and went about his business. He was not one to pry into others' affairs.

TELLER and his closest comrades found themselves in the narrow siq leading to Petra. Stone walls rose high on either side. Only a narrow sliver could be seen of the sky above. Stepping out of the passageway, they paused in awe to gaze at the sight. Rising hundreds of feet high, covering the adjacent cliff wall was the front of a massive Roman building. It was carved into the stone itself.

"Indiana Jones was here?" Costel asked.

"The *actor* who played Indiana Jones was here and his name is Harrison Ford," Abdullah corrected.

"Cool. Let's go see if we can make it through the booby traps." The twins disappeared into the main entrance to the Roman structure.

Teller shook his head and turned his attention to the Rose City in the distance. It was not truly a city. It consisted of many small hollowed out caves not far from the Roman edifice. The caves reminded Teller of swallows' nests on the side of a rock face, only much more colorful. Red and white veins ran through the sparkling sandstone making them shimmer with a vibrant rose color in the sun — hence the name, the Rose City. These caves had once been an apartment-type complex for Bedouin people.

"Do those two not know the difference between movies and reality?" Abdullah asked.

Teller shrugged. "Who knows what goes on in their heads?"

"Or what doesn't go on in their heads?"

Teller laughed. "To them, life is one big movie or video game, I suppose."

"In a way, I envy them. The world is nothing more than a big playground to them. Long before movies or video games they moved through life with ease — not a care in the world."

Teller nodded. "That would be nice, in some ways."

Abdullah frowned at all the rose colored caves. "How do we know where to start digging?"

The twins appeared. "We could not get past the first challenge," Costel admitted.

"It's sealed tight," Cosmin said.

"You do realize that Indiana Jones is not real? It was a movie. They shot some scenes in front of the great carved building and then the rest was filmed in a studio. It's fake," Abdullah explained.

"No! You mean there are no booby traps in there?" Costel was crushed.

Teller ignored the twins or at least tried to. He studied the caves in order to decide where to start.

The screech of a hawk pierced the air. He watched the graceful red hawk land on the ground and hop into one of the caves. *This is odd behavior for a predator of the sky.* The hawk seemed to be staring at Teller. He screeched again. "That's the cave. That's where we'll find the scroll." Teller pointed to the hawk.

"How can you be so sure?" Abdullah asked.

"Sergiu is showing us the way."

Abdullah narrowed his eyes. He did not know what to make of Teller's new way of looking at the world. He thought his oldest and dearest friend may be losing his mind after all these years. "Very well."

They dug quickly at first.

"Careful," Teller said. "We need to slow down. I don't want to damage the scroll with the shovels.

They dug out most of the small cave floor so they would not miss the artifact. They found bones and a couple of gold coins. They were most likely only a couple hundred years old. They had to dig deeper. They needed to go back almost two thousand years. If Theodora knew of these scrolls or even hid them here herself, then they had to dig much deeper, as she was the empress of Constantinople in the 6th century. Once they had dug a hole as deep as they were tall, Abdullah's shovel scraped against something that was not dry dirt. He quickly swept away the earth around the object in order to learn its size and shape. He forced his shovel underneath it and freed a large terra-cotta jar from its ancient resting place.

Teller seized the pot. "This must be it." He headed out into the sunlight and dropped the jar, causing it to shatter. As predicted, it contained a rolled up parchment.

The parchment was so dry that it was difficult to unroll without destroying it. They carefully managed to spread it out on the ground. Teller recognized the language of the scroll. He also knew what it was about and roughly how old it was after reading the first sentence. The language was Aramaic, the language of Jesus. It had to date to around the time that Christ walked these lands and to further confirm this, the first sentence read, *When Jesus of Nazareth traveled to Magdalena he found his love.*

Hebrew and Arabic had many common roots in Aramaic. The Aramaic alphabet had been used in this region for a very long time so it was easy for these very old Arabic-speaking vampires to make out the meaning. Teller and Abdullah read the second sentence out loud together. "Jesus and Mary of Magdalena were married in the spring of the following year."

"This is blasphemy," Abdullah said.

"Indeed. That's why it was safely hidden away. The early church destroyed any documents that contradicted their beliefs."

Teller took pictures of the document with his phone.

"Sergiu Pasha truly did lead you here to find this?" Abdullah asked.

Teller nodded. "I told you that already. Well technically it was Empress Theodora."

"So you did see our Pasha? And he's well?"

"Better than well." Teller narrowed his eyes. "You, of all people, didn't believe me?" Abdullah might as well have slid a dirk in Teller's back.

Abdullah lowered his head. "I'm terribly sorry. I never should have doubted you. You must admit, you have been acting strange these past months. I was honestly worried you had gone mad, especially when you started talking about seeing our deceased Pasha."

Teller smiled. He *had* made some drastic changes recently. It must seem very odd to his old friends who had known him to be constant for so long. "I'm sure I would have thought the same thing had it been you," Teller said. "Yet, you followed me here without question."

"We will always follow you."

CHAPTER 50 MIDDLE EAST 2034 AD

Once Teller was sure he had the entire document photographed on his phone, he tore off a small piece of the parchment that contained no text and placed it in a plastic bag. They carefully rolled the scroll and sealed it in a glass jar. Teller placed it gently back in the hole in the cave.

"You're not going to take it with us?" Abdullah asked.

"The only reason this parchment still exists today is because it has been preserved in this dry climate. The wet Amazon rainforest would destroy it in no time. It is safer here."

They reburied the scroll and took flight for home.

"I can't believe there are no traps inside Petra," Cosmin's voice was full of dismay.

"We found an ancient religious text and they are upset because an old movie 'lied' to them." Abdullah shook his head.

Teller laughed. The mission had been a success and Teller could hardly wait to read the script in its entirety.

As SOON AS they returned to the tunnels, Teller went straight to Aaron. Teller handed him the bag containing the piece of parchment. "Can you date this for me?"

Aaron rubbed a piece of the scroll between his fingers to get a feel for the texture and then tasted his finger. "It's very old, possibly thousands of years. I can run some tests and get you a more exact date."

"That would be much appreciated," Teller said.

Teller sat in his small room and began to read at once. He had been completely lost in the text and didn't notice that Abdullah was standing behind him trying to make out the small writing on the phone.

"You don't have to do that. I backed the photos up on my computer. You can read them from there."

This Abdullah did. Neither one moved a muscle until they had read every word.

Teller finished first and was speechless. He simply stared into space.

Abdullah closed the laptop. "Holy shit."

Teller nodded.

"Do you think this is true?"

Again, Teller only nodded.

"What does this mean for us — for humans? If this is true then Elda is right. Vampires were meant to rule the earth."

"Not necessarily. I don't think that's why we were created. Think about it, we had to be created by something and for some reason. Some of us are good and some are terrible, like humans. So why would we not have the same creator or perhaps creators...?" Teller had never given much thought to *why* vampires existed — they simply did.

"Perhaps it's only a myth, like Greek mythology," Abdullah said.

"That could be. Yet vampires are not myths." Teller knew in his heart that the words on the scroll told a true story. It was the origin story of the first vampires. Teller was not sure others would be ready to hear it. "Let's not tell anyone about this — for now."

"That does seem wise. No one would believe us anyway. In fact, I'm going to try to forget I read the damn thing." Abdullah left. Teller picked up his phone and began to read the scroll again. He had to figure out what it meant and why Sergiu thought it was so important at this time.

CHAPTER 51 NORTHERN CANADA 2034 AD

Even though Vera and Veva had been born twelve years earlier, they were developmentally about six years old. They were very smart; with four teachers, the girls read well. Valentina would bring them a fresh round of books from the abandoned library with every trip she made for supplies. The girls would then devour them. They loved children's books about geography and history the most. This was their only way to know the outside world. They never left the inside of the volcano.

The only electricity they had went to preserving the blood supply. They did not waste precious energy to watch movies or play video games. Books were it and Vera and Veva — who preferred to be called Eva — lived for them. Val would often speak Greek or Latin to them. The girls were well educated and knowledgeable about the world despite never having seen it.

While Eva, the smaller one, was content in her quiet and humble home, Vera was not. She wanted more than anything to experience the world. She would beg and cry and even scream at times but their grandmother would insist that it simply was not safe and that they must stay in their secluded little valley. They were like two princesses, locked away for their own good. Vera did not buy it.

"I sense that our time is running out here," Angela said after the girls were fast asleep.

"We will not be here forever. That I have always known," Sasha said.

"How could someone possibly find this place?" Val asked.

"I have no idea but we must be prepared to leave at once. Let's go through our emergency packs to see if they're missing anything. I'll head to town tomorrow if needed," Valentina said.

"We can't stay here forever, as our blood supply will eventually run out," Val said. Angela and Sasha added to it when they could but the supply was still dwindling. Once the girls stopped breastfeeding Val went back to a diet of blood. "It takes fourteen humans to comfortably sustain a vampire. It's easy math. Two humans can't feed us forever." This had been a growing concern of Val's. She was relieved to finally voice it.

Valentina's brow furrowed. "Perhaps we should leave as soon as I return from town tomorrow? We should not sit here and wait to be found. Our goal was to get the girls to their thirteenth birthday. That day is quickly approaching."

Val felt a twinge of excitement. "Where will we go?"

"To your most trusted allies, of course. We have succeeded in keeping the girls safe for this much of their lives. It was our greatest chance of keeping them alive this long. Let's hope it was enough. If it is Elda who is about to discover this place then the girls are not likely to be a secret for much longer. They will be relentlessly hunted. They'll need all of their family's protection."

"You mean their father's protection as well?" The worry for her girls came second as Val was filled with joy. *I will get to see my family again. I get to return to them ... to him! How will Elijah receive me?* She felt as if she might explode from all the emotions overwhelming her, anticipation, excitement, fear ... to name but a few.

Val could not sleep that night. She tossed and turned, paced, checked on the emergency packs at least fifty times and checked on the girls a hundred times. When the sun was rising, Val drifted into an uneasy sleep. She saw Elda's face, many times larger than life, glaring down at her. She woke with a start and ran to the girls' room. They were not there.

"Girls!" Val called as she tracked their scent. Val stopped in her tracks as she passed the seeing stone. It was uncovered — open to the world! Her heart raced as panic fully set in. *How could the crystal be uncovered? Everyone here knows the danger of leaving it uncovered and unattended. Without its cover, others could see us as well — Elda can find them!* Val sped to the crystal to cover it. *Maybe it's not too late.*

Staring back at her from the crystal was Elda's face.

"You must bring the girls to me." Elda's voice was calm, almost pleading.

Val covered the crystal to stop Elda from seeing any more and ran for her swords.

Angela and Sasha were tilling the land with hoes.

"Where are the girls?" Val demanded.

"I thought they were inside with you? Valentina should be back from town any minute."

"Get your packs and get out of here! I'll find the girls."

"What's wrong?"

"The crystal was uncovered! Elda has found us. Her men are most likely on their way as we speak." Val yelled this as she sped away, following the girls' scent.

She took flight but remained low to the ground so she would not lose the path Vera and Eva had most recently taken. She flew up the steep side of the volcano wall. As she spotted her daughters, a loud sound rang out. It was as if she were under a giant cymbal at a rock concert. Val covered her ears and looked up to find vampires flinging themselves into the layer of protection above. One of them placed their hand on the protective layer and chanted. Val could feel their spell weaken. *They're coming through!*

Her wings could not carry her to her children fast enough. A vampire grabbed both girls, each by the back of her shirt, and lifted them into the air. Val did not slow as she moved forward at full force. She cut the vampire's head off and turned to catch her babies. Their screams stopped as they landed in Val's arms. Val flew out of the volcano toward the south.

"Is that you, Mama?" Vera asked.

"Yes Baby, it's me." Val tried to reassure her with a smile but her long fangs and bright yellow eyes did not help to comfort the terrified girls. The girls had seen their mother and grandmother in this form before and it was always scary but under these circumstances it was doubly so.

The vampires chased after Val. They were only interested in the children. Val could not fight them off with her girls in her arms and they would eventually catch her, as they were not carrying a load. Val barely touched the ground as she set the girls down.

"Run! That way." Val pointed south.

This they did without question.

Val had a moment to survey the attackers. Eight remained. She wished she had grabbed her gun. She could at least slow some of them down with it. Her trusty swords would have to do. She swung them around, readying them. In a blur, she moved toward the closest of them. She did not want them to get any closer to her daughters.

They exchanged a couple quick blows but Val was more skilled, not to mention she was a mother protecting her young. Her assailant's head fell to the ground. She only had enough time to tackle the nearest vampire. They fell to the ground. When they landed Val's sword was in her opponent's chest. With her second sword she finished the job. The other vampires were forming a circle around the girls who had not made it far.

Valentina sped overhead, "To the girls!"

Val had never moved faster. In a flash, Valentina and Val stood with their backs to each other and the girls in between them. Valentina readied her shield.

Six vampires surrounded them. "Hand over the girls. They will not be harmed. Elda needs them alive."

Valentina fired several rounds hitting two of the vampires. Gunfire whizzed back at them. Valentina kept several bullets from finding their mark with her shield. However, Val was unprotected. She dodged one bullet but a second one hit her shoulder. She charged forward, taking off the head of the gunman. She spun around to face two other vampires. She charged after them. Her injured shoulder would not let her fight well. She was barely able to block blows with that arm, and in no way able to attack at full force.

Valentina decapitated the vampires she shot and was fighting the last of their enemies one on one.

Val kicked the legs out from under one of her attackers as the other ran for the girls. With her good arm she threw her sword into the girls' attacker. With the last of the strength in her bad arm, she cut the head off the one she had just knocked to the ground. Val sped to the vampire closest to the girls and snapped her neck.

Valentina decapitated the last of the assailants. The girls screamed as the head landed at their feet.

They ran to their mother who flinched in pain as she tried to hug them.

"I have to get that bullet out before you heal around it." Valentina looked around. "I have no tools to extract it." She unceremoniously stuck her fingers into the wound.

Val moaned. For a moment she thought she might pass out.

"It's too slippery. I can't get a tight enough grip. The bullet is lodged in bone." Without warning, Valentina bit into Val's shoulder.

Val screamed.

"Mama!" Eva yelled.

Valentina ripped the bullet out with her back teeth and spit it out. Val fell to the ground. Valentina caught her and straightened her out so she would be more comfortable, while she rested and healed. The two girls stared with open mouths at their blood-splattered grandmother who had dark red blood dripping from her chin — their mother's blood!

"Don't be afraid, my darlings. You're safe and your mother will heal quickly." Valentina made an attempt to wipe the blood away, which only smeared it. The girls were too frightened to move.

Sasha and Angela had followed the sound of gunfire and made their way to the battle. The girls ran to them. At least they were not covered in blood, only sweat from their long hike up and over the volcano wall. Sasha and Angela took the girls into their arms as they surveyed the gruesome scene — eight headless bodies and Valentina covered in blood.

"Val!" Sasha ran forward. "Will she be okay?"

Valentina smiled with relief at seeing them. "Yes. She was shot. The bullet was in her bone and apparently touching a bundle of nerves, as she passed out from the pain when I removed it." Valentina gave a shiver at the thought of her daughter's agony. "But she will be fine. Let's get out of here. We'll clean up by the stream and you two can help Val to heal while I return to the cabin one last time for anything we may need. We'll need to leave as soon as Val is able." Valentina gently lifted Val into her arms and carried her to a nearby stream to wash her.

CHAPTER 52 NORTHERN CANADA 2034 AD

When Val woke, she jumped to her feet in a flash.

"The girls are fine. We're all fine," Valentina said in a calm voice.

The girls raced to hug their mother. Val felt the soreness in her shoulder and arm when she wrapped it around Eva.

"But we must leave at once. Can you fly?" Valentina said with urgency.

In no time, they headed south. Val carried Sasha on her back and Eva in her arms, while Valentina took Angela and Vera. The humans carried the packs. Valentina sprinkled dust behind them to cover their scent.

More of Elda's followers would be headed this way. Val knew they had only killed the ones who had been close by. Others were on their way from farther off.

They flew late into the night.

"I don't think I can hang on any longer. I need to rest," Angela said.

Val did not want to stop. She wanted to get as far away from Elda's men as possible. She was also more than anxious to see her other family — her ancient family. She could hardly contain the jittery feeling in her stomach.

They unrolled four sleeping bags. Angela was barely in hers before she was snoring. The girls had slept some as they flew. They all — save Angela — worked to set a protective shield around them and the Court's tunnels in the Amazon.

"Poor Angela. Her age is finally catching up with her. This trip will be rough on her," Valentina mused.

"Mama," Vera's voice was barely audible. "I'm so sorry." She began to sob.

Val took Vera in her arms. "What are you sorry for?" Val asked, although she had a good idea what the answer would be.

"I just wanted to see the world. I wanted to see what was outside the volcano."

"What did you do?"

"When we woke and you were asleep and Grandma was gone, I knew that was our chance to see what was over the volcano wall and ... I took the cloth off the crystal. I wanted to be found so we would no longer have to hide. I thought it would set us free." Vera buried her head in her mother's chest.

"And you ran off without telling anyone?"

Vera nodded. "We can't sneak past you and Grandma. You always hear us but we did get by Sasha and Angela."

"It was easy," Eva added.

Val gritted her teeth. "You put us in real danger, Vera." She was surprised at how upset she was over her daughter's betrayal. "You did not trust us. You thought we were keeping you in the volcano to be cruel, when we were only trying to protect you."

Vera started sobbing again. "I know, Mama. I'll never doubt you again."

Val felt her heart soften as her anger waned. Her daughter was truly sorry and she had learned a valuable lesson — she knew who to trust. Val hugged Vera tight. "Well, you are in the real world now. Our secret is out."

"No!" Eva said. "I want to go home. I want things to be the way they were."

"That home is gone forever. We can never go back. It will never be safe again."

This caused tears to fall from both girls.

"And don't think you have gotten out of trouble, Eva."

"I didn't do anything! It was all Vera's idea."

"Yet you went along with your sister. You did not try to stop her."

"That's not fair. It's all her fault," Eva snapped.

Val glared at Eva. Eva put her head down. "I'm sorry, Mama. I should have told Angela and Sasha."

"I'm sorry that you two are not normal children — that you are not free to see the world. You're very special and we're going to have to work extra hard to protect you now," Val said.

Sasha lit up. "Perhaps our sight was unclear because we were not looking for a betrayal from within."

"We sensed that change was coming but could not see when or who was behind it. We were not looking for one of the girls to reveal us to Elda," Val added.

"That does make sense. However, the word *betrayal* is a bit harsh. After all, they're only six year old girls who wanted to see the world," Sasha protested.

"Vera wanted to see the world, not me. And we're thirteen," Eva corrected.

"You're not thirteen yet and you are entirely too short to be twelve," Valentina said.

"But we're smart," Eva and Vera said in unison.

"Yes, you're very smart for six-year-olds but this morning you acted like six-year-olds," Val said.

"Now all I want is to go back to our old life," Vera cried.

"This world is dangerous and you two will need to be strong in order to survive. Yet, we'll have a new life. Things will be different and different does not mean bad. It can be good but it will not be like our old life." Val paused and looked to her mother, who nodded in return.

"We're taking you to meet some very old and very dear friends of mine. They have been like family to me and …"

"What is it?" Vera prompted.

"Well ..." Val sighed. "You know how I have always been ... vague when you asked about your father?"

"We get to meet our father?" Eva's emerald eyes danced, as Teller's eyes had when he gazed upon Vallachia.

Val smiled at the memory and nodded.

"Tell us about him! What's he like?" Eva asked.

"Oh, you have heard of him," Valentina said.

"We have?"

Val glared at her mother. "Don't you dare. They have had enough fright for one day. And Teller is not who he once was a long time ago."

"You're not going to tell them that their father is the infamous Dracula?"

Sasha choked on her water and they all looked to Val with wide eyes.

"Dracula? Really?" Vera said.

"They need to know the truth," Valentina said.

"Our father is Count Dracula?" Eva looked terrified all over again.

Val shot one last glare to Valentina. "No. Not anymore and count is a newer term. He once went by Prince Vlad for a number of years but —

"Cool! Our dad is Dracula," Vera said.

"Not anymore. He goes by his given name — Teller — and he's very kind and loving, not someone to be afraid of."

"So what's he like," Eva asked with trepidation.

"Your father and I are about the same age. We grew up together in a small village called Ludus. Ludus is in the country now known as Romania. Teller and Mari — whom you will also meet — are my two oldest companions. Your father and I had fallen in love but then I was turned into a vampire ..." Val continued to tell her story until the girls were fast asleep.

"Thanks for that, Mother." Val was still upset with Valentina for mentioning Dracula.

"Please, don't call me 'Mother'. It sounds so ... cold. And it's better that they know. We can no longer keep them sheltered from the world. They would have found out and it's better they hear it from you."

"That was a brief and insignificant time in Teller's life." Val snapped.

"Or some might say it was his most significant time. It's what he'll always be remembered for."

Val didn't want to admit that her mother might be right.

"Imagine how proud I was to learn that my daughter was in love with Vlad the Impaler." Valentina's voice was full of sarcasm.

"Shut up, Mom," Val whispered.

"That's better." Valentina laughed. "You know I prefer to be called 'Mom'."

They stayed up to keep watch throughout the night.

The next morning Vera woke full of energy. While Sasha cooked breakfast over a campfire, Vera threw punches and kicks into the air. "I didn't know you and Grandma could kick butt like that. I want to be like you!"

"You thought we kept swords and shields around simply for show?" Valentina said.

Vera grabbed one of Val's swords. She could hardly lift it.

Valentina took the sword from her. "Not yet, little one. You'll hurt someone or, more likely, you'll hurt yourself."

"But I want to learn. Can you teach me? Pleeeease!" Vera's emerald eyes glittered with excitement.

"We'll start with something much less dangerous. Why don't you run along and find us two sticks that will work for fencing practice?"

"I'm sure I'll be a good fighter. After all I'm Dracula's daughter." Vera ran off on a mission to find the perfect sticks.

Eva curled up on Val's lap. "I want to go home, Mama."

"We are going home — to a new home."

"But I want our old home back."

"I know, Baby, but you know that can't happen."

They took flight as soon as it was humanly possible, which was entirely too slow for Val. Having to stop to rest and eat greatly slowed their journey to the Amazon.

~

WHEN VAL and her new family made their way across the open skies of Colorado, she noticed a distant humming sound. It was a sound she had not heard in a long time. It was a sound that she realized had all but vanished after vampires took over the world.

"Do you hear that?" she asked her mother.

Valentina closed her eyes to focus on what could be heard. "It's electricity and a lot of it."

Val pointed to a large power plant in the distance. "That plant is still operational.

"It must be vampires who maintain it. They will not be friends to us. Let's travel far around it," Valentina said.

"What could the plant be powering? Colorado Springs appears to be abandoned," Angela yelled over the wind blowing by her.

"Is that Pikes Peak?" Val asked.

"Indeed," Valentina said.

Val narrowed her eyes at the highest point in the mountain range. An uneasy feeling came over her. "Let's get out of here."

CHAPTER 53 NORTH AMERICA 2034 AD

Deep beneath Pikes Peak, Elda and Silvia had been debating about heading out on their own to find the former queen and her children.

"If we can't rely on others to find them, then we have to do it ourselves."

"We were so close," Silvia said. "We finally found where they were hiding. They couldn't have gone far."

Two of Elda's guards marched into the conference room. They roughly grabbed Elda and forced her arms behind her back. They slapped thick iron shackles around her wrists.

Silvia stepped toward Elda. "How dare you —

In the next heartbeat, Silvia found herself in the same position.

"What are you doing? Have you gone mad?" Elda demanded.

"Unhand us, you fools!" Silvia spat.

"We have not gone mad, my dear. Indeed it's quite the contrary — we have come to our senses." John rounded the corner, entering the conference room with the rest of Elda's entourage, who once had been her trusted guards.

"It has been decided that you're not fit to lead. You're misguided. You only care about finding two tiny little girls, when you should be worried about finding our enemies. Elijah and his resistance are a real threat but you only care about two harmless children."

"You are a fool. Those girls will have the power to destroy us. They're the only things that can stop me."

"You're wrong. *I* can stop you. Imprison her!" John commanded.

"No! We must find the chosen ones. You don't understand," Elda said.

"This time you're correct. I don't understand your obsession with these children. In all my years, prophecies of every kind have been foretold and guess what? They're only the false musings of crackpots. That's what you are — a crackpot — and we have decided that you're not fit to rule the world."

"And you are?" Elda spat.

"I am the oldest amongst us. I have ruled the vampire race for fifteen hundred years. Obviously, I'm *highly* qualified."

"You never ruled. You were a mere servant to the true leaders. You're nothing but a traitor!"

"That's quite enough." John's cheeks turned bright red. "You should be happy that I'm not going to kill you. We," John pointed to Elda's former guards, "agree with your law which declares that it's a crime for vampires to kill one another. If we are to truly be an honorable race then we can't run about slaying vampires like savages — as the Court once did. That's why I'm locking you up. I can't risk you interfering. Take them away."

"John, wait! It's not a prophecy. My visions have always come true —

"Vision, prophecy, there is no difference. Besides I thought you lost your *sight?"*

"I did but this was a very strong vision that I used to have before I took over and my ability to see the future … vanished," Elda choked.

"You have wasted enough of my time." John flicked his wrist and Elda and Silvia were dragged out of the room."

"John, please!"

~

ONE MONTH AFTER BEING IMPRISONED, a guard came to give Elda and Silvia their meager ration of blood.

Silvia jumped to her feet in order to serve her beloved Elda. "So it's not okay to kill us but it's okay to starve us?" Silvia yelled after the guard as she retreated down the long hallway.

The guard did not respond.

Carefully and quickly Silvia poured one of the glasses of blood into the other and turned to give it to Elda.

"What happened to your portion?" Elda asked.

"I already drank it. I was too thirsty. Please forgive me."

Elda smiled and downed her glass — both portions. "It's not your fault." Elda rubbed her throat, which was still dry. "It's not nearly enough. You know those girls are the only chance of undoing what we've … what I've done?" Elda said.

"I know. We'll find a way." *Or rather you will.* Silvia kept this last part to herself. She was growing weak — slowly starving to death.

A MONTH PASSED but this time when the blood rations came Silvia did not get up to retrieve them. Elda was weak and tired. She barely woke enough to say, "It's here."

Silvia did not move.

"Silvia!" Elda crawled to her side. Elda shook her. Silvia's head fell forward and Elda gasped. Silvia's cheekbones were greatly sunken. There were dark circles under her hollow eye sockets.

"No," Elda whispered.

"That's what happens to vampires who don't feed," a woman's voice came from the other side of the tiny barred opening of the thick iron door.

"We petrify?" Elda asked.

"Aye. It's not pretty but she's not in pain and she'll wake when a copious amount of blood is poured down her throat."

"Why am I not petrified?"

"Your faithful servant must've given you her blood rations."

Elda gasped. *Of course! Silvia had been giving me all the blood and taking none for herself.* Moisture formed in Elda's eyes. "How do you know all this about what happens to us when we don't feed?"

"You really don't know, do you?"

Elda heard the heavy steel rod as it was removed from barring the door and the door latch made a deafening noise as it was released. A woman entered only to glare at Elda. She was the guard who often watched over them or more accurately, came around every couple of weeks to hand out blood.

"What don't I know?" Elda demanded. She may be in prison but she was still royalty.

"What it's like out there on the streets. Blood is scarce and many vampires have mummified, like your precious Silvia."

"That's not true. There are millions of humans left. There is plenty of blood to go around."

"If one can afford it."

"What are you saying?"

"He who controls the blood controls everything. That's the world you've created."

"I didn't set any limits on blood rations. It should be free to all, as it has always been."

"Exactly. You have done nothing to stop your men who guard the human prisons. They can name their price and only those who pay a ridiculous amount can get humans to feed from. Being a guard is a dangerous job with those rebels out there. At least this is how the prison guards justify what they do. Those who can't afford to pay the guards' price, well ..." the woman pointed to Silvia.

"This can't be." Elda had heard word of unrest but surely things were not as bad as this woman said. "Are you here to kill me?"

The woman laughed. "No. I supported you — in the beginning and I still believe that vampires should not kill their own kind. I'm here to free you."

"Why?"

"You need to see what you've done." She grabbed Elda roughly under the arm.

"I can't leave her!"

The woman sighed. "Here, you'll need this." She pulled a pint of blood out of her coat pocket. Elda almost lost control at the sight of it.

The woman tossed it to Elda. When Elda ripped open the bag the scent was all consuming. With shaking hands she impulsively put it to her lips. *No! I must revive Silvia.* Elda put the torn opening of the blood bag to Silvia's pale, dry lips.

"Don't do that! That's not enough to wake her. You'll need an entire human for that. The blood is for you. It will give you enough strength to carry her out. Which I can't do because I have to distract the guards along the way."

With one last conflicted look at Silvia, Elda guzzled the blood in a matter of seconds. She felt some life flow back into her body. Now she fully realized how weak and tired she had been. Yet the guilt of not giving the blood to Silvia was unbearable. "How are we going to get out of here?"

"We don't have to hurry as much as we need to be careful. The guards most likely won't come this far into the cellblock for weeks — to hand out blood rations. I know the guards' whereabouts. I can get you out but you have to do as I say. The guards trust me so I'll make idle conversation with them. Once our backs are turned you'll sneak by."

"Why go through all this trouble for me?" Elda asked.

"Because it's been said that you can fix this mess of a world. I once thought it would be nice to be free, to be able to be ourselves and not have to hide but I see it now — the Court was right all along. If humans thrive so do vampires. I don't particularly care about humans but I don't want this for my race."

"I don't know if I can help, let alone change the world."

"You did it once. You can do it again."

Elda carefully lifted Silvia over her shoulder. "I can't make any promises, other than that I will try."

~

Elda's mysterious rescuer, who would not reveal her name, helped Elda find a small abandoned apartment in Colorado Springs. "I wouldn't stay here long if I were you. But this should work for now." The woman headed for the door.

"Wait. You're not going to help me?" Elda's heart jumped into her throat.

"I've risked too much for you already. I have to look after myself. It's a vicious world out there. Good luck saving us." Under her breath she added, "If you can even survive." Then she vanished.

"Great." Elda looked around at the dusty old apartment in dismay. *It's terrifying not knowing what the future holds. What in the hell do I do now?* Elda had never been alone before.

CHAPTER 54 SOUTH AMERICA 2034 AD

Teller always thought that it was Elijah whom Vallachia would return to. Her very infrequent communication was only to him. She truly loved him. Teller had long since accepted that fact. Yet Elijah was not the first one she returned to.

Teller was in the garden outside the tunnels when Vallachia's arms went around his neck. He had not even registered her scent.

"It's wonderful to see you," she whispered.

Once he fully realized that it was truly Vallachia, he put his arms around her waist and hugged her tight, breathing in her scent. She was not entirely the same. Although, he could not place what was different. The only thing he knew for sure was that everything was about to change. Whether that was for the best or not was impossible to tell. Sometimes change could not be labeled as good or bad, it was simply change and one must always be ready for it. Teller hoped he was ready for what was coming.

Like being on autopilot — as if it was the most natural thing in the world — Teller bent down to kiss her but she moved to place her lips on his cheek instead. This was when he realized everything about her gestures were purely platonic. This confirmed what he already knew,

She cares for me, even loves me but not in the way she loves Elijah. This thought sent a sharp pain through his chest.

"There are two people I have been waiting a long time to introduce you to," she whispered.

With his hands on Vallachia's waist he held her back in order to look into her large blue eyes. They danced with joy. Her eyes had always been one of his favorite things about her; they made her irresistible. She was positively stunning. Her expression was candid and excited. Her long flowing white dress appeared to make her light up. For some reason, Teller was reminded of the mysterious lady who had saved him from Neacsa.

Vallachia took Teller's hand and led him to a small clearing. Her long flaxen hair swayed gracefully along with her dress as she moved. She was like something out of a dream. *Maybe this was a dream and Vallachia was not truly back?* Teller would follow her anywhere. This had always been the case and he had no idea why. He didn't even care where they were going.

Teller was surprised to find himself facing two small girls.

"Girls, I want you to meet your father," Val said.

Teller's head reeled. *This must be a dream.* The girls appeared to be about six years old; they looked at him with curiosity and earnestness. They reminded Teller of Vallachia when she was a little girl but they had large emerald eyes that sparkled in the sunlight — they had *his* eyes. The girls were virtually identical. The only noticeable difference was that one was slightly smaller than the other. This was the one who hid behind Vallachia, shyly peeking out from around her mother's dress.

The other girl, the slightly larger one said, "Father!" She ran to Teller and jumped on him. He instinctively put his arms out to catch her. She threw her tiny arms around his neck.

Teller was petrified. The child's scent was mostly familiar — that of his and Vallachia's and something else — something unidentifiable and … not human. He slowly put his arms around the small child, as he realized that she was his — the daughter he thought he could never have.

Teller closed his eyes to stop the tears. *I have a daughter – I have two daughters*, was his first thought. This was all that mattered – they were all that mattered. The change inside him was instantaneous. The fact that Vallachia would not choose him was insignificant. The past seven hundred years fell into place. He and Val had had that inexplicable connection because they were meant to have these two beautiful girls. He had even seen these two perfect spirits before, whenever he had touched Val. Granted they looked different than they had in his vision – nevertheless it had been them – his children – their children.

All Teller wanted now was to be a father, to love them and protect them. "My daughter," he said to the little girl as he put her down. When he looked to Val for explanation, he was surprised once again, as there were two of her standing side by side. He was seeing double twice over, with two small Vallachias and now two grown Vallachias.

"What in the hell is going on?" he asked.

Val laughed at his wonderment. "You two have met before but let me formally introduce you to my mother, Valentina."

"'Mom.' I'm your mom," Valentina corrected.

"It was you who saved me from Neacsa?" Teller managed to put together some of the pieces.

Valentina nodded a yes and glided forward. She appeared to float through the air. "It's a pleasure to meet you." She extended her hand to Teller.

Now that she was closer Teller could see the differences between her and Vallachia.

"And you've met Vera," Val gestured to the larger of the two children. Vera had taken Teller's index finger and was holding it tightly in her tiny hand. It was as if she did not want to let go, now that they were finally together. Teller hoped this was the case, as he did not want her to let go either. She gazed up at her father with wide expectant eyes.

"And this is little Veva," Val said, as she gestured to the smaller mostly-hidden girl.

"Eva," the small girl's voice was quiet yet stern. She was clearly irritated by the name Veva.

Who could blame her? Teller thought.

"Of course, my dear, Eva," Val said.

Teller knelt down on one knee, trying to appear less intimidating. "It's a great pleasure to meet you Eva."

She hid her face in her mother's dress.

"Eva, say hello to your father. Remember what we taught you? When you meet someone new, it's customary to shake hands," Val said.

The little girl shook her head, which was still buried in Val's dress. She refused to say hello or shake his hand.

"Let's not push her," Valentina said. "She'll open up to you in her own time."

"Of course," Val and Teller said in unison. They looked at each other and smiled.

It was difficult for Teller to look away from Val and her new radiance. He didn't think it was possible but she was even more stunning somehow. Oddly though, Teller felt differently towards her. His desire for her had faded and there was only … love; as one would love a sister or a mother. He didn't understand it or have the words for it. It was similar to how he felt about Sergiu, Abdullah, the twins, as well as some of his other men.

"Motherhood suits you. You look better than ever," Teller said.

"Thank you." Val studied Teller for a moment. "You look wonderful as well. You appear … free."

"I have made some major changes lately. I suppose you could say that I've recently come to terms with myself."

"You've finally defeated the demons within. I knew it; you look happier, content even."

"I'm no longer burdened by the past."

"That's wonderful. I'm happy for you." Val hugged Teller. "Well, I'm sure you have many questions. Let's take a walk." She put her arm in his as they used to do so long ago back in their village. Back when they were nothing more than two young lovers, before they became vampires and a prince and a queen.

Valentina tried to take Eva's hand but Eva clung even tighter to Val's leg.

Val bent down. "Give us a minute, my sweet. We won't be long I promise."

"Don't leave me here in this strange place," Eva said.

"I'm not leaving, only going for a walk. I'll be right over there. I need you to be brave and you won't be alone," Val said.

Reluctantly Eva moved to hide behind her grandma — who in no way resembled a typical grandmother.

Vera looked disappointed that her father was leaving already.

"Keep an eye on them and we'll be back in two shakes of a lamb's tail," Val said.

Vera nodded. "Okay Mamma, only two shakes."

Val told Teller everything about where she had been and why she had stayed away. She told him about learning her mother's ways. To Val's surprise, Teller believed her when she told him that she had learned to do magical things. He had witnessed Neacsa's future-telling ability. He had fought skeletons that would not fully die. Tomoc had had a type of magic as well. Not much would surprise him after all that.

"Go to him. He needs you," Teller said. "Besides, that will give me time to get to know my daughters." His eyes shone bright with excitement.

"Thank you." Val kissed his cheek. "But I told the girls that I would be right back. I've never left them before."

"Then it's time you did. You need a break from being a mom and they have a dad now. Come." He took Val's hand and led her back to the garden where Valentina had taken the girls.

Valentina was inspecting the garden with a critical eye.

Vera jumped into Teller's arms at once. She was fine with her mother leaving. Eva, however, threw an outright fit. Her mother had never left her before. She had not ever been more than a couple hundred yards away from Val. Now her mother wanted to go who-knows-where for who-knows-how long? This was unacceptable.

"It's okay. I will see Elijah eventually," Val said.

"No. Go now. We've got this," Teller spoke loudly over Eva's screams. "She has to get used to being away from you at some point."

"Well, maybe not today." Val could not stand the anguish this was causing Eva. "This is all so new to her. I should stay."

Valentina held Eva tightly. "Now is as good a time as any. Go so I can calm her."

CHAPTER 55 SOUTH AMERICA 2034 AD

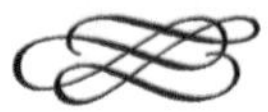

Vallachia ran as fast as she could through the tunnels, until she caught the familiar scent she was looking for. The girls would be safe with Teller and Valentina but it still felt odd leaving them. *I pray Eva has calmed down. They need to get to know their father and ... I need to see my husband.*

His wonderfully familiar scent led her to a closed door. *Should I knock? What if he is not alone? I should not go barging in on Elijah after all these years.* Finally, she decided to take her chances, the need to see him was stronger than these concerns. She slowly opened the door. *There he is!* He was sitting at a desk writing. Val could not help herself, the excitement at seeing him was too much. In an instant she was standing behind him. Then trepidation invaded. *What if he is furious with me? No one could blame him – after everything I have done.* Her heart thudded loudly in her chest.

He caught her scent as she hesitated. He quickly stood. Val smiled and he wrapped his arms around her tightly. "Is it truly you?" Elijah whispered. Then to answer his own question, he inhaled sharply and added, "It is."

Val laughed with delight. It was wonderful to be in his arms again, even though he was holding her so tight around the upper body that she could not hug him in return.

"I can't believe it. You're back."

"For good," Val whispered. He eventually loosened his grip so Val was able to wrap her arms around him. She started to say the many things that she knew needed to be said, "Oh, Elijah, I'm so sorry —" was all she got out before he pressed his lips to hers. She kissed him back and let herself enjoy his hungry touch.

"There's much to tell you. I need to explain — " she tried again.

"I don't care," he interrupted. "All that matters is that you are here … with me."

Elijah's wonderful gray-blue eyes were full of love and longing. Val could not help herself. She needed him. She pressed her lips to his and jumped up on him throwing her legs around him. They did not make it to the bed. They eventually melted to the floor in a tangle of arms and legs as clothes came off …

Eventually, Val lay with her head in her favorite place, Elijah's bare chest. She gently ran a finger across his skin, outlining his tattoo.

It had been a long time since he had had a woman's touch. He closed his eyes and his body felt fully relaxed for the first time in years — all but his arm, which held her close.

Elijah might never let her go; she hoped he never would. She wanted to stay like that forever. "I missed you so much," she whispered.

"You have no idea."

They heard loud footsteps coming down the tunnel, headed their way. They were too loud to be that of Vampires.

"Oh, boy. Here we go," Elijah said. With his free arm he quickly yanked a blanket off the bed to cover them. After only a brief knock, his door opened.

A loud human voice said, "Elijah —" but her words were cut short at the sight of the reunited lovers. She was a human with short black hair.

"Oh my God … you're back." She seemed to know who Val was but

Val had no idea who she was. Whoever she was she was not happy to see Val and her eyes filled with tears as she ran out of the room.

"Do you need to tend to that?" Val asked.

"No. That was Bray. She's a friend, nothing more."

"She fancies you."

"Aye ... hopefully now she will leave me alone." Elijah wrapped his other arm around Val and pulled her in closer. "She wants me to turn her into a vampire because she thinks I'll finally be with her if she's one of us. I've told her many times that it's not allowed to turn humans and that it would not make me want to be with her. Yet nothing I do or say deters her. She's hung on for all these years. Now she will see, you're the only one for me. Hopefully she'll move on and find a nice human boy." Elijah pressed his lips to Val's.

Val didn't care what Elijah had done while she was away. After the sin she committed, she had no right to expect that Elijah had remained faithful to her. She was only relieved that he was with her now. He wanted her back and that was all that mattered. She didn't care about the past fifteen years. That was Elijah's business, not hers.

Val cherished every second of this, as it postponed her having to tell Elijah about the girls. *How will he react to them? Will he reject them because they're Teller's and therefore reject me?* This was an unbearable thought. For now she would lose herself in him for as long as possible.

IT WAS like being newlyweds again. Val and Elijah did not leave his room for an entire day. He would not allow Val to talk about why she was gone for so many years or why she was back now. He would say, "Don't, not yet. Let me enjoy this a moment longer." It was as if he knew he would not like what Val had to say.

"I must see everyone else. How are they?" Val asked.

Elijah released Val for the first time from his iron grip. "I suppose we can't postpone the inevitable any longer." So they dressed quickly. He stopped suddenly as he was about to pull a shirt over his head and looked at Val as if for the first time. "There's something different about you."

Val shrugged. "What's different?"

Elijah smiled at her beauty — how he had missed it. She appeared radiant. Perhaps it was simply because he had not seen her in so long — he had forgotten how stunning she was.

Val felt her heart might burst when Elijah gave her his crooked smile.

She was anxious to see her other friends. Not surprisingly they tracked Riddick down in the weapons room. "Riddick!" Val ran toward him.

Riddick narrowed his eyes. When Val grew close he backed away. "So you finally decided to show up." His voice was full of accusation.

"Riddick, it's so nice to see you. I've missed you."

"Not that much apparently or you would have come back sooner."

"I had to stay away. Please let me explain —

"I don't care to hear anything that you have to say. You're nothing but a selfish whore."

Riddick's words were like an arrow through Val's chest. She recoiled as the full impact of his words hit her.

Elijah appeared at her side. "That is quite enough!"

Riddick glared at Elijah. "Honestly, you're one of the most intelligent people I know. You, above anyone else, should be wise to her tricks. Yet you're blinded by her charms. You can't see her for who she truly is."

"Riddick, please?" Val reached for his arm. He quickly pulled away and continued to speak to Elijah, as if Val was not there.

"You see, this is what she does. She looks at us with those big blue eyes and we do whatever she wants. I was under her spell for far too long but not anymore, do you understand? She's nothing but an evil temptress!" With that he turned and stormed out.

Val bent over and tried to breathe. Her stomach wrenched.

Elijah held her. "Don't worry he will come around."

"Riddick's a brother to me and now he hates me." Val's tears fell to the floor. “He’s right. I’m a wretched person. You should be as furious as Riddick — even more so.”

“Nah, Riddick is angry enough for the both of us.” Elijah tried to reassure her with a smile. “And you’re far from being a wretched person.”

It was amazing how Elijah’s arms comforted her. At least she could breathe normally again.

After Riddick’s reaction to her return, Val could not face her other friends. She feared they would be equally upset.

“They will be elated to see you.” Elijah rubbed his forehead. “Then again, I didn’t think Riddick would react in such a manner.”

CHAPTER 56 SOUTH AMERICA 2034 AD

It didn't take long for the rumors of Val's return to spread through the tunnels. Mari was the first to burst through the door into Elijah's room.

"You *are* back! Mari pulled Val up from the chair she had been seated in and threw her arms around Val, momentarily lifting her off the ground. They embraced for a long time.

"How have you been, Mari?"

"How have I been? Well, this place is simply awful but we're managing. The question is how have *you* been? We were worried sick about you!"

"I'm fine. As a matter of fact, I am better than fine." Val turned to Samuel and gave him a brief hug and a warm smile.

"It's great to have you back," Samuel said. "We've really needed you."

"It's wonderful to see you all," Val moved to greet Sonia and Aaron but was almost knocked over by a sudden embrace. Val found herself face to face with Mary.

"Where in the hell have you been?" Mary demanded after her crushing yet thankfully brief hug. "You're a crazy bitch for leaving us at a time like this. All we did was worry; worry about you, worry about the end of the world ..."

"Thanks Mary, it is good to see you too. I sent word that I was fine. Did you not get my messages?"

Mary punched Val in the arm — quite hard. "You mean the goddamned vague notes tied to a bird's leg? Aye, we got those. They didn't put us at ease. Don't ever do that to us again."

Val rubbed her arm where Mary had hit it. "Hopefully I won't have to." After more embraces there were happy tears running down Val's face and she was not the only one. Being reunited with her ancient and familiar family was a tsunami of comfort, safety and belonging all in one.

Val was relieved that her old friends were glad to see her — well, all but Riddick. Not surprisingly, he was nowhere to be found.

"So tell us, what have you been doing for the past fifteen years?" Elizabeth inquired.

Val took Elijah's hand for reassurance. "Well ... you would not believe me anyway, so I had better show you instead. There are some people I would like to introduce you to."

Val led them down the tunnel until she caught the scent of her daughters. This place was vast and Val would have been lost without her super vampire sense of smell. This led them toward Teller's room and Elijah gave her a concerned look.

Val took a deep breath before entering. *There will be no turning back after this.*

Eva lit up at her mother's return. "Mommy, Mommy, there you are!" She had been playing Monopoly with her father, sister and grandma.

Val had to let go of Elijah's hand in order to catch her daughter. "Hello, my sweet baby girl. It appears you are getting along well."

"It's not so bad." Then Eva notice the crowd of strangers Val had brought with her and blushed. She buried her head in Val's shoulder.

"We were beginning to think you might never return, Mama," Vera said.

Val shifted Eva on her hip and placed an arm around Vera. "You know I would never leave you, my lovely daughter." Then Val turned to her friends. "I would like you all to meet my twin daughters. Vera and Eva."

Mari looked as if she might faint and the others stared with open mouths. It was Elijah's reaction that concerned Val the most. He backed away. With a glare toward Teller, Elijah shook his head no, as he began putting the past fifteen years together.

"This is my mother, Valentina and her companions, Sasha and Angela." Val finished with a gesture to the ladies.

Angela looked overwhelmed as she surveyed all the people. She was used to living in isolation. Val didn't know how she would handle all this.

This was all too much for Elijah. Val did not understand the concerned look that he gave Valentina before he disappeared in a flash. Val set Eva down; the little girl immediately clutched her mother's leg. Val stared after Elijah but Teller grabbed her arm.

"Elijah, please! Wait," Val called.

"Eva needs you," Teller said. "She really missed you."

"Yes, it will be best to give him some time anyway," Valentina said.

Val looked back to where Elijah had disappeared. Having only gotten him back moments ago, she did not want to lose him again. She needed him. *Why can't they see that?* Yet one look into Eva's bright green eyes told Val that she had to stay and be a mom first. Without a word, Eva begged Val not to leave her with all these strangers. Val gave her a reassuring smile and picked her up again.

Mary and Elizabeth exchanged a worried glance. Mari's mouth still hung open.

It was Sonia who found her manners. She stepped toward to Valentina. "I'm Sonia. It is a pleasure to meet you."

Val introduced her old family to her new family.

It was Mary who quickly started in with the many questions, "How could you possibly have daughters and where in the fuc… hell did your mother come from?" Mary usually cursed like a sailor but she managed to hold back in front of the young ears — somewhat.

"Allow me to explain." Valentina stepped forward. "Why don't you take the girls and finish playing Monopoly?"

"I've never played," Val said.

Vera took her mother's hand and then Teller's. "Come on Mama. We'll teach you."

Eva sat quietly on Val's lap while Vera chatted away merrily about the rules of this fun new game her father had taught her.

Val could hear Valentina in the other room talking about what happened the night Val had run away and how they had stayed away to keep the girls safe from Elda.

"Who was that man, Mommy — the one who left before we could meet him?" Vera asked.

Val glanced at Teller for help but he shrugged and tilted his head in an expression that said, *Good luck explaining this one.*

"Well, he's our king, the leader of our kind or rather the leader of what is left of our followers and ..." Val hesitated, "he's my husband."

"What?" Vera said. She had been laying belly down resting on her elbows concentrating on the game. She jumped to her feet. "You're married to a king? That means you're a queen and that makes us princesses!" She grabbed Eva's hands to pull her up. They danced around as Vera sang merrily about being a princess.

"So does that mean we have two daddies?" Eva asked.

Val rubbed her forehead with her thumb and index finger, a habit she'd picked up from Elijah, who in turn had learned it from his father. These difficult questions were bound to be asked and Val dreaded having to explain this to the girls.

CHAPTER 57 SOUTH AMERICA 2034 AD

Teller spoke up and spared Val the anguish of having to answer her daughter's tough question. "Yes. You do have two fathers. Elijah, your mother's husband, may need some time to get to know you. You are quite a surprise. This is a lot for everyone to take in."

Val gave him a grateful smile. The girls were happy as they continued to sing and dance about being royalty. Val's friends soon joined them as they were very interested in the two miracle children. Eva did not enjoy all the strangers staring at her and retreated back to Val's lap to hide her face. On the other hand, Vera relished the attention. She spoke freely and confidently with these new vampires, whom she easily won over.

In no time she was sitting on Mari's lap showing her how she could braid a doll's hair. Mari looked as if she were holding back tears.

"They are simply lovely."

"And intelligent."

"They look like mini-Vallachias."

"Yet, they have Teller's eyes."

"Are they vampires?"

"Can they fly?" These were some of the many comments circulating about.

Once Eva had fallen asleep in Val's arms and Vera, despite her desire to stay awake, was yawning uncontrollably, Teller and Val tucked the girls into Teller's bed as everyone else quietly left.

"It's frightening that Elda knows about them," Val whispered. "Yet I'm grateful that you get to be in their lives. I wanted this for all of you for so long."

"I'm glad you're back and that you brought them to me," Teller said. "It's strange; since the moment I realized they were mine, everything changed. They're the only ones who matter."

"That's good, because they're going to require a lot of protection — by all of us." Val smiled at the two beautiful sleeping princesses. "I know exactly what you mean. I felt that way ever since the day I first heard their faint heartbeats. They will always come first."

Teller put his arm around Val's shoulder. "You're the wonderful mother I always knew you would be." He chuckled. "I bet you grew incredibly fat while pregnant with twins."

Val laughed. "I was enormous."

"I would have given anything to see you like that." His face grew serious, sad even. "I wish I could have seen them come into this world."

Val placed her head on his shoulder. "I know. I desperately wanted you there. I hope you can have a long life with them now."

"Since Eva is asleep, you should go to him."

Val nodded. "I need to find Elijah … to talk with him."

"Good luck," Teller said. "Don't worry, he'll come around."

Val searched everywhere but could not find Elijah. She asked people she came across if they had seen him and no one had. As she passed by, she overheard comments such as, "That's her! That's the Queen! She's returned."

Finally, she found the girl with short black hair sitting in what appeared to be a mess hall. A hand full of other humans sat around her. *What was her name, Bree, no ... Bray?* Val appeared in front of the girl. "Sorry to interrupt but have you seen Elijah?"

It took the girl a moment to focus on Val and another moment for it to sink in that Val had asked her a question.

Humans are annoyingly slow, Val thought.

The girl narrowed her eyes. "Don't tell me — he has seen you for what you really are and has left you already."

"It's *who* you really are not what." Val could not help herself; people no longer spoke proper English.

One of the men let out a long low whistle as he eyed Val and another said, "Damn."

Men in this day and age are so crude. They have no idea how to be proper gentlemen, Val thought. "That's no way to treat a lady."

"Good thing you're not a lady, then," Bray snapped. "You're nothing but a cheating wife."

Bray is obviously not going to be of any help. The girl would not tell me where Elijah is, even if she did know. Val turned to leave.

"Bray, don't you know who that is? She's fought for humans for centuries; show her some respect." A young man stood and held his hand out to Vallachia. "Never mind her, ma'am, we have not seen Elijah all evening. My name is Marcel and it's a pleasure to finally meet you."

"Thank you Marcel." Val gently took his hand. "Now if you'll excuse me, I need to find my husband." Val sped away.

"I know who she is and I don't care." Val overheard Bray say. "You don't deserve him!" Bray yelled after Val.

In a flash, Val returned. She was only an inch from Bray's face. "And you think I don't know that?"

Bray jumped back — wide eyed.

"There is nothing you can tell me, little girl, that I don't already know." Val disappeared.

Once there was no place left to look in the tunnels, Val resigned herself to pacing in Elijah's small room. Mari eventually found her. She wanted to keep Val company while she waited for Elijah. It was wonderful to talk with Mari. Val had missed her company. Mari wanted to know what motherhood was like. She listened with a hint of envy as Val described the joys of having two sweet and beautiful baby girls to care for.

Mari told Val of the hardships of losing the mansion and the servants. "I'm actually expected to clean my own room in this dreaded dungeon. Well, most of the time Samuel does the cleaning," she added with a smile. "There's no way to truly clean our clothes. The river is too muddy, so we are forced to wear filthy gowns at all times."

Mari moved to the small chipped mirror on the wall. She gently patted her cheekbones and pushed the skin upward. "I swear, I have started aging since we came to this dreadful place."

"Don't be silly, Mari. You look as lovely as ever." Val joined her and peered into the mirror.

"Not like you. You're simply glowing." Mari frowned at Val's reflection.

"Perhaps it is motherhood."

Mari was still Mari and Val was glad of that. She was also a wonderful distraction, as Val was starting to worry about Elijah. *Where could he be? Perhaps he's in trouble?*

CHAPTER 58 SOUTH AMERICA 2034 AD

She had children with him! How can that be? It's not possible. But they resemble her. Looking at the girls was like looking at Vallachia when she was child. *Yet their eyes ... they had his eyes.* It was the emerald eyes that haunted Elijah. They would always be there — a reminder of who the father was. *So that's why she stayed away, to give birth to them, to hide them from me.* Even as Elijah thought this, something about it didn't ring entirely true. Confusion overtook him. He could not make sense of any of it.

Sex was one thing but to have someone else's children — that was another matter entirely. One he could not forgive. *Maybe Riddick was right; I should not trust her. Perhaps I have been fooled by her all this time?* For the first time in a long time, Elijah thought of his father. *What would he have to say?* The answer to this was all too clear. *He would have killed Teller a long time ago, perhaps Vallachia as well. Or perhaps he would have kept her alive to torture her in some terrible fashion. Father tried to kill Teller before Val and I were married. He would not stand for any of this. I wish he were here now, to do what I have not been able to do. He had the courage to take action and I am weak — when it comes to her. I should have killed Teller when I had the chance; if only Samuel had not pulled me off of him fifteen years ago, I would have torn his head from his body. I should have!*

What are you waiting for? A voice in Elijah's head rang out. *I did not raise you to be a coward.*

"Father?" Elijah asked.

Yes, my son, it is I.

Elijah had been aimlessly walking through the jungle but now he ran. He headed straight for Teller's living quarters, knowing exactly what he needed to do. It was as if he was possessed. He was only able to see his anger and nothing else. It was easy for him to sneak into Teller's room and hide behind a curtain. *He will be going to bed at any time.* Elijah only had to wait a short while before Teller entered the room. This was the perfect opportunity; he had no idea Elijah was waiting with a broadsword.

Elijah could only see Teller — his focus was on his prey. Nothing else in the world mattered. *Only him and me,* Elijah thought.

Elijah waited until he was sure Teller was fast asleep. Then in a flash Elijah was at his bedside — sword drawn. A sure way to kill a vampire was to sever the head from the body. Elijah had done this tirelessly for centuries fighting the Black Plague across Europe. Killing vampires was all too familiar and all too easy. *So why not him? Why not now?* Elijah placed his sword near Teller's throat.

A movement came from the bed. A tiny little arm draped itself across Teller's large chest. Teller placed an arm around the small girl. They both continued to sleep —peacefully. Elijah withdrew his sword. Teller's daughter was protecting him in her sleep without even knowing it.

Elijah noticed the second girl, the smaller one. She seemed to keep her distance, so innocent and beautiful. With their eyes closed the girls did not remind Elijah of Teller, only Vallachia — his lifelong love. Elijah shook his head to try to clear the confusion. *How did I not notice the twins until now — their sweet scent, their heavy breathing? Have I been out of my mind — a crazed madman?* Elijah looked around the room. *I shouldn't be here. I can't kill Teller. What am I doing?*

But the voice in Elijah's head returned — his father's voice. *Since when is a son of mine afraid to kill? If the girls are in the way then you kill them as well. I did not raise you to be so weak!*

"Shut up!" Elijah said.

Teller stirred and Elijah disappeared in a flash. Elijah headed out of the tunnels. He walked the dark jungle for hours trying to reconcile with himself. *Did I fail to act? Am I a coward? Or have I done the right thing by not killing Teller ... again.* The confusion was unbearable.

When Elijah finally returned to his room Mari was chatting away. Val sat frowning at the floor. Mari fell silent and they both stood when he entered. Val looked relieved and Mari looked uncomfortable. Elijah glared at Mari and pointed toward the door, "Get out."

Mari gave Val a concerned look. Val nodded for Mari to leave.

Reluctantly Mari exited.

Val approached Elijah. "I'm glad you're back. I was concerned —

Her words were cut short by the sword Elijah pointed at her chest.

She gasped and took a step back. "Elijah? ... What's going on? Please talk to me."

"You had *his* children. Then you hid from me. That's what's wrong. How do you expect me to feel?"

"I never hid from *you*. Elijah, I would never do that. We were hiding from Elda but she found us. That's why I came back. So that I could be with you, now that the girls were no longer a secret from our enemy."

Elijah studied her; she seemed sincere. *Who to trust?* He let out a yell of frustration and threw the sword across the room. It made a loud clattering sound against the rock wall as it fell to the floor and Val gave a start. *I shouldn't have scared her.* He fell in a pile on the floor and she moved in sync with him, half catching him and half falling with him. She held him.

"Why couldn't it have been me? You should've had my children."

"Shhh, I know. I know," Val whispered.

Elijah eventually fell asleep in her arms. In the past it had always been her in his arms.

He woke abruptly as if the previous night was one long nightmare. He found himself sitting upright in bed. Elijah didn't remember how he had gotten there. Vallachia stirred by his side. He watched her intently for a moment. *I know that she truly does love me.*

Elijah felt more like himself after resting, yet still a part of him worried that he had failed. He was not entirely sure how or more accurately, whom he failed. *Father,* he guessed. This remaining confusion was unsettling. But at least he knew that he would not kill Teller and he would not harm Vallachia. *I could never hurt her.*

Val sat up and put her arms around his waist. She kissed his neck. "How are you faring?"

Her touch was wonderful — familiar. Elijah could have easily let himself get lost in her caress, as he had always done. He shook his head, as he recalled Riddick's words, "evil temptress". *Is she toying with me — using me?* These thoughts allowed doubt to enter his mind. This also allowed his father's voice to return. *Val is the traitor. She must have been working with Elda the past fifteen years or even longer. How else did she know when Elda would attack? She most likely betrayed us, long ago. Val was the one to tell Ramdasha that I would be in the rear of the army during the battle of 1551. She is responsible for my death.*

"No." Elijah said to the voice in his head. Nevertheless, he removed Val's hands from his waist.

"Elijah please, don't push me away," Val said.

Think, my son! Who had more cause to hate me than Lady Vallachia? "I need some time — to sort things out." Elijah could not look her directly in the eyes because she would have been able to weaken his resolve. Surely he would give into her crystal-blue eyes, as he always did; well not any more.

Val nodded. "I understand. I'll be here for you if ... or when you need me." She brushed a tear from her cheek and quickly left the room.

Her children would be waking soon. She needs to be getting back to them. This thought filled Elijah with spite. He lay back down and tried not to think. He let himself go numb — forcing himself to not feel or think. All he wanted was for Vallachia and the stupid voice in his head to leave him alone.

CHAPTER 59 SOUTH AMERICA 2034 AD

Vallachia left Elijah alone for a couple of months, hoping every day or rather, every second, that he would come for her. She prayed he would at least try to get to know the girls. He did not. With every moment that passed, she became more concerned that he would leave her for good. It was all she could do to stay away but she had promised him his space, as he was once gracious enough to grant her.

Val was giving the girls a school lesson in the garden when Samuel appeared behind her.

"Mari asked me to find you. She needs to see you," Samuel said.

Val nodded. "Where is she?"

"In the meeting room."

There was an urgency in his voice that caused Val to stand and excuse herself. The girls, well Eva mainly, as Vera had been fine from day one, were getting used to this place and their newfound father. Eva was more comfortable with Val leaving. In fact, she hardly looked up from her math problem to say goodbye. Val could not help but feel a bit disappointed. Her baby no longer needed her as much. On the other hand, Val knew that it was a good sign that Eva was adjusting.

"What's wrong?" Val asked.

"She would not say," Samuel replied.

He looked guilty. *They are up to something,* Val thought.

Once she reached the meeting room, Val turned to Samuel but he had disappeared. She cautiously entered. It quickly became apparent that Mari was not waiting for her in the meeting room, as only Elijah was there. *So that's what's going on,* Val thought. *Mari and Samuel are trying to get us to talk. Surely they are hoping to get their two best friends back together.*

Val smiled at Mari and Samuel's slyness. "Hello," Val said.

Elijah who had been sitting in a chair poring over a large map glanced at Val briefly and looked away.

"I was hoping … well I came here looking for Mari but apparently you're who I was meant to find," Val said.

"Then you had better go find her." Elijah's voice was flat.

"It's you I want to see. Can we please talk about this … about us?" Val pled.

Elijah would not look at her. She slowly sat down in the chair across from him.

There was a long awkward silence. "You drive me insane, literally certifiably mad. I can't …" Elijah blurted.

"And I am sorry for that, I truly am. I never meant to hurt you. The past fifteen years have been out of my control. There is a part of me that would give anything to go back to those perfect years we had together — when there was nothing between us."

"There has always been something between us or rather someone. I used to ignore it, your love for Teller but I can't do that anymore."

"I don't love him — not like I used to. I care about him and I want my daughters to know their father but I no longer long for him. Now that my relationship with Teller is no longer romantic, you're going to reject me? Please don't push me away. You're the only man I love, the only one I want."

Elijah still refused to look at her. He began to rub his forehead with his thumb and index finger. This familiar gesture made Val want him all the more. She wanted to comfort him — to ease his pain.

"You see Teller and I had a connection and once the girls were conceived that connection was broken. We were meant to have them and that's all. It's over between us. We'll never be together again. We don't even want to be together as we once did. Now that I'm entirely yours, please don't give up on me!" Val resisted the urge to wrap her arms around him. *Why won't he look at me?*

"I want to believe you. I do. But what if Riddick is right and I'm nothing but a fool, blinded by you? What if you continue to hurt me?"

"Elijah, I won't ever hurt you again. You're my true love. We're mated for life."

He shook his head. "I can no longer allow anyone to have this much control over me — driving me mad. Do you know that I actually thought I heard my father's voice?"

"What did he say?" Though Val had the feeling that she didn't actually want to know.

"That I should kill Teller and that you are a traitor."

Val's lips parted. "Please tell me you don't believe him."

"I don't know what to think. All I know is that you hamper my ability to govern. In case you hadn't noticed, we're at war. I have a job to do." Elijah's voice rose with each sentence. "I can't be bothered with this nonsense. I have to be done with you!" Quietly he added, "It's over ... we're over."

Val wished he had stabbed her with his sword, as that would have hurt less. *How will I live without him?* She had never really been without him. He had always been there, throughout the vast majority of her entire long vampire life. Her world grew foggy. She slowly stood and walked out. She wanted to run but her feet would not let her. She wandered the tunnels not knowing where to go. *What happens now?* She did not want her daughters to see their once strong mother like this; heartbroken and numb. She questioned her ability to be a mother at all.

Her eyes were dry. She was beyond the pain of tears.

Val wasn't sure if she could stand to see Elijah and not be able to touch him, hold him, kiss him. *Perhaps, I should leave ... again? I'm of no use here. I'm not a leader anymore.* She wanted to get away and try to sort out what she should do with her life. Her life had been defined by her relationship to Elijah. The two of them had acted as one for centuries. If she was no longer his wife then she was no longer the Queen. *If I'm not a wife and I'm not a leader, then what am I? Losing Riddick was bad enough; now Elijah?* The pain would have been overwhelming if not for her trusty mask of numbness.

Val decided that she had to leave. She didn't want the few people who still cared about her to worry, so she went to Valentina. Val quickly and quietly pulled her mother aside as the girls played merrily with Teller.

"I have to get out of here," Val said.

"My dear, you look terrible! Your light … it's faded. What's wrong?"

The words would not come. Val could not bring herself to say the unimaginable — that Elijah no longer loved her. "I need some time — to myself—to sort things out."

"Of course dear, how much time, so I can let the girls know when you'll be back?"

"I don't know, a couple of days, maybe more. I'll send a message if I'll be longer."

"Take care of yourself." Valentina wrapped her arms around Val and kissed her cheek.

Val disappeared.

CHAPTER 60 SOUTH AMERICA 2034 AD

Val was in a grey haze as she flew over the dense jungle. The world around her had dimmed. She no longer saw the colorful trees or the sparkling rivers. She didn't want to believe that her marriage was over. That was something — the one thing — that was never supposed to end. Marriage did not change in her world. Vampires never left their mates, not that she had seen anyway. Yet after all that had happened, how could she expect anything else? She deserved to lose Elijah. In fact, she had never deserved him.

Val landed by a small stream. Water rushed over and around large boulders as it made its way into the mighty river — the Amazon. She needed to meditate. She had to try to clear her thoughts and figure out what to do. *How do I move forward ... without Elijah?* This question was her focus when she went into a deep trance to ask the Great Goddess for guidance. However, the only answer she received was the clear image of Pikes Peak — the huge mountain in Colorado.

Val shook her head. "No, I don't care about some random mountain." Yet even as she said this she knew it was not random. She was reminded of the odd feeling that had overcome her when she last saw the enormous peak a couple of months ago. *It had been humming with electricity. Was it another prison for humans?*

Vallachia tried again. *There must be something I can do to save my marriage?* She was barely insightful enough to notice that in this brief time her focus, her desire, went from moving on from her marriage to trying to salvage it. She didn't truly want to get over Elijah, she wanted him back.

Yet again, she received only the image of the cone-shaped peak rising high into the sky, clear, unmistakable.

And again Val resisted. Many hours passed.

"As you wish. You have always shown me the way. Thank you Great Mother of us all." Val was not naive. She knew that whatever awaited her in Colorado Springs had nothing to do with her ruined relationship and she also understood her gut-turning feeling about the mountain — it was dangerous. She headed north at once. She trusted the Great Goddess's guidance. Even though it was likely that enemies awaited for her, she knew she had to go alone. She did not need her army — if it was still hers to command.

At sunup, Val landed on top of the highest peak. From fourteen thousand feet she surveyed the land. There was nothing out of place except the faint vibration of electricity. It seemed as if the mountain was electrified or at least large amounts of energy were being pumped into it. *Why does someone need so much energy — within this mountain or perhaps underneath it?* Val decided the entrance must be hidden at its base somewhere. It would be heavily guarded and sealed tight. She hoped that she had not been spotted already. She decided it would be best to blend in. The city in the distance appeared largely vacant but it could be crawling with vampires by night.

Val made the short flight to Colorado Springs. She rummaged through some vacant apartments until she found a pair of jeans and a blue t-shirt that fit. She quickly changed out of her white dress. She tucked her long blond hair in a baseball cap. Of course she always wore sunglasses.

"There. I could be anyone," she said to her reflection in a mirror. She hid her pack, which contained some basic provisions — mostly blood bags. She had learned that if she drank a pint every five to six days she could get by on five pints a month, rather than the allotted six pints. This didn't seem to affect her strength, her energy level or her ability to control her thirst. She didn't know how long she would be gone so she planned ahead.

At dusk she walked the streets looking for signs of life. She didn't have anything of value on her, save her usual weapons — a long sword and her knife belt. She carried no blood and no money for blood. These were the only things her desperate kind cared about. They would do most anything for blood. Still she was a queen or a former queen; she could be in danger out in the open like this. She had watched over the world from afar — through the seeing crystal. Yet, she was not entirely sure what she would find on the streets.

A handful of bodies with dry wrinkled skin lay about but there was no sign of healthy vampires; until she heard a distant sobbing. Val drew her sword and followed the noise into a narrow alley. She had never grown to like guns. Her sword was an extension of her arm — natural. It was as if she had been born with it. The sword was difficult to give up. It had always protected her. Not to mention guns were entirely too loud.

At the end of the alley there was a figure of a small woman. She hovered over more petrified vampires. The vampires must have come here with what little strength remained to comfort one another. Some had fallen into their starvation sleep as they held each other. Some of them had most likely been lovers. This once had been a coven that cared deeply for one another. Val could almost see herself and her family, her coven, in their sunken faces. For the first time she felt sorry for the mummified vampires. Val had always looked at them as traitors to the Court. Val could see now that they were not all deserving of this fate. Some were simply caught in this awful new world, with no way out. And this could be her family's fate if things did not change.

Val kept her sword pointed at the woman as she cautiously approached. The small figure sang a gloomy melody…

The pieces are in place

The pawns are ready to play
No more, no more
The chains are broken
The chains are gone
How brief the war
A simple late frost
The color was lost
What was not seen
Without the color
There is no green
The life force itself
No more, no more
Better left unknown
Better left undone
The pieces are in place and
The pawns are ready to play

TEARS FORMED in Val's eyes, perhaps a drop spilled over. She quickly blinked the moisture away so that it would not impair her vision.

The woman slowly turned. She must have caught the scent of another. Large honey-colored eyes peered up at Val. The rather small woman had full red lips. There was the hint of a dimple. Val was sure it would be a deep crevice in her cheek if only she smiled. But there was no smile. She was stunning; even more so than her image on TV or the hazy figure in the seeing stone.

Vallachia inhaled sharply and then tried to exhale the jealousy away. *Teller married this woman. Had he loved her?* Val was ashamed of this intrusive thought. This was of no importance in this dire moment. She was facing her greatest enemy and was overwhelmed with shame that her first reaction was as petty and horrible as jealousy. Jealousy was the most evil of all emotions. She was humbled to find that it could still overcome her.

Val was sure that all her hard work to become more "enlightened" would make her immune to such primitive emotions. She took another deep breath to regain her insight — her wisdom of years, her father's and now her mother's teachings came back to her. She had to reject the darkness that had churned from within. Val could almost hear her mother say, "One is never completely free of negative and harmful emotions. It's what one does with them that matters."

CHAPTER 61 NORTH AMERICA 2034 AD

Vallachia raised her sword to Elda's throat. Elda remained motionless, she did not even blink. *Elda does not care if her head is removed from her body. In fact, she most likely wishes for it.* Val swiftly sheathed her weapon, as it was obviously not needed. There was no fight in her enemy. *If your enemy wants death then that is the last thing you can give them.*

"I had it you know?" Elda whispered.

"Had what?" Val was filled with confusion. *Am I honestly going to have a civil conversation with the woman who is hunting my children — the woman who most likely wants them dead?*

"For about a year, the blink of an eye for us, I had the perfect life. It was just my two faithful companions and me. We lived simply and in peace, then *he* found me. I was such a foolish girl. Perhaps I still am, as I did all this *for* him. Men ..." Elda trailed off.

"Not all men are terrible and it's rumored that Ramdasha truly cherished you." Val could not believe the words that fell from her lips.

A tear ran down Elda's cheek, which was already soaked from previous tears. "I suppose so."

"We do foolish things for love."

"I never thought I would love a man but then like an earthquake, my world went from simple and peaceful to wild and chaotic. And the strangest thing of all was that I was fine with it. In the time it takes to snap your fingers he changed me forever. It's odd how men can do that to us."

Val could almost see it; Elda falling in love with the dark and handsome stranger, the second she gazed upon him. Val guessed the feeling was mutual. Ramdasha surely fell equally hard and fast for the pale and lovely young maiden, with her large honey-colored eyes.

Elda sang again. It was a glorious sound. Val recognized the ancient Eastern European song — one she had not heard in hundreds of years. By the second verse Val joined in. Musings of misguided love, longing, regret and unfailing companionship rang through the air.

Elda remained on her knees long after the singing stopped. "How can I possibly live with the realization that my entire life's work, meaning hundreds upon hundreds of years, was nothing but a foolish pursuit? I studied how to raise the dead — which was not an easy task. Then I had to wait for the right time. It was all that drove me after I lost them in the great war of 1551." Elda gestured to the mummified bodies. "Look at what I've done. These are my people. I did this for him, to make him proud but even Ramdasha would not have wanted this. He loved his fellow vampires. We never thought that vampires would be so greedy and cruel to their own kind. We're supposed to be the honorable race or so I once thought. Blood has always been plentiful. We never thought that would change."

A derisive chuckle escaped from Val. "You mean to tell me that you thought setting a bunch of bloodthirsty monsters loose on the world would somehow end well? It took less than a decade for vampires to ruin everything."

"The Court warned that if humans thrived so did vampires. I thought that was only propaganda so they could remain in control and keep vampires suppressed. Yet, it's true, Ram and I were wrong. And now I am paying the ultimate price. If only my sight would have stayed with me. If I would have been able to see this future I never would have done what I did."

Val nodded. Elda appeared to be telling the truth. "You said you lost *them* in the war. Whom did you mean?" Val realized that they had been speaking in their ancient native Romanian dialect.

"I had several ... companions before I married Ram..."

Val took Elda's hands and raised her from her knees.

Elda's cheeks flushed as she continued. "I not only lost my husband in the war but I also lost my ... friend, Adela. You see, Adela and Silvia were my faithful servants and ..."

Why is she so hesitant to speak about Adela and Silvia? Oh, that's right. Teller mentioned Elda's unusually close relationship to her chambermaids. "I understand. Society has always wanted to pretend that such relations don't exist, yet they always have." Val was surprised at Elda's continued reluctance to discuss her former lovers. Of course, gay and lesbian couples were not fully accepted even now but much more so than they ever had been since Greco-Roman times.

"Silvia!" Elda's face lit up. "Can you help her?"

Val's jaw dropped. *Elda is asking me for help!* "Do you know who I am?"

"If you're suppose to be disguised it's not working. Every vampire knows who you are. In fact, I'm still baffled that you didn't chop my head off a moment ago."

Now it was Val's turn to blush. She should have known her "disguise" would not fool anyone. She took the ball cap off and her long blond hair fell down her back.

Elda's large red lips parted. "As beautiful as they say." Then her eyes widened. It was as if she had been dreaming this entire time and now she was awake from her state of deep grief. "The girls!" she almost yelled. She looked about frantically as if she might spot them.

"They're safe."

"But they're not here — with you?" Elda's voice was full of panic.

"No." Val's voice hardened. "They're far away and well protected. You'll never find them."

"Thank God! You need to get away from that mountain as well." Elda took Val by the upper arm to lead her away.

"Why? What's in the Mountain?"

"It's my headquarters — or former headquarters, as John has taken over now."

"John!" Val spat out as she stopped in her tracks. She wrenched her arm free of Elda's grip. "I thought he was dead."

Elda flinched away at the anger in Val's eyes. "We were both betrayed by him." Elda raised her hands up slowly in a defensive gesture. "I'm sorry, I thought you knew. Please, there is a reason you found me. Perhaps your sight led you here. If we work together we may be able to fix this awful world I've created."

"Of course, it was that snake who betrayed us." Val muttered, as if Elda was not even there. She forced herself to take a deep breath. If only John were in front of her now she would wrap her fingers so tight around his scrawny neck that he would never take another breath.

"Lady Vallachia, please. It's not me you want. You need me. Together we can help each other ... to get what we both want."

Val suddenly focused on Elda, as if remembering she was there. "And what is it you want?" Val spoke through clenched teeth.

"To save my dearest friend. She's all I have left in this entire miserable world." She knelt down on one knee. "Please show me mercy, My Queen. I don't deserve it but I beg of you." She cautiously pressed her lips to the back of Val's hand.

Val's shoulders relaxed and her jaw unclenched. When Elda gazed up at Val all that could be seen was sorrow and desperation in Elda's eyes. Val swiftly grabbed Elda by the shoulders and lifted her to her feet. Val only gave her a slight nod of acceptance and understanding.

"Thank you," Elda whispered. She glanced around for signs of others and saw none. She took Val by the wrist and moved toward a door at the far end of the alley. "You're not safe out here. If they were to find you — take you to John ..." Elda shivered.

Val let Elda lead her away. *This is insane*. Of course, Val worried that it could be a trap. *Perhaps Elda put me under a spell of sorts?* Yet, Val had never seen this kind of despair in another before. The Great Mother had led her to Elda for a reason and that reason was not to kill the woman. Val had to find out why the Great Mother wanted her here.

CHAPTER 62 NORTH AMERICA 2034 AD

Elda led Val through an abandoned apartment complex. She passed many doors and when she came to a blank space in the wall, she paused and began chanting. She waved her hands over the wall. There was a brief flash of light, as if lightning filled the rectangular shape of a doorway. And that's what appeared in the wall — a door.

"A concealment spell," Val muttered. They passed through the now visible door and Val helped Elda to conceal the door once again. Elda wobbled on weak legs and Val had to catch her. "What's the matter?" Val watched as dark circles formed around her eyes. "Elda, when was the last time you fed?" It dawned on Val that she and Elda had touched more in the past ten minutes than Val had touched many of her close friends. There was never a hand kiss from Riddick or Samuel, even Mari. She had never held any of them as she was now holding Elda. She wanted to chuckle at the thought. Val didn't expect her first meeting with Elda to go like this.

"I'm fine." Elda struggled to her feet. "It must be the magic — it can take a lot of energy." She moved slowly to an old sofa and pulled the blanket off a mummified figure. Elda knelt and took the dried hand in hers. "Her name's Silvia. She's all I have left and I'll do anything to get her back. It's because of me that she is in this state."

Val studied Elda and the corpse that was Silva. She half expected to see Elda petrify before her eyes. Val made a sudden decision. "Stay here. I'll be right back." Val vanished before Elda could question her.

Elda had begun to doze and woke with a start when Val returned with her travel pack. Val took out a pint of blood and handed it to Elda.

Elda only shook her head no.

"You said you could help me. If we're going to … figure out a way to undo this mess of yours, then I need you to be healthy."

Elda still didn't move.

That's no matter. She's starving. Val knew how to get a hungry vampire to feed. She ripped the top of the bag open and the delicious scent of human blood filled the room.

In a flash Elda's hands were around the blood bag. In another instant, the blood was gone.

Val quickly tossed her another pint.

Elda ripped it open with her teeth and downed it. She sat down hard on the floor with her back against the couch. She panted with relief, revealing her long fangs. Val sat beside her and handed her another bag.

"I'm … I'm better now." Elda struggled not to reach for the third pint.

"You'll need your strength for our journey."

Elda took the blood with more composure this time.

Val opened a pint in sync with Elda and held the bag up. "Cheers."

Elda shook her head but nonetheless tapped her bag to Val's.

"To saving the world."

The blood disappeared as fast as before. Elda put her head down. "How did we get here?"

Val chuckled. "I never could have predicted this in a thousand years."

"Neither could I and at one time, that would really have been saying something."

"Teller told me of your ability to see the future. He said that even as a human your sight was strong."

Elda's face darkened. "You mean Vlad."

"He no longer goes by that name. Once again he's Teller."

"He stole my rightful name."

"But he does not use that name anymore. It has long since been lost over the years."

"Until Bram Stoker uncovered it."

Elda is clearly still bitter about the misuse of her family name.

"Well, Stoker's account of Dracula is clouded in myth and besides Teller is no longer the same person he once was."

"You're blinded by your love for him. He's nothing but a monster."

"You may be right. Then again, all vampires are monsters." Val gave her the slightest smile.

The corners of Elda's lips turned upward in a half smile. Now that her strength was back, her freckles seemed to pop off her pale skin. Val could see her cute dimple as well and she could not help but feel protective of this petite woman. Val was growing weary of all the conflicting emotions she'd felt since she found Elda. *How could this be my mortal enemy?*

Val studied the vampire sitting next to her and tried to see the evil witch who managed to destroy the world — who managed to dethrone the High Court of the Elders after fifteen hundred years of rule. The only thing Val saw was a broken woman. "Perhaps you should give up the name Elda and take back your rightful name — Neacsa Dracula."

"Vlad stole more than just my name, he took everything from me, my beloved father, my homeland, my entire kingdom. He ripped my identity away. I was forced to find a new name and Elda suits me just fine."

"Yet Teller also gave you eternal life. Perhaps it's time you gave up that identity and became your true self — Princess Neacsa, who only wanted a simple, peaceful life."

"Hmmm, simple… peaceful…" Elda's head fell onto Val's shoulder.

Val jerked at the odd gesture and then realized that Elda was fast asleep. Val laid her on the floor in a more comfortable position. Elda's comfort was the last thing Val ever thought she would be concerned about. *Poor thing. She probably hasn't slept in days.* There was nothing to do now but wait for her to wake.

CHAPTER 63 SOUTH AMERICA 2034 AD

For the most part, Elijah was relieved. With Vallachia out of his life she could never hurt him again. The pain would end eventually and never return — so he hoped. The other part of him could not stand the thought of a future without her. He also feared that he would become like his father — alone, heartless, bitter — never truly caring for a companion. He knew Val was right, they were mated for life. This appeared to be the way love worked for vampires. He'd never seen any evidence to the contrary. So without her, he would never find another. He would be alone, as his father had been. Nevertheless, this was better than being hurt by her. *Wasn't it?*

Elijah left the tunnels one sunny morning. It was always a relief to step out into the fresh air after being cooped up all night with a bunch of humans and farm animals. But on this morning he found himself face to face with a small girl — a miniature version of his wife or former wife.

Eva greeted him with a sing-songy, "Good morning," as she smiled up at him.

Elijah furrowed his brow and sidestepped her with ease.

"Where ya goin'?" Eva's sweet voice rang out.

Elijah cringed. "What do you want?"

"I want to do whatever you're doing." Eva spoke proudly, completely oblivious to Elijah's annoyance.

"Why?" Elijah stopped walking but kept his back to the girl.

"Because you're a king, how cool is that? You are a king aren't you?"

Elijah rubbed his forehead. "No. I once was but now... I don't know. Not anymore." He resumed walking.

Eva skipped along beside him to keep up. "Then who is king?"

"You really want to get into politics, kid?"

She put her hand in his. "Well you're still the leader around here. That makes you a king to me."

Elijah resisted the urge to jerk his hand away. Instead he gently removed her hand from his and turned to face her. "Where's your mother?" he snapped.

Eva shrugged her tiny shoulders. "I don't know," but it came out as a series of M sounds.

Elijah looked around in hopes of finding Val so she could get this child away from him. Perhaps he could learn to tolerate the twins, if only they didn't have their father's eyes. When he looked at them he was reminded of Val's betrayal. It was difficult to be civil to this child when all he felt was pain when he looked at her.

Eva put her head down and focused on kicking some pebbles. "Grandma said that Mama had to go away for a while."

Good, was Elijah's first thought; then concern set in. "Where did she go?"

Eva shrugged. "She has never left me before and well ... Vera and Dad, they get along great. They're always doing stuff together, dumb stuff like sword fighting and boxing ... and well ... I was hoping we could do ... I don't know, something together. You know something fun, that doesn't involve trying to hurt someone."

"Why me?"

"Because you're our dad too. I was hoping that you could be *my* dad."

At some point Elijah's mouth had fallen open. "I … I'm not your father."

"You're our stepdad. I've read about it in books. That's still a dad, right?"

Elijah inhaled sharply. "Ahhh." He couldn't recall anyone leaving him speechless before — let alone a child. She was pulling at his heart. Finally he managed, "You know what, have you ever ridden a horse?"

Elijah's beloved horses had been lost when the mansion in New York was attacked. He had noticed that many of them escaped as the barn caught fire but he hadn't had time to rescue them and some had most likely perished. Elijah could not go without horses in his life for long. He knew where a group of formerly domestic horses tended to graze. Horses weren't native to the jungle. They found the thick vegetation difficult to maneuver. They preferred the rolling grassy plains that were a relatively short flight to the south. Elijah had set some of these horses free from their corrals after their owners were rounded up by Elda, thirteen years ago.

Eva's eyes grew so big Elijah thought they might fall out of her head. "I've asked Mama for a pony every day since I can remember but she always said we couldn't feed a pony and ourselves."

This was the first glimpse that Elijah had into what life had been like for Vallachia while she was away. They had all made great sacrifices but no daughter of Elijah's, step or otherwise, would go without a horse. He swooped her up into his arms and in only a short time they were flying over a herd of horses that ran through a green meadow.

They landed on the back of one of the spooked horses. They raced across the field, with Eva riding safely in front of Elijah. When they reached the trees, Elijah gently pulled back on the mane to slow the horse.

"I call him John," Elijah said. "I named him after someone lost to me. I have worked with John a lot. He's the tamest horse in the herd. It's easy. Move the base of the mane to the right to steer him in that direction. Obviously, a left tug of the mane leads him left. Tap his sides gently with your legs to get him to walk and a bit harder and faster to run. You already saw how I stopped him. Pull back on his mane but not too hard."

Eva nodded in concentration, taking it all in.

"Now." Elijah slid off the horse. "You give it a try."

"Wait! No." Eva's voice was higher than normal . She knew what her mom and grandmother were capable of. Eva knew she was safe as long as Elijah was with her ... but alone — on a horse?

Elijah had to move in front of the horse and pat his nose to sooth him. "You have to remain calm in order to ride a horse. They know if you're scared. I'm right here. This horse can't outrun me. I'll be here if you need me." Elijah nodded with encouragement.

Eva swallowed hard and nodded in return.

"Gently tap John's flanks."

"What's a flank?" The panic crept back into her voice.

"Tap his sides, with your legs."

This she did and Elijah walked alongside giving her further instructions. After an hour or so she and John galloped across the meadow. Eva laughing with delight.

When the sun was high in the sky, it dawned on Elijah how long they had been gone. He stepped in front of John to stop him. He patted the horse for a moment and fed him an apple from his pocket. "Thank you friend," he whispered. Then to Eva he said more loudly, "We have to be getting back."

"But did you see how good I'm doing — all on my own? This is so much fun — the most fun I've ever had!"

"We've been gone a long time. Your family will be looking for you."

"But you're my family and I'm with you, so it's okay."

A child's logic. Elijah spotted three dark figures flying straight for them. Soon he was face to face with a furious Teller, a tearful Valentina, and Abdullah — who shifted uncomfortably from side to side.

Valentina scooped Eva up into her arms. "We were looking everywhere for you. I'm so glad you're safe."

"Teller. I'm sorry. I thought we would only be gone for no more than an hour. Eva was doing so well and time got away from me ..." Elijah tried to explain.

Teller's face had been stern but it softened as he nodded to Elijah.

Valentina had put Eva down. Eva was telling her grandmother about her amazing day and all she had learned.

"Eva." Teller's voice boomed.

Eva shut her mouth and put her chin to her chest.

"I don't care how much fun you had. You *must* tell us where you're going and who you're with at all times," Teller said.

Eva was most likely too frightened to move, let alone speak, which was for the better.

Teller knelt down on one knee. "Eva. Look at me. While you were having a great time, do you know what we were doing?"

No response.

"Eva?"

She forced her head up and did the only thing her body would allow her to do, she shook her head no.

"We were terrified. We thought something bad had happened to you. We asked everyone where you were. We searched the perimeter of the camp and finally caught your scent and tracked you here. While you were having a blast we were going through hell. We thought we lost you."

This haranguing made Elijah feel terrible. He could only imagine how the tiny girl felt.

Eva sobbed as she clung to Valentina's leg. They waited patiently for the girl's crying to slow. It was all Valentina could do not to hold her and tell her that everything was fine. This was a lesson Eva needed to learn.

"Next time you want to go running off what will you do?" Valentina asked.

"I ... I'll let ... you know ..." the girl managed in between hiccups.

"That's my girl." Valentina hugged her granddaughter tight.

Elijah touched Valentina's arm to get her attention. He spoke quickly and quietly, "This is my fault. I should've told you. I'm terribly sorry." He doubted Eva could hear him.

Valentina gave him a warm smile. This was good for her daughter. Now that she knew her granddaughter was safe, Valentina was pleased with this turn of events — Eva and Elijah bonding was good for the family. Valentina headed for the safety of the tunnels with her precious bundle in her arms.

CHAPTER 64 SOUTH AMERICA 2034 AD

That evening while the last meal of the day was being prepared for the humans, Eva joined Elijah by the campfire. "Thank you for teaching me to ride."

"I'm sorry I got you in trouble."

"It was worth it."

Eva's smile reminded Elijah of Val. An intense longing consumed him. "Well, next time we'll go about it the right way."

The girl nodded in agreement. "It's hard you know. My sister is so confident. She steals all the attention. I didn't think anyone would even notice that I was gone. Vera is so … perfect. Everyone instantly loves her, but me …"

"Well, I think you're perfect." Elijah gave her a gentle nudge with his shoulder. "Besides you're a natural with horses."

"Do you really think so?"

"I know so."

Eva leaned against Elijah's shoulder.

~

FROM THE SHADOWS of the tall tropical trees Val watched, in disbelief, as her most delicate flower seemed to be getting along well with her husband, if he was still indeed her husband. Her stomach heaved at this thought. *What on earth happened while I was away?* Then she looked to Elda at her side. *Well, it's not any more unbelievable than this. A lot can change in a short amount of time.*

"I can't just go marching into your camp. They'll rip me apart." Elda said this as if being ripped apart was fine with her.

Val nodded.

They found a large tree not far off. Elda was to wait high up in it with Silvia, well, with Silvia's petrified body. When Val entered the camp she was greeted by her daughters, her mother and Mari. They all expressed their relief at her safe return.

Once the excitement died down she pulled her mother aside. "There's something I have to show you." Val took her mother's sword from its sheath and leaned it against a tree.

"What are you doing?"

"I don't want you to ... act impulsively."

"I'm not impulsive."

"Not usually but ... this is a very delicate situation ... come, you will see."

She led her mother out of camp. Val glanced back. *Hopefully no one will follow* us. Val needed time to figure out what to do next.

THE INSTANT VALENTINA saw Elda perched on a branch high in a tree, she reached for her sword and Val was glad she had disarmed her.

"You led her to us?"

"Mom, please, if anyone can understand, it's you. Elda may be the only one who can help us."

Valentina studied Elda.

"Mom, you don't have to trust her but please trust me."

Valentina looked deep into her daughter's eyes and took a deep breath. But then someone called Val's name. It was a familiar voice and Val normally would have been overjoyed that he was looking for her. Her heart jumped as she turned to face Elijah. He landed gracefully on the branch next to her.

Val stepped between Elda and Elijah in hopes of obscuring his sight.

"Elijah!" Val said with alarm.

"What's going on?"

"I needed to sort something out with my mom. What can I do for you?" This came out too harsh for a possible reunion or what Val hoped would be a reunion.

Elijah was taken aback for a moment at Val's odd behavior. "I'm glad you're back. I was beginning to worry about you and I was hoping we could talk ... alone."

"Elijah, I would love to but ..." She stepped forward in a flash and took his sword from its sheath.

"What are you doing?"

"First there is someone you should meet."

"Without my sword?"

"Yes, without your sword. We need her alive." Val stepped aside to reveal Elda sitting on the tree branch with her friend's lifeless body draped over her lap.

"Is that who I think it is?"

"Yes; Elda."

Elijah lunged for his sword in Val's hand and she barely kept it out of his reach by tossing it out of the tree.

"What are you doing?" he roared.

Val stepped close to him and took his hands. He ripped them away. She stepped in closer until their bodies touched. "Please, Elijah. She's here to help. She's our only hope. Together we may be able to stop John."

"What did you say — John?"

Val nodded. "I'm so sorry Elijah. John has been helping our enemies for a long time and now he has overthrown Elda."

Elijah wavered and placed his arm on Val's shoulder to steady himself. "No."

Val's heart ached for Elijah. For the majority of Elijah's boyhood he had been raised by John; John had always been by his side.

Elijah flashed back to shortly after the war, when his father was killed. John had knelt before Elijah and declared, "I proudly served your father for many years. Now it will be an honor to be your faithful servant, My Lord." Elijah's face quickly changed from shock and sorrow as it hardened in realization. He turned on Elda. "How long did John help you?" but he did not give her time to answer. "He was the one who told Ramdasha that my father would be in the rear of the army in the battle of 1551?"

"Yes, My King." Elda spoke softly and slowly moved to kneel. "John worked with ... us for a number of years leading up to the great vampire war. I'll tell you everything, My Lord."

Elijah stepped forward, as did Val. But he stopped and clenched his hands into fists, as if it was the only thing he could do to keep himself from wrapping them around Elda's tiny neck. "Like what? What use can you be to us?"

"There's another turncoat amongst your ranks."

Val had been intent on Elijah, making sure she could intercept him if he attacked Elda. But now she turned to Elda with wide eyes.

"What?" Valentina asked.

"Who?" Elijah demanded.

"I don't know. It was only recently that he came to us — to John really. John protected him by keeping the spy's identity a secret. John claimed to hear from him only on rare occasions, as he was deep in your ranks — close to you. The last time John met with him the informant told John you were in the Amazon but would not say where exactly. John has had scouts searching the jungle skies at night for you. I assumed it was a protection spell that kept them from finding you."

"You don't know the name or the identity of the traitor."

Elda shook her head no.

"She's of use to us — as long as she's alive," Val cautioned.

Valentina had been standing back to see what would happen. "Elijah, she can be locked up until we're sure we can trust her. She is clearly not an immediate threat. There's no fight left in her."

"Very well, lock her up. Valentina, retrieve some shackles." But Valentina was not a soldier Elijah could command so he added, "Please."

Valentina nodded and took flight.

"Elijah, may I have your word that she will not be harmed?" Val asked.

"There will be no need to harm her, as long as she cooperates."

"In exchange for her help, I offered to revive her friend." Val pointed to Silvia.

Elijah furrowed his brow. "What does it take to bring a vampire back from this state?"

"Nine or ten pints of blood," Val said.

"That's a lot of blood. We shouldn't be so liberal with our rations."

"Please, Elijah. I gave her my word."

"You want to use our dwindling blood supply to bring back one of our enemies from the dead or whatever you call that." Elijah pointed to Silvia.

"Silvia has learned the art of magic over the centuries. She has become very powerful. She can help us to defeat John," Elda pled.

"The fact that she's powerful does not make me want to revive her."

"Lock them up. Do what you must. But please give Elda a chance to prove herself to us."

Elijah studied Val and then Elda and finally gave the slightest of nods.

"Thank you." Val wanted to throw her arms around him and bury her head in his chest but she refrained.

They covered Elda in a hooded cloak. She willingly let Elijah bind her arms behind her back. They wrapped Silvia in a blanket and Val carried her. They discreetly made their way into the tunnels.

Once locked in a cell with solid rock walls and thick steel bars for a door, Elda told them of how John took over and how she used to have visions of the chosen ones. "They're the key to restoring the balance and overthrowing John," Elda ended.

"What does that mean?" Val asked.

"That's what I'm going to help you figure out," Elda said.

Elijah leaned against an adjacent wall with his arms crossed. Val could tell he was barely listening to Elda. The storm raged in his steel-grey eyes. "How could John do this to me?"

Elda pursed her thick lips in concentration. "Let's see, when John first came to us in the sixteenth century, he said —

Elijah flinched. "He has been working with you for that long?"

"Are you sure you're ready to hear this?" Elda asked.

Elijah nodded. "Continue."

"Well, essentially he was bored. He said life was the same thing, day and night. He wanted change, if for no other reason than to see what would happen. He thought for sure, as we all did, that the Court would fall in the great vampire war. Him divulging your plans would give us the ability to win — so we thought. Most likely he had two motives. He wanted to be on the winning side, so no matter which side won he would still come out on top," Elda paused.

"I see now that his second motive was to become the supreme ruler of the vampire world. Over the years he often complained about how the Court was too powerful. He didn't know how to defeat you. Vampires loved their queen and king and were faithful to you. So you proved to be much more difficult to overthrow. Yet, it's clear that his plan all along was to take control. He didn't want to be in your shadow any more — or mine, for that matter. I have a feeling that he worked hard this past decade to turn my men against me."

Elijah looked tired. He nodded slightly and walked out of the small room which held the cell in the back.

"Elijah, I'm sorry," Val said to his back. Val was not as heartbroken as Elijah. John had never been among her favorites. But he and Elijah had been very close. Val was angry about the betrayal and now even more indignant because of the pain it caused Elijah.

CHAPTER 65 SOUTH AMERICA 2034 AD

The camp was abuzz at the news of Elda's capture. It took several times for Elijah to get it through to everyone that their hiding was not over and that John had taken her place and was still very much in charge. "It's still not safe to leave the tunnels," Elijah yelled over the loud humans for the fifth time.

Val guarded Elda's cell and listened to the crowd outside. "I'm glad you're in there, for your safety. It'll make it harder for an angry mob to get to you."

Elda did not answer as she most likely didn't care if an angry mob was able to reach her or not.

Val slid down the outside of the bars and sat staring intently at the door leading to the tunnel and the sound of the chaos.

"You gonna' just sit there?" Elda asked.

"Yep." Val replied. There was no reply but Val could feel Elda's stare so she turned to look at her through the bars.

Elda's large downturned lips mouthed, "Thank you."

The sound of someone running in their direction caused Val to jump to her feet and draw her sword.

Teller slowed and held up his hands indicating that he had only his phone on him. "Is it true? Did you capture Neacsa?"

"'Capture' isn't the right word. She came willingly. Elijah locked her up."

"Thank God she's here! For the past couple of nights, maybe even a week, Sergiu has been telling me … in my dreams…" Teller clarified, "that Neacsa is the only one who can help us. I was overwhelmed with the idea of trying to find her and now I don't have to."

Teller approached the cell and Val raised her sword again.

"Vallachia, I mean her no harm. I know as well as you do, that we need her alive if we're going to save our daughters."

"Save our daughters? I thought this was about restoring the world or at least defeating John," Val said.

"Our daughters are the key to accomplishing that," Teller said. "The two are connected. Our daughters must be the chosen ones. That's the only explanation for their miracle birth. Don't you see, they're the only ones who can fix this world?" Teller slid his finger across his phone to open it. "According to this …" he held up the image of the lost scroll to Val. "Well, you need to read it for yourself. It can help us piece everything together … I hope."

Val took the phone. She thought the text was Arabic at first but she could not make out most of the words. Next she tried Hebrew but it did not help; then again these were not her strongest languages. This was an ancient language, one that was no longer used. "Aramaic?" she guessed.

Elda had turned her back on Teller but she could not help but turn in interest at what was on the phone. "Aramaic, the language of Jesus. I have studied many ancient languages, including that one."

"I've never learned it," Val admitted. "What does it say?"

Teller took the phone from Val and held it out to Elda through the bars.

She quickly turned her back on him again, refusing to take the phone.

"Neacsa, please, read it. Perhaps you can help us figure out why it was so important that a dear friend bothered to contact me from beyond the grave to tell me where it was hidden."

"My name is Elda," she snapped.

"There's the fire I remember."

"I won't help you."

Teller put his forehead against the bars. "Elda, I'm very sorry for who I was back then and everything that I did to you. I was young and selfish and cruel —

"You were far from young. You were, what a couple hundred years old?"

"Yes, well I'm a slow learner. But now I'm like you."

She snorted.

"We're alike because I too have lost the people closest to me. I lost my dearest friend and I lost my chance to be with Vallachia. Now I fear my daughters are in trouble. Every day I pay the price for my past. Just as you're paying for your actions."

Elda's tense shoulders fell a bit.

"Do you remember why I spared you back in 1456?"

She didn't answer.

"I told you that you were smart and full of life. That you weren't like other girls I'd met. That's all true. Your strength is admirable."

"You didn't spare my father."

"What can I do to make it up to you?"

Elda didn't hesitate. "Give me Silvia back."

"I'll break into the blood bank myself if I have to."

"And I'll help," Val added. "We'll return Silvia to you."

Elda snatched the phone from Teller. Her lips parted in awe. "Where did you find this?"

"I was led to it by Sergiu. It was preserved in a Middle Eastern desert."

"He spoke to you from the other side." Elda sounded envious. She began reading aloud and Val listened carefully. …

AN ANGEL APPEARED before Mary of Nazareth. The Angel told Mary of the miracle that was to come. "The Great Mother and Father have chosen you to bear and raise their child. This child will be special. He will do many great things." The angel waved her hand over Mary's stomach. A bright light flashed. The angel kissed Mary's forehead before vanishing.

MUCH OF THE story was familiar, Joseph married the pregnant Mary of Nazareth and they journeyed to Bethlehem, where Baby Jesus was born in a manger.

Teller often argued with Elda over the exact meaning or connotation of some of the words. They were like an old married couple, the way they snapped harmlessly at one another. Technically they were an old married couple.

"When the twelve apostles joined in the ... final meal..." Elda struggled for the correct words.

"It's the 'last supper'. The text is referring to Jesus's last supper — the one in the Bible. You know, the night before he was sacrificed —

"I know that! And that's what I said," Elda sneered.

"It's not 'the final meal'. No one calls it that."

"I'm tired of you correcting me." Elda threw the phone at Teller's head. "You read it."

Teller snatched the phone out of the air. He began reading more smoothly than Elda had. ...

JESUS PLACED a knife to his hand and cut it open so that blood flowed from him. He let his blood fill a silver chalice. "This chalice contains the new covenant in my blood."

Before they drank, each apostle individually recited, "The precious blood of our Lord Jesus Christ, preserve my body and soul unto everlasting life."

The twelve apostles drank of the blood of everlasting life. Mary of Magdala and Mary of Nazareth chose to drink only the wine that their beloved husband and son had made for them. They chose to remain mortal. They did not want to stay on this earth forever without Jesus. They dreamed of the day they would be reunited with the Great Mother, Father and Son — the Holy Trinity.

Jesus addressed his faithful followers, "I have been sent here to accomplish two tasks. My Mother and Father wish for me to die for the sins of mortals. This I will fulfill tomorrow. Yet my beloved parents sent me here to carry out one other task. Now that you have drunk my blood, my second purpose has been fulfilled. From this day forward you will be the most powerful creatures in existence. It will be your job to maintain the balance across these lands. There will come a time when humans have overrun this earth. They will destroy the land if there is no one who can stop them. When humans grow too many and resources grow too few, you will know that it is your time to act. Until then you are to remain a secret. You are given the gift of eternal life by the Great Mother and Father of us all. They have sent me here to create you — the first upyrs to walk the earth.

Val's mouth hung open. "Upyrs? You mean the first vampires?"

Teller nodded in confirmation.

CHAPTER 66 SOUTH AMERICA 2034 AD

Teller waited patiently for the two women to process all that they had heard.

Val looked at Teller with wide eyes and then turned to Elda. After a long silence the two women broke out into an explosion of excitement.

"Vampires are divine!" Elda exclaimed.

"It simply can't be." Val said.

"This confirms it. I knew it! We are the Great Mother's creation. She loves us." Elda was almost in tears.

Val narrowed her eyes at Elda. "We couldn't have come from the blood of Jesus! We are demons …"

"You see, as soon as you tried to say it you knew it was wrong. You and all the good you have done for people, you aren't a demon. You're a creation of the Gods, the Great Mother and Father. All vampires are."

Val sat silently with wide eyes, trying to see the truth. All those years, centuries even, searching for information like this and now she wished she'd never heard these insane words.

Teller spoke softly which was in contrast to the excited women. "Val, it's true."

"You believe this — this scroll from who knows where?" Val spat.

"I do."

"How are you so sure?"

"Sergiu told me. He was there."

"There? You mean at the last supper?"

Teller nodded. "Sergiu's given name was Peter."

Val's mouth fell open again. "He told you this?"

"Peter, as in the most prominent of the apostles?" Elda asked.

Teller nodded. "All of the original vampire apostles changed their names to protect their identity. Vallachia, this all makes sense. Sergiu's scroll confirms what other texts have found. The text of Nag Hammadi was buried in the desert as well and it states that Jesus used to kiss Mary Magdalene. They could have been married. The church destroyed many scrolls; keeping only the ones that fit their needs. However, there are scrolls that have survived. Like the text of Nag Hammadi and the Dead Sea Scrolls, this scroll also would have been destroyed, if it hadn't been hidden away."

Val glared at Teller, not buying it.

"Aaron tested the parchment for me. He found that it dates back to just after the time of Jesus, sometime between 100 and 300 A.D.," Teller said.

"This is amazing!" Elda said. "Early Christian texts were destroyed in order to write women out of religion. And now it appears texts were destroyed to write vampires off as well. It has always infuriated me that before Christianity there were powerful Goddesses and High Priestesses. Christianity worked hard to destroy the Goddess. They eliminated the Great Mother, reducing her to a ghost. The 'Holy Ghost', because they killed her!" Elda's breath was rapid.

"So you believe that it is not the Father, the Son and the Holy Ghost, but rather the Father, the Mother and the Son who make up the Holy Trinity?" Val asked.

"Of course," Elda said. "Let me ask you this. If we didn't come from The Holy Trinity then where did vampires come from? Satan? You don't truly believe that?"

"I have met some vampires who were highly likely to be doing Satan's work," Val said.

"And some humans are psychopaths; so what?" Elda argued.

"Where are these original vampires?" Val asked.

"A few are still alive but many have been killed over the years, according to Sergiu. Sergiu had a love for vampires. He helped them. He understood that we're here by God's ..." Teller glanced at Elda, "and the Goddess's will."

Val narrowed her eyes. "So you mean to tell me that what Elda did was the work of God? That this apocalypse was Gods' will?"

"Yes. You see, the Mother and Father only protect the balance. Vampires were created to maintain that balance — to make sure that human populations remain sustainable. We're the only natural predators of humans. We were to keep our identity a secret until humans overran the earth, then it was our job to reset the balance. This is why Sergiu did not warn me before the attacks on Europe and the Court, as it was time for vampires to rise. He's helping me now because it's time to let humans rebuild."

Elda's breathing was still heavy. "My life's work — it was not a waste."

"Then who's going to stop vampires? This world can't be the one the Great Mother wanted for humans or vampires." Val's cheeks grew red.

"You're right, it's not. Vampires have ruined the earth in just thirteen short years. Now both humans and vampires are suffering. So the reign of the vampires needs to end. Once again, balance must be restored," Teller said.

"How do you know this?" Val asked.

"Because Sergiu told me."

"Enough!" Val held up her hand. "I've heard all I can stand." She headed for the exit. She needed to do some serious meditating to sort this all out. Her heart would tell her the truth, even if she did not want to hear it. But the sound of a body hitting the floor, caused Val to spin around. Elda lay limp on the floor.

"Elda!" she yelled. She ran to the bars and shook them. "Open the door!"

Teller was already heading for the keys hanging on the adjacent wall.

Val quickly undid the protection spell. Teller unlocked the door. Val propped Elda up in her lap. "Her heart is still beating."

Teller locked them all in the cell.

"What are you doing?"

He straightened out on the empty cot, Elda's cot. "There's nothing to do but wait for her to wake. We still need to figure out what to do next and Elda is the only one who can help."

After a long silence Val ventured, "It's our children isn't it? They're the key to restoring the balance."

"I'm afraid so."

A tear ran down Val's cheek. "So this text of yours implies that our girls must sacrifice themselves as Jesus did?"

"I hope not but, quite frankly, I'm terrified that it does."

Perhaps an hour had passed before Elijah could free himself from all the questions about Elda. He entered the small room that contained the cell, only to find Val and Teller locked up with an unconscious Elda. "What is going on?"

Val sighed. "It's a long ... long story."

CHAPTER 67 SOUTH AMERICA 2034 AD

Elda woke with a start and Elijah ran to the bars.

"Don't worry. She won't hurt us," Val said.

Elda shook her head and rubbed it. "It's back," she whispered.

"What's back?"

"My sight. Only ... now it includes memories, ones I have long since forgotten."

Val helped her to sit up.

"There was an angel; she visited me one night when I was a small girl. She told me that one day, when the time was right, I would have to use the Curse of the Powerful to set the world right once again."

"The Curse of the Powerful?" Teller repeated.

Elda jumped to her feet and Elijah drew his sword.

"It's okay," Val said.

"I see it now. I know what I have to do. The Curse of the Powerful is one of the many spells and incantations in my grimoire."

"You mean you don't know it by heart?" Teller said.

"The more powerful the magic the more complicated. No one could possibly memorize them all. Plus I never imagined a time when I would use such a curse."

"Why?" Teller asked.

"Because it's deadly to vampires. I had completely forgotten about it. Many centuries ago when I came across it for the first time I almost ripped it out of my grimoire and burned the pages. Thankfully I didn't. I wanted vampires to rule the world, not be destroyed. So I pushed the terrible curse out of my mind."

"Where's this grimoire?" Val asked with dread.

"In a vault far beneath Pikes Peak."

"Shit," Teller said.

"Never fear." Elda glared at Teller. "I have a Precious Possession spell on it. I can summon it to me."

"Great. Then do it," Teller demanded.

Elda narrowed her eyes even more. "You don't know much about magic do you? The next full moon … which is in about two weeks … Yes, that will work. I can perform the Precious Possession spell at that time and retrieve my grimoire. The full moon should give me enough strength. Oh and I will also need her." Elda pointed to Silvia, who was spread out on the adjacent cot.

Val nodded. "This retrieval spell, is it good magic or dark magic?"

"Everyone here is so new at this. There's no such thing as good or evil magic. There is only magic and it can be used for just purposes or evil ones. Intent is everything."

Val's eyes widened. This was exactly what her mother believed.

"What nonsense is she speaking?" Elijah demanded.

Val took Elijah's hand through the bars. "I will tell you everything, I promise but now we need enough blood to bring Silvia back. Please give it to us."

Elijah studied Val for a moment. "How much do you need?"

"A humans worth."

"That's over eight pints."

"Better make it ten to be sure," Val said.

"That's a lot of blood."

"Please, Elijah."

"I can't believe I'm doing this," Elijah muttered. He turned to the key hanger. "Where in the hell are the bloody keys?"

Teller jingled them in the air.

"Then you can let yourselves out." He stopped abruptly. "But not her." he pointed to Elda. "She is to remain in custody."

Val nodded. "Of course." She wanted Elda in here for her own safety.

~

ELIJAH PASSED PINT AFTER PINT of blood through the bars of the cell door. Val helped Elda pour each bag down Silvia's throat. They watched as life flowed back into the mummy. Her cheeks filled out and her dry skin slowly became a silky pale color. By the sixth pint Silvia devoured the blood herself. In no time, Elda embraced Silvia, as tears of joy ran down her face.

"Let's give them some time." Val said as she put her arm in Teller's. It was a habit from her youth.

Val resealed the cell with a protection spell once she and Teller were out and Elda and Silvia were locked safely inside.

"Go." Teller nodded to Elijah. "You two need to talk. I'll keep watch to make sure no one hurts them."

~

VAL FOLLOWED Elijah through the tunnels.

"We'll need to call a meeting," Val said. "Everyone needs to hear this ... story of Teller's. I would rather do it all at once. I can't stomach repeating it fifty times. Besides I don't know how I feel about it. We have time. It appears there's nothing we can do until the next full moon anyway."

Elijah nodded. "Then there is no hurry and I need to talk to you ... about well ... that Eva, she's really something."

Val smiled. "I know."

Once in Elijah's room she waited for him to go on; he obviously had more to say. She prayed that it was that he loved her and wanted her back.

"I wanted you to know that I would have done the same thing."

Val tilted her head in confusion.

Elijah sighed. "This is difficult for me to say but I understand why you disappeared. If I had been blessed with a daughter like Eva, I would have done what I thought was best to protect her — at any cost. Val … I'm sorry. Can you forgive me?"

Thank you Eva! If anyone could win Elijah over, of course it would be her. Val wrapped her arms around Elijah's neck. "No."

Elijah pulled away. "No, you can't forgive me?"

"I mean, no, you should not be the one who is sorry. I'm sorry that you were hurt because of this whole mess. I'm glad you understand why I had to stay away. I never stopped loving you. I never stopped needing you. It was hell to be away. But I would do anything for my wonderful daughters."

Elijah knew her well. She was genuine, sincere, she always had been and he could feel how much she loved him. He pulled her closer and gently pushed her long hair back from her neck. She buried her head in his chest for comfort as she had always done.

Elijah lifted her chin with his index finger so he could kiss her. She exhaled in relief.

"Please don't hurt me again. You drive me insane and you may push me over the edge next time. I fear that I may become like my father. I'm choosing to trust you."

"You have my word," Val whispered. Tears of joy ran down her face.

The sight of her perfect face and her bright blue eyes made his heart ache for her. He knew he had made the right decision. She was his and only his.

"I have something for you." Elijah moved to retrieve the wooden box that he had stashed away.

Val slowly opened the beautifully carved box to reveal her father's hand-carved patriarchal cross. "You were able to save it?"

"I went back for it before we came here."

"Thank you." She gave him a hug. She felt whole again with Elijah back in her life and now this little piece of her father. It was the only thing she had left of him. She held the cross to her chest. All that had happened, all that had changed, her world had been turned upside down by finding Elda and learning about Teller's mysterious manuscript. All she knew and held dear was being threatened. Now Elijah was forgiving her. It was too much. She felt overwhelmingly tired. She curled up on his bed.

~

VAL WOKE to Elijah's handsome smile and she quickly wrapped her arms around him. She needed him to look at her like that. She was grateful that the love was back in his eyes. Then she remembered the cross. She felt around for it.

"Don't worry. I put it back in the box for safekeeping," Elijah said.

Val grabbed his collar and pressed her lips to his. He fell on top of her as she wrapped her legs around him. She wanted to lose herself in him. She didn't want to think about where vampires came from or what a Curse of the Powerful looked like or who else was betraying them. Then there was the greatest concern, what all this meant for her daughters — the chosen ones. She could put her worries aside when she was in Elijah's arms. Together they would get through this. They always had.

CHAPTER 68 SOUTH AMERICA 2034 AD

Within a week a meeting was held, in which Val and Teller informed everyone about the scroll and what Elda had told them. This caused much debate and eventual arguing. Val offered no opinion. She didn't have all the information she needed to determine if vampires really came from the blood of Christ and maybe she never would. Ironically, she didn't even know if she cared, with everything else that was going on.

Val sneaked out of the meeting. She was no longer comfortable in crowds. Her quiet life with only a handful of females hidden away in an isolated volcano had spoiled her. She didn't like how loud the humans were or the cramped and dank tunnels. She longed for fresh mountain air.

Val headed for Elijah's room — well, their room. She wanted to see her father's cross — to hold it. It would help calm her. She ran her fingers over the wood that her wonderful father had carved in 1260 A.D. She could almost hear his words of comfort. She wasn't sure how long she stood there meditating with the cross in her hand.

When she placed the cross back in its protective box she heard a hollow thud. She picked the box up to examine it. It sounded as if there was a false floor — a hidden chamber in the bottom of it. She pushed on a notch that seemed out of place. She thought it might be a button that would open the secret compartment. Nothing happened. Finally, she waved her hand over the top. "Reveal what is hidden."

The bottom of the box popped open like a second lid, exposing a single piece of parchment.

~

ELIJAH ENTERED to find Val staring at the wall with a piece of paper in her hand. "Well that sure caused an uproar. Do you believe this nonsense about the twelve apostles being the first vampires?" When Val did not respond or even move he went to her side. "Val?"

"You knew my mother?" Vallachia's voice was flat. She did not think she had any more tears left.

Elijah shoulders sank. "Valentina didn't tell you?"

"No and it was not her job to tell me. You should have." She slammed the parchment into Elijah's chest and turned to leave.

"Val wait. I thought she was dead. You thought she was dead. I didn't think the past mattered."

Val rounded on him. "Well she's not dead! And it does matter. I was a fool. I thought it was a 'mysterious coincidence' that both my mother and I became vampires. But it was no coincidence, was it?"

Elijah shook his head no.

Val fled the room.

Elijah looked at the parchment — it was a love letter to Valentina — one that was never delivered.

Val searched the tunnels for her mother's scent. It eventually led her to the main entrance. She found her mother in the garden.

"I know, I should not be outside at this hour," Valentina said. "But I dearly miss the open night sky." When Val did not say anything she turned to find her even more pale than usual. "Darling, what's the matter?"

"You knew Lord Chastellain?"

Valentina sighed.

"No more vague answers Mother. I deserve to know."

"Unfortunately, yes, I did know him. And please don't call me 'Mother'."

"Did … did you love him?" Val asked with trepidation.

"Oh, goodness, no." She took a deep breath and patted the tree stump beside her, indicating for Val to sit.

"He turned you?"

Valentina nodded. "Not long after your brother Josiah was born, Chastellain came to town presenting himself as a wealthy merchant. He tried to court me. He was arrogant and thought he could impress me with his wealth.

"Sounds familiar," Val muttered.

"As you are aware, Lord Chastellain does not take no for an answer. Once it became apparent that I would not leave my beloved husband and family for him, he dragged me out of the house in the middle of the night and forced me to drink his blood."

Val only nodded, she could see it. Perhaps it was because it was similar to her experience.

"What did you do?"

"Like you, I ran. But unlike Elijah who let you go and only followed when he knew you needed help, Lord Chastellain hunted me. He would never let me be free of him so…I faked my death. The only way for me to be rid of that monster was to make him believe I was dead." Valentina smiled weakly. "I'm really quite proud of how I managed it. It took a lot of my own blood, so it would be the correct scent." Valentina showed her daughter a long thick scar on the underside of her forearm.

Val inhaled sharply through her teeth. "That had to hurt."

"My blood also led them to the corpse. I used a skinned and mostly burned bear carcass."

Val gave her mother a questioning glance.

"Yes, well I had learned that bears look like humans when they are skinned and hanging on a meat hook. I had to get rid of the head of course. The long snout would've given me away."

Val shivered. *She faked her death by cutting herself and decapitating a bear — which she apparently then skinned and burned. She must have been desperate to get away from Elijah's father.*

"Well, it worked. Lord Chastellain stopped looking for me."

"And so did father."

"My dear, you know how hard it is for a young vampire. It was best that everyone thought I was dead. I feared I would hurt someone I cared about and it was best for your father to have closure. He needed to think that I was dead rather than holding on to a false hope that I would return."

"And that's why you could never come back, even after you learned to control your thirst? And it's the reason you could not come to me after I was turned? Lord Chastellain needed to continue to believe that you were dead."

Valentina nodded. "What I said before was true as well. You didn't need me until now. As much as it hurt me to stay away, I knew our time together would come. I have cherished every moment with you."

Val looked up at the hundreds of stars that could be seen in the small opening between the trees.

"This is not Elijah's fault, my dear. He had nothing to do with it, except that he tried to reason with his unreasonable father."

Val nodded. "But he should have told me. You both should have."

"Honestly, I did not want to relive that terrible time. Losing my family, having to resort to extreme measures to escape. It was the most terrifying and depressing time of my life. I have never been as lonely as I was then. I've all but blocked it out to save my sanity." Valentina took a deep breath and exhaled the sorrow away.

"So all those times we took spring flowers to your grave it was a bear buried there?"

Valentina chuckled. "A bear has never been so mourned by people before."

"No wonder Father never told us the details of your death. He thought you had been decapitated, skinned and burned." Val shivered. "Thank you for telling me the truth. I know it was difficult for you." Val headed back into the tunnels. She paced aimlessly for a time and checked on Elda and Silvia; they were safe and happy to be reunited. The girls were fast asleep in Teller's room. With nothing left to do she headed to Elijah's room.

CHAPTER 69 SOUTH AMERICA 2034 AD

Elijah sat at his desk and smiled when Val came in. She curled up on his bed with her back to him. He gently moved to the bed.

"Father loved Valentina very much," he whispered.

"Apparently to the point of obsession."

"Father was convinced that Valentina was meant to be with him. Her 'death' changed him — made him crueler. He never loved again. Vampires appear to be monogamous with their mate. We can take a long time to choose our mates and we don't leave them once we find them."

"What's your point?"

"One thing I've learned these past couple of years is that if you're out of my life I would never love again and I would become like my father."

Val stopped staring at the wall to look at Elijah. One look into his stormy eyes and she knew it was true and that she could not live without him either. They were indeed mated for life.

"Relationships are work and we were lucky. For many centuries we did not have to work hard at our marriage. It's okay that we're now having to fight for our relationship," Elijah said.

Val issued a weak smile. "We had it good for a long time didn't we? Is there anything else I need to know about the past?"

"No, we didn't know your family before Valentina."

"No more secrets?"

"I promise."

"Why was the letter in that box?"

"The box was my father's. I wanted to keep something of his. I thought it was fitting that your father's cross be stored in something that belonged to my father."

Val frowned. "It's ironic. They both loved the same woman and neither one could have her."

"Valentina belonged to your father. She loved Adam and only wanted him. I tried to convince father of this and that he needed to leave her alone. But you know how well he listened to me."

Val snorted. Lord Chastellain was never one to do much listening. She rolled over turning her back on him once again.

"What is it you need me to say?"

"I need to hear that you're sorry and that you realize you should have told me about this back in 1260."

"I am truly sorry. I should have told you sooner. I had plans to tell you after Valentina rescued me from Elda and I learned she was alive but I didn't have a chance, as you ran away. Life has been insane since your return — you introduced me to your children, then ran off only to lead our enemy right into our camp. Not to mention this mysterious scroll that … well, who knows what that's all about? I've been rather distracted. There has not been any time to worry about something that happened almost eight hundred years ago."

Val turned enough to glare at him. "That's a lot of excuses."

"Very well, I'm sorry, I should have told you about your mother when you were first turned into a vampire."

"Thank you. Now I can forgive you." She sat up and put her arms around his neck. "We belong to each other — for life."

Elijah laughed. "You're only now figuring that out?"

Val pressed her lips to his. She would never take Elijah for granted again. She hoped they were done fighting for a long time. With all they had been through, they could overcome any obstacle and always find their way back to each other. She pulled him down on top of her.

Elijah's hands made their way to her breasts when they heard company coming.

Eva and Vera entered the room full of energy.

"Look at what Aunty Mari did to our hair," Vera exclaimed.

Val and Elijah were siting innocently apart from one another on the bed. Val gasped, "Forget your hair! What did she do to your faces?"

Mari entered with her chin held high. "Don't they look lovely?"

"Lovely! They look like harlots," Elijah said.

The girls had bright red lips, red cheeks and their eyelids had been painted with purple eye shadow. Their hair was curled in tight golden ringlets.

"What's a harlot?" Eva asked.

"Never mind that." Val shuffled the girls to the washbasin. "Get that junk off your faces."

"But Mom!" Vera whined.

"Listen to your mother, girls. The makeup looks terrible," Elijah said.

"Well, you two know how to ruin the fun," Mari pouted.

"Their hair does look lovely, though." Val smiled at Mari.

CHAPTER 70 SOUTH AMERICA 2034 AD

On the night of the full moon Silvia and Elda were escorted out of the tunnels to perform the spell that would retrieve Elda's grimoire. It was rather simple or they made it appear so. Elda held a crystal in each palm and Silvia placed her hands over the tops of the crystals. They chanted in an unfamiliar language. It only took a couple minutes before a large leather-bound book appeared at their feet. Elda smiled down at the book, as if greeting a long lost friend. Back in her cell, she went straight to work.

Val, Elijah, Teller and Valentina waited patiently.

Marcel approached.

"What's on your mind?" Elijah had to ask because Marcel seemed nervous. It was as if he wanted to say something but was afraid to.

"I've been thinking, you know, about the scroll and all. I know I'm not as old or intelligent as you but I thought it might be helpful to have a human's perspective on this matter. I don't know if other people feel the way I do but ..."

"It's okay. We want to hear what you have to say," Val encouraged.

"Yes, out with it already," Teller said.

"I'm sorry. You're so ... I mean, the King and Queen of Vampires and Dracula — wow," Marcel said.

Teller rolled his eyes.

"You're intimidating. I mean what could I possibly say that you don't already know?" Marcel continued.

"Don't be intimidated. What is it?" Elijah asked.

"Okay, when I lived with my mother in Natal, I hated the city — the littered streets, the polluted air. I was surrounded by people and yet felt alone. They were all strangers. There was no sense of community. I remember hearing on the news that they ran out of room in the landfill, so they started dumping the trash in the ocean. City officials decided that this was a bad thing, so they approved to clear-cut more of the forest for a new landfill site. It's crazy, they cut down thousands of trees just to have a place to toss all our shit. Sorry — it still infuriates me."

"What's your point, Marcel?" Teller asked.

"Well, I came back to live with my family here because this makes sense to me. We live simply. We use everything, nothing is wasted or thrown away that is not biodegradable. My people live as one with the earth. We respect each other and the forest which provides all we need."

"And?" Elijah prompted.

"Okay. The point is, ever since your kind took over the world I can't help but think that it's for the best. Humans are no longer screwing up the world."

"So you, as a human, agree that vampires should keep people in prisons and feed off them?" Elijah asked.

"Well, not exactly. I … I'm just saying I can understand the whole 'balance of nature' thing. Human life as it was … was not sustainable. Something needed to stop us before it was too late."

"Wow, even the human agrees that vampires should rule the world," Silvia said.

"Here, the Curse of the Powerful." Elda interrupted. She had been focused on her grimoire and had heard very little of the conversation. She read quickly for a moment, then added, "There are different types of sacrifices. It depends on the spell; some require blood, alone. That is a blood sacrifice, of course. That would be preferred, as we would only need to draw blood from your daughters and use it to create the spell or in this case a curse. I was hoping for this type of sacrifice. But, as I had feared, a powerful curse like this requires a full sacrifice. That is the first bit of bad news. It clearly states that it will take a bloodletting and then the death of the chosen ones."

Val and Teller exchanged a desperate glance.

There was no need for Elda to explain further but apparently Elda felt the need to elaborate. "This type of sacrifice requires the blood and the life, like Jesus bleeding to death on the cross."

"We get it!" Val snapped. She put her face in her hands to keep herself from falling apart.

Elijah rubbed her back.

"There are a couple other things to note. The grimoire uses the term saviors, so it is plural. In case you were thinking that only one has to die. It appears they both must be sacrificed —

"No. We were not thinking about which one has to die and which one gets to live," Teller spat.

Elda was oblivious to Val and Teller's troubled reactions. She was alight with the excitement of magic and solving the mystery. "There's one more bit of bad news."

"How could it get any worse?" Valentina muttered.

"The curse, once unleashed, will issue a plague. The plague will spread across the earth killing all vampires it touches. It will not discriminate against the good or the bad. However, there is good news —

"What could possibly be good about this?" Val glared at Elda.

"Like Jesus, the saviors will be resurrected."

Val knew nothing of this grimoire but she did know the Bible inside and out. "Resurrected! And we are supposed to be happy about that? The Bible is vague about how Jesus came back to life and in what form. In some accounts he is an apparition. In others he comes back in the flesh. In none of the accounts does he appear to stay for long before he disappears again." Val was on the verge of a breakdown.

Teller looked at Elda. "You appear to know a lot about this sort of thing. How do you know so much about sacrifices and curses?"

"I've studied … a lot. You could say I'm an expert. I raised the dead in order to take over the world, didn't I?" There was no pride in her voice. Elda was only stating a fact.

So Val could not be mad at her, though she would have loved to vent her growing desperation and anger on someone.

"This all makes sense!" Elda's honey eyes shined bright. "The scroll that Vlad found filled in the missing information —

"Teller! I go by Teller."

"Whatever. Jesus's blood created the first vampires and vampires helped to keep human populations under control, with plagues throughout history and by being the only predators of humans. Yet we still reached a time when humans overpopulated the earth and the world was being destroyed. This is why vampires exist. They have done their job — a bit too well and now the balance is upset once again. Vampires are too strong and neither species can survive like this. Eva and Vera were miracle births, like Jesus. They must have been born for this. Now vampires have overrun the earth and the girls' purpose is to reset the balance by destroying vampires."

"The Great Mother only protects the delicate balance," Valentina recited.

Val's mouth fell open and she turned to glare at her mother. Valentina actually believed what Elda was saying.

"She appears to know what she's talking about." Teller's arms were crossed and his brow was furrowed in deep thought.

Val shook her head in refusal. "No. No and no." She looked to Valentina, then Teller, then Elda, each in turn. "No one will hurt my girls. Their sole purpose in life is not to be sacrificial lambs. They will not be killed only to be resurrected to find all of their family dead, due to a plague that they released. We kill them, so they kill us. None of this makes sense. There's nothing good about any of this! You're all crazy for even entertaining this nonsense!" Val was yelling by the time she finished.

"The Great Mother loaned us these two marvels. But She wants them back." A tear ran down Valentina's cheek.

Val lunged at her mother. She would have thrown Valentina

against the wall but Elijah and Teller each held one of her arms. Which only infuriated Val more. It was a good thing she did not have her sword on her or someone would have lost a head.

Elda reached through the bars and gently placed her hand on Val's arm.

The gesture surprised Val, which worked to distract her from her fury.

"I will find another way. Your daughters will not be sacrificed."

Val's lips quivered. "You will?"

"You have my word. I will not rest until I find another way to enact the curse."

"But this curse will kill *all* vampires," Elijah reminded them of the second problem they faced.

"That's the easy one to get around. You see, it says here," Elda pointed to the text, "'the curse will kill all vampires it touches.' This tunnel alone will most likely be enough to protect us from the 'touch' of the plague. Our basic protection spell will also work to stop it. So we will be doubly safe if we stay inside the spelled tunnels."

"Does that book of yours say how long the plague will last?" Elijah asked.

"Forty days and forty nights."

"Of course." Teller sighed at yet another Biblical reference.

"So we'll have to stay sealed in here for forty days?" Elijah asked.

"And forty nights," Elda confirmed. "The curse will not affect humans, so they will be free to leave. No vampires will be able to hurt them once the ritual has been completed. We must make sure we have enough blood to last that long," Elda said.

"Then we can all be free," Elijah said.

"Great. Then all we have to do is find a way *not* to kill my daughters." Val said through gritted teeth.

"We will." Elda reached for Val's hand.

Val swiftly seized a knife from Elijah's belt and slashed Elda's hand open. Then she did the same thing to herself. This happened in the blink of an eye and in one swift motion. Val wrapped her fingers around Elda's — pressing their bleeding wounds together. "Promise on your blood."

"No!" Silvia protested.

But Elda didn't flinch or hesitate. "I promise on my life that we'll not enact the Curse of the Powerful unless we can do so without taking the life of your children."

"Thank you," Val whispered.

"So if we can figure out a less gruesome way to perform this spell, when will it take place?" Valentina asked.

"It cannot take place until the chosen ones have come of age on their thirteenth birthday," Silvia said.

"They will be thirteen in two weeks," Val said.

Elda paced. "Then that is precisely how much time I have to come up with another plan." She plopped down on her cot and began scouring through her grimoire.

Elda needed to work and Val needed to think, so she headed out. There was nothing else to do at this point anyway. As the room slowly cleared, Val overheard Silvia whisper, "Why did you promise with your life? You know there *is* no other way."

Elda did not reply. She continued to read with great determination.

CHAPTER 71 SOUTH AMERICA 2034 AD

A week later Val went in for her turn at keeping watch over Elda and Silvia. This was to make sure no one tried to assassinate them rather than out of any worries about them trying to escape. Val greeted Samuel, who appeared to be more than ready to get off duty. Elda and Silvia were asleep on their cots. As soon as Samuel was gone Elda sat up and ran to the bars. She glanced back to Silvia, checking to make sure she was truly asleep.

This filled Val with hope. "Did you find something that can save my girls in your Grimoire?"

"No."

Val's shoulders dropped.

"But as I have said before..." she spoke softly. Val had to lean in close. "My sight is back." Elda looked over her shoulder again. She clearly didn't want Silvia to know what she was about to say.

What would Elda possibly keep from Silvia? Val wondered. "At least your sight is back. All I see is grayness when I try to look into the future," Val had fallen into despair this past week. She knew if her girls died so would she. There was no way she could give them up. Yet how could she be so selfish? This was their chance to save the world.

Val felt as if the Great Mother had abandoned her entirely. She could no longer see the sky when she looked up, let alone the future.

Elda whispered in Val's ear. "I have seen how we'll do this. The key ingredients are the twins' blood and two deaths. It may not need to be your daughters' deaths but two others."

"Will that work?"

"Shhh. It may but it's a serious spell. This will be like cheating death because the two girls are meant to die. There may be consequences for such trickery."

"You mean, two others can be sacrificed in Eva and Vera's place?"

"It's worth a try and it very well may work."

Hope flooded back into Val. It felt as if a light from her core was spreading through her body.

"So you will draw blood from the girls, a pint each should be plenty, then *we* will perform the sacrifice."

Val shook her head not fully understanding.

"We, as in you and me. We are the only ones who can know about this."

"Why?"

"Because we'll take the girls' place."

Val nodded. "I will gladly die for my children but why you? You don't need to die. Teller will volunteer. He will die for them."

"Yes. He would ... but gender is very important in sacrifices. The female lamb is the most precious of offerings. She could go on to produce many sheep while a ram is more easily replaced. Herds can thrive with only one ram while prosperous herds had many females. One female is worth thirty males to a herdsman. When sheep would give birth, prayers would be made asking for the lamb to be a female. Of course half the time it was male. There was no need to feed so many rams so male lambs would often become dinner. Rams were virtually disposable and therefore not a real sacrifice."

"We aren't sheep and this is no longer biblical times."

"Either way, it would be too risky to replace what is meant to be a female with a male. It needs to be two females."

"You would die for this?"

"It's the price I must pay for what I've done. This is the only way for me to set things right."

Val studied her deep golden eyes and decided she was telling the truth.

"We can't tell anyone of our plan, as they will interfere. This is the way it has to happen." She glanced nervously at Silvia, who remained fast asleep.

Val nodded. She had had the feeling since she first found Elda that they were together in this until the end — whatever that might be. Finding Elda was the beginning of the end and Val knew they would finish this — one way or another — together. The only two queens to have ever ruled the vampire world had a duty to make things right. It all made perfect sense. *This is the way it has to be.* Val placed her back to the bars and slid down them to sit on the cool tunnel floor.

From inside the cell, Elda did the same. She began to sing her solemn song, which was in contrast to her lovely voice. …

The pieces are in place
The pawns are ready to play
No more, no more
The chains are broken
The chains are gone
Better left unknown
Better left undone
The pieces are in place and
The pawns are ready to play…

Val's first thought was that she was grateful to have had twelve, almost thirteen, wonderful years with her girls. She was glad that Teller would get time with them now. *Thankfully they have a loving father and grandmother. They have aunts and uncles who will look after them.* Val frowned. She was not sure that Mari and Mary would be the best influences on the girls. Mary would teach them to curse and Mari would teach them to dress and act as "proper ladies". Val chuckled at the thought. She didn't know which one was worse.

They also had a stepfather. Val knew Elijah would be there for them. He might outright claim little Eva as his own. He cared deeply for her.

The thought of Elijah made Val's stomach turn. She rubbed at the pain in her heart. They had confessed their eternal love for each other — not that there was ever much doubt. They had been together for so long and been through so much. Not even death would change their love. Val didn't want Elijah to become like his father. She pictured Eva helping him to remember how to love. Eva would help to remind Elijah that he was not his father. Val took some comfort in knowing this.

After a long silence Elda asked, "Are you thinking of all that needs to be done before we unleash … the curse?"

"It's going to be hard to say goodbye."

"You can't do it in person. They'll stop you."

Val nodded. "So what are we going to tell everyone? I mean, how will we keep this a secret."

"I've been planning." Elda slid a note under the door and whispered. "I don't want to risk Silvia waking and hearing us.

Val read quickly...

It will happen on their thirteenth birthday. The girls' blood will need to be drawn on this day — the fresher the better. It will need to be kept warm. You will let me out and we will keep Silvia in here — locked up safe. We'll have to sneak out at dusk or shortly after. First we will cast a spell to keep vampires sealed in the tunnels, a circumscription spell. It will be a magical barrier, protecting them from the curse as well. Humans will still be able to come and go at will. Neither the curse nor the circumscription spell will affect them. Your vampire coven will not be able to follow us this way. As you are well aware, crystals are powerful conduits for magic. This will be a difficult curse for only two to perform. It will take a lot of energy, so bring as many high quality crystals as you can find. Now burn this note.

"You have been busy," Val said. Val held the note in the palm of her hand. She focused on the paper until it went up in flames. "Won't others like my mom, her companions and Silvia be able to undo the barrier curse?"

"Perhaps but it will be too late by the time they figure it out. We'll have enacted the curse. You can warn them of that in a note, once we are out."

Val was rather impressed with the plan. *I suppose she does not have much else to do, locked in a cell.* Val dreaded having to draw her daughters' blood. Eva would not like it. What would she tell them? She would have to think of something. She also had to figure out a way to warn their other allies in time. She could not let Hector, Shantanu and Jinlan's covens succumb to the curse. Val sighed. The next week would be the worst week of her life, as they had exactly one week until the girls' thirteenth birthday.

CHAPTER 72 SOUTH AMERICA 2034 AD

Val tried hard to enjoy every last moment with her family but she felt little joy. She focused on what needed to be done. Val made a run for supplies; heat packs, a small ice-chest for the girls' blood, crystals and some other provisions. Over the years, supplies grew harder and harder to find. The tricky part was planning the exact time to send her messages, via crows, to their allies overseas. She could not warn them too much in advance or they would contact Elijah with questions. But she needed to warn them in enough time so they could secure themselves in their hideouts. After much calculating she had a plan that she hoped would give them just enough time but not too much. Then there was nothing left to do but practice the odd incantation for the curse.

The night before her daughters' birthday Vallachia crafted a note to Elijah. She was surprised at what came out as she wrote. …

My Love,

I have lived many wonderful lifetimes. Thankfully, I was able to spend them with you by my side. You were always a wonderful, fair and loving companion. No one could ask for a better partner than you.

If your father were here, I would thank him for the life he gave me. You are nothing like him and you never will be. Keep our family around you and you will be fine.

VAL'S THOUGHTS turned to Riddick. He had made an oath to protect Val. He was determined not to fail, as he had once failed his wife. Val knew that Riddick would not remain mad at her forever. He would most likely take her death doubly hard. He had been largely missing since Val's return. She knew that this was temporary. He would return in his own time and he would forgive her. She could see a bigger picture now that she was about to die. Knowing the date of your death changes the way you think. She was not stuck in the present; she was only concerned for the future of the ones she loved and Riddick was very dear to her. She continued writing….

IF RIDDICK RETURNS in time please tell him that my death was not his fault and that there was nothing he could do to save me.

After the curse, you will be the leader of vampires once again. Send our people back into hiding. After a couple of generations, vampires will pass back into myth and humans can prosper once again.

I'm sorry I will not be there to see it. I love you more than anything!

Val

SHE DID NOT CRY. This was too painful for tears — beyond tears. She could not bear the thought of writing letters to all her other family. She was emotionally drained after writing this. Elijah would have to say goodbye for her.

P.S. PLEASE TELL everyone that I love them and will miss them terribly.

. . .

BY THE MORNING OF HER DAUGHTERS' birthday Val had become numb. Her face was emotionless. She moved with purpose and determination. Val only allowed herself to focus on the task at hand. She had to do what needed to be done and she could not allow emotions to mess things up, give her away or cause her to hesitate on what she *had* to do. This mission was too important — saving her daughters and the world — restoring balance, once again.

First she had to get through the birthday celebration. She and Elda would not leave until dusk. Somehow Val had to make it through this entire excruciating day. The only possible way was to allow herself not to feel — anything.

Vera and Eva greeted her with a hug. Val placed her arms around them but there was no feeling in the gesture. She could barely force a smile as she said, "Happy birthday, my lovely angels."

Eva cocked her head. "Are you okay, Mama?"

"I'm fine ... darling." *Just go through the motions — stick to the plan. That's all that matters.* Val thought she might be getting used to making herself numb. She'd had to do it a lot lately.

Elijah narrowed his eyes at her.

Val snatched his hand more forcefully than she had intended. "Let's celebrate." Again she struggled to force a smile across her lips. She headed out to set up for the party. *Just stay busy.*

THEY PLAYED games and ate a cake that Valentina had baked for the girls. Val did her best to act normal. She was aware that she was not overly convincing but convincing enough. Val gave Vera her favorite sword.

Elijah continued to watch Val closely.

"My first real sword? But Mama this is your best sword."

"That's why I want you to have it."

"And for you my dear..." Val handed Eva the ancient patriarchal cross.

"Your grandfather made this and I want you to take good care of it."

"My grandpa's." She held it close to her chest. "I will take really good care of it, Mama."

Vera playfully thrust the sword at her sister with surprising force. Vera appeared to be much stronger today. Before Val could reprimand Vera, Eva threw her hand up and a bright light flashed, sending Vera flying backwards. They stared open-mouthed at the girls for a moment trying to understand what had happened.

Val ran to help Vera to her feet.

"They have come into their own," Valentina said.

"What does that mean?" Val snapped.

"On their thirteenth birthday they gain their power. It also means they're ready to do what they came here to do."

Val glared at Valentina. "We have been over this. Elda did not find another way so there will be no curse!"

Valentina looked skeptical but she trusted her daughter. "Very well, we'll find another way to defeat John and set humans free."

Eva looked at her hand as if it was a snake. "Mom! What happened? I didn't mean to do that. I just … thought I was in danger when I saw the sword coming at me … then Vera went flying…

"It's okay dear. Your sister is fine. Your grandmother, I mean we, will teach you to control your new powers," Val answered.

"Powers? Cool!" Vera said. "Will we be able to fly, like you?"

"I don't know. This is new to us as well. Only time will tell." Time that Val did not have. *What does this mean? The girls are not simply slow growing human children. They are powerful. It doesn't change anything. Other than the fact that they will be able to protect themselves. That's a good thing but it changes nothing.*

Valentina, Sasha and Angela bombarded the girls with magical tips and advice. Val stood back and watched. *They're in good hands. Surrounded by many loved ones.* The slightest smile, a real one, crept across her face for the first time in a number of weeks.

CHAPTER 73 SOUTH AMERICA 2034 AD

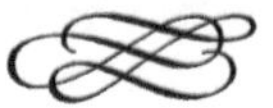

Not long before sunset and the curfew for all to be underground in the protection of the tunnels, Val pulled her girls aside. "Now that you're big girls, it's time for you to start donating blood. Every person who is able needs to do their part." This came out mechanically — a rehearsed lie. It was the first time Val had lied to her daughters and it would also be her last.

The girls were glad to help. Eva was determined, yet she still worried that the needle would hurt. She was thrilled when it was only a tiny prick.

"I can do this!" Eva exclaimed with a broad smile.

"You can do anything, my love. I'm proud of you two. Thanks for being brave." For the first time Val thought she may cry. Val gave them each a sucker. "Now run along to your father."

Val had the last ingredient — the most important ingredient and it was time for her and Elda to go.

First she had to change into more appropriate attire. She took her dingy blue jeans off and dressed in a long velvety crimson gown. *Perfect for a sacrifice — blood red.* Val studied her reflection in the mirror.

She gathered her pack, which contained a dozen premium quality crystals, a cloak and the small ice-chest with two pints of blood surrounded by heat packs. She headed for her "shift" to watch over their "prisoners".

Before she reached the cell. Elijah stepped out from around a corner.

Val jumped.

"What are you up to?" Elijah crossed his arms in front of his chest.

Val tried to keep her heart beat normal. "It's my shift to watch Elda and Silvia."

"Dressed like that?"

"I wanted to feel womanly for a change." This was very unlike Val and she knew Elijah would not believe her.

"I don't know what's wrong or what you're planning but whatever it is you can tell me." Elijah placed his arms on her shoulders.

"Thank you but I'm fine." She moved away.

He gently took her by the arm. "Please talk to me. Something is amiss; you have been acting strange — giving away your most prized possessions. What's this about?"

Val forced herself to look into his troubled eyes — the grey storm was raging. The silly things they had been fighting about these past months had been an utter waste of time. It could have been time that she spent in his arms. Val regretted that. "You have to trust me," she finally whispered.

Elijah nodded and released her arm.

Val had to command her feet to walk away — no kiss or even an embrace goodbye. If he were to hold her to his chest, she would falter. *I have to save my daughters and set the world right,* she reminded herself. Love swelled inside her as she was reminded that Elijah truly loved her. He had always let her make her own way. He knew something was terribly wrong but let her go anyway. *He has never tried to force his will over me.* This thought made her feel warm and overwhelmed with sadness at the same time. She regretted that their last years had been filled with turmoil. *Yet we did have many happy lifetimes together.* She tried hard to focus on those years as she made her way to Elda's prison cell.

Samuel was glad to be relieved of his shift, as always. He didn't even look twice at Val's unusual attire.

As soon as she was alone with the prisoners, Val unlocked the cell door and handed Silvia a folded piece of paper. "Please give this to Elijah tomorrow but not before."

Silvia looked confused which gave Elda time to slip out the door and lock Silvia in.

"What's going on?" Silvia demanded.

Elda reached for Silvia through the bars. "I love you." Elda ran her hand down Silvia's cheek.

"Elda … no."

"Goodbye."

"No!" Silvia tried to grab Elda's hand, narrowly missing it as Elda pulled away.

Val pulled a black cloak from her pack and swung it over Elda; then they were speeding through the tunnels avoiding others when possible. They could hear Silvia rattling the bars, trying to free herself.

At least Elda gets to say goodbye. Val tried to push away the bitterness.

In order to get through a couple of crowded areas Val and Elda had to slow down. Elda shadowed her face with the hood of the cloak and Val tried to act normal. Soon they were outside. They performed the spell of Circumscription. No vampires would be able to leave the tunnels. In no time they were heading to the nearest clearing.

SILVIA QUICKLY GAVE up on the thick reinforced steel bars. She did not want to yell; that would only draw attention to whatever it was Elda was doing. She did not want Elda to get caught. Silvia only wanted to be with her. *Why would she leave me? I can help.*

Silvia flipped through the grimoire. *There's something I remember seeing in here. It was a spell of ... transport — or was it transference. Here!* She ran her finger quickly through the text to find what it required. *Only a possession of great importance to the person you wish be with. Perfect. I have Elda's grimoire.* Silvia began chanting the spell from the ancient book.

CHAPTER 74 SOUTH AMERICA 2034 AD

Vallachia and Elda made their way south to the open meadow where Eva had learned to ride horses. They placed a circle of ten crystals around them. Each woman held a crystal in her left hand and the blood in a copper chalice in her right. The copper helped to keep the blood from going cold too quickly.

"We pour the blood on the ground at the same time, then recite the incantation," Elda said.

Val nodded. "Sounds simple enough." She wanted to get this over with as quickly as possible, before she did something crazy — like change her mind.

Elda suddenly looked to the sky. Vampires and lots of them were headed straight for them. "Now," she said.

They poured the warm blood on the ground and dropped the empty chalices. Elda took Val's free hand and chanted. Soon John and his men surrounded them. Val tried to concentrate on the incantation but then she caught a glimpse of Riddick. His arms were shackled in front of him and he was on his knees.

"Riddick!" Val yelled and she moved toward him.

Elda tightened her grip on Val's hand. "We have to complete this — now!"

A puff of white mist obscured Val's view of John and Riddick. This caused everyone to pause. As the mist evaporated Silvia appeared before them.

"What... How..." Val managed.

"Cast a protection spell around us so that we can complete the curse," Elda yelled to Silvia.

Silvia did just that as several bullets whizzed by, the last of which bounced off the green see-through shield that now surrounded the women.

"Stop ... whatever it is you're doing," John's voice rang out.

Val and Elda resumed their chanting.

"You're going to enact the curse? But where are the girls?" Then Silvia's eyes widened. "You're going to sacrifice yourselves?"

"Stop now or he dies." John held a sword to Riddick's throat.

"No!" Val yelled.

"Focus! Once this curse is unleashed they're all dead anyway," Elda said.

Val and Elda continued reciting the spell until a hole formed in the earth between Val and Elda, at the place where the girls' blood had been spilled. Golden sunlight swirled until it became an eddy in the ground.

"We did it! It worked," Elda said.

Val instinctively stepped back from the vortex. But Elda jumped, disappearing into the golden light — the self-sacrifice.

"No!" Silvia yelled.

Val was glad it was not a grotesque and painful sacrifice, simply a leap into an abyss. She stepped into the vortex. Val's last thought was that she wished she could save Riddick.

Val found herself dangling in a sea of spinning bright light. She looked up to find that Silvia held her by the wrist. It was all that was keeping Val from falling into oblivion.

"Let me go!" Val demanded.

"Elda! Where is she?"

Val looked down. There was no sign of Elda, only a bright yellow abyss. "She's gone."

Silvia's closed her eyes tight and moisture escaped from them. She struggled to keep Val from falling.

"Let me go. Two must die or this will not work."

Silvia shook her head no. She looked around, desperately trying to decide what to do. She pulled Val upward.

Val tried to grab onto something to stop her ascent out of the hole but there was nothing to grasp. "Please stop! You must let me go. Don't let Elda die in vain." Val twisted her wrist trying to free it from Silvia's grip.

"There's no need for you to die." Silvia lifted Val out of the hole and threw her with all her force. Val tumbled across the ground. She leapt to her feet and ran for the hole but Silvia stepped into it. The hole disappeared behind her. Instantly a loud explosion came as a column of golden light shot from the ground into the sky. Val was thrown back, as were John and the others.

The deafening silence rang in Val's ears after the shock of the blast. She tried to focus. There were claw marks where Silvia had dug her fingers into the ground in order to pull Val out of the vortex. Val looked up to see a strange light raining down like a giant umbrella across the night sky. It began to spread and spread quickly. *The Curse of the Powerful. The deadly light will move throughout the entire earth.* "Riddick!" Val yelled. She ran to where John and Riddick were. They still looked dizzied after the blast. She leapt into the air and kicked John in the chest sending him flying backwards. Silvia's protection spell had vanished with her, so Val bent over Riddick and put up her own protection spell as golden yellow rain fell around them. Val felt herself tire. All this magic was draining her. She would not be able to keep the protection spell up for long. Let alone for forty days and nights.

John and his men screamed in agony as the rain pelted them. Val watched as red welts formed on their skin. A sizzling noise could be heard as the vampires eventually caught fire. Val covered her ears and shut her eyes to block out the torturous screams. "John," she whispered in sorrow, "I should have saved him...

"No." Riddick said. "You shouldn't have saved me either." He averted his eyes.

Val collapsed and Riddick caught her with his bound arms.

"I haven't saved you yet. We have to get to the tunnels ... before ... I don't know how long I can keep the curse out," Val managed.

Riddick glanced around. "It's difficult to see through the light or the rain or whatever it is."

"You have to try. I'm growing weaker by the second." Val's head fell against his shoulder.

Riddick took flight. Val had to concentrate to keep the spell around them as they sped through the air. They could see the rain rolling out across the land faster than Riddick could fly. No vampire would be able to outrun the curse. Riddick was barely able to make out the odd bends in the river that told him where the tunnels were."

"We're almost there. Don't give up."

Val closed her eyes. *Don't fall asleep. Don't fall asleep.* It was as if the curse was fighting against her protective barrier. Blow after blow, it pounded against her powers. It took all her energy to keep it intact.

Riddick shook Val. "My Lady, please don't leave me."

"Will you ever stop calling me that?" Val muttered.

"No."

"That's what I thought." Her voice was barely audible, even for a vampire. *My Lady is a better title than whore, which was what he called me the last time I saw him.* This thought helped to distract her from the relentless pounding rain.

It seemed like ages passed before Riddick barged into the tunnels with a severely weakened Vallachia in his arms.

The Circumscription spell only keeps vampires locked in, it doesn't keep them from entering, Val noted with interest.

As soon as she was under the more powerful protection spell over the tunnels she gave up her fight against the curse. It was as if she had been holding the weight of an entire ocean on her shoulders and the water suddenly turned to mist and vanished. She stood from Riddick's arms and took deep breaths. She was still tired but no longer to the point of passing out.

There were many curious humans and vampires at the main entrance.

"We can't get out."

"Where did you go?"

"What's going on?"

"Elda and Silvia escaped." These were but some of the many comments thrown at Val and Riddick.

Elijah made his way through the crowd.

Val ignored everyone and ran to embrace him. The tears could finally fall but now they were tears of joy, not despair.

CHAPTER 75 SOUTH AMERICA 2034 AD

Vallachia told everyone what had happened and that the curse was spreading quickly over the earth. "Vampires must stay in this tunnel for forty days, unless they wish to die."

"What about us?" Bray asked.

"Humans are free. The curse will not hurt you. Any vampires out there will not survive. You may leave the tunnels forever and begin to rebuild your lives."

"You know this, that if we leave the tunnels we will die?" Elijah asked.

Val nodded. "Yes. I saw John and his men perish. It was ... a horrific death."

Elijah closed his eyes and pursed his lips. "John."

"I'm sorry, Elijah. I know he was always by your side for most of your life."

"He truly did betray us," Elijah said.

This brought Val's attention back to Riddick. "Why were you with John?"

Elijah's head snapped up. "You were with John?" He rounded on Riddick.

Val stepped in between them. "Riddick had been imprisoned by John. Please let him speak."

"Elijah's right, you should throw me out of the tunnels and let the curse take me." Riddick knelt in front of them.

Val's eyes widened. "You were the second betrayer?"

"No," Elijah whispered. "Not you." The despair on Elijah's face was almost more than Val could take.

"I was angry ... at you." Riddick lifted his head to gaze at Val. "I was angry that you slept with Teller. I was angry that you abandoned us. Months ago I decided that I had had enough of this place. ... that I would go to the winning side. Not to mention, it was a way to get back at you. Of course, I didn't find Elda. I found John. I only told him that what remained of the Court was hiding in the Amazon. His scouts searched every night. It was only a matter of time until they found us during the day when we were out and about. Then I would be on the winning side, once again."

Elijah placed a knife to Riddick's throat. Elijah clenched the handle tight as he considered using it.

Val placed her hand over Elijah's to stay him. "Why did John have you as his prisoner?"

"I returned to the tunnels one day, only to find two beautiful little girls who looked like you. Everything all fell into place. I understood why you did what you did. In order to have them you had to be with Teller. In order to protect them you had to stay away. It dawned on me that I would have done the same, if it meant getting to have children of my own. I regretted going to John. The lovely girls reminded me of my wife when she was young. Perhaps our unborn child would have looked like them." Riddick shook his head in sorrow.

Elijah and Val only stared at Riddick, so he continued. "John expected more information. He wanted exact locations and details about our camp and he wanted to know the whereabouts of our allies overseas. I withheld this at first, dangling a carrot, playing the game. I could not hold him off much longer. At our next rendezvous, a couple of days ago, I had promised to tell him everything he wanted to know. I went to tell John that I would no longer help him. I had hoped, even begged for him to kill me. But John, with his stupid law about not killing vampires, kept me alive but not free. He imprisoned me. He and his men brought me back to the jungle. His plan was to torture me until I led him to the tunnels. But there was no need, as we caught your scent and followed it to the meadow, where we found you."

"I'm so sorry I hurt the two of you. That was never my intention." Val hooked her arm in Elijah's and placed a hand on Riddick's shoulder.

"What I did can't be forgiven," Riddick said.

"You forgave me," Val said.

"But what I did was much worse. You can never trust me again. I'm nothing but a piece of shit traitor."

"I forgive you." Val then turned to Elijah for his reaction.

"I don't know what to think." Elijah lowered his knife. "All I know is that I can't kill you."

Like Riddick, Elijah didn't have any fight left in him. He was solemn and even more pale than usual. This broke Val's heart twice over. *Time will heal them,* she thought. *At least we are alive and together.*

THE AIR WAS thick with excitement as the humans prepared to leave the tunnels — for the last time. They were finally free. There was much work to do. The first order of business would be to set the remaining humans free from their prisons.

Valentina ran to her daughter and hugged her tight. "I knew you would find another way. I'm so proud of you!"

"Thanks for believing in me, Mom." Val then turned to greet her daughters. She scooped them up into her arms. She thought she might never let them go. There was no holding back the tears.

Bray had her pack loaded with provisions and all of her belongings, which didn't amount to much. She approached Elijah and the others. "This looks like a terrible time but…"

Elijah turned to find Bray staring at him.

"I wanted to say … thank you for everything and to … say goodbye."

Elijah shook her hand. "Good luck out there."

"Our goal is to set as many people free as we can."

Elijah nodded. "Good — they may not make it forty days in their cells without food."

Bray looked back one last time with a longing look before she disappeared in the crowd of humans who were heading out.

"She's truly fond of you," Val said.

"Aye, she's a sweet kid."

"She's not a kid, she's thirty something, isn't she?"

"Yes and I am a millennium and a half, so how do you think that would work out?"

Val chuckled.

Elijah put his arm around Val. "You're the one I belong with, haven't you figured that out by now?" He drew her in close.

Val buried her head in his chest.

CHAPTER 76 THREE DAYS LATER

Mary and Mari rushed into Elijah's room. Val and Elijah had been playing a game with the girls. Eva was showing them how she could move the cards without touching them.

"You have to see this." Mary pulled Val from her seat.

"All right, all right. What's going on?" Val freed herself from Mary's grip.

They moved quickly through the tunnels to where Elda and Silvia were once held. The barred door was wide open. And inside the cell stood Elda and Silvia.

Val's mouth fell open.

"Oh ye of little faith." Elda laughed.

"You're here. You're back?" Val ran to them. She thought her arms would go right through them when she tried to hug them but they did not. "You're here — in the flesh?"

"Yes but only for a short time. We were sent to give you a message." Elda said.

Val stepped back. Many vampires gathered around. They were already growing restless and it had only been three days. Any excitement was of much interest.

"What's it like on the other side?" Val asked.

"It's wonderful. Yet, as you can imagine, the Great Mother and Father were not happy to see us. They were anxiously awaiting the return of their beloved daughters. It took some convincing — on the Great Mother's part — but they have decided to be merciful. The good news is that your girls can stay here with you."

"I'm assuming there's bad news?" Teller asked.

"You see the problem is that the girls are very powerful. They were not meant to live past their thirteenth birthday — the time when they awakened to their true potential. They have the ability to cause immense damage.

"What damage?" Val asked.

"What the Great Mother and Father hold most dear — nature's delicate balance."

"We would never do anything to hurt the earth," Eva said.

Val had scarcely noticed that the twins had caught up with the vampires.

"Well, as long as that's true, the two of you may remain here on earth," Elda said.

"That's not bad news," Vallachia said.

"There's more. The girls are not vampires, as you well know, and they are not fully human either. They are divine. Yet they will age, though be it slowly. They will continue to grow and eventually die. They are not immortal."

Val looked at Teller and smiled. "Then we'll enjoy every moment we're allowed with them."

Teller picked Vera up.

"We have to go," Elda said.

"Wait!" Val ran forward.

"Don't be sad for us. We're right where we belong. Adela, Ramdasha, even my father, we're all together." Elda took Silvia's hand and they began to evaporate into white smoke.

"Thank you." Val whispered, as she reached for Elda. Her hand found nothing as it passed through the smoke.

EPILOGUE FORTY DAYS LATER

Vallachia and all of her companions emerged cautiously from the tunnels. The golden light of the curse was gone. Val headed straight for the meadow to the south. The crystals remained in a perfect circle, as if nothing had happened. No sign of John and his men could be seen. It was as if they had simply vanished. The meadow was normal and peaceful. Val knelt down next to the spot where Elda and Silvia had disappeared and the great curse had risen from the earth. While stuck in the tunnels, Val had carved a patriarchal cross out of a large rock. It was the size of a headstone. She forced the cross deep into the ground. "I can never thank you enough. You saved me. You saved us all."

The End of Book Three

If you enjoyed this book please write a review on Amazon.
Sign up to Lynne's email list at www.lynnehill.com to get a free eBook. Plus, never miss a new release.

A WOMAN'S WORLD SERIES

Wonder Woman meets Divergent

Baya is being groomed to become the next ruler of the world.

Her life is one of constant pressure to become who her mother wants her to be.

This requires Baya to train relentlessly as it will take all her magical abilities to survive the ancient and deadly trials, which all future leaders must pass.

However, it's not in her mother's plan when Baya falls in love.

So it's time for Baya to escape with the man she loves.

But is love enough to keep them alive?

Get your copy today!

What critics are saying...

"A truly marvelous and engaging YA Fantasy novel that perfectly introduces readers to a brand-new series. The incredible new mythos that this author has brought to life will feel both familiar and original all at once..."

— The Verdict

"A mesmerizing, addictive, and engaging read."

— Anthony Avina

"A really pleasant surprise! I couldn't predict not even one twist and turn from this ride."

— Mihaela Constantinescu

"Absolutely recommended to fans of easy-to-read-but-not-dumb Fantasy!

— Lilli Stähle

ALSO BY LYNNE HILL

<ins>The Lords and Commoners Series</ins>

Of Lords and Commoners Book 1

Of Princes and Dragons Book 2

Of Gods and Goddesses Book 3

A Gods and Goddesses Novelette

<ins>A Woman's World Series</ins>

A Woman's World Book 1

Lost Powers Book 2

A Collision of Worlds Book 3

LIST OF CHARACTERS

The High Court of the Elders
King Elijah (son of Lord Chastellain, deceased)
Queen Vallachia
John (trusted advisor)
Riddick (commander in chief)
Samuel (Elijah's closest friend)
Mari (Val's closest friend)
Sonia
Aaron

Teller FKA Prince Vlad Dracula
Abdullah (Teller's commander in chief)
Cosmin and Costel (twins)
Sergiu Pasha (Teller's trusted advisor, deceased)

English Branch of the Court
Lord Alexandru
Hector (trusted advisor)
Mary (former commander in chief)
Elizabeth

Foreign Courts
Jinlan (head of the Chinese branch)
Shantanu (head of the Indian branch)

Servants of Aggadad
Elda (Ramdasha's wife) FKA Neacsa Dracula
Silvia (Elda's trusted companion)

Servants of the Goddess
Valentina
Angela
Sasha

Humans
Tomamacowee (Tomoc for short)
Marcel
Bray
Jack
Ramon

ACKNOWLEDGMENTS

Many thanks to all my preliminary readers. A special thanks to Elaine, Claudia and Michelle. Your advice has helped me to become a much better writer. You offered a different perspective that was much appreciated. I wish you the best of luck with your future writing!

A good editor can be hard to find. Many thanks to my wonderful editor Marcia Kwiecinski. David VanDyke is a great author, who has given me much needed advice. He has provided invaluable wisdom about the industry. Thanks David for helping your fellow writers!

Last but far from least: I would not have been able to accomplish all I have without the loving support of my family and friends. I am very blessed to have you all in my life!

ABOUT THE AUTHOR

Lynne Hill is the author of the *Lords and Commoners* series and the *Woman's World* series. She made the short list for the Chanticleer Book Awards and was awarded a 5 Star Reader's Favorite Award. She was born in Colorado and raised in a small town of eight hundred people. Lynne holds a Doctorate of Psychology in criminology and justice studies. She is an advocate for Restorative Justice, a theme that is incorporated into her novels. Her extensive travels overseas and her work as an American Peace Corps Volunteer in Jordan helped to inspire her writing.

Find out more at www.lynnehill.com and sign up to her email list to get a free eBook. Plus, never miss a new release.

www.ingramcontent.com/pod-product-compliance
Lightning Source LLC
Chambersburg PA
CBHW030626310726
48979CB00003B/894

* 9 7 8 1 7 3 6 7 2 4 9 7 2 *